G000135877

THE SEVERING SON

BOOK ONE OF THE SUNDERED NATION TRILOGY

VAUGHN ROYCROFT

To Johan —
I hope this story is
fitting to the Library of a Viking!
thanks for all you do

[signature]

AVALON COTTAGE PUBLISHING LLC

Copyright © 2022 by Vaughn Roycroft

All rights reserved.

No part of this book may be reproduced in any form or by any electronic or mechanical means, including information storage and retrieval systems, without written permission from the author, except for the use of brief quotations in a book review.

Cover image by John Anthony Di Giovanni

Graphics by Three Star Smoked Fish Company

Paperback ISBN: 979-8-9865264-2-3

For Maureen,
Without whose inspiration and support
This book would not exist.

PRAISE FOR THE SEVERING SON

"Fans of the Banished Lands, Westeros, and the Omehi Peninsula, get ready to journey to Dania! With a fast pace and sweeping battle sequences, not to mention one of the best duels in fiction, The Severing Son will appeal to action-hungry readers of such authors as John Gwynne, George R.R. Martin, and Evan Winter. The character work is memorable and endearing, with painful choices that change the course of whole peoples. Friendship and love form in the crucible of battle, giving rise to vengeance, courage, glory, and loss."—*Philip Chase, PhD. (YouTube's Dr. Fantasy)*

"The author blends history with imagination to create a dramatic and engaging story. The Severing Son will appeal to lovers of historical fiction and epic fantasy enthusiasts alike."—*Juliet Marillier, author of the Blackthorn and Grim and Warrior Bards series*

CHARACTER LIST

The Gottari

The Amalus Clan (the lions):

Vahldan (Eldest son of Angavar the Outcast)

Vahldan's Family:

Angavar (father, Former Lion Lord, Banished)

Frisanna (mother, wife of Angavar)

Eldavar (younger brother)

Mara (little sister)

Kemella (infant sister)

Desdrusan (Lion Lord of Dania, cousin to Angavar)

Teavar (Rekkr, royal guardsman)

Jhannas (Rekkr, royal guardsman)

Arnegern (Rekkr, son of Vildigern, a landholder)

Badagis (Landholder/herdsman, friend of Angavar)

Lefric (Vahldan's uncle, former horse master of Danihem)

Vahldan's Cousins:

Belgar

Herodes

Attasar

The Wulthus Clan (the wolves):

Thadmeir (Wolf Lord of Dania)

Thadmeir's Family:

Urias (adopted brother and captain of the longhouse)

Aomeir (elder brother, deceased)

Theudaric (father and former Wolf Lord, deceased)

Amaseila (wife and Priestess to Freya)

Hloed (merchant, prominent member of the wool guild)

Gizar (prominent member of the Elli-Frodei, an order of shamanistic scholars)

The Skolani

Elan (Blade-Wielder, daughter of Ellasan – a healer)

Keisella (Queen of the Skolani)

Icannes (Princess, daughter of Keisella, near-sister to Elan)

Sael (Wise One, a Dreamer/seeress, grandmother to Elan)

Annakha (Wise One, a healer, near-sister to the Queen)

Sochana (Blade-Wielder) Annakha's Daughter

Ursellya (apprentice healer) Annakha's Daughter

Anallya (Blade-Wielder and royal guardian)

Kukida (Blade-Wielder and royal guardian)

Alela (wet nurse)

Hildeanna (Blade-Wilder, captain of the scouts of the eastern borders)

The Foes of Dania

The Carpans (High-hill dwellers, displaced of the Womb of Danaae):

Túkash (Priest of the Enarei, guardians of the Duhadai)

Kochia (The Duhadai – Spirit-walker of the goddess Zemele)

Sakasha (sister to Kochia)

The Spali (Steppe nomads, driven west by climate change):

Auchote (known as Death's Grin, chieftain of the Paralatoe, royal clan of the Spali)

PLACE NAMES & GLOSSARY

Place Names:

Dania—A river valley formed by the Pontean Mountain range to the south and the Carpan Mountain range to the north. Home of the Gottari, Skolani, and Carpan tribes.

Danihem—A stockade-fortified village in central Dania, on the Danian River. The longhouse of Danihem holds the seats of the lords of the ruling clans of the Gottari tribe.

Afletam—An ancient forestland, to the east of Dania. Thought to be uninhabited by the Gottari, many are superstitious that these lands are haunted.

Oium—A sprawling grassland, relatively featureless beyond its gently rolling hills.

Pontea—A province of the Tiberian Empire, Pontea encompasses the lands adjacent to the northern shoreline of the Pontea Sea, from the Pontean Straits in the west to Akasas in the east.

Akasas—An ancient, walled city on the northern coast of the Pontean Sea. Located at the mouth of the Berezan River, Akasas was once a prominent port for Hellain traders.

Thrakius—An ancient, walled city on the northern coast of the

Pontean Sea. Due to its enclosed harbor, and the marvel of its ancient seagates, Thrakius was long the eastern stronghold of the Hellain navy. It remains a prominent trading port of the Tiberian Empire. Though Thrakius is but a shadow of its glorious past, it remains the largest imperial city in Pontea.

Illyrica—the mountainous realm of the Illyrican tribes, located to the north and west of Dania.

Vigs-Utan—An aging stronghold at the head of the trail that leads through the Pontean Pass, consisting of a stone tower and ramparts surrounding the gateway to Dania. The tower remains the home of the Elli-Frodei—the order of the Wise Ones of the Gottari.

Other Terms:

The Ananth-jahn—A trial in the form of a sword duel, granted to a petitioner to the dais chair and the Rekkr's council, to settle a perceived wronging or a slight of one's honor. The challenged has the right to select a champion to fight in his stead.

The Fulhsna-Utanni—a part of the Mithusstandan (see below), in which the Skolani agree to supply Blade-Wielder guardians to the scions of the Gottari's ruling clans. Considered archaic and obsolete.

Futhark—Any runic missive intended to convey a shared oath or law. To the Gottari, *The* Futhark is the shared oath between the two ruling clans of the Wulthus and Amalus. The runes of the oath are inscribed on rings, fastened to the hilts of the two futhark swords, borne by the Lion Lord and the Wolf Lord.

The Jabitka—The mobile village of the Skolani. During the time of Vahldan and Elan's tale, the Jabitka is located in eastern Dania, south of the Danian River, near the ford at Red Rocks.

Mithusstandan—the ancient oath between the Gottari and the Skolani, in which the Skolani agree to safeguard the borders of their shared realm in exchange for Gottari weaponry (primarily the vaunted Gottari blades, prized by the Skolani Blade-Wielders).

Qeins—A woman bonded to a Rekkr or chieftain of the Gottari, often of noble or landed birth, a qeins is a wife with rights and an inheritance outside of her marriage. Indeed, some qeins are more wealthy or prominent than their husbands. Esteemed priestesses are also granted the status of qeins.

Rekkr—A Gottari warrior who has claimed his name, pledged himself to one of the two ruling clans, and who owns his own weaponry and at least one warhorse.

The Urrinan—The prophesied calamitous end of the era, in which the Tutona peoples shall rise to prominence from the ruins of the so-called civilized world of the imperials. To be wrought by the Bringer of Urrinan, who is foretold to arise from among the Gottari tribe.

"When Mighty Lion is cast aside
    The Severing Son restores his pride
    Thunder wakes when blades collide
    The steed on which Urrinan rides..."
    —*from the Song of The Severing Son*

PROLOGUE—THE SEERESS

"The girl has arrived." Urias stepped into the small room where Thadmeir sat in wait, and did as bidden when Thadmeir motioned to close the drapes behind him.

"Must we really do this?" Thadmeir asked his brother, once the infernal rumble of voices from the longhouse chamber was muffled.

"It's the only way to appease the petitioners."

"By granting an audience with a witch? Rile them, more like."

Urias smiled. "Calling her a witch is bound to rile them."

"If I'm to consider all of their wild claims possible, what else should I call her?"

"You could say *seeress*. Or name her as the Amalus themselves do, as a priestess."

"*Priestess*." Thadmeir rolled his eyes. "You said yourself, she's little more than a girl."

"The Amalus herdsmen are superstitious folk, and they're afraid. These Spali raids—"

"Bah." Thadmeir stood and waved him off. "Superstitious, I'll grant you. But afraid of Spali hoodlums seeking to make off with a few lambs? Raids like these are a seasonal ritual, as reliable as the spring rains. No, they're baying for a fight. Father always said that if the realm goes too many seasons without war, sure as a tick finds its way to the hound's ear, the Amalus will find their way to a conflict. That's what this is about."

His brother pressed his lips tight, refusing to continue or concede. It was a familiar tactic of his. Thadmeir slipped into the ceremonial robe that Urias held up for him, then peered through the draped partition to the longhouse chamber, scowling over the assault of the stench and noise. "Let's get on with it."

Urias followed him to the front of the dais, where Thadmeir's counterpart, the Lion Lord, sat waiting. Desdrusan stood as Thadmeir arrived before his own chair, radiating contempt for a meeting his clan had forced by circumventing their lord's will. Thadmeir, as the Wolf Lord, would have been just as angry had their places been reversed—if his clan had forced a formal hearing with another clan's lord, publicly airing what should've been in internal grievance. Particularly with a spectacle like this—parading a self-anointed mystic before the entire council.

"Rekkrs!" his brother called. The chorus of voices faded as everyone in the longhouse stood. "Hail and heed Desdrusan and Thadmeir, lords of the Amalus and the Wulthus—the ruling clans of Dania."

"Hail to our lords," came the droning refrain. The Amalus petitioners and their supporters sat back down without so much as a bow of the head.

"Be seated," Thadmeir said, glaring at those who'd already done so.

Benches creaked and murmured conversations restarted. Thadmeir scanned the Amalus side of the Gottari chamber, disgusted by the slovenly posture and cold glares of the warriors who called themselves lions. As usual, the lions' benches were already crooked and misaligned. He suspected they did it on purpose just to annoy him. One of the lions in the front row was actually scraping sheep shit from his boot with his belt knife. Behind the benches of the

Amalus and Wulthus councilmen, a throng filled the dim recesses of the chamber. Seemed every far-flung Rekkr with a warhorse and a secondhand blade had come for the tawdry show.

"Let's get this done. Bring forth the girl," he called. His brother, standing at Thadmeir's shoulder, pointedly cleared his throat. "Priestess," Thadmeir amended. "Or witch, or whatever she is," he muttered under his breath.

The great wooden door at the far end of the longhouse swung open, letting in a gust that set the torches flickering. A grizzled herdsman entered, steering a waif by the arm through the parting warriors. The girl bowed her head and held closed an overlarge woolen cloak.

The pair made their way up the center aisle and several on the Amalus side bowed as she passed. Thadmeir leaned to whisper to his Amalus counterpart. "The witch commands more deference from them than you do." Desdrusan frowned but didn't refute it.

The herdsman drew the girl to a halt before the two dais chairs and bowed. "My lords, I have brought my daughter Amaseila before you, as bidden."

"Tell them why," someone prompted from the Amalus benches.

"She has seen much of what is to come," the herdsman offered.

The girl stood hanging her head, her lank orange hair curtaining her face. Desdrusan presumed to speak first, but he gave voice to Thadmeir's own doubts. "Why should we believe her?"

"Believe as you will," the herdsman said, "but I've heard and seen. My daughter knows things before they happen. She hears Freya's own voice. Inside her head."

Those on the Wulthus side leaned to one another, grumbling and scoffing.

"Well?" Thadmeir prodded. "What say you of your father's claims?"

"What more can be said of such a simple truth?" The witch's face slowly rose. Her hair fell away, and torchlight spilled over her milky complexion. Her eyes met Thadmeir's and latched onto them. He drew his next breath as a gasp.

Desdrusan stirred in his chair. "By the gods, she *is* possessed. If not by Freya, by something."

The eyes that held Thadmeir captive were the oddest he'd ever seen. The pale gray irises were nearly indistinguishable from the whites, and the large black pupils bored into his. In contrast to her eyes, a delicate nose rode on taut, freckled cheeks. She had a long neck and a firm, centered chin. Her lips were pink and full. Her face was perfectly symmetrical, till one side of it quirked in a wry smile, spoiling the effect.

He found his voice. "So the claim is indeed yours, that you commune with Freya?"

"You may name it a claim, my lord. For me, it is a way of life. One not of my choosing."

Thadmeir was transfixed, and Amaseila's smile said she knew it. This was no girl. This was a woman of age and intention. Again, he fought to focus his thoughts.

"Why would the goddess pick you—a simple herdsman's daughter?" he asked. "Why not someone more prominent?"

"She tells me not why, my lord." Amaseila cocked her head. "Nor is it my place to ask."

Thadmeir found himself nodding and smiling.

Urias bent to his ear. "Perhaps the priestess could share what she claims the goddess wishes to say?"

Amaseila said, "Yes, you have but to ask. Freya has much to say. Perhaps there is a certain matter that troubles my lord?" She spoke as if he and his brother were the straight players in a mummery. Perhaps they were.

"You've been saying that Dania faces grave threat from the Spali?" Urias prompted.

"Ah, yes, the Spali. The marked among them are already here. They ride within Dania's borders even as we speak. If only to heed invitation." She laughed as if she'd made a joke, revealing straight white teeth. "These first few are but the sparks. The flames they ignite shall be fast and bright. Beyond the imagining of he who sought a simple fire."

Desdrusan harrumphed. "This is riddle-speak. Send her back to her flea bed, my lord."

Thadmeir stroked his beard. "The marked. You speak of the Spali's tattooed warriors? Some of them are here, in Dania?"

Amaseila raised her brows. "Oh yes."

It could be true. But the typical Spali raiders were unmarked boys, seeking to earn their first tattoos. "These raiders—you say they shall set fires?"

"Fast and Bright," she repeated ominously.

"Can this be avoided? Tell us what Freya wishes us to know."

"You wish to hear her for yourself?" Amaseila asked, a note of amusement in her tone.

Thadmeir threw up his hands. "Why not?" He looked up at Urias. "May as well get the whole act." His brother shook his head in disapproval.

Amaseila's chin fell to her chest. The chamber grew silent.

"My lord," Desdrusan began. "Must we really—"

"A moment." Amaseila held up a finger. "She is near." Her shoulders rose and fell with her breath. When she raised her face, it was an oval mask with vacant eyes. She slowly closed her eyelids. The smooth skin of her face began to twitch in a most unnatural way. When her eyes sprang open, they had transformed to the fierce eyes of a raptor, darting around the chamber. Her toothy smile was almost savage. She raised sinewy arms and her weathered cloak fell behind her shoulders, revealing a slender but womanly figure in a clinging shift. A voice that was no longer a girl's rang through the chamber.

"Long have Spali sons come as shadows in the night, counting stolen sheep as coup to earn their marks. But so too have they shed the blood of my children. The tattooed have grown a thirst for carnage and dominion. So too do they covet what they've seen of my valley. The common now follow where the marked lead. The Spali move as a people. Long were they disjointed, fighting amongst themselves. No longer. Need drives them. They come in the greatest migration their kind has ever known."

The words echoed in the stunned hush. The being before them seemed taller, almost radiant. She vibrated more than trembled. Thadmeir sensed that she was brimming with divine energy. This was beyond any playacting skill.

The transformed being gracefully swept an arm overhead, her wide, unblinking eyes scanning the rafters above. "Forced by blight, out across the windswept plains, they come in great caravans of man, woman and child. With herds and wagons and beasts of burden."

Suddenly Thadmeir saw it—a vision overhead—as if from a waking dream.

"Across grasslands that stretch to every horizon, on toward the very edge of their known world. What they seek is refuge—a home-land. First come warriors, seeking a foothold. More and more will follow, gathering in the east until—"

"Until what?" Desdrusan slapped the arms of his chair, banishing Thadmeir's vision.

Amaseila drew the sharp breath of a diver reaching the surface. She dropped her arms to her sides and her chin to her chest. "Until one of our two peoples is defeated, and driven from the land." The girl's voice had returned.

Desdrusan shifted his bulk in his creaking chair. "You see? More nonsense."

"I *did* see," Thadmeir whispered.

"What we saw was an act, my lord. Everyone knows that Spali seek only easily won prizes. If any are truly here in Dania, I promise you, they will be no different. Bloody their noses and they'll slink away, same as ever." The murmur of grumbling conversation renewed.

Thadmeir looked down and rubbed his eyes, wondering if he'd

been the only one. He opened his eyes to Amaseila. She was watching him, looking forlorn and gaunt, as if she'd spent her very flesh in channeling her goddess. Thadmeir found that he longed to comfort her. Though he didn't dare reveal that he'd seen the vision as she described it. Instead, he asked, "If they come, who shall prevail?"

She raised her chin, firming her countenance. "It depends."

He sensed she knew more but was afraid to say. "On what?" he prompted.

He still saw her fear, but it became tinged by sorrow. "On so much," she said. "So much must yet be endured. So much anger and hate, strife and confusion. So much death."

Desdrusan groaned and theatrically rolled his eyes. "Ah, the perfect answer. Perfectly meaningless. I beg of you, my lord—end this farce." A swell of concurrence rose from the Wulthus side of the chamber.

"It is no farce!" The lion named Arnegern leapt from his seat on the aisle. "Did you not hear? Already there are Spali warriors here, in our homeland. Already they bring fire and death. Our patron goddess has chosen to speak through this priestess in an attempt to warn us, to tell us that the worst is yet to come. The danger will only spread should we fail to act. Till flames rise and blood is shed in every Gottari settlement. Even should you remain uncertain, the sane choice is to act! To seek to avert the risk, however remote you think it. Even a partial mustering—"

"For the hundredth time, we do not need a mustering!" shouted the Wulthus Rekkr Hloed from across the aisle. "*Any* mustering will cripple the wool and grain yield. Not only would we lose the labor of the young men who ride, but this action would keep all but the boldest few from a second planting this summer. Setting warriors loose to gallop hither and thither would only cause honest, hard-working men to fear the trip to Danihem with their shearing. They'll sell at a loss to any cheat with the guts to come calling. All in the name of hunting down a few rogue savages. How will those you claim to protect then feed their families come winter?"

"Are the Gottari no longer one people?" Arnegern rejoined. "Will the Wulthus care only when the fields they lease for grazing are burned? When the flocks that supply their fullers are slaughtered or stolen? When the blood that's shed finally affects their precious earnings?"

"You see, my lord?" Hloed addressed Thadmeir directly. "He admits there is no real invasion. Raiders have ever posed a threat to those who risk grazing the far reaches of the valley. It is a risk they take to avoid paying fairly set tariffs. This is naught but a cunning maneuver."

"Enough!" Thadmeir raised his hand for quiet, then turned again to Amaseila. He felt there was something more at work behind this—something that had yet to be said. He needed her to speak out. "Please," he softly prodded. "Tell us what you see. Tell us what truly comes."

Amaseila seemed to seize. She squeezed her eyes shut. "What truly comes?" The words came as a threatening growl. Her eyes sprang open, raptor-like once again. "Urrinan!" The word resonated, and the chamber fell still. "A king shall arise from among the king-less, born of exile."

The drone of the crowd resumed and grew, sounding of shock and alarm.

"She speaks of the son of the Outcast," someone called from the recesses of the chamber.

"Treason," Desdrusan hissed, his lip curling and eyes hard.

"The Outcast is but a wandering beggar," the Amalus Rekkr Jhannas said from the front row. "Who can say if the boy yet lives?" Imposing as the man was, all knew Jhannas was one of Desdrusan's lapdogs.

"By Freya's will, he lives to ascend!" a herdsman cried from the restive mob at the back.

"Treason *and* blasphemy," Desdrusan proclaimed, sitting up, clutching the chair arms.

The savage grin overtook Amaseila's face again. She spread her arms and laughed, loud and long, the sound of it leaving no doubt: this was Freya's own laughter. The being's voice rose to its greatest resound. "In glory shall he rise, and glory shall be his song. Accept him and the glory is yours. Renounce him and share in his doom!" The last word seemed to echo, as if into the depths of a canyon.

Then she slumped, pulling her cloak tight and panting like a storm-frightened colt. Thadmeir's voice came hoarse and meek. "Amaseila? Tell us true. Of whom does Freya speak?"

Amaseila, a girl once again, raised wide eyes, her face shiny with tears and sweat, as pale as unskimmed cream. "The Bringer," she said. "He comes."

CHAPTER I—DUTY-BOUND

" O ne cannot know the Gottari mind without grasping the Urrinan's place in it. In the days before the assent, every Gottari parent both dreaded Urrinan and yearned for its outcome for their progeny. It was to be the upheaval that remade the world, the darkness that renewed the faltering light.

It is true that the Urrinan foretold the rising of all of the Tutona tribes, but it held a particular fascination for the Gottari tribe, as it was long told that the Bringer of Urrinan would appear and ascend from among them.

For the Gottari, that these things would come to pass was beyond doubt. And yet, as foretold events began to occur, many refused to accept that it must happen to them."—from the Saga of Dania, as recorded by Brin, known as Bright Eyes

VAHLDAN PUSHED THROUGH THE GATE, walking across the sunbathed compound as fast as he could without spilling the milk. He'd gotten an early start. None of the goats had given him any trouble, and milking them was his last chore. His little brother was filling a basket in the bean field, and their little sister was *helping* by crawling down the rows with her stuffed horse doll.

Best of all, his father was nowhere in sight.

The top half of the cooking shed door was open. Vahldan's mother stood facing the hearth. He reached in and quietly set the milk pail behind her, turned and set off.

"Vahldan," his mother called.

He was tempted to pretend he hadn't heard, but he couldn't refuse her now—not in her condition. "Yes?"

Frisanna's profile revealed her swollen belly. "Your father is looking for you."

"I'll go find him in a bit." Vahldan started again toward the sleeping cabin.

"Hold it." He stopped. "What's going on between you two?"

"Nothing." Frisanna's expression told him she wasn't going to let it go. "It's just that I know what he wants. To fight, same as always."

"You used to love sparring with your father."

It was true. But his father had been different since his return. Vahldan supposed he'd changed, too. "I'm just sick of it." Not just the sparring. Vahldan was sick of hearing how corrupt the Gottari lords were; how unjust his father's banishment had been; how righteous and honorable Angavar's restoration would be.

"I miss seeing you two having fun together," she said. "What happened to those days?"

Vahldan could hardly recall it. "That was before I knew what he really wants from me."

"Your father wants you to be your best."

"What he wants is for me to be like him."

Frisanna paused and frowned. "He just wants you to be prepared. He knows—"

"No, he doesn't know. You don't either." His mother recoiled. "I'm sorry. I just want to finish this carving. He can rough me up afterward."

"Oh, Vahldan."

He hated how sad she looked. But was she sad for him or for his father? Or was it that things had changed? That even made him feel sad sometimes. "I'm kidding. May I please finish my carving if I promise to find him right after?"

Frisanna laid her hand on his cheek. "You know what I always say about this. Your life is your own. Don't ever let anyone tell you differently. Understood?" He nodded. "Go on. I never saw you." She turned back to her kettle.

Vahldan hurried off, silently thanking the gods that Frisanna understood both his need to carve and his reluctance about his father. He slipped inside the cabin door, scanned the room, and closed it behind him.

He was alone.

The fire in the hearth was banked, but the coals glowed orange. Too warm. He rushed to the window and flung open the shutter. Sunlight and fresh air streamed in. He dropped to his knees and lifted the bench lid, illuminating the treasures within.

Vahldan set the woodpecker and the horse on the windowsill, in plain sight, to motivate him. He'd carved the woodpecker himself. He'd been inspired by the tenacity of the real one that hammered away at the protruding end of the ridgepole of the stables. The horse was the work of a master—the finest Vahldan had seen. The intricate horse pushed him to seek the details that brought a piece of wood to life.

He drew his belt knife and checked its edge. Then, at last, he pulled out his unfinished piece, examining its texture and grain in the sunbeam. It would be his finest yet. He'd come upon the lucky chunk while chopping firewood. The axe had stuck in a burl, and when he knocked it loose with a mallet the raw piece fell away.

Vahldan had instantly recognized the head, body, and tail of the hawk. Even the color was right. Better still was the slab of wood extending from either side, which was slowly becoming the wing-span. His first bird in flight. Carving the hard oak down to the required sleekness was taking longer than expected, but today he would finish.

The young raptor in question was both his subject and his muse. Just as the woodpecker had been the prior year. The hawk had made almost daily appearances since the spring. He liked to think of the raptor as a spiritual messenger, appearing to remind Vahldan of the freedom that would be his once his father regained his status as the lord of the Amalus clan.

Vahldan lifted the knife and set it to a wing, then hesitated. Capturing the hawk would be like capturing a piece of the sky. He visualized the feathers beneath the surface, rippling in the wind, pressed the knife's edge into the grain, and peeled off the first long shaving.

It felt like cutting the cords that bound his anxious spirit.

He set the knife in place again. The door crashed open and the knife slipped.

"What's this? Playtime?"

Vahldan spun to face his father. "No. It's nothing." He set the hawk on the bench.

Angavar's silhouette filled the doorway as he ducked in under the timber lintel. "Haven't I been saying how few days are left?" Angavar held two practice swords. He threw one at Vahldan's feet. "Come. Time to focus."

"I'll be out shortly," he said. "I'm almost finished."

Angavar strode in, boots thumping, raising his practice sword. Vahldan scrambled out of his way. The sword swished. *Clack!*

"You're finished," Angavar said. "It's time to set aside childish things."

His hawk had been deftly knocked into the coals of the hearth. Flame leapt from the spot. Vahldan lunged to yank his treasure out and throw it to the flags. One of the wings was black and smoldering, the other missing. The broken wing on the coals was swiftly engulfed in flame.

Vahldan's body clenched. The ugliness within him was making

itself known. It rose from his belly to squeeze the air from his lungs. It rose up to lurk behind his face, heating his cheeks.

"What?" Angavar's smile was mirthless. "It makes you sad, losing your toy?"

This wasn't sadness. Vahldan pushed down the ugly rage. He made himself blank and faced his father. "It wasn't a toy."

"You think I don't know how it feels? You think I never enjoyed life, that I don't regret what's happened?" Angavar's stare hardened. "They took everything from me. From us. We don't have the luxury of doing things to amuse ourselves. Do you understand?"

Vahldan held himself very still and gave a single nod.

Angavar loomed over him. "You promised to stand by me, as my second in the trial. Do you hold to your vow?"

Vahldan raised his chin. It felt almost like defiance just to have grown nearly as tall the man who lorded over his life.

Then he saw it—the plea in Angavar's eye. It made this intense bully into his father again. His hero. The man who'd been wrongly accused of murder. The man who'd sacrificed all for his family, his clan, his people.

Vahldan bowed his head. "Yes," he said. "I hold to it."

"Good. Because this is bigger than you and me. This is about duty. And honor. I need a man of duty and honor to stand with me. Can you be that man?"

"I just said I would," Vahldan snapped. Angavar's glare drifted to the other carvings on the sill. "It's just that I need to finish—"

His father's blade deftly knock the horse and woodpecker from the sill, out the window. "This is a distraction. You need to devote yourself to duty. Can you give me that?"

Vahldan stiffened, pushing down what Angavar sought to goad.

Angavar's smile was wry. "Well?"

"Yes sir," he said.

"Good. Now, pick up that sword. Get your shield and meet me in the sparring circle." Angavar turned and left without closing the door.

Vahldan bent and grabbed the smoking hawk by the head and tossed it onto the coals. He made himself watch it burn, taking slow, even breaths to cool the forge in his belly. As the flames of the ugliness sputtered, he looked out the door to the main gate. He imagined himself running—out the door, through the gate and up the road, all the way to the river. He imagined wading into the flow, letting the current carry him away. On and on he'd go, till he came to the sea, wide and open and free. Someday, he would go. Somehow, he would get there.

But he'd given his word. Before he left Dania, he would stand with his father.

He retrieved his shield and snatched up the practice sword. Vahldan gripped the hilt, resenting how natural it felt—how it became like a part of him. Holding a knife he made beauty. Holding a sword he only made trouble. A knife had a thousand uses. A sword had only one. His father always said that the best way to keep swords from spilling blood was to be the best at wielding one. The words rang hollow, considering what it was they trained for, especially as the solstice continued to draw nearer.

The trial was his father's fight. Vahldan just had to get through it. Then he'd leave.

Angavar stood at the far edge of the sparring circle, adjusting the arm-straps of his shield. "Ready?" Angavar asked without looking.

"Do I have a choice?"

His father paused, staring off. "I fear none of us does. Not really."

Angavar faced him, got into his stance and nodded. Vahldan mirrored his mentor, squatting into position behind the shield. They circled one another. He felt self-conscious.

Angavar smirked. "Are those feet or hooves? Gods help us, you really do need practice."

Vahldan got onto the balls of his feet, adding vigor to his step.

"Still sad about your toy?"

"No sir."

"You're lying, but it doesn't matter. Remember, sadness is weakness. Better to be angry than sad." Angavar stepped into a feigned thrust to bait him. "Come on, boy. Get angry. Show me what we both know you're hiding."

Vahldan held fast to the hilt, and to restraint. Angavar dipped his head and delivered an overhand blow that slammed his shield. Vahldan retreated to the edge, shaking off the tingling in his arm. The forge in his belly was restoked.

Angavar stopped on flat feet. "That should've brought a counter. How many times must I tell you? You hesitate, you're dead." His father only circled a moment before repeating the lame attack, this time striking harder. Vahldan absorbed it, rolled his shoulder and countered with a lunging thrust.

Angavar's down-stroke easily knocked it aside. "Oh please." His father barked a laugh. Then, fast as a striking snake, Angavar whipped his sword-arm up and around. *Thwack!* Vahldan barely blocked the powerful blow. The shock echoed up his arm to hum in his shoulder.

"You awake?" Angavar said. "You'd better get serious, boy. Those who want us dead certainly are." His father resumed his stance. Vahldan grit his teeth, raised his shield and circled. Angavar leaned in. "Getting angry?"

"No."

"Yes you are. Use it!"

"You know I don't like going there," he said, hating the whine in his voice.

"There's no choice. The time to fight for what's ours has come."

"It's got nothing to do with me."

Angavar laughed. "You don't think so? You're my son. It's got everything to do with you. What if I fail? What will you do when they come for you?"

"I'll reason with them. We're not beasts. The Wulthus are Gottari, too."

His father's laugh was bitter. "Reason?" Angavar whirled and swung. Vahldan shield-blocked and scurried away. "That's your mother's word. Trust me, there's no reasoning with wolves. And when the time comes, you'll have her to protect, too. It won't be the other way around. If you won't fight for yourself, will you fight for her?"

Vahldan shook his head, circling, crouched behind his shield. "It won't come to that."

"It will! Are you going to let them hurt her? Put her in chains? Sell her? Are you going to let them win? You've got to fight, dammit!"

The forge burst, spewing flames of rage through him. Vahldan lunged with a tilt of his head and a flinch of his shoulder. Angavar pulled his shield around to block, but just in time. His father was off balance. The sight of the opportunity was like a bellows. The flames flared and Vahldan pressed the attack. His world became a blur of chopping, grunting, swinging, their blades clacking louder and harder, pushing him to more—hotter, fiercer, stronger.

The ugliness had consumed him.

His father finally caught Vahldan's blade in parry, twisting it and trapping it down, both tips grinding the stony turf. The pause was like waking from a nightmare. Angavar's eyes were full of concern. Vahldan hated when he lost himself like that. He leapt back and danced away, tamping down the flames.

"That's not fighting, it's flailing. You've got to maintain control." Angavar sighed and retook his stance. "Again."

Vahldan's words came in huffs. "Now? After what just happened?"

"Yes, especially after that. You need to harness it. You've got to stay mad and stay sharp. Look at you. You're like a scared boy again. No foe will give you the chance I just did."

Afraid of letting the ugliness return, Vahldan leapt to the attack without a plan. He managed to stay on the balls of his feet. The only move he could think of was to signal an overhead strike and then bring his blade around in a low swoop, targeting his father's exposed hip. Angavar easily blocked again. Vahldan backpedaled, barely blocking another hard counter-blow coming for his head. The desperate retreat caused him to stumble and he nearly fell.

His father dropped his guard, and stepped back. "Really? This is all you've got? After all this time. All of this training. What a waste."

The ugliness returned like a thunderbolt strike. Vahldan sprang with a roar, slamming his shield into Angavar's, his blade flying toward his father's head.

Angavar fully absorbed the blow, his blade holding Vahldan's aloft. With a deft flick, Angavar wrenched Vahldan's blade from his hand and sent it clattering to the ground. The ugliness vanished as quickly as it had arrived. His father glowered, his wooden sword at Vahldan's chin. "You just can't keep it harnessed, can you?" Angavar flicked again and the practice blade's tip tore Vahldan's cheek.

Raw, bright pain flared. Vahldan's hand flew to his face. His fingers came away bloody. The fire was doused. He felt like a helpless child. "Why? Why can't I ever please you?"

"Because you refuse to focus, to go deep enough."

"I've given you all I've got."

"It's not enough," Angavar shouted. "Don't you get it? You are the blood of the Amalus kings. It's your legacy. You've got to be the best or they'll tear you apart."

Vahldan touched his cheek again, causing a sharp sting. "I didn't ask for any of this."

"Face up to it—it's yours."

"I've been trying. What else do you expect me to do?"

Angavar started pacing. "I expect you to dig. I expect you to find it inside you."

"What? That I'm a killer like you? What if I want to be better than that?"

Angavar slumped. In his father's look of disappointment Vahldan recognized the man he'd all but worshipped. He also saw that he'd failed him.

Vahldan dropped his chin to his chest, unable to face his father's judgement.

Angavar's next words were whispered, but Vahldan heard them clear enough. "Gods, what will come of us if this falls to you?"

Angavar's thrown practice sword clacked against Vahldan's own abandoned weapon. When Vahldan looked up, his father was halfway to the stable. He wanted to call after him, but no words came. The stable door closed with a thump, and he was alone again.

Vahldan looked down at his hands, swollen and bloody. They didn't look like the hands of a carver. They looked like the hands of a killer.

CHAPTER 2—FALLING TO YOU

"*Scholars ascribe a broad meaning to the word futhark. They use the term to describe any runic missive of the Tutona peoples, and will perhaps concede that most futharks convey oaths or laws. But any Gottari tribesmen will offer a much more specific meaning. For the Gottari, there is only one futhark. It is the futhark—the oath between their nation's two powerful ruling clans, the Wulthus and Amalus. The futhark not only resolved generations of tribal infighting, it made their people whole. And mighty.*

History did not record the name of the carver who first wrought the words—Two become one, Together to stand, Forever to lead, Brothers unto Urrinan.—upon the rings affixed to the hilts of the two futhark swords, borne by the ruling clans' chieftains. But all Gottari grasp the importance of the tenet."—Brin Bright Eyes, Saga of Dania

VAHLDAN STARED at the closed stable door, feeling empty. All had been burnt out of him, leaving only the soot of his spent rage. His shield clattered to the ground. He shook his tingling hands, trying to feel again, to no avail.

He ran. Ran as he wished he had before the sparring match. He ran out the gate, and up the road. The way grew steeper but he kept going, pounding uphill till his legs grew wobbly and his throat was raw. He crested the ridge and the view of the Danian valley opened before him. He beat to a halt and dropped his numb hands to his knees, panting for relief.

He wanted to keep going, until he found the sea and sailed away. To a new life.

No, dammit. He'd given his word. He would stand with his father.

Vahldan looked back at the hidden compound in the alpine vale, at the cabin and the outbuildings and the wall surrounding it all. It looked so small from up here—safe but confining. He watched his little brother, chasing chickens in the yard; heard his mother's call, riding on the wind. She would be starting meal prep. His father emerged from the stable doors and Vahldan's little brother ran to him, pestering as they walked to the cooking shed. His father grabbed Eldavar by the waist, lifted him, and swung him over his shoulder. Angavar held his son by the ankles, carrying him like a sack of grain. Eldavar's squeal and giggling drifted up to Vahldan.

Vahldan couldn't move, couldn't go back. Not because of the intense warrior, the mentor who'd goaded forth his ugliness. Rather, it was because of the man who lifted and carried his young sons overhead. The man who'd given Vahldan a belief that anything was possible. Who'd taught him the meaning of honor. That was whom he couldn't face. Not just yet.

It started again. The ugliness stirred, low in his belly. Fighting it made his face muscles sore. His feet started to tap. He shook his tingling hands.

Vahldan looked along the ridge, to a stand of scrubby jack pines. He spotted what he needed in their shade. He scampered over the rock to grab the stick beneath the boughs. It was a bit old and soft, but free of pitch. He sat, drew his knife, and cut a slice of bark. Then another, revealing the yellow grain. His inner churn started to quell.

He sat whittling away the old pine stick, relishing its scent, until it was half its original size. Until the sun began to dip toward the mountaintops. He brushed the shavings from his lap, sheathed the knife, and tossed the remainder down the mountainside.

Vahldan knew the change that came couldn't be avoided. He'd long understood that his father was at war with the past. It was clear that Angavar now wanted to declare war on the present. Even if he wagered his family's future in the bargain.

Seemed Angavar was determined to make Vahldan a weapon in his widening war.

As much as Vahldan hated working in the mine, and resented the loneliness of living in hiding, he felt reluctant to face life beyond the little compound in the hidden vale.

Life beyond banishment would be fighting and trials, deception and danger.

He stared down, past the foot of the canyon. The Danian River carved through a green and lush landscape. Dania was his father's homeland. Vahldan only vaguely remembered living down there. He was sixteen now, which meant he hadn't been in the valley for a decade. But he remembered swimming in the river, cold and swift. His mother said it ran to the sea, that it could carry him right through the mountains, out of Dania, and into the wide world beyond.

The idea had stayed with him, that leaving the compound could mean finding his way to someplace distant and exotic. Someplace free of his father's grievances, plots, and expectations.

Vahldan had never been to the village of Danihem, home of the Gottari longhouse, seat of the lords of Dania. He'd been born after his parents had been ousted, while they still fled from place to place, living lawlessly on the fringes of a homeland from which they'd been exiled.

He simply couldn't imagine that the risk of venturing back to Danihem was worth what the place might have to offer in return. It wasn't just his father's risk. He couldn't image what going back would require of him. Or maybe he was unsure what might be coaxed from him.

He shook off the thought. He lifted his gaze, out beyond the river valley, across the mist-shrouded mountains that formed Dania's southern border. Sometimes he imagined he saw glimpses out there, of a blue deeper than any sky.

Like carving, just the thought of the sea could soothe. It haunted his dreams—vast and sparkling, lined with white stone cities strewn with bright banners, rippling in the wind.

Vahldan reached to touch his cheek. The wound burned and his eye watered. It felt like a brand. Angavar only cared about his legacy. It was all he saw in Vahldan.

Angavar's legacy demanded justice, restoration, reparation. That his legacy somehow depended on his skill with a sword had never been in doubt. Now it seemed Vahldan's skill with a sword was vital, as well. If his father was right, the very survival of their people stood in the balance. Vahldan didn't want to believe that justice required bloodshed. Accepting that led to too dark a place to contemplate. There simply had to be a path to peaceful resolution. There had to be a way out—a way to break free of the shackles of legacy.

The familiar, high-pitched screech echoed through the stone canyon.

Vahldan looked up, shielding his eyes. The golden hawk swooped down from the heights and hovered overhead. "There you are," Vahldan said. The hawk rode the south wind a moment before diving toward the valley and then banking to swoop back. He hovered nearby again, seeming to beckon Vahldan to follow. The image of the charred wing sprang to mind. He said, "I wish I could. But I can't. Maybe there was never a choice after all."

The hawk screeched again. It sounded scolding. "Well, you're free to go."

With a final cry, the hawk soared on toward Dania and the sea beyond it.

"Maybe I'll see you there someday," he said, watching the raptor grow smaller in the sky.

He was just about to head back when something caught his eye. Movement. On the mountainside to the east, a swirl of dust. Horses. A host. Riding uphill fast.

Vahldan scrambled to hide behind the outcrop and peered over. A glint from one of the lead riders revealed a crescent shield.

Spali!

DESDRUSAN KNEW where the priest would be. He signaled a halt and reined in. "I'll go on alone," he said to his two guards. Teavar, the larger of the giant men, raised an incredulous brow. Desdrusan had to admit, dismissing his own security wasn't like him. "It's fine. Ride a perimeter. Stay close." Jhannas, always compliant, simply bowed his head, and the two big warriors reined into the forest in opposite directions.

Desdrusan awkwardly drew the futhark blade from its sheath at his hip. He was no swordsman. He only began carrying one when he ascended to the Amalus chieftainship, but he'd quickly grown fond of it. It wasn't just that this particular blade was a revered relic. As wearing swords generally did, it also conveyed menace. And Desdrusan had indeed become a dangerous man. He'd worked long and hard to make himself so. He'd risen by using his wits rather than blades and brawn. He would soon prove to Dania which was more dangerous.

He didn't expect trouble tonight—particularly not from a crippled priest. Nor from the other Carpans Desdrusan presumed were monitoring his approach. They were sneaky little demons, but they weren't warriors. Tonight the bare blade merely served to set the tone.

He urged his mount to walk through the clearing toward the cave where he'd first found the man. How well he recalled the night.

Túkash had been wounded, bleeding out. The wretch had crawled into the cave to hide from Angavar's rampaging brutes. Túkash hadn't realized then that Desdrusan had been hiding, too. The only difference was that Desdrusan had been hiding from his own clansmen, to avoid the danger of the hunt.

That was before he'd become dangerous.

The low mouth of the cave glowed among the shadows, a small fire burning just within. Dismounting with the blade in his hand was no simple task, but he managed to lift his leg over and slide from the saddle to land on swollen feet. He flung out his arm to keep from falling, and the horse skittered away a few steps.

Desdrusan feigned a lack of concern, ignoring the shrieking pain in his feet as he strode toward the fire. Sure enough, there sat the Carpan, his crippled leg stretched out before him—the leg Desdrusan had tied off with a tourniquet, saving his life. Sure, the leg was all but useless now. Luckily for Desdrusan, that didn't diminish the man's debt to him.

"Mirëmbrëna, a'Madha," Túkash said. The Carpan didn't rise, but he bowed from a sitting position with his palms pressed together. It seemed respectful enough.

"None of your gibberish," Desdrusan said in Hellainic. "You know I hate that."

The priest tilted his head. "Forgive me, my lord," he replied in Hellainic, their only shared tongue. Túkash smiled solicitously, leaned to grab a skin and a cup. " Please sit. I have wine. It's fairly—"

Desdrusan thumped the tip of the sword on the ground. "Save it. I'll stand. This is no happy reunion, for either of us. Just tell me. You found him?"

"I did, my lord."

"You showed our ally the way?"

Túkash bowed his head. "My scouts guide him and his host there now."

"What price does Auchote seek to do our bidding?"

"His people seek food. This is why they come in such numbers."

"Can you not simply pay him in gold?"

The priest's eyes grew fierce in the firelight. "I told you, Zemele's gold is sacred. It cannot be used to pay heathens for murder."

Desdrusan brought the tip of the blade up to tickle the Carpan's whiskerless chin. "Watch yourself, my friend. I told you to do whatever it took. You owe me that. Besides, you wouldn't want things to return to the way they were when Angavar led his thugs to hunt your people and steal your gold."

"Forgive me again, Lord of Lions." The priest wore a penitent smile, but there was scorn in his eyes. "I fear that coin means naught to Death's Grin. I also fear that—should you not supply the price he demands—Auchote is a man who takes as he sees fit. Perhaps more, should he feel he's been cheated. What the Spali now seek, only the Gottari can pay."

Desdrusan lowered the blade. "I suppose you're right."

"What shall I tell him, my lord? I vowed that once the deed was done, you would make things right with him."

Desdrusan gave him a mirthless chuckle. "Tell Death's Grin that he may take with him whatever he can reap from the flea-infested homesteads of the eastern marches."

The priest frowned. "What are you saying, a'Madha?"

"I am telling you to tell Auchote he has free reign to raid."

"Among your own people?"

"As long as he stays in the east, I will see to it that no force is mustered against him," Desdrusan said. Those in harm's way would be the very ones who'd been causing his problems.

"A man such as he," Túkash began, eyes darting. "I doubt Auchote will be satisfied with such an answer."

"Perhaps not." Desdrusan's smile was genuine. "We shall soon see. Will we not?"

The priest looked down. "I suppose we shall."

"Good. I'll consider your efforts in this regard to be another installment toward fulfilling your debt."

The priest bowed in his seat again. Desdrusan turned to leave, hoping his horse hadn't wandered far. It would be a shame to spoil the lordly effect by calling his guards for help.

"A'Madha, I must ask." He spun back, surprised Túkash had dared to speak again. The man's eyes were earnest, almost pleading. "You understand... the scourge you have unleashed? Upon your own people, and mine."

Desdrusan considered it a moment. For the Carpans, he cared not a whit. And the Gottari were a divided people. The futhark was dead. It was but a matter of time before more blood was shed. Angavar would see to it if Desdrusan didn't first. Men of blades and brawn always did.

He smiled. "I do, actually. Better a foe from without than treachery from within. Best get your people hidden in their mountain caves." He turned and set out again.

Vahldan kept low as he scrambled along the ridge. He vaulted onto the road and ran downhill as fast as he could, barely able to stay over his feet. He crossed the clearing and ran along the wall. He pounded to a halt inside the main gate and spun to slam and bar it.

"Spali!" he cried as he ran to close and bar the smaller north gate that led to the mine path. No one answered or appeared. The buildings of the compound crouched in late-day shadows. Vahldan ran to the stable and burst through the door, startling the horse. His father stood before his gear spread out in the straw at his feet. He didn't even look up. "I saw Spali!"

Angavar dropped his chin to his chest. Vahldan ran to his side. "Did you hear me? They're coming up the road from the confluence. They won't miss us. They'll be here soon!"

His father finally turned to face him with haunted eyes. "I heard."

Vahldan nodded at his gear. "Grab your bow. Mine's in the cabin. I'll get it on my way to bar the west gate. You take the northeast corner, and I'll take the southwest."

Angavar shook his head. "No. You're taking your mother, brother, and sister up to the mine. You'll guard the entrance. Don't come out. No matter what."

"What are you talking about? You always said we only need to bloody one Spali to set them into flight."

"Not this time." His father snatched up his hauberk and pulled it over his head. "I'm staying alone. The rest of you are going to hide."

"We should handle this as you always said we would. From the two corner platforms we can cover all four walls. One man can't—"

"Enough!" Angavar's eyes blazed. "I'm telling you how we'll handle it now. Can't you just do as I say for once?"

"I don't understand."

Angavar's expression firmed. He snatched up his sword belt. "I know what they're coming for. There's only one way through this now."

"What do you mean? They're raiders. They're coming to pillage."

"No. These Spali won't leave. Not until..." Angavar looked away, buckling the belt.

Vahldan pulled his father's shoulder. "Until what?"

Angavar rounded on him. "Listen to me. This may be the last thing I ask of you."

"Don't talk like that. We'll get through this."

Angavar grabbed the front of Vahldan's tunic in his fists and yanked him close. "Listen! Promise me you'll stay in the mine. Protect your mother and your brother and sister. Don't set foot outside it until you're sure the Spali are gone. Then find a way to get word to Badagis."

"Badagis? How? I haven't seen him in years."

"Just find a way. And stay alive. It's the only way to save everything we've worked for."

"Stay alive? Of course we will. We all will."

"Gods, you're still not listening. Have you heard any of this?"

Clearly there was no use arguing. "All right! I hear you."

Angavar released him, and his fierce gaze faded. "This is my fault.

I should've seen that you..." His father frowned. "Just stay true to me. Badagis will show you how."

Vahldan shook his head. "I don't know what you're talking about."

"I'm asking you to trust me. Can you do that?"

"Of course." It was the only answer left to him.

Angavar nodded. "Good." They both knew things were far from good. "Now go. Hurry."

VAHLDAN'S little brother's body trembled. Having Eldavar so close made the mine's entry tunnel feel even smaller. Vahldan's arms ached from holding up his bow.

"This is dumb," he whispered. "We'll be trapped if they find us."

"Father says it's the best place to hide and defend ourselves. Raiders steal and run."

The smell of smoke drifted in on a breeze. Vahldan had to do something. "This isn't a raid. I need to go see." He started crawling for the opening.

Eldavar grabbed his ankle. "We're not supposed to leave. No matter what!"

"You stay. I'll be right back." He shook his leg free.

"Vahldan, you can't leave me." It hit him. His brother was terrified. Eldavar was four years younger—too young to have so much thrust upon him.

"I'll go and have a look, and then I'll come right back. I promise." Vahldan reached and took his brother's hand, sealing their deal. "Keep your bow up," he said brightly. "See first, then release. Just like when we're hunting rabbits." Eldavar nodded, trying to look brave. Vahldan turned and crawled out.

The smoke grew thicker as Vahldan hurried down the path to the compound. Halfway down he left the path and crept along the tree-line of the north slope, staying out of view. He came to a shelf of rock topped with gorse, perched over an open slope that rose from the clearing outside the wall. It was a spot from which he could get a look at the entire vale.

He slowly rose to peer down. The sight was jarring.

Everything was on fire. Every roof inside the compound spouted a pillar of black smoke. Dozens of Spali galloped back and forth on the slope outside the east wall, shrieking and waving their javelins and bows. Angavar stood on the nearest corner platform, aiming his bow. A fallen horse and two Spali bodies were strewn across the clearing. One of the Spali lay on his back with an arrow protruding from his face, a hand grasping the shaft.

So much for the blood of one Spali putting the rest to flight.

Off to Vahldan's left, two Spali sat ahorse watching over the attack. Their black hair was tufted, as the elite Spali warriors wore it. Both riders' muscled torsos were covered in elaborate tattooing. The nearest one looked into the setting sun, displaying his profile. His entire face was either tattooed black or painted white to transform his façade into a grinning skull. This could be none other than Auchote—the infamous Spali warlord known as Death's Grin.

Based on all he'd heard about the Spali, the loss of their leader should end the attack. Perhaps it was the only thing that would. It was a long shot, but makeable. Vahldan fumbled for an arrow, nocked it and drew the bow. Gods, had it really come to this? Could he really kill?

He squeezed his eyes shut, quelling the flopping in his belly, seeking control.

When he opened them, the Spali duo was cantering along the hillside, heading out of range. Vahldan squinted through the smoke, lowered the bow, and hissed a curse.

A series of war-whoops was followed by a wordless roar from his father. Auchote sent a squad of his men to charge the main gate. The riders shot as they wheeled in retreat. His father ducked, then popped up to fire a parting shot.

The attack looked half-hearted. The Spali were biding time.

Vahldan scanned the rest of the vale and spotted movement to the west, beyond the back wall. A trio of Spali had dismounted. They ran in a crouch toward the back gate. One of them carried a coiled rope with a hook dangling from it.

The attacks on the main gate were to hold Angavar's attention. The sneaking trio would be up and over the back wall in mere moments. It wouldn't be happening if Vahldan had been on that back platform, as they'd always planned in the event of an attack like this.

He hopped through the gorse and skittered down the steep rock face. He lost his footing and landed on his butt at the top of the grassy clearing. He pushed off and ran. His bow was still nocked with an arrow. The ground leveled, and he loped through knee-high grass toward the wall. The small gate to the mine path was burning. He might be able to kick it open.

He was halfway there, sure he was going to make it to safety, when he heard it. Not a battle cry, but a warning call. He turned to look.

Several Spali on the slope above the east wall pointed and shouted. The Spali chieftain and his companion were the closest to Vahldan. They were looking right at him. As one, the pair started to gallop straight for him, their javelins raised to be thrown. The grin tattooed on Auchote's jaw seemed to grow.

Vahldan panicked. He dropped down in the grass, but instantly realized it wouldn't hide him. He fought to gather himself, to run again or aim his bow, but his appendages felt floppy. He had to do something, but terror seized and bound him. He rose up to find that Death's Grin was almost to him.

His father had been right. What Vahldan had inside him wasn't enough. He couldn't summon it or control it. What he had was useless ugliness, nothing more.

"Auchote!" The call echoed across the clearing. "It's me you want!"

His father had leapt from the wall. Angavar ran at an angle to intercept the attackers. Both Spali reined toward Angavar, who stopped and drew his bow. The chieftain's companion threw first. Angavar released his bowshot and dove clear of the thrown missile. The Spali rode on, gripping the arrow protruding from his chest. Angavar landed in a roll, but Auchote bore down on him.

Vahldan heard the thud of the Spali chieftain's javelin, watched as the tip pierced his father's flesh. He cried out, sprang up, and ran to his father. Auchote reined for another pass, drawing a curved sword. Vahldan grabbed the jutting javelin shaft and yanked. His father's roar sounded more animal than human.

Vahldan stood on wobbly legs to face his fallen father's attacker, gripping the bloody javelin. Auchote's grin grew again as he came around to face them. "Ah, the little rabbit stirs!"

Vahldan had only heard two humans speaking Hellainic. The first was his mother, during their insufferable lessons. But in spite of his struggles with the language, he understood Auchote well enough.

Auchote laughed and brandished the sword, his horse prancing sideways, ready to charge. "This rabbit is hardly worth a bother. But the crippled priest will be pleased by his pelt, I think."

The second person with whom Vahldan had spoken Hellainic was his father's escaped captive—the Carpan Túkash. The man who'd originally led them to the mine. A crippled priest.

The attack was part of a plot. Banishment hadn't been enough. These Spali had been sent to kill his father. And Angavar had known it was coming.

His father's words echoed in memory. *"This has everything to do with you. You're my son."*

This chieftain believed Vahldan would freeze and fail. Again. He was next.

Auchote kicked his mount to a gallop. Hot energy surged through Vahldan, down into his wobbly limbs. He felt it flow through his hands into the javelin's shaft. He held the missile over his shoulder. Every muscle in his body felt like a drawn bow.

The horse came on, faster, Auchote's sword poised to swing.

Vahldan waited, coiled to launch—waited till he saw the Spali's arm twitch, bringing the blade into motion.

Vahldan hurled the javelin and threw himself over his father. The horse screamed and hooves beat past them. His father groaned. Vahldan raised up, realizing he hadn't been cut. Nor had the hooves kicked either of them. Auchote's cry was of frustration. Vahldan glanced to find the horse rolling to the ground, dumping his Spali rider. He wrapped Angavar's arm over his shoulder and heaved, pulling him up.

Angavar growled as Vahldan dragged him to the gate. Thankfully, his father got his feet moving under him, speeding them. Vahldan focused on getting to the smoldering ruins of the gate, all the while waiting to be speared or chopped down.

Both he and his father were gasping as they stumbled over the burnt ruins of the gate. Once inside, they tumbled to the turf. Vahldan grabbed Angavar under the arms and dragged him away from the opening, to the partial shelter of the inner wall. He drew his carving knife—his only remaining weapon—ready to face the attack that was sure to follow. Outside the walls, the ground shook with the rumble of hooves; the thundering was pierced by odd, high-pitched cries.

The noise faded. Moments passed, and no one appeared in the gateway. It grew strangely quiet. Vahldan ran to the gateway and peered out. The clearing surrounding the compound was empty. The crackling of the nearby burning stable was the only sound.

His father slid down onto his back, groaning. Vahldan rushed to him, sheathed the knife and dropped to his knees. Angavar's face had grown frightfully pale, and though he clutched the stab wound with both hands, blood was oozing between his fingers.

"You're bleeding fast. We've got to get you to the mine."

Angavar shook his head. "That's not happening."

"This is my fault," Vahldan said. "I'm sorry."

His father actually laughed. "Your fault? Hardly."

"I shouldn't have left the mine. I'm sorry I didn't listen."

Angavar's gaze locked with his. "You did what you had to. As did I."

It was so much worse, though. "I'm sorry that I froze."

"Doesn't matter."

"It's why you jumped down," he said. "It's why you got hit."

"But you didn't let it happen twice. I trust it will never happen again."

"I'll never be as good as you."

Angavar huffed another laugh. "I doubt that's true. All I care about is your oath. Stay true to me. *That* we both know you can do." Angavar reached to grab Vahldan's hand. His father's hand was sticky with gore. "Can we agree?" The intensity was gone. It was a father's plea.

"Of course. Always." Vahldan pressed his lips tight. Gods, it sounded so final. This couldn't be happening. He had to do something. He scanned the compound. The stable was a blackened wreck, but in spite of the smoke billowing from the roof, the cabin still stood. "I'll go find some bandaging." He started to rise.

"Don't!" His father's grip tightened. "It's too late." Angavar gestured downward. "It's time. Take the blade."

"No. This can't be happening."

"Take it! I can feel the poison. We both know what needs to be done."

"I can't."

"You can!" Angavar pulled him closer. "I know why you fear it. But it's in your blood. Grant me a warrior's death, and you need never fear it again. Understood?"

Angavar released him and nodded toward the hilt. Vahldan drew his father's sword from the sheath at his hip. He pulled up Angavar's hauberk, and then the blood-soaked tunic, baring his torso. The wound gaped, dark and ugly. Vahldan stood and straddled him, bracing himself.

Angavar's eyes locked on his. "Now promise me. Promise you'll heed your legacy. Restore our honor. Claim your rightful title. Lead our clan to glory. Take it back. Glory is the way."

This was all wrong. Angavar of the Amalus could reclaim their glory. His father was a leader, not him. "You were right. About everything. There is no reasoning with them." Vahldan shook his head and gulped for breath. "I'll never live up to you."

"You will!" Angavar clenched and convulsed. "Trust me, I know what's inside you." His bloody smile was grim. "Because it's inside me, too."

"No." It came as a voiceless breath. All that was in him was ugliness and fear.

"Remember, Badagis will show you the way." Vahldan opened his mouth, but Angavar held up his bloody hand. "There's no time. Come, before it's too late."

He was right. The poison couldn't take him. Vahldan pressed the tip to the base of his father's sternum. He hesitated.

"In and up," Angavar said. "I'll suffer but a moment."

Vahldan steeled himself, the tip of the sword riding up and down with his father's ragged breath. "You're sure?"

His father gave a single nod. "This is where I end and you begin."

Tears blurred his vision. He drew a shaky breath and pushed. The blade slid in and up. Angavar gasped, eyes wide. Gods, how could it be so easy, like halving a firm round of cheese, to pierce the heart of the Gottari people's greatest warrior?

"Be bold. Go all the way," his father whispered. There was love in his eyes.

Vahldan yanked the blade out, as if it were possible to take it all back. He dropped to his knees and grabbed his father's hand. "I will. I'll try, I promise." Blood flowed free, forming rivulets across pale flesh.

His father huffed his final words. "Seize... your... destiny." His grip went limp, and the love in his eyes became a blank stare.

Vahldan squeezed his eyes shut, the rage surging more intensely than ever. He tilted his head back. "No!" he cried to the sky and the gods. "I won't let them get away with it. I won't let them win!"

He lifted the sword and squeezed, watching his knuckles turn white. Gods, he hated them—all of them: the wolves, the guildsmen, and most of all the Amalus traitors. He used to hate how good the hilt felt in his hand, but now he relished it. Now he grasped how it would serve him. "I won't let them win," he repeated, making it a vow.

Vahldan drew himself up to face what they'd made him do. His father's skin looked waxy, his face slack. He couldn't look anymore.

He turned to survey the wreckage they'd wrought. He walked to the cabin, feeling the heat of the smoldering ruins. He bent outside the window, picked up the horse carving. He fingered the intricate mane, fashioned by a master. He tossed the horse in through the window, into the flaming wreckage. Then he found the woodpecker. The work of his own hand. He held it close, studying it. It wasn't as good as the horse, but it was good. In another life, he would've gotten better.

His lip curled. "You were right, Father. There is no choice." The ugliness flared and he hurled the bird into the coals. The flames rose, consuming it.

Vahldan pushed down the rage and returned to his father. Night was falling. He had to move, to stay alive. He unbuckled Angavar's sword belt, pulled it free, and wrapped it around his own narrower waist. He sheathed the blade. It may have felt good in his hand, but wearing it still felt awkward, heavy. Unearned.

It was time to get used to it. Time to grow up. Vahldan stood at Angavar's feet. "I guess it's fallen to me, Father. Just as you feared. But I gave you my word. I'll try to live up to you."

Vahldan gleaned a shush of movement. He spun and glimpsed a ghostly form in the smoke and shadow, just as it disappeared from the gateway.

The rage flashed like a thunderbolt, fresh and hot. The blade was out and he was running through the gate. Hemlock branches swayed across the clearing. He ran for the spot and crashed through the boughs with the sword before him. The brush was stirring further on.

He stood catching his breath. This chase would only grow darker and more dangerous. He could best defend himself and his family at the entrance to the mine.

He headed back, the thrum of his anger fading. His father's voice echoed in his head: *'Trust me, I know what's inside you. Because it's inside me, too.'*

Vahldan was startled by the terrifying truth of it. He hadn't hesitated. He'd boldly embraced it—the curse of his legacy. Where his father had ended, he began.

He was the blood of a killer.

CHAPTER 3—THE DUTY AND DEEDS OF THE SKOLANI

"*The old songs tell of the coming of the Gottari to Dania, and of their ill reception by the Skolani. The two tribes spent generations in mistrust and in bitter strife. Much blood was spilled before they came to terms with one another. To most Gottari, the Skolani remain mysterious and somewhat frightening. Which is just as most Skolani prefer it.*" —Brin Bright Eyes, Saga of Dania

VAHLDAN WOKE with a start to the sound of shuffling. He'd fallen asleep just inside the entrance to the mine he was supposed to be guarding. Outside, the sky grew gray with the morning twilight. He lay perfectly still, his hand on the sword hilt, straining to hear beyond his pounding heart. He swiftly realized that the sounds came from behind him, up from the tunnel.

His mother's form appeared. She was crawling toward him, her belly hanging low, huffing with the effort. "What are you doing? You should be resting." Telling her about her husband's death had been just as difficult as being the instrument of it. He'd had no idea how to respond to her tears—the first he remembered seeing from her. It made his chest hurt. After they'd said the prayers to Hel together, he'd used the excuse of having to take up the watch, and left her. Which made the ache worse.

He still hadn't told her that he'd been to blame for what had happened.

Frisanna came into the light of the entrance. Her expression was hard. "There's no time to rest. Time to get on with it."

"Get on with what?"

She frowned. "With life." She gazed out through the entrance. "Is it clear?"

"As far as I can tell." He had no idea how long he'd been asleep.

Frisanna crawled past him. "Wait." Vahldan hurried after her. "You shouldn't go out there."

His mother stood outside the entrance with a groan, holding her back as she stretched. "What should I do? Lay in a stinking hole?"

Vahldan followed her to the path to the compound, sword in hand. Smoke rose from the vale, but all was quiet and still. She started down the path.

"Mother, wait." She kept going. He hurried to catch her by the shoulder. "Please."

"Wait for what?" she snapped. "To die up here?" Her eyes were puffy and her face was pale. "I have to go down there. I need to feed my children."

"There are stores up here," he said tentatively. Of course she knew it.

His mother drew a deep breath. "I have to see what's become of my home. I have to..." Her face crumpled. "See for myself what's become of my husband." Tears streaked her face and dripped from her chin. "Damn him. We should've run. He knew they'd find out. He knew they'd come. He should've known that damned Carpan would never stay quiet."

Vahldan longed to comfort her. He sheathed the blade and warily wrapped her in his arms. She surprised him by leaning in and burying her face in his tunic. He had to tell her. "It wasn't his fault."

She drew back, firming herself. "Of course it was. A banished man is supposed to leave. He could've just walked away, started again elsewhere. But he couldn't let it go."

It wasn't what he meant, but still. "He stayed because he was innocent."

Frisanna closed her eyes and shook her head. "He might have been innocent of Aomeir's murder. But he was far from innocent. He..." She opened her eyes. "Wanted too much." Her smile was sad. "They were never going to accept his ambition."

He thought he knew, but he had to ask. "Who?"

"All of them. Every man who puts himself over others. Every Rekkr who draws profit from the bent backs of their fellow Gottari. Wolves and lions alike. They were either in on it, or they stood by. Which makes them all guilty. And now a true leader—perhaps Dania's best hope—is dead. They all have his blood on their hands."

She was right. Vahldan had to remember his vow. They wouldn't get away with this. It was time to grow up. "Let me go down there. You stay here with Eldavar and Mara. Let me bury him. I owe him that much." And more.

Without looking, Frisanna gripped his hand and nodded.

VAHLDAN CLIMBED down to the spot overlooking the vale, where he'd first seen the raid unfolding—where his string of failures began. He peered through the mist. The clearing was empty. The fallen Spali were gone. Had the foe come to claim their dead? Dread filled him when he thought of his father. Had they defiled his body?

Vahldan drew the blade and returned to the path. His head swiveling from side to side, he strode to the north gate. He paused outside the compound, listening. He heard only crows cawing. He braced himself and stepped over the wrecked gate.

The view stole his breath, but not for the reason he'd expected.

His father was not defiled or mauled by scavengers. He was gone. The Spali must have taken him.

Vahldan ran to the spot, searching for tracks or any sign at all. There was nothing new, just the bloodstain where Angavar had lain when Vahldan left him. He spun in place, his heart galloping. He knelt to study the scuffs in the moss. There was nothing telling. The marks could've happened before, during, or after the battle.

"Vahldan!" His brother's call echoed through the canyon.

He sheathed the blade and ran. He flew through the north gate and headed up the mine path. He heard rhythmic thumping behind. A galloping horse. It had to be Spali. Without slowing his pace, he left the path and darted into the pines and scrub at the base of the rocky slope. He crashed through the brush, shielding his face with his hands. Once he figured he was out of sight, he drew the blade and turned to see if he was being followed.

He peered through the branches to find not Spali, but a sight that seemed to have sprung from legend. The rider reined a sorrel warhorse to a halt, exactly where he'd entered the brush. A sword hilt rose over the rider's shoulder. Long braids swayed as the rider leaned in the saddle to gaze right at him. "We've no time left to play our game, Young Lion."

A woman. Her words were accented, her tone stern but not hostile.

Vahldan instantly knew she was Skolani. He next realized that hers was likely the ghostly face he'd seen the prior night. If she'd intended him harm, he'd be dead. The Skolani were among Dania's most vaunted warriors. If anyone hated Spali more than the Gottari, it was the Skolani.

He didn't move. He would not blunder into danger again. But neither would he fail to act. "Our game?" he called.

"Stalk and chase. Though I admit you've some skill at it."

"What do you mean, no time left?"

"Just that." She cocked her head. "The Spali are coming back. If you wish to live, we must flee." Her urgent warning belied her calm demeanor.

"Vahldan!" His brother called again.

"My family." He took a step and halted, still uncertain of her.

"Your family is safe, for the moment. The Spali are riding up the road from the ford. But your brother's yodeling isn't wise. They're likely to have scouts. Come, ride with me."

He stood evaluating the situation. What could she really want?

"Come, come." She beckoned. "Have you learned nothing? Standing and gawping is seldom wise."

Damn, that stung. How did she know? Had she seen? "I wasn't—"

"You still are. Be sensible and come with me, or flee. Either would be wiser than this."

He raised his chin and strode to her.

"That's better. Now, sheath that blade."

He found himself doing as bidden. Even as he took the final steps, she reached to him. He put his hand in hers. It was larger than his mother's. And strong. She vacated a stirrup and, just as his foot found it, she pulled him up with astonishing ease. The instant his rump hit the horse she clucked and they were on the move.

He had no choice but to grasp her waist. Her tunic was close-fitting doeskin, her waist firm. Thick auburn braids hung a hand's width from his nose and nearly down to his hands. Her scent came to him, exotic—spicy and earthy. He found focus on her blade hilt. It was of Gottari make, intricately ornamented. A legacy blade. It made her a Blade-Wielder—one of the elite guardians of the realm. They said the Skolani trained with weapons from the day they could stand, and rode from the day they could stay in the saddle unaided. Yet only the fittest among them ascended to the ranks of the Blade-Wielders.

She seemed young, perhaps a few years older than him. It made her status all the more impressive. Her mount was calm and well-trained; the warhorse adeptly stepped onto the narrow path and started to climb the rocky slope. His grip must've been too tight. She turned her head, her eye angled, like a predator's. He eased his grip and she looked away.

In mere moments they came to the plateau just below the entrance to the mine. The steepness of the final stretch made the footing for the horse too dangerous, and the Skolani reined to a halt. Without waiting for him to dismount, one of her legs folded and slipped over, and she was off. She tied the reins to a sapling and started up the path. He hurried after her.

She hadn't spoken since he came to her. The questions were like a swarm of eels, slithering about him—so many he couldn't find grip on a first. "You are...?" he started before faltering.

"Elan," she said without turning. He didn't know what she meant. She looked back. "My name," she said. "I am Elan, daughter of Ellasan—a Blade-Wielder of the Skolani."

"I am Vahldan, son of Angavar."

"I know who you are, Young Lion." Her tone was wry.

The path to the mine leveled. Elan stopped, her gaze on their surroundings. "Your brother wouldn't be foolish enough to shoot at me, would he?"

"Sorry. I can never be sure with him."

"Call to him."

"Eldavar, it's me!"

"Who's she?" His brother's high pitch betrayed his fear.

"A friend," Vahldan said, hoping it was true.

Elan strode on. "Your mother. Is she in labor?"

"I'm not sure," Eldavar said, sounding worried. He appeared from behind a rock above the entrance, his nocked bow in hand. "She's in pain again."

"Let's hope not," Elan muttered, and turned to Vahldan. "Take me to her. There's little time. We must be over the western crest and down into the next canyon before sundown."

"The western crest? We're running?"

She scowled. "What would you suggest? Rebuilding the gates? Hoping they'll ride on?"

Heat rose to his cheeks. "No. It's just, I doubt my mother can handle the climb."

"We'll have to put the lioness on Hrithvarra. That too is dangerous, but it's a risk we'll have to take."

He frowned, then realized. "Hrithvarra. Your horse."

"Yes, Hrithvarra has been my friend since she was a colt and I was a pup. If I ask it of her, she will gently bear a stranger."

He dropped down to enter the mine. "Freya help us," he murmured.

Elan was right behind him. "Mind a bit of advice? Don't bother putting your trust in the gods. They don't give a damn. When it comes to life and death, best to trust to mortals. We have more to lose."

"I should trust you, then?"

"You should," she said, without hesitation.

He had to admit, he admired her certainty. Besides, there were few other choices.

Fate seemed to have delivered her. Just moments earlier he'd wondered how they would survive. Now it seemed they'd gained a vaunted warrior to guide them in flight. He supposed having only one choice was better than having no good ones.

THE OUTCAST'S widow emerged from the mine with a groan, hefting a leather sling filled with straw. "Bring only what you must," Elan pleaded. "We need to make haste." The swollen-bellied woman glared and set about tying the sling to the donkey.

Once again, Elan questioned how she'd ended up leading a family in flight from seemingly relentless killers. The worst part was, she'd all but volunteered for it. It had been exciting enough when her host's scouts gleaned they were hunting none other than Death's

Grin. But then when Elan had learned where Auchote's band seemed to be headed, Elan had felt a little thrill. She'd long heard the tales of the Outcast. A dashing Gottari chieftain, ousted by rivals who feared his growing power—the man was a legend. Although the clash between the legend and the infamous killer had resulted in tragedy, she'd been witness to a tale that would be told for generations. And now she was with the son. Many whispered his name in regard to prophecy.

But in all of the excitement, she'd gotten too mixed up in the affairs of outsiders. Such lapses were not the Skolani way. Skolani protected their fellow Danians, but without interference. She'd waded in too deep to avoid a growing current. One that threatened to sweep them all away.

"Eldavar, take a basket to the lower dig and fetch the cheeses I've laid up. Vahldan, go to the spring and fill all of the skins." The widow still hadn't spoken directly to Elan.

"No, please, there's no time." Elan held her arms out to block their way. Both brothers tensed, eyes wide.

The Outcast's wife rounded on Elan, her anger animating her beauty. "What, pray tell, do you propose I feed my children?"

"I have enough food to get us through the day."

"And then?"

"If we don't go now, there'll be no need to worry about food."

The lioness glared. Elan sensed her mistrust and understood it. It was a Skolani-like attitude. "How old are you?" Frisanna abruptly asked.

Elan returned her stare. "Old enough to save your family. But only if you put yourself in my hands. Starting by leaving now and bringing nothing."

The woman sighed. "If you can save my family, I'm at your command." Frisanna's hands drifted to her belly. Gods, when would that babe come? Elan couldn't save a babe. Her mother could have, but not Elan. She was no healer, in spite of what so many seemed to wish of her.

Elan directed the boys to unload the donkey. They left the poor beast behind with all the straw. She still wondered if it was wise to lead them out. Maybe she should leave them and ride to find her host. Or perhaps together they could hold the mine. There was only one good path up to it. If the boys could hold the entrance, she could delay the Spali's arrival with ambushes, then harry them from the heights. Perhaps the foe could be forced to give up and move on.

There was no choice that didn't involve risk. Flight offered the least.

"I think we're ready," Vahldan announced, helping his brother don his pack.

"Lady Frisanna?"

The woman gazed at the lingering smoke over the vale. She finally faced them and nodded.

The little girl, Mara, stared up at Elan with wide eyes, clutching two woolen dolls, one under each arm. Vahldan lifted his little sister onto his shoulders. "Lead on, Blade-Wielder," he said. "We're in your hands."

Gods, this was all on her now. The fate of Angavar's legacy was in her hands.

They started down the path, and Elan soon realized she'd gotten way out ahead. She stopped. They came along so slowly. The little brother looked unsteady under the load. His baggy cloak and thin legs made him look like a newborn heron, learning to walk. Vahldan kept a hand on his mother's elbow, and she kept both hands on her belly. Even once they managed to get the mother ahorse, it might not speed them enough. Elan got an idea. There was a stand of young larches along the plateau where she'd tied Hrithvarra.

Arriving ahead of the others, she retrieved her axe from the saddle and made her selections. She swiftly felled and stripped the limbs from three straight poles. Vahldan caught up and set the girl down. Without hesitation or questions, he came into the stand and started dragging the poles to the clearing. She pulled the last out, and began cutting it into sections. She retrieved a roll of cording from her saddlebag and tied off the first crosspiece. She laid the next one in place, beginning a ladder-like sequence.

Vahldan knelt and held the crosspiece. "Like this?" She nodded and tied it. As she finished off the knots, he cut the next crosspiece.

Working together they quickly finished. She cut a section of rope to fasten the first of the projecting side rails on Hrithvarra's saddle while Vahldan held the other on the far side. The makeshift litter was strong enough to carry the pregnant woman. But until that became necessary, it would carry their supplies and the girl. Elan worried about the tracks it would leave. She'd simply have to try to erase them for a time and then focus on speeding their flight. She finished tying the load, and her gaze rose to the Young Lion's forced smile.

"This will help. We'll make it now." He sought to reassure her. He sensed her fret.

She smiled back. "Of course." Her smile was just as forced. Surely he saw through it.

Elan turned to the girl. "And you can ride on top. Would you like that?" The girl wore a wary look, hugging her dolls to her chest. She'd need to hold on with at least one hand. Elan leaned on her knees. "What are their names?"

Mara held out the girl doll. "This is Saarin."

"And her friend?" Elan pointed to the horse.

"Neeha."

"Did you know that Hrithvarra here has always been my friend, just like Neeha has been for Saarin?" The girl shook her head. "What if we were to have Hrithvarra protect Neeha? I could put her in a special place, in Hrithvarra's saddlebag. Would that be all right?" The girl looked at the dolls, considering. She nodded and handed her the horse.

Elan took Neeha to her saddlebag and stowed it. "See? She's safe."

Vahldan lifted his sister up and helped her to get settled. He turned to Elan. "Thank you. That was kind. She's never met another woman before."

Elan knew how Mara felt. She'd never met an Amalus before. She'd often heard other Skolani prattling on over the royal clansmen —their rowdy and sometimes volatile temperaments, their good looks and fine physiques. Particularly during the approach of a full moon, when the fertility ceremonies loomed. She had to admit, the son of Angavar was handsome. A bit lanky yet, and his flaxen beard wasn't quite full. A hint of his mother's beauty softened the father's rugged features. He wore a recent wound on his cheek, but it looked like it would heal without leaving a scar.

It took both Elan and Vahldan to get the mother into Hrithvarra's saddle, but once they set out again they did indeed make better time. In the early going, Elan decided it was wiser to stay with them and urge their pace, rather than leave to scout the foe.

Once they crested the ridge, Elan backtracked to the forested heights above the compound. The Spali had arrived, but they seemed more intent on scavenging for loot than survivors. She had to presume they would find their trail and start after them again. And based on the level of destruction at the compound, they'd resume their hunt soon.

She returned to find the family had stopped. Frisanna sprawled on a flat rock clutching her belly, her expression twisted with discomfort. Vahldan explained that once they began to descend, she'd been unable to stay in the saddle at such an angle. By the time they settled the lioness on the litter, Elan's fears that she would give birth along the way were all but assured. Once again, Elan found herself missing her mother, and wishing she'd paid more heed to Ellasan's lessons.

All too soon, the sun dipped behind the western hilltops. Dense trees loomed below. She had hoped to make it to the safety of the far banks of the river before dark, but that had been wishful thinking. They were far from it. And crossing the ford in the dark was ill-advised.

With a nocked bow, Elan led them into the twilit forest. Vahldan followed, leading Hrithvarra. The girl sat in the saddle, legs dangling, and the brother walked beside his mother.

Elan sensed Vahldan watching her, and turned. "Just so you know, the Skolani consider it rude to stare."

His cheeks flushed as he looked away. "Forgive me."

"I get it. You are all quite different to me, too. But if you meet another of us, you should remember it. Most will be less understanding." She went back to watching the way ahead.

"Why were you there?" he said. She tensed but kept moving. "Last night. It was you at the gate, wasn't it?"

Now it was her turn to flush. She told herself to just answer the question. He wanted to know why she was there. Fair enough. "Our host was hunting the Paralatoe that attacked your compound. Their leader is a dangerous warlord."

"Death's Grin." She nodded once, hoping it would suffice. "So where's your host now? Why are the Spali still chasing us?"

It hadn't sufficed. "I presume my host is still hunting. The Spali who are following us today are not Paralatoe. Though they may be at Auchote's command."

He shook his head, clearly bewildered. "Why are you not with them?"

Gods, if he only knew. But he mustn't. "I'm a guardian, commanded to stay behind to see to your family's safety."

Vahldan was silent for a moment. "What can you tell me about the Spali?"

"What would you like to know?"

"Why now? Why so many? Why our compound?"

She walked on a moment. It wasn't her place to speculate. "No one is certain why there are so many Spali this year. Or even if the various bands are working in league. Perhaps this warband's scouts stumbled upon your home. Perhaps they guessed it was built for mining. Perhaps they hoped for easy plunder."

Vahldan scowled and looked ahead. "That seems likely." His tone was sarcastic. She said nothing. "Almost no one knew of the mine," he added.

"Seems prudent."

"Your queen knew."

She turned a hard eye on him. "Are you making an accusation, Young Lion?"

He sighed. "No. I'm just looking for answers."

"I understand. I am a Blade-Wielder. As is our queen. The Blade-Wielders' oath is twofold. We swear to protect the innocent, and to avoid interfering in the lives of others."

She glanced at him and he looked away and nodded. Again, he seemed far from satisfied.

The path grew less steep, but became muddier and closely lined with trees. They were forced to drag the litter directly over the streambed, through cattails, the pole ends plowing the slop. Her boots grew heavy with water and muck.

As the twilight faded, Elan gleaned a foreign sound over the splash of the horse hooves and the scrape of the litter. She halted and raised a hand for silence.

In the stillness she heard it again. Human voices.

The family heard it too. She sensed their terror. She signaled for them to stay put and she set out. She crept high along the slope of the gorge before stalking downhill toward the voices. She came upon the Spali about two hundred paces ahead. Four of them.

Elan studied the steep, wooded slopes of the stream gorge. There was no way around. The Spali appeared to be hunkering down for the night. They'd chosen a secluded spot, but it wasn't the best ground to defend. Their ponies were tethered, grazing a nearby patch of grass. Two Spali sat slumped against trees while one leaned over the muddy bank, drinking and washing from the center flow. The fourth seemed to be set as their watchman. But he only watched downhill. Perhaps they feared pursuit.

The watcher was the only one armed with a blade. The others had bows and daggers. The one in the stream muttered as he washed a wound. One of those sitting held a bloody cloth to his bicep, the arm laid across his lap. His quiver was behind him, nearly out of reach. They appeared to be exhausted. These boys had been in a fight. And it hadn't gone well for them.

All of it boded well. But the best bit was that they weren't Paralatoe. Their tattooing was slight or absent. They wore beards, and their long hair hung lank, not tufted or tied back as the warriors wore it. These were herdsmen. Perhaps they were raiding to seek wealth, or status. Perhaps they were beholden to some raiding chieftain—perhaps Auchote, but she doubted it. It was said that Death's Grin had little patience for untrained warriors.

None of which helped to explain their presence. Had they been chased here? Were they part of a larger host that had been scattered? Were they waiting for others?

Something buzzed inside her. The warrior in her couldn't ignore the acclaim that taking a Spali scalp would bring. It would make a much better tale than having been the one who'd insisted on ruining a perfect ambush, and then being assigned as a nursemaid to those she'd insisted on saving.

And yet, there were four of them. All Spali were dangerous. Taking on all four by herself was no small task. With the family's hunters surely on their trail by now, retreating the way they'd come was out. Waiting in hiding was risky, too—a nightmare if the lioness's babe came.

However it had come to pass, she'd bound herself to this family. Whatever fate held in store for them, she'd firmly tethered herself to it. There was no easy solution, but there were still choices to be made.

Elan made her first decision and headed back. She would test the eldest son's reaction, and then make her second decision based on that. She arrived to find the lioness writhing, with little Mara gripping her mother's hand. She waved both brothers to her. "There are four Spali up ahead," she whispered. "They appear to be there for the night. I see no way around them."

Vahldan didn't hesitate. "We'll have to eliminate them." A wildness flashed in his eyes. "Tell us what you need of us."

It was exactly the response she'd hoped to hear.

THADMEIR STILL FELT RESTLESS. Too restless to go to bed. Instead he sat in the dais chair, drinking and thinking. The evening's session in the longhouse had been another contentious one, but at least tonight he'd ended the ongoing debate. Which left no one happy with him.

It had gone on too long, but it was finally done. He had finally decreed that the Amalus Rekkrs could muster a force and ride.

Yet the lions of the eastern marches were still angry. They'd been pushing for it since before the snows melted, and he'd imposed yet another delay. Not to mention their annoyance that he'd imposed limits on their numbers and on the scope of the mission. The wolves, the landholders, and the guildsmen were livid that he'd given in.

He'd heard the rumors, that the priestess Amaseila somehow held him spellbound. It was difficult to deny or hide his fascination. Which was why the eastern herdsmen kept bringing her. Those who believed it thought him a fool, or at least feebleminded.

Thadmeir knew he was neither. It was worse. He was more like a lovesick teenager. He actually had trouble keeping himself from looking at her. Tonight all the lions had done was position her on the front bench. All she'd done was stare and emote. She hadn't uttered a word.

It had been enough. He was loath to admit that she'd had an effect, even to himself. Best to console himself that he acted with prudence, regardless of his inexcusable crush.

It had grown late while he wrestled his conscience. Most had left the longhouse. There had been none of the usual song and drink after they'd adjourned. Many had stormed out right after his decree, Desdrusan leading the outraged pack. Even the victors had not lingered. Young Arnegern, the leader of the upstart herdsmen, had left the longhouse with most of his cousins and supporters in tow, likely to plan their next steps. Even Urias had gone straight to bed.

Thadmeir was grateful they were gone. The months of bickering had left him exhausted.

He sat mulling the mess he'd allowed. What bothered him most was his inability to halt the rancor that kept the Gottari nation divided. Tonight's session had ended with an undeniable hostility between the ruling clans. The Gottari were edging toward calamity. Again.

It pained Thadmeir that many considered the futhark to be broken. And most who considered it so, on both sides, thought it stemmed from the incidents surrounding Angavar's exile, for the murder of Thadmeir's brother. It should be ancient history, but the raw feelings born of it lingered on. The Outcast's supporters continued to call Aomeir's death accidental, and considered Desdrusan a usurper—a puppet to the Wulthus-dominated wool guild. Thadmeir had to admit, he sometimes wondered how it had come to this.

Not that he didn't believe Angavar responsible. Nor that the former Amalus chieftain didn't deserve being deposed and exiled. After all, the man had time and again proven himself a reckless leader, not to mention the realm's most volatile warrior. Angavar had always sought and relished any reason to spill blood.

But nearly a score of years later, there was no end in sight. The divisions formed on the day of his brother's death seemed to grow deeper and more irreversible than ever. The past simply would not leave them be.

Perhaps the futhark really was broken. Perhaps it was foolish to believe that the Rekkrs' council could ever go back to the way they'd been before they were so divided.

Perhaps his attempts to find ways to compromise made him the biggest fool of all.

Thadmeir was gazing at his reflection in his cup when it suddenly went dark.

Someone had snuffed the nearest torch. All of the torches were
out, actually; the only light now came from the dying fires in the two
hearths and a few families' candles. Several dozen attendees from
far-flung settlements had bedded down on the longhouse floor. Even
in this the lions were slovenly, like twigs scattered by a gale. Thadmeir couldn't wait to have the place swept and scrubbed. And aired
out! Gods, did these people ever wash themselves?

The sojourners whispered as they settled in. Thadmeir brought
his cup to his lips and gulped down the stale dregs. Going to bed was
the only sensible thing left to him. He stood, wobbly with drink and
exhaustion. He gathered up the nearest abandoned cups and stumbled through the cloak and blanket-wrapped bodies, heading toward
the sideboard and his washtub. May as well get a start on the
cleanup.

Thadmeir set the cups in the cold water. He resisted the impulse
to keep cleaning and headed for the residence drapes. Rounding the
center hearth, he came upon two benches slid together and outfitted
with blankets as a cushion and covers. He stepped closer, drawn to
the curvaceous blanket-wrapped form. Blood pounded at his
temples. Had he found her by instinct or accident? Either way, there
was no harm in a final look. After that he would banish her from his
mind. She'd likely never be back, now that the lions had gotten
their way.

He hesitated when he spotted the father's boots sticking out
from beneath her bench bed. Thadmeir stooped to look. The
herdsman was wrapped in his cloak, snoring. Amaseila's face
appeared from the top of the blanket. "Come to wish me pleasant
dreams, my lord?" Her blanket slid an enticing finger's length off of
milky bare shoulders. His shame burned on his cheeks. He couldn't
reply or turn away.

She chuckled. "Or perhaps you would have me dream of the
coming of the Spali—something of use to the realm?"

He shook himself free of her spell. "Sorry to have disturbed you.
Good night."

She propped her head on an elbow, revealing more skin. "So, you believed me after all."

He knew he should walk away, but he couldn't. "It was never a matter of my belief."

"Why then?"

He straightened, raised his chin. "It's expedient. The risk outweighs the cost."

Her smile quirked. "Ah. The cost. Am I a part of the risk, then?"

Gods, she was alluring. "I don't know what you mean."

"Surely I'm not expedient." Alluring, but also taunting him, apparently to amuse herself.

"I should go to bed. And you should leave at first light."

"Surely you know by now. You can't be rid of me so easily. It is as it shall be, my lord."

His feet were leaden. His voice came as a croaking whisper. "Who are you, really?"

Amaseila raised her brows. "You really need me to say? I could never hide. Not from you." The sly smile returned to her lips. "You know what's coming, same as I."

A snore issued from below, jarring Thadmeir free to turn and flee. He hurried across the dais and on through the residence entry. He went straight to his sleeping chamber, closed the drapes and gasped for breath. He stood there, seeking calm. At last, he was in a place where everything was in order. He stepped to the basin and splashed his face.

Somehow he had to get to sleep. He pulled the ceremonial robe from his shoulders, folded and smoothed it flat, and closed the chest. He sat on his pallet, still unable to lie back. He sat stroking his beard and staring at the lamp's dancing flame.

The outer drapes rustled. He froze, both hoping and dreading. Padding bare feet approached.

Amaseila was wrapped in the blanket, those lovely white shoulders jutting from the top. Gods, this was so wrong. He should have told her she was mistaken—that he never believed any of it. He should turn her out. The scandal of it. The disorder this could bring to his life.

Her pale eyes were kind now, her smile no longer wry. She wasn't a mischievous girl, but a purposeful woman.

Amaseila halted just within arms' reach and leaned in. The blanket dropped just enough, and the cleft of her breasts beckoned. Thadmeir raised both of his trembling hands and stopped just before touching her.

His eyes searched hers. What did she want of him? If he surrendered, would she use his weakness against him?

She gave him the faintest nod. It was more than an invitation. It was a command. There was knowing between them. This couldn't be avoided. Even if it led to upheaval.

Thadmeir surrendered. He grasped her waist, the curve of her hips firm and familiar. He drew her to him and plunged his nose into the inviting cleft, breathing in her glamour. His head swam and his heart soared.

She ran nimble fingers through his unbound hair. He sought the opening of her wrap. One hand explored the curve of her bare belly, the other snaking to cup a butt cheek. Amaseila shivered. Her skin was hot but dry and smooth. His hunger for her became ravenous.

She let the blanket fall away and, for Thadmeir the rest of the world fell away.

He ran his hands over her every curve. The softness of her buttocks and the taut small of her back, the firm roundness of the tops of her legs and the boniness at the front of her hips. He lightly kissed her stomach and let his fingers roam and explore, sliding into the downy curls at the base of her abdomen.

A tear slid down his cheek. Amaseila said, "Ah yes, you feel it too. The blessing of the goddess flows between us. My heart fills near to bursting with it."

She adeptly pulled his tunic over his head, then bent and pulled down his leggings. She climbed atop his lap, her knees straddling him. She spit in her hand, reached down to smear it on his engorged cock, and then lowered herself onto him. There was a moment of resistance, and Thadmeir had the presence of mind to realize that she was indeed a maiden. She pressed her cheek to his and gasped into his ear. He feared he'd hurt her and went still, but she began to raise and lower herself. A slickness soon enveloped their contact.

Thadmeir caught fire, clutching her, thrusting his hips, eager to have every bit of her. She slowed and controlled him, as if she were the elder. She took his face in her hands and kissed him deeply. Her mouth tasted of summer-berry wine. An urgency came to him through her kiss, and her rhythm increased. It was like a rider allowing a spirited mount to gallop.

He released inside her with a moan. Eyes closed, she slowed, chanting in prayer, "Glory to you, Mother, for the joy of the reaping of my soul-mate's seed. Blessed is Your womb in this humble body. Blessed are we two for the chance to embody Your grace. Blessed are we who carry out Your bidding."

She slowly lifted herself, and they both shuddered as he slipped from her velvet enfolding. She drew him into embrace, then stood, her hands lingering on his face before severing their contact. He slumped, his rapture fading for the loss of her touch.

Amaseila bent to retrieve the blanket. Rather than wrapping up, she held it open behind her. She smiled under his devouring eyes, her flesh now pink with the abrasion of his hands and beard. She was savoring his hunger. She relished her power. It frightened him. For she was right—she had him now. She'd brought havoc to his door. This was messy, and could not be made orderly. How had he let it happen?

She finally wrapped herself. "I can answer your query now. That is, if you still wish it spoken aloud, my lord."

He was dumb. Was she toying with him? Amaseila smiled. "Earlier, in the hall. You wanted me to voice what we both know. Do you still wish it?"

Thadmeir sat with his leggings still tangled at his ankles. "Freya —She really sent you?"

Amaseila laughed. "Of course, my love. I am Her gift to you. Just as you are now my gift. Our communion this night is but the beginning. I am to be your qeins."

He instantly saw it as truth. Perhaps betrothal was the only way to keep some semblance of his rein on the situation. "What have I done?" he murmured. "I was to marry a highborn, to strengthen the Wulthus line."

"Oh, my darling. Surely you know there can be no other. Not just yet, anyway. There will be only one other woman in this life who will receive your truest love and devotion. But fear not. For strength shall be found in our bond. Strength we shall need in order to face what comes. Only in legacy will such strength be matched. Know that through our union She blesses the Wulthus line as no other coupling could."

He frowned. "What must we face?"

Amaseila's smile faded. "War, of course. And the Urrinan with it. The Bringer, he comes."

"So you've said," he grumbled.

"As it shall be. And soon." Amaseila bent, her lips brushing his. "But there is time enough to rest, my ravenous wolf." She started to leave.

"Who else?" he asked. She turned back, holding the bedchamber drapes open. Now she was puzzled. "What other woman will I love?"

She laughed. "Why, our daughter, of course," she said, and the drapes fell closed.

CHAPTER 4—
OVERCOMING,
BECOMING

" Long have the seers told of the Bringer being born an outcast. One *would surmise that the girl-child of Ellasan would have heard such tales, lingering at the skirts of the Wise Ones in the queen's pavilion, as Elan did prior to her training."—Brin Bright Eyes, Saga of Dania*

ELAN KNEW time was running out. The elder brother looked shaken, but he was at least unhesitant. The younger boy went still, eyes wide with terror. It was nearly dark. The Spali who likely pursued them from the compound might catch up at any moment. To the boy, Elan said, "Can you stay and protect your mother and sister while your brother and I go ahead?"

The boy nodded, his relief apparent. She feared his task might not prove so easy, but she simply returned the nod. They'd have to make this attack quick and hope for the best.

"Do we take bows, shoot them from hiding?" Vahldan asked.

Elan shook her head. "Too risky. Even if we take out two with the first shots, we'd have to run the others down. Chasing in the dark is dangerous. There may be more of them about. All four must fall, and swiftly. Surprise is our only asset. We'll have to charge them with blades."

Even a protégé would have realized it. His chin dropped. Elan wasn't sure if he was abashed or having second thoughts. She needed to know. "Can you do this thing, Young Lion?"

Vahldan drew himself upright and nodded. She set out. No good could come of delay. Elan knew she took a great risk. Why overthink it? He instantly followed. She was glad for his lack of hesitation. At least since the moment he faced Auchote outside the compound walls.

He wouldn't let that happen again. Would he?

She halted uphill of the Spali camp. Vahldan crouched beside her. He looked frightened. It wasn't necessarily a problem. Everyone was frightened in battle. She had no choice but to hope he'd act in spite of it. Every good warrior had to find their way to doing just that.

The Spali had lit a small fire. The one who'd been washing was now seated, leaning against the same tree as the one nursing his arm. The third sat two span from the fire, and the fourth still stood watch. The seated trio conversed in low tones, all still wide awake. At least none had left to scout and no additional Spali had joined them.

Elan wrapped an arm around Vahldan and drew him near. She pointed, and breathed into his ear, "The pair near the fire are yours. Strike the right first, then the left. Surprise and speed are all. Your first stroke must kill. The other is wounded but has a dagger. Stay here until I get in position. When I go, you go."

He nodded. He was shaking.

"Look at me."

His eyes found hers.

"I need you. We need each other. If we fail, they'll kill your family. We can do this. Do you believe me?"

His eyes hardened. "Yes," he hissed, and she believed him, too.

She stepped away, repositioned her buckler straps and drew her blade, going through her pre-battle routine. She stretched her neck and loosened her shoulders. Hers was an heirloom blade named Biter, passed down from her mother. Elan focused on her grip on Biter's hilt, feeling the blade's enduring power, passed into it from generations of strong hands holding it. Power that now flowed into her and up her arm.

She looked over at the Young Lion, still staring at the Spali. His expression was unreadable, but he held his blade very naturally. He was no novice. This might just work.

Elan briefly gripped his shoulder and moved off into the darkness, leaving the young man into whose hands she had just placed not just her reputation, but her life.

VAHLDAN STARED AT THE SPALI. The dim glow of their fire made them look like a distant image from a story, as if he saw them through a portal that led into one of his father's tales. Elan touched his shoulder, startling him. She gave him a nod and set off into the darkness, leaving him. This was really happening.

He still couldn't see himself actually fighting these foreigners. This would not be sparring. His belly flopped. He was poised between the ugliness and a shrieking fear that kept him woke from it. The woke part of him begged him to do anything but what he'd agreed to do.

He couldn't surrender to the ugliness. If he lost himself, he could lose it all. Not just his life, but his family. His honor. If he lost himself here, he might never recognize himself again.

'I know what's inside you. Because it's inside me, too.'

Vahldan tightened the grip on the hilt. It was possible. Just two thrusts. He could do what Elan needed *and* not lose himself. He scanned the wooded hillside for Elan but couldn't see her. Everything was silent. He looked back to the Spali, at the one he was supposed to attack first. The Spali chuckled and nodded. He was amused, relaxed. He was no creature, no beast. He was a man—they all were. He looked older than Vahldan, perhaps Angavar's age. He wondered if the man had a wife, or children.

Angavar. His father was dead. Auchote killed him. He clearly recalled the Spali chieftain's glee in killing, his savage grin as he bore down on Vahldan. Auchote would've happily killed again—he'd tried his best to run a spear through Vahldan. These so-called men were invaders, killers, just like Auchote and his host.

The forge in his gut flared. He imagined these Spali were laughing about his father's death, imagined they considered him a little rabbit. He relished the grip on the hilt, that the sword felt like a part of him. He could do this.

Commotion stirred, off to his left. Elan. Fighting in the darkness. A muffled grunt.

The Spali heard, too. They sat up straight, craning, alert. It was time. Time to act.

ELAN RAN TOWARD THE SENTINEL. She went into the trance of stealth, her training taking possession of her moves, each footfall landing in perfect silence. She slid from one position to the next, paused, listened, went on. Her back to a tree on the third stop, compulsion gripped her. She looked back to find Vahldan's face in the moonlight. He stared, transfixed by the Spali. She shouldn't have looked. She sensed his fear, his reluctance.

Elan's mind raced as she neared the sentinel. Why wasn't Vahldan watching her? How would he know when to attack? What had she been thinking, sending an untried boy against two experienced warriors? His death, or even an injury, meant failure. She would be blamed for any harm that came to the Outcast's family. What if Vahldan really was the Bringer, as so many claimed? Could her failure now ruin the coming of the Urrinan? How could she have risked so much? Why was she so fixated on proving herself?

She stopped before she needed to, behind yet another tree. She had to refocus. She thought of the lioness—waiting, frightened, in pain. And the girl, so helpless. She thought of how the Spali came to her homeland to steal and burn and kill. Finally, Elan thought of her mother—how the Spali had murdered an unarmed healer as she tended to those they'd wounded.

She set out again, moving swiftly and silently. By the time she gained the final position, the controlled fury of Thunar's Blessing thrummed through her.

She crept to a thicket, twenty paces from her target. This was it. She couldn't see Vahldan. It didn't matter. She had to trust that he'd act. She ignored the prick of the thistles and her fret. She regulated each breath, waiting for the watcher's head to turn away. Instead his head twitched toward her and locked, seemingly staring directly at her. Had she given herself away? Her head was awash with white noise.

Finally, he slowly turned away. Elan ran, closing in long strides.

His head snapped around, but too late. Her roundhouse swing struck his neck, and his attempt to shout came as a gasp. His hand flew to the wound. She kicked his chest. He grunted and crumpled to his knees. She'd severed his windpipe. He was out of the fight.

She ran on. Confusion stirred the night. She focused on her next target, assessing his confusion, calculating his probable reaction. Someone bellowed. Had it been Vahldan? Her head instinctively swiveled. Everything below was a shadowy blur.

Vahldan forced himself to keep running. His first target got to his feet. The other was already up, moving in Elan's direction. Vahldan couldn't see her. A vibrating current thrummed within. Rather than the ugliness, fear had seized him. Over halfway there, and he still couldn't conceive of what he needed to do. He raised the blade. It was real. It was steel, with an edge. He sought to cut human flesh. The thought was surreal.

His first victim lingered warily by the fire. With only steps to go, Vahldan caught a glimpse of the third man, facing away with an axe raised over his shoulder. The Spali threw and realization dawned. His target was Elan.

A jolt of energy surged, and the rage seized him. A roar erupted from him as he set the blade swinging with his final steps. The closest Spali was the one he'd been told to strike first. His targeted victim turned, eyes wide. *Thunk!* The blade hit the flesh of his shoulder. It sounded like the wood axe hitting a saturated cedar stump. Droplets pattered his bare skin, and the man fell, crying and crawling, scrambling to escape.

Why hadn't the bastard died? The rage boiled. He got over the fallen man, raising the blade. The thing that had just seemed to be a man was slithering on his belly. It was a beast after all. Vahldan swung again, like chopping wood. The blade bit into flesh between the shoulder blades, and stuck. The beast lurched again; Vahldan roared again, yanking his blade free, his only thought to keep chopping.

Too late he saw the knife, flashing at the edge of his vision, arcing toward him. Before it struck he saw the snarl of his attacker, seeking to end his life.

Elan barreled downhill, returning her focus to her second victim. But too late—this time for her. Her target had not only become aware of her, he'd thrown something. A spinning hand-axe skipped off the rocky turf and hurtled toward her. Unable to dodge, she threw up her buckler. The bedamned thing glanced off the bottom edge of the shield and punched her in the abdomen. The impact to her breastplate stole her breath.

Elan sucked for air that couldn't be drawn. Worse, she'd dropped her blade—a Blade-Wielder's most inexcusable offense. First shame, then rage, infused her. Her target fled. Still uphill of him, she sprang. Her head and shoulders hit his legs, knocking him to the turf.

The man wriggled around to face her, swinging and punching at her tucked head and shoulders. The blows made the sin of losing her blade all the more painful. She managed to roll, her buckler pinning his calf. He tried to kick. She snatched her belt dagger and stabbed him in the groin. He howled and rolled, trying to get away, but she stayed atop of him. She grabbed a fistful of hair with her shield hand and jabbed with her right, puncturing his neck just below the ear. He made a gurgling noise, and his body flopped like a landed fish. Victim number two.

Elan tried to regain her breath as she retrieved the sword. Relieved to have Biter in hand, she turned to seek her ally. Sparks flew and smoke billowed, and two bodies twisted amidst it. She couldn't even be sure one of them was Vahldan. She ran on.

VAHLDAN REACTED to the coming knife by jerking back. His foot slid, and he fell into the fire. He rolled as his pursuer came after him, tripping through the hot coals and swinging again. He landed on his back and kicked, catching the Spali on the thigh and causing him to stumble back. Vahldan pushed off with his free hand and was amazed to find himself back on his feet. Realization hit him—his sword was in his hand. Another roar erupted from him as he swung.

His rival jumped back, and Vahldan trudged on, swinging. All of his thought and motion, his fear and rage, came to a simple binary: kill or be killed.

The Spali danced from his wild swipes through the trees. The Spali held his knife at the ready. Vahldan didn't care. The tricky beast kept a tree trunk between them. Vahldan lunged around the trunk. Again, the slippery bastard dodged. As he pulled back the blade, the sneak slashed. The Spali blade bit into his arm. He didn't care. Kill or be killed. Vahldan was still alive. He couldn't swing his sword so he threw his head, cracking into the surprised Spali's face. His nemesis stumbled back and Vahldan followed.

A raptor-like shriek rent the air as a flashing blade struck the staggering Spali at the base of his neck. Vahldan's opponent was slammed to the turf, his hands drawn up to protect his face. Vahldan saw the opening, sensed the kill, and thrust. The blade slid in with such smooth satisfaction. The foul creature made the sounds of dying, and Vahldan roared again, his heart soaring. It was the stroke that his father had taught him, in and up from the sternum.

He yanked the blade out and raised it again.

Someone grabbed his forearm, and he spun to face the new threat. "It's me!" He stopped, heaving for breath, sword still overhead.

She moved closer, her face near. "See me?"

He shook his head, trying to clear it. Gods, he still wanted to chop, but not her.

"Come back to me," Elan said, her voice calm. His sigh came as a growl. His head reeled, the energy leaking from his arms as he lowered the blade, letting it hang limp at his side.

"ARE YOU HERE?" Elan asked. Vahldan stared, wild eyed. "See me?" she repeated. He finally nodded, apparently struggling to come clear of imbuement. She scanned the area, making sure the four were still down, and that no other Spali had appeared. Silence. Nothing but their own labored breathing and the stirrings of the Spali's tethered ponies.

She was coming clear of imbuement herself. But it was done. She'd done it! *They* had done it. She straightened, stretching her aching abdomen. He had a gash on his arm, and his head was certain to hurt. But they'd survived a fight to the death against twice their number. Elan felt herself grinning.

She faced her fellow victor. His tunic and face were splattered with gore, and blood trickled down the bridge of his nose. He stared down at their last victim, his face pale, gulping for air. He turned from her and doubled over, retching. She put her hand on his back as he spit and gasped.

He straightened, wiping his mouth. His eyes were still a bit wild. Clearly he'd never been taught control. Accepting Thunar's Blessing was not to be taken lightly. It could be intoxicating— addictive, even. The gods were fickle, their gifts as much a danger as a boon.

She moved in, filling his field of vision. "Hear me?" The daze in Vahldan's eyes continued to clear. He nodded again. "Good. You must listen. With Thunar's Blessing, learning to let go is as vital as embracing it and acting within it. Understand?"

Vahldan drew a deep breath and nodded again, his gaze drifting back to his victims.

"It's hard, I know," she said. He pressed his lips tight. "You fear it?"

"Yes," he hissed.

"Good. That is wise." She dipped her head to make him look at her. "It is wise to not take it lightly. But your family is alive. Because of you."

Elan reached for the tunic of their last victim and cut a strip from the hem. She bent to the stream, wet it and wrung it clean, and tossed it to Vahldan. "The blood, wash it away. But never dismiss it. You spilled it so that others need not shed theirs."

Vahldan wiped the blade as she'd bidden him. He noticed that his arms were splattered with blood, too. Elan cut anther strip and held it out to him and pointed to the top of his forearm. It was cut and bleeding. "You'd best clean and wrap that. Is it deep?"

He shook his head as he wiped it. "I didn't even feel it."

"You will." He did already. "Here, let me," she said. He held his arm out to her. Gods, it hurt even more when she touched it. "Well fought, Young Lion," she said.

His stomach churned again. *'Get ahold of yourself! That's not fighting, it's flailing!'*

He threw aside the bloody cloth. Elan finished wiping her own blade and sheathed it. She strode to one of the bodies and pulled her belt knife. She knelt, grasped his hair in her fist, and started cutting the skull along the hairline.

Vahldan swallowed back his gorge, then gulped for air. "That last one was yours," she said as she cut. "He put up a better fight. A trophy from him holds more honor."

Vahldan didn't move. He fought for calm. He'd heard the tales, that the Skolani practiced scalping. But Elan seemed so different from the Skolani of the tales.

She finished cutting and tore the scalp from the skull with a sickening sound. She stood to face him, her posture and expression proud and defiant. "I forgot that taking trophies isn't your people's custom," she said.

"No, it isn't," he managed, and raised his chin. Why did her words shame him?

Elan cleaned the dagger and tucked the mass of hair into her belt. "It honors the gods, you know. For the Skolani it acknowledges Horsella. Only through the goddess are we given the strength and courage to vanquish our foes."

"It's for honor?" Seeing the aftermath, killing didn't feel honorable. Necessary maybe, but not honorable.

Her eyes narrowed. "You said before that you feared it." She touched the hair at her belt. "This is to show the world that you will go there. Once others see and believe it, you will need to less often." She took him by the arm and led him to the Spali ponies in their makeshift corrals. They shied and stepped back. Elan pointed. "See that, on the brown's reins?" A mass of hair topped with a patch of rusty-brown leather hung there. He realized it was another scalp. Likely a Gottari scalp.

Still holding his arm, she said, "When you've seen enough of those, having these"—she pointed at her own again—"reminds you why you go there. And why you only go when you must. Understood?"

She released him. He drew his belt dagger, took a deep breath, and strode back to the first Spali he'd felled. He knelt and gathered the hair. He paused, thinking about his dead father, about Auchote's murderous grin, about his mother and sister, alone and afraid. He drew another deep breath and began cutting. Elan stood over him, offering a hum of approval as he cut. "Go around a second time," she suggested. "Now pull back not up, hard and quick. That's it."

Vahldan stood and shook the gore from the hideous thing. Saliva filled his mouth. He swallowed and tucked the ghastly reminder into his belt as she had.

She clapped his shoulder. "Well done, Young Lion. For your first time, that is."

He bristled. "I am Vahldan, son of Angavar, rightful lord of the Amalus."

"Clearly so." Elan looked taken aback.

"I mean..." he said, and she raised her brows. "I'm not my father. Call me Vahldan."

She smiled. "As you wish. Vahldan. Call me Elan."

"As you wish. Elan."

"We should get back to the others," Elan said.

He nodded and surveyed the scene, his gaze stopping on the white bone of the skull he'd just exposed, glowing in the moonlight. He'd ended two lives.

"Don't worry," she said. "It gets easier."

"That's what I'm afraid of." He'd lost himself and had taken lives. The ugliness had won. Easily. It would win again.

CHAPTER 5—A COLD JABITKA HOMECOMING

"*In those days, the upbringing and training of a Blade-Wielder was more brutal than most in today's world can conceive. Protégés are selected in their sixth summer, and taken from their mothers into a life of endurance, pain, and deprivation. Devotion to duty necessitates not just the hardening of their bodies. So too must their hearts and minds be inured to suffering—their own, and that of others.*

Some say that Elan inherited Ellasan's healer's heart, making her inurement all the more difficult, her life as a Blade-Wielder all the more trying."—Brin Bright Eyes, Saga of Dania

"I AM TAKING you to the Jabitka," Elan declared. "We have no other choice." Vahldan thought it sounded like she was convincing herself. He was a little alarmed by it. He'd presumed that she was leading them to her Skolani tribal home all along.

Thanks to the addition of the captured Spali ponies, they were all mounted and moving much faster. Elan had rigged his mother's litter on longer poles between the sorrel and one of the ponies. Eldavar was able to ride the smallest one solo, and Vahldan rode with his sister before him, huddled in his arms asleep. His mother was resting quietly, too. Even at the faster pace, Vahldan feared the birth would come too soon. He had no guess what they would do when the time came.

They crossed the river ahorse without incident, and beyond the far bank the terrain leveled. Dense evergreen forest gave way to sparse hardwood groves. "We are very near now," Elan announced. "We'll soon be challenged by a sentinel. Remain calm. The Skolani scorn those who show fear."

Eldavar straightened in the saddle. Elan noticed and said, "Rest easy. It'll be fine. They'll likely turn you and your brother away, but they can't turn away your mother. She'll soon have the help she needs." Again, she sounded like she was convincing herself.

"Turn us away?" Eldavar frowned. "We have to stay with her. It's our duty."

Vahldan shushed him. "Elan means they'll take her for the birth. She'll be in good hands. We can trust the Skolani." He wondered if now he was the one trying to convince himself.

Eldavar said no more, but he didn't look convinced. Vahldan hadn't really convinced himself, either. The Skolani in the tales of his youth were so fierce and cold. Elan had surprised him. But even she had a sternness that made him feel self-conscious. Would the Skolani even care about a pregnant outsider? And what if the babe was a boy? Vahldan had gleaned there were rumors about what became of the males born to the Skolani. The secrecy of such talk seemed ominous.

They rode across a small meadow and Elan signaled a halt before the next treeline. She cupped her hands to her mouth and voiced an owl's call. Another owl call answered. She dismounted and motioned for he and his brother to do so, as well.

The forest began to stir. From the darkness came a menacing voice. "Hverr swa?"

Elan stiffened. Vahldan found it odd. After her reassurances, she was the one who'd become apprehensive. "What did she say?" he whispered.

"I'm being challenged," Elan said through gritted teeth.

"Is my family safe?"

"Yes, I'll see to their safety. It's just that... well, this sentry is..."

"She's what?"

Elan's smile was a grimace. "She's challenging."

"Svara!" The voice became cross. "Hverr swa?"

"You know who it is, Anallya," Elan replied just as crossly.

"Hverr gera thu foera?"

Elan sighed. "Elan, daughter of Ellasan, brings forth the family of Angavar the Outcast. I was assigned as their guardian after their home was attacked by Spali. The Outcast has been slain. Our mission is urgent. His qeins is near to childbirth."

The brush stirred again. Vahldan sensed movement all around them "Do not speak unless spoken to," Elan whispered. "And don't stare."

"Staring is rude," Eldavar recited.

"To some Skolani, like these, it's beyond rude. It's..." She shook her head. "Never mind."

"What?" he pressed.

"It's a challenge, of sorts. Just don't do it."

Three tall women appeared, seeming to have stepped from the gates of the nether world. They were mere forms and shadows at first. But the moonlight in the clearing revealed that they were painted in browns and greens, blending their skin and garments perfectly with the forest. Their braided hair was tangled with leaves and boughs. They each had a sword hilt rising over a shoulder, but each held a drawn bow. Worse, each bow was trained on Vahldan and his brother. He raised his hands and Eldavar imitated him.

The largest one in the center strode toward him wearing a scowl. He dropped his gaze to the ground. She only stopped when the arrow was an arm's length from his throat. "Why bring them here?" she growled. "You know it's forbidden." The accent in her deep voice was more pronounced than Elan's.

It wasn't just that this Anallya person was large. She radiated belligerence.

Elan stepped between Anallya and him. "There is nowhere else to take her. She needs a healer. Soon. The signs foretell a difficult birth."

Anallya sneered and lowered her bow. "But *you* are a healer, Elan, aren't you? Wasn't that the reason Hildeanna chose you?" Her tone was clearly mocking.

Elan stepped chest to chest with her. Anallya stood a hand taller, forcing Elan's chin to rise. The woman outweighed her by half again. Whether staring was an insult or a challenge, Elan clearly wasn't backing down. "Whatever her reason for picking me, what she got was a Blade-Wielder." She tilted her head and looked down at the Spali locks tucked into her belt.

Anallya fleetingly glanced at the trophy. Her smirk faded. "Anja, escort this... *Blade-Wielder* to the Jabitka so she might seek an apprentice to aid this foreigner. See that she doesn't bother any of the Wise Ones. Not while there are wounded Skolani to be attended. Kunna and I will keep watch over our charming guests." More mockery.

Elan turned to Vahldan. "Stay together, right here." She lowered her voice. "Hands off weapons. Do not speak unless addressed. And *do not* stare." He nodded and she set off at a fast trot, leading the woman assigned to escort her. They quickly disappearing into the night.

Anallya's second companion disappeared from sight as well. Vahldan ventured a quick glance at Anallya to find her still glaring. He swiftly looked away. She laughed.

∿

ELAN HATED LEAVING them with the blood-bitch. But there was no time to figure another way. Even Anallya wouldn't dare to harm those under guest rights. Not even Elan's guests.

Would she?

She hurried to the center of the Jabitka ahead of Anja, who left off her escort as they passed through the outer sleeping shelters.

Most of the outer shelters were canvas build-outs from the wagons that transported the Jabitka seasonally. The adjacent corral was crowded with horses, and sentries strolled its perimeter. It was a sure sign of the tribe's high state of alert, as horses were normally allowed to roam the Jabitka and the nearby meadows. She came to the larger pavilions of the elders and the prominent Blade-Wielders. They were all well-lit, and several bonfires continued to blaze in the commons. As late as it was, the Jabitka buzzed with quiet activity.

She spotted Ursellya hurrying across the commons carrying a basket, and called to her.

They ran to meet. "You're unharmed! Thank the gods." Ursellya gripped the arm Elan extended to her. "Sochana brought word that you'd been left behind to guard a family of innocents. They went back for you, but you were gone. What became of the family?"

Sochana was Ursellya's sister, another young Blade-Wielder who rode in Elan's host. Sochana was often utilized as a scout and a messenger. "The Spali returned first, so we fled. The family is at the perimeter. I had to leave them with Anallya."

"You brought them here? Oh, Elan."

"It couldn't be helped," Elan snapped. She composed herself and went on. "The matron will give birth any time now. The signs aren't good. She needs a healer. Perhaps your mother?"

"Mother is far too busy. As is every Wise One. Wounded from the patrol hosts have been trickling in for days. Every new messenger reports more Spali incursions. It's getting spooky."

"It is! We ran into a second small band while fleeing the first. But this woman is—"

"Elan! I thought I heard you." Elan turned just in time to be wrapped in her near-sister's powerful arms. "Praise Horsella you're home." Icannes kissed her cheek and pulled her tighter. Ursellya stiffened and looked away. Elan and Ursellya got on well when they were alone together. But Ursellya had resented Elan's closeness with Icannes since they were protégés.

She didn't care. It felt wonderful being in Icannes's arms. Relief suffused her. Icannes smelled of the cleansing paste—a mixture of pounded cedar leaves, cypress bark, and ground frankincense. The aroma reminded Elan of her own exhaustion, body and spirit. She relished the thought of a cleansing ceremony, but it would have to wait. "I'm relieved that you're here," she said. "I thought you were still out there."

Icannes released the embrace but held Elan's hands. "We arrived home at nightfall. We scattered one Spali band, only to chase the remnants into another. There was another brief fight, but the lot of them fled. We pursued the bastards all the way to the confluence. Our friends could be driven no further, so we had to come back."

"I'd say the warriors need the rest as much as the horses," Ursellya added. "You should be in bed, my princess."

Icannes waved her off. "You know I don't sleep. There's too much happening. Every time I sit down I hear a new arrival. Besides, there's much to be done to get ready for our next patrol."

The thought worried Elan. "You have to get some rest before you go back out."

"We can rest when this is over. These Spali raiders can't keep raiding at this pace. They're too far from home. If we keep them on the fly, they'll have to go back. If only to unburden themselves of what they've managed to steal."

Elan shook her head. "I just keep wondering why? Why so many at once? It's never happened before. Is Auchote behind all of it?"

"Mother seems to have her suspicions, but she's not sharing them. Not with me, anyway. Speaking of Mother, she just asked about you. She'll want to see you right away."

A knot formed at the top of Elan's chest. She hadn't prepared herself to face the queen. Which reminded her of why she'd come. "The Outcast's family—I brought them here. His wife, she's about to give birth. I left them at the first perimeter on the trail to the ford. With Anallya."

Unlike everyone else, Icannes didn't question her decision. "Ursellya and I will head over there." Ursellya clenched her jaw. "Now go," Icannes ordered Elan. "Mother won't be pleased if she finds out you didn't come straight to her."

Elan sighed. Icannes had taken control, as always. But that left her to face the queen alone. She hurried to the royal pavilion. The guard at the entrance seemed unsurprised. "Elan." The woman held the flap open without announcing her, which meant Keisella wasn't alone.

Elan ducked inside. She rose to a warm and brightly lit interior, fragrant with the cooking of cleansing spices. She was always surprised by how colorfully Queen Keisella kept her pavilion decorated. Instead of the rich furs and oiled leather so many of the Blade-Wielders favored, the queen draped her pavilion with doeskins dyed in bright colors and cut and sewn into decorative patterns. The queen was similarly attired, in colorful Gottari-wool robes, soft and loose. Keisella reclined on cushions, conversing with her nearly blind guest.

Elan fell to her knees and bowed before Keisella, nose nearly to the woven mat. "My queen. You sought my presence?"

The queen's aging guest clapped her hands and cackled. "Simply speak of Loki, and she appears! Did I not say?"

"Yes, yes, Sael. So you said." Keisella waved the old woman off. "Rise, Elan. I presume you are unharmed?"

"I am well, my queen. Nothing a bit of sleep won't heal."

"Good. Then you'd best properly greet my guest, or we won't hear the end of it."

Elan turned to the white-haired woman. "Grandmother," she said, and fell into Sael's widespread arms.

"Ah, my dear heart." Again, Elan was engulfed in comfort. Again, she found herself wishing she could simply go to sleep wrapped in loving arms.

"You were worried?"

Sael laughed. "About you? Never. You walk through too many of my Dreams, child. But, oh how my heart leaps over its coming to pass. Everything proceeds just as I've foreseen, with you at the center of it."

VAHLDAN UNROLLED the blanket from Hrithvarra's saddle and wrapped Mara in it. The child instantly dozed. Eldavar yawned. "It's okay. You can sleep." His little brother shook his head, but settled in beside Mara, pulling his cloak close. He fell asleep almost as fast as his sister had. Anallya paced the edge of the clearing, glancing often but keeping her distance.

Vahldan went to his mother and took her hand. "It's not your fault," she said softly.

"I'd stay with you if I could. But I know they'll help you through this."

Frisanna shook her head. "No. What happened, with your father. It's not your fault."

"I've been meaning to tell you..." He swallowed. "There's more." He'd failed in the crucial moment, and he'd failed to tell his mother of it since. No longer.

"It doesn't matter," she said.

"But you don't know—"

"I know what matters. I know you wanted to do the right thing. He knew it, too."

A sigh escaped him. "I guess I wanted to show him that I'm worthy."

"Oh Vahldan. I admit you were right about one thing. Your father always thought it was just a matter of time until you became a younger version of him. I tried to warn him, but he never dreamed you'd be your own man. Angavar was not a patient man. And yet, he waited."

"Waited for what?"

"He could've gone back and demanded a trial at any time. But he wanted everything to be just right. He wanted you to be his second, standing at his side. He spent years in patience for it. For you."

It explained so much, about Angavar's intensity, his frustration. "I guess he wasn't pleased with what he got."

She shook her head. "He never really understood what he had in you."

"Maybe that's because you were always telling him I was normal."

"Of course you're normal."

"You know I'm not. I've always lost myself. It frightens me. It happened again, when I killed those Spali. Worse than ever. Father kept saying I should learn to control it, but I can't."

His mother squeezed his hand. "You'll learn. Trust yourself. I know your heart. You're stronger and braver than you know."

"No," he whispered. "I'm not." He knew what he had to say. Why was he choking on the words? "He died to save me. I froze. He took the javelin meant for me."

"Of course he did." Frisanna forced a smile, but it made her look sad. "He may not have understood you, but he always knew the struggle would fall to you. And now it shall."

'Gods, what will come of us if this falls to you.'

"You know I don't want what he sought. I don't want them to get away with what they've done. I said I'd stand by him, but I'm not going to play his game. Or theirs."

"You don't have to. Focus on what you know to be true. Don't ever let anyone convince you that anything is ordained. Your choices are your own." He looked away. She pulled his hand, forcing him to look. "Are you hearing this?"

"I hear. But—"

"No buts. Remember, my son, that a journey can only be taken step by step." She winced again, in evident pain. "I fear nothing will be easy for you. Some of them will have it in for you, simply because of who you are. Others will try to rein you, to use you. Don't let them."

"Who?"

"All of them. Wolves, lions—the Amalus who betrayed him, even your father's friends. They'll come at you from all sides." She lowered her voice and glanced at Anallya. "Even the Skolani have an agenda."

"You know I don't believe the fables. I trust in balance, and reason. You taught me that."

"Yes, you should reject the fables. But never forget, you come from two of the most noble bloodlines of your people. It comes with a responsibility." She raised her hand to his cheek. "You are beautiful. And you are a part of me. Just as I am a part of you. As are your brother and sister." She looked down at her belly. "Just as your new brother or sister will be." She gripped his hand again. "I am so fiercely proud of you. Never forget it."

"I won't," he vowed.

Her face contorted as another spasm of pain hit and passed. "Now it's your turn to be patient. Remember, your family must come first." Her smile was forced as she looked down, rubbing her belly with her free hand. "Life is about to get more complicated." Her smile faded and her gaze went distant. "With your father gone, I need you. Now more than ever."

Gods, things really were getting complicated. He'd been so worried about living up to Angavar of the Amalus, warrior and chieftain. He hadn't even considered living up to his father's role in a family with a newborn. "Don't worry. I'm here." He masked his emerging fret.

"Don't you worry, either. Your destiny will be revealed in time. And it'll belong to you and no one else." His mother put her free hand over their clasp. "Who knows? It may yet lead you to the sea." Frisanna managed another smile. "Perhaps we'll even get there together."

Her words soothed his troubled soul. She knew him so well.

Approaching footsteps caused Anallya to raise her bow. Two women appeared. Neither was Elan. Anallya stowed her bow and bowed her head. The smaller one hurried to his mother. She had a bag hanging across her shoulder—obviously a healer. The second woman stopped to talk to Anallya. She was as tall as Anallya, and her braids were fair.

The healer bent to Frisanna. "I am Ursellya," she said. "I'm here to help." She seemed little more than a girl. Ursellya boldly pulled aside the blanket and her hands roamed over Frisanna's belly.

Vahldan kept gripping his mother's hand. In spite of the strangeness of it all, Frisanna seemed relieved. "Is there pain here?" Ursellya asked.

His mother grimaced. "Yes."

"How long between the bouts?"

Powerful hands latched onto Vahldan's shoulders from behind. "Come away, Young Lion." The voice carried authority, but was not without empathy. He allowed her to guide him out of the way. His captor asked, "How is she, Ursellya? Will her cub come soon?"

"Yes, my princess. This babe must come out. An incision is needed, to help her in her labor." His mother groaned.

"No! You can't." He wasn't about to let this girl cut his mother open.

His captor's grip tightened. Ursellya ignored him, and said, "We'll have to take her to my mother's pavilion. We need good light and boiled vinegar. And she'll need dosing for the pain."

"Please," he said, "there must be another way."

His captor's voice came low in his ear. "Of course our healers will only do what must be done. Your mother needs you to be strong now. Help me assure her that you and I will care for her children while she's away."

He felt both scolded and enjoined. "We will. All will be well, Mother."

"Take her," the princess said. "Anja, lead the horses, quickly." The sentinel led the tethered mounts into the darkness, the healer hovering at his mother's side.

A sigh escaped him.

"Look at me," the woman commanded.

Vahldan turned to her. He'd thought Elan to be stern, and Anallya to be intimidating, but this woman was both. She was the embodiment of authority. "Know this, Young Lion: Ursellya is a trained midwife. Our Wise Ones study and practice healing throughout their lives. There is no safer place for a woman in all the realm than the Jabitka. Do you believe me?"

In spite of being told not to stare, he was unable to pull his gaze from hers. She raised a brow and he forced his chin to his chest. "I do," he mumbled. She was younger than he'd thought. She wore a close-fitting doeskin shift and boots without leggings. Her fur cloak was thrown behind broad shoulders. Her arms were bare other than a pair of silver torcs, one on each of her sculpted biceps. She was more muscular than Elan but more feminine than Anallya.

He stole another glance to find her smiling. "Good. We understand one another, then." She turned from him. "Anallya, see that the lioness arrives safely, then return with my weapons and more blankets for the cubs. Leave word for Elan, as well. She and I will set them up in the visitors' campsite, and keep watch through the night."

"Aye, my princess." Anallya sounded sullen, but turned and set out at a run.

~

"You brought them here?" Keisella's eyes narrowed on her. Elan tried not to fidget.

"Yes, my queen. I felt I had no choice."

"No choice? Come now, Elan. Surely choices were made."

"I feared for their lives. Particularly those of the mother and her unborn child."

"So you brought the prey that all the hounds hunt to our very door."

Elan bowed her head, not knowing what to say. Did Keisella mean that Vahldan and his family were the reason all of the Spali had come? Were they merely a part of something larger? The silence lingered. "Forgive me if I erred," she ventured.

"You did what you thought best, I suppose," Keisella conceded. "No doubt you're anxious to return to Hildeanna's host."

"Only when my queen deems my duty done."

"You've been busy, I see." Keisella reached out and flicked Elan's trophy with her fingertips. "Found a way to prove those who've doubted you wrong, have you?"

Elan's cheeks grew hot. "I did not seek it, my queen. Four Spali were camped on the ravine trail we chose in flight. There was no way around them."

"Such an opportunity." The queen's sarcasm couldn't be missed.

"It didn't feel like opportunity. I felt... worried. The family was so vulnerable. It weighed upon me, more than any decision I have ever made."

"Allow me to guess. After all of your mooning over tales of the Outcast's part in the prophecy, you found being a custodian to a helpless family in wartime to be less than romantic."

"I suppose so."

"You suppose?"

"I mean, yes—it's been less than romantic. But I'm honored to serve. And..." She bowed her head.

"Go on," Keisella said.

"The Outcast's eldest son is far from helpless, my queen."

Keisella huffed a laugh. "Perhaps returning to your host isn't what you want, after all."

Sael came to life. "Ha! You see? So you fought beside him, Elan—you and the Young Lion?"

"Yes, Grandmother."

The old woman grinned, her rheumy eyes staring upward. "And

victory came of it. Ah, that is fitting, child." Sael turned to the queen. "Was I not right about this one? And the boy, too! Admit it." The old woman cackled again, causing herself to cough.

Still staring at Elan, the queen raised her brows. "I admit only that you're a meddlesome old crone. I find it no laughing matter. I've said time and again that the Skolani cannot allow ourselves such an entanglement."

Sael shook her head. "Ah, but we are entwined already. And all the moreso shall we become, before the end. And my queen well knows of her own hand in it."

Keisella waved her off again. "Pah-sha. I said only that I'd do what I could for him. Now he's dead. Little good it did him."

"Yes, the sire is gone, Woden welcome him. The Outcast's passing is but a prod to the Bringer. It is as it shall be. Whether you find it to your liking or not, my queen."

Vahldan was startled by a hand on his shoulder. It was Elan. "Is there word?" he blurted, and struggled to his feet. His legs tingled from sitting cross-legged too long.

"Of your mother? Sorry, no. But she's with our most esteemed healer. The queen sent her near-sister Annakha to attend her." Vahldan nodded, trying not to look worried.

"Sorry to sneak up on you," she offered.

"Old habits can be tough to break." He smiled.

"So it would seem." She looked freshly scrubbed, her auburn hair combed and rebraided. How long had she been gone? Had he dozed? She'd removed her breastplate and wore a doeskin frock under her cloak. He couldn't help but notice how shapely she was. Their wiry, agile warrior-guide had been replaced by... a woman.

He looked away, hoping he hadn't been caught staring again.

He'd been meaning to ask her about the breastplate she no longer wore. He's come to suspect it was made up of interconnected horse hooves, laid up like fish scales. He wondered how they were made. It could wait. He caught a whiff of her—earthy but spicy, same as before but stronger. It was a clean smell. It was *her* smell.

The Skolani were more feminine than he had imagined. They were capable and confident; frank and yet mysterious. And Elan was one of them.

He glanced again and she pulled her cloak closed. Damn, had she noticed his noticing? "I met Princess Icannes," he said, trying to move past it.

"And?"

"I'm impressed."

"It's hard not to be. Either impressed or intimidated, I suppose."

"Oh, for me it's definitely both," he confessed, and they both laughed. "You two are close, I take it?"

"Since we were small. I've known her all my life. My mother served hers. But our true bond came after I began my training."

"You trained together?"

"No, not exactly. She's a few years older, and my own training began later than most. And Icannes is... Well, she's Icannes. It's difficult to describe."

"So she trained you?"

"In part, yes. We all learned from her, but..." Elan looked away. "Let's just say, Icannes took me under her wing."

"A nice place to be, I imagine."

"It is. Or was. Before tonight, I hadn't seen her in months. We ride with different hosts now." Elan's gaze drifted to the starry sky.

Again, the silence lingered. "Sorry," he said. "I didn't mean to pry."

"Ha. I'm the one who appeared at your house, remember?"

"Thank the gods."

"Didn't I tell you not to bother?" she said, and Vahldan laughed.

He was too intrigued to let it drop. "So you're still friends—you and Icannes?"

"Of course." She furtively glanced. "Icannes and I are what the

Skolani call near-sisters; not sisters of the womb, but bound for life. There's a ceremony. We made a pledge."

"A pledge? To one another?"

"Of course. I would do anything for her." Vahldan playfully raised his brows. "Within reason, of course," she rushed to add. Was she blushing?

"I get it. She bid me to wait here. I wouldn't dream of disobeying."

Elan huffed a laugh. "Good choice. She's building a fire, at a campground we sometimes use for visiting males. It's not far. I'll take you. Shall we?" She nodded toward his sleeping siblings. He woke Eldavar, pulled him to his feet and helped him onto the Spali pony. Then he lifted Mara up to sit before her brother. His sister barely woke.

Elan took the leads and set out at an easy pace. Vahldan walked beside the siblings to make sure they didn't fall. His mind reeled. This warrior, who'd only a short time ago led him into his first real fight, and had then taught him how to take a scalp, was a part of this strange, hidden world. The Skolani had princesses and rivals, midwives and Wise Ones, training regimens, a camp for male visitors, and... a ceremony to pledge to sisterhood? The only way he'd bothered to imagine them was in battle, as they were described in tales. How foolish of him.

They soon came to an opening under the sprawling branches of a half-dozen ancient oaks. Icannes wasn't there but flames danced merrily in a stone-lined fire pit. He helped Eldavar dismount and wrap up in his cloak between the roots at the base of the oak nearest the fire. Elan carried Mara, still wrapped in her saddle blanket, and laid her close enough to stay warm.

Vahldan held his hands to the flames while Elan fetched more logs from a nearby stack. The canopy seemed to capture the light, making the campsite feel like a cozy room. He felt his muscles starting to unclench. Since the attack their lives had been a blur of terror and strife. There hadn't even been time to mourn. Through it all, he'd felt the burden of new responsibility.

Strange and uncertain as it all was, at least his family was safe, if only for the night.

Icannes reappeared and sat on her haunches behind Elan, massaging her shoulders. Elan grasped one of Icannes's hands, and smiled up over her shoulder. The Skolani had a reputation for being stern, harsh, or even cruel, and everything he'd seen since they arrived supported it. Until that moment.

An owl call pierced the night. Icannes answered with an impressive call of her own. Anallya led a horse bearing a bundled pack to the edge of the campsite. Anallya released a strap and came around with blankets, some of fur, some woolen. Vahldan accepted his with a nod of thanks. Anallya went to Elan last. Elan glared and refused the proffered blanket with a low word that sounded like a growl. Anallya smirked, tossed it at Elan's feet, and left. Vahldan tucked Mara's around her and Elan did the same for Eldavar. Neither child stirred.

Icannes said to Elan, "Let's have a bite first, and then walk the perimeter. After that, you're getting some sleep." Elan nodded and Icannes produced a skin from the saddle bag, pulled the cork and drank. She offered it to Elan, who drank before offering it to Vahldan. The spirits stole his breath. He coughed as he handed it back. Both women laughed.

"Warm you up a bit?" Elan asked.

Unable to argue, or even speak, he nodded and wiped his watering eyes.

Icannes dug in the bag, handing off items to Elan for unwrapping and parsing.

From the sack came a loaf of risen bread and a round of cheese. Elan broke off a chunk of bread and passed it to Vahldan. It was crusty and dense, still warm inside. And delicious. Icannes drew a belt knife and Elan held the cheese out while Icannes cut wedges, which Elan then handed around. The cheese was flaky and white, tangy but nutty. "This is good," he said. "I've never had its like."

"Mare's milk," Elan said, and laughed at his startled reaction.

Sitting and eating offered an opportunity to watch them without staring. The pair's movements spoke of familiarity. Appraising them together, in spite of the contrast in their appearances—Elan darker, long and lean; Icannes fairer, thick and muscled—they actually did seem like sisters. Their bond was clear. He found it fascinating. And enviable.

Harsh as they seemed, they'd shown genuine concern. For him, for his family.

A young Skolani girl arrived at a run and beat to a halt at the edge of the clearing. She bowed and waited. Icannes said, "I'll go." The girl spoke to her in low but urgent tones.

"Vahldan." Icannes beckoned him.

He rose, his mind racing. A lump of bread seemed caught on the way down, and made his chest ache.

Icannes appraised him gravely. "There's no time to waste, so I must be blunt. Your mother's babe is coming, but the head is not coming first, as it should."

It seemed he should know what to say, or do. Instead he stood dumbly.

Icannes went on, "The Wise One fears for saving both mother and child. As we understand your people's custom, it falls to you to decide whether to have Annakha strive to save your mother or your new sibling.

"So tell me, Young Lion, how will you answer to such an ill choice?"

CHAPTER 6—THE COMPLICATIONS OF BIRTH

"Frisanna was ever a subject for the riving of wolves and lions. That she was the fairest maiden in Dania was never in contention. For the wolves, she'd been deceived and despoiled by Angavar. Among the lions, she was the temptress that lured their fine young chieftain to his downfall. But those who knew her children would've heard of the couple's fierce commitment to one another and their undying love. Which would lay both quarrels to ruin."—Brin Bright Eyes, Saga of Dania*

"MOTHER!" Vahldan woke with a lurch. He yanked back the hood of his cloak to bright morning sunshine. His brother and sister were still wrapped in their blankets, asleep.

He remembered. His mother was with the Skolani. She was having trouble with the babe.

Vahldan scanned the clearing. No Skolani in sight. But fuel had recently been added to the fire. He stood and stretched. His muscled ached. The hideous trophy tucked in his sword belt reminded him of what they'd endured to get here. It seemed like weeks had passed since they left the mine. But it was only about this time the prior day.

Surely daylight would bring tidings. He hated the thought of his mother suffering, or distressed, and he couldn't be sure if the babe had survived childbirth or not. Either way, they would soon have to move on. The question was, to where?

It had troubled him all through the night. He'd long known his mother disliked Badagis. She thought Angavar's former right-hand man was behind many of his mistakes. But Vahldan could think of no one else who might help them. After Angavar's banishment, Badagis had renounced his status as an Amalus captain and had moved to Dania's eastern foothills. Vahldan had heard that his homestead was within the Skolani hunting grounds, so it couldn't be far.

Vahldan simply had to convince Frisanna to change her mind. Surely she would see that their options were limited. One thing she couldn't deny was Badagis's loyalty. He'd walked away from his old life for it. Where else could they find anything resembling that sort of loyalty? Where else might they turn for aid?

At the least, his father's former first captain could provide shelter and protection.

Which would offer a chance to try and figure out who was behind his father's murder. Auchote's words revealed that it hadn't been a random attack. Death's Grin had also provided a starting point. Vahldan needed to find the Carpan priest. Túkash was the first step. Whatever the scheme had been, Túkash was at the heart of it— the worm at the rotten apple's core.

He found his water skin and drank. The thump of horse hooves had him reaching for his hilt. Elan stepped from boughs nearby. "You won't need that," she said. He pushed the blade back into the sheath. He wondered if Elan had slept. It made him feel guilty for having slept himself. Indeed, he was surprised he even managed to fall asleep, after having been asked to make the dreadful decision that may have led to his unborn sibling's demise.

The newcomers took shape in the mist, coming from the Jabitka. Icannes led Elan's sorrel, still outfitted with the litter that led the Spali horse. The horse bore a rider—a Skolani woman. The second walker was the healer, Ursellya. He saw with relief that his mother was laid out on the litter, and that the lone rider held a bundle that was likely a swaddled babe.

He smiled to Elan. "And a princess to escort them. Such an honor."

Elan didn't return the smile. In fact, she looked troubled. He followed her gaze, and noticed that the princess's countenance was grave, too.

Vahldan stifled the sob that rushed to the top of his throat. He ran to his mother's side. Icannes drew the procession to a halt.

Frisanna's face was unnaturally white but oddly peaceful. Vahldan instantly knew she wasn't sleeping. The sob escaped. He fell to his knees beside the litter. His bones felt as limp as willow branches. He reached under her cloak and took her hand. He held it to his cheek, as she so often did. Her hand was cold, unresponsive. It sent a chill straight to his heart.

Ursellya said, "I'm sorry for your loss, Young Lion. The bleeding grew worse after the birth. We did all we could, but it was just too much. She was too weak and fatigued."

He stared at her, as if he could somehow will her to wake up. "You can't leave us." He closed his eyes. They burned under the lids. "You'll never see the sea," he whispered. It felt like an admission that he never would, either.

Vahldan buried his face in her frock. Frisanna was his guiding light. She'd taught him so much. She'd been his truest ally. She'd not only taught him the value of balance, she'd provided it—for their family, for him.

Her love was his only constant. It was gone now. He'd never felt so alone. Or aimless.

"May your new sister be a consolation in the days ahead," Ursellya offered.

As if hearing herself referred to, the babe began to cry. The woman holding her to her breast cooed soothingly. The ugliness stirred deep inside him. A consolation? How could this helpless creature be anything but a burden? This was someone's fault. His mother had lived—indeed thrived—through three childbirths. Had the Skolani botched it? Was it something about this babe?

Elan gripped his shoulder. His body tensed. "I'm so sorry, Vahldan."

"Your sister is hearty and hale, thank the gods," Icannes said. She turned to the woman holding the babe, and pointed. "Alela, let Vahldan hold her."

The ugliness came to life as the woman held out the strange little pink being. His vision blurred. How had such a needy little being survived when his mother—so caring, so strong—had not? The woman frowned, waiting for him to take the babe. He finally accepted her in his hands. The babe wiggled. He couldn't even look. It was so fragile. So weak, pathetic. It occurred to him that he could easily crush this creature.

"The lioness has named her Kemella, after her own mother," Icannes said. He made himself look, sought for focus. The babe's face contorted and it squeaked. "The queen said she is the very image of your mother as a girl."

'It comes with a responsibility,' his mother's voice echoed. 'You are a part of me. And I am a part of you. Just as your new brother or sister will be. I am fiercely proud of you. Never forget it.'

He studied her scrunched little face, then looked back to his mother. He saw it. She did have Frisanna's cheekbones and nose. The ugliness settled back into his gut. He drew the babe to his chest, and she settled, too. He touched her hand with a fingertip, and she grasped it.

"You see?" Icannes said. "Hale. Already a bold one, this girl." A surge of pride flowed through him, and the ugliness receded.

Ursellya said, "Your mother wasn't alone, at the end. We stayed with her, and she held the babe till she passed. Your mother was brave, and she beseeches you to also be brave. The lioness asked us to remind you that family comes first, and that all else will come clear in time. Know that her final thoughts, the last of her strength, were dedicated to her children."

Kemella wiggled again, and he nestled her closer. "Why didn't you call for me?"

"There wasn't time." Ursellya frowned and looked away. He wondered what she might be hiding. *'Even the Skolani have an agenda.'*

A world without his mother was impossible to imagine. And now he alone must care for his family? A family which now included an infant. *'I need you. Now more than ever.'*

"I'm here for you," he whispered to the babe, hoping his mother would somehow hear. He cradled Kemella close and bowed his head over Frisanna, to pray to the goddess at the bridge. "Oh great Hel, I know you will recognize this woman's strength and courage, for they are well known. Also remember that her love was mighty—as vast and beautiful as the sea. And oh how she was loved in return. Please, guide her to her truest love, who has already passed before you."

Vahldan's new sister burrowed into his tunic. She was a part of his mother, and his mother was a part of them both. A surge of love and protectiveness filled his chest, and then melted in crucible along with the ugliness that simmered there, making it something wholly new. Something that felt less ugly. He knew that if he had to, he would fight—and kill—for her. For his family. For their honor. It made him want to learn how to avoid losing himself in it.

Mara squeaked wordlessly behind him. Eldavar said, "What's going on? Mother?"

His brother and sister came running over. He knew his mother's bidding of him began now. He drew himself up to face them. "Our mother is gone. The goddess Hel will guide her spirit across the bridge. She'll soon be with Father again. But she left our new sister here to remember her by." He nodded down to the child in his arms.

Eldavar gaped. "Gone? Who will take care of us?" He was bewildered, unaccepting.

The ugliness momentarily flared, and he tamped it down. He couldn't be cross with Eldavar. He knew his anger was born of fear. He didn't have the answers. How would he comfort them? All he had were his mother's words. "We are of our people's greatest bloodlines. It comes with a responsibility. We'll make her proud, won't we? As proud as she is of us."

Neither child responded. Mara stood clutching her doll, tears streaming down her cheeks. Her face was a mask, her crying silent. It made him even more frightened. Kemella mewled. He rocked her, and said, "Come, Mara. See your new sister. Let's make Mother proud of us."

Mara kept staring at their mother. Vahldan knelt beside her. "Look, Mara, she's as small as Saarin. Will you help me to raise her, to be strong like you?" She still didn't look. "Please. You're so good with Saarin. Your sister and I need you."

Mara's eyes found focus on the child. "What's her name?"

"Kemella. It was your grandmother's name, and she was strong, descended from the shieldmaidens of old. We must be strong and make our ancestors proud of us. Will you help me with her?"

Mara nodded, wiped the tears from her face with her tunic sleeve, and reached out to caress the babe's cheek with gentle fingers.

Eldavar's brow was furrowed. Vahldan gave an imitation of their father. "Eldavar. Will you also help with Kemella?"

At the sound of the command in his voice, the babe started to bawl, and Eldavar's gaze locked onto his new sister. Vahldan saw it —beyond the fret he saw the protectiveness, the pride. "Well?" he prodded, and his little brother's expression firmed. Eldavar nodded.

The nurse dismounted and came to him. "Perhaps she's hungry," the woman said. He handed the crying babe over. The nurse sat at the fire, slipped her shift from her shoulder and offered the babe her breast. The return to silence was swift. Mara sat beside the nurse and babe, rapt. The sight made him wonder how they would continue to feed her.

More importantly, where would they now go?

CHAPTER 7—A LEGACY OF BANISHMENT

"*Most outsiders believe that the Skolani queenship is inherited, but it isn't so. Candidates are selected by the acclaim of the many, often in the light of their deeds. Beyond battle prowess, candidates are considered for their wisdom and compassion. From those who are winnowed, only the elders can then name one regnant.*

Such was the case with Keisella, whose mother was neither queen nor an elder. Keisella was not only a vaunted warrior, but a clever one. She knew that offering a pragmatic voice for her common tribeswomen could lift her, even beyond the disapproval of several elders. She saw the need for an insular tribe's ability to adapt. Her progressive stance often put her at odds with the tradition-bound elders. Some who are wiser than I am have asserted that only through Keisella did the Skolani survive the tumultuous days of her reign."—*Brin Bright Eyes, Saga of Dania*

FROM THE SILENCE created by the cessation of the babe's crying came the rumble of approaching horses. Vahldan gripped his hilt again. Icannes casually craned to look. "This must be Mother. She wanted to see the Outcast's children."

A procession of riders emerged from the trees, two by two. Those in front sat bolt upright, chins high, scanning the scene as they reined to a halt. One called, "Kneel for the coming of Queen Keisella!"

Ursellya and Elan instantly dropped to a knee, and Alela cradled the babe and carefully moved to a kneeling position. Vahldan knelt and beckoned Eldavar and Mara to do the same. Elan whispered, "Speak only when spoken to. And don't stare."

Resentment filled his mind, pushing aside his grief. He had to deal with this now? No one could tell him not to watch the arrivals canter into view. He certainly didn't need to be told which was the queen. The woman was showy as she reined a shiny chestnut warhorse to a stomping halt. Keisella instantly dismounted and strode toward them, leaving others to handle her feisty mount. Her golden braids were pulled from her face and tied in a great bundle behind her head. Her doeskin tunic was artfully rendered in green, red, and orange angular patterns. A bearskin cloak was pushed behind her broad shoulders.

The queen's keen gaze locked onto him. He looked down, feeling his pulse in his temples. Polished boots halted directly before him. "Arise and be at ease." He rose to find she was as tall as him. "Elan, introduce our guests to your queen."

Elan stepped forward. "My queen, may I present Vahldan, eldest son of Angavar of the Amalus. And these are his brother Eldavar, and sister Mara." They each bowed in turn.

Keisella said, "Children of Angavar, know that the Skolani mourn both your father and mother. I've been fond of your father since we were but children. And I thought your mother brave and loyal. She was ever the cooling urn to the flare of your father's forge. What has happened is unjust, as was much that befell them. Honor them, and cherish their memory. Their love for you weighed heavily in all of their striving."

The queen stepped closer. She placed her fingers under Vahldan's chin and lifted his face. Their eyes met. Blue ferocity, bright as the heart of flame, radiated from her tanned and weathered face. He felt his pulse again. He wondered how long he should hold her gaze.

The others waited in silence. Keisella's expression softened. "You are well-formed and bright of eye, Young Lion. Your father held lofty aspirations for you."

Vahldan swallowed. "He did." His father's face, so full of disappointment after their last sparring match, flashed in his mind's eye. He wondered how much Angavar had said to the Skolani queen, and when he'd said it.

"What will you do now, son of Angavar?"

"Find a place to shelter my family."

"It may takes weeks yet for the Blade-Wielders to root out the last of the Spali." She eyed him. "Do you believe they still hunt you?"

"I do." Her directness had startled the truth from him.

Keisella nodded. "Good. At least you can see that traveling alone would be foolish. So tell me, Young Lion, why would ignorant savages trek long miles and venture across patrolled borders simply to hunt your father? And why would they still hunt you and your family?"

Was she baiting him? He might have asked her those same questions. What could he say? He had no real proof that Túkash had led the Spali to the compound, let alone that the Carpan priest had been put up to it. No matter how certain Vahldan was that Túkash had been directed by the usurper, it was Amalus business, as Angavar always said.

"I can't be certain, my queen. Not truly." Vahldan bowed his head again. Keisella was surely clever enough to sense his evasion, but he could think of nothing else to say.

Keisella's stare beat down on him like hot sun. "I am not your queen, Young Lion. This, I think we might agree, is our problem." She sighed. "Ah well. Have it as you will. Hunted or not, there'll be no returning to that forsaken mine. The place was a folly for him, and would be doubly so for you."

The thought of going back hadn't crossed his mind, but her criticism rankled. He reminded himself how much he hated the mine, how little they'd actually gotten from it.

Keisella said, "Your parents never mentioned kinfolk you might turn to?"

"None that I recall, Queen Keisella." Rather, none that could be trusted. "Before my father passed he spoke of seeking Badagis."

"Master Badagis was indeed your father's loyal friend. But word came to me some moons ago that Badagis has left his home. I suspect he is in hiding, though I'm not sure where or why." She raised her brows, eyes alight. "Perhaps your father mentioned it?"

Vahldan shook his head. "He said only that I should seek him."

Keisella waved a hand in dismissal. "It matters not. Badagis has no womenfolk. And clearly you are in need of womenfolk." She glanced at the wet nurse Alela and the babe.

The queen went on, as if to herself. "If you cannot or will not confirm who is behind the Spali's pursuit, I don't know how to keep you safe. Not without causing a stir among the strutting cocks. And yet... A part of our oath with the Gottari pledges us to the safeguarding of members of the royal clans. Regardless of the scandals of the past, you are still that."

Keisella looked off to the west. "I suppose there's only one of them who can be relied upon. He's as stubborn as the sire, but with half the bitterness, at least. And perhaps his being a stickler serves us for once. If nothing else, he can be trusted to adhere to custom and decree."

She faced him and her tone brightened. "It's well that you took up your father's blade." She nodded toward his hilt. "The question is: will you seek Angavar's rightful sword?"

Vahldan hesitated. It felt like a betrayal, to voice his father's ambitions. Just a few days ago, he'd considered Angavar's plan for regaining the futhark blade to be a foolish risk. Now reclaiming it seemed all but impossible. "I must see to the safety and wellbeing of my family. At the moment it's all that matters."

Her gaze was arch. "At the moment," she repeated. Keisella

stepped closer and spoke softly. "You understand that the tenets of the Mithusstandan require my restraint from interference." He nodded. "Your birthright, Vahldan of the Amalus, should be worth more than the banishment you've been forced to reap. It would be a shame if you showed yourself unwilling to strive to make right such a wrongful legacy." She narrowed her eyes, and hissed, "Even an outsider can see it. The Gottari are not whole. Ambition and rancor has blinded both sides. There can be no balance in Dania without your effort."

Without *his* effort? He'd suspected, but now he knew—the queen felt as his mother had in regard to the futhark. And her words seemed like both a ridiculous challenge and an unfair burden. What in the gods' names could he do about it?

Vahldan bristled. "My mother saw to it that I understood the role of the futhark."

Keisella offered a wry smile. "Ah, that is well. Look at you. So much resting on those slender shoulders. And here you and I stand." Her eyes narrowed. "Much hope has been placed on what may come of you. Your father seemed so sure, once. Ironically, Angavar's rising doubts actually gave me hope. And yet, I fear for more folly, more wishful thinking. Still, I see it in snatches, like sunlight streaking through the rustling leaves."

His head swam. "My father? He spoke of..." He shook his head. "Never mind." Of course Angavar voiced his doubts. *"Gods, what will come of us if this falls to you."*

"He was hard on you, I'm sure. He pushed you, even as he protected you. Indeed, he was wishful. Still, he kept you like a newly forged blade he secretly whetted for a future battle. His ambition reveled in the augurs of your birth. Through all these long years, you are the reason he tarried and bided—striving to make ready for the challenge he knew must be faced."

"And they killed him for it."

"Yes," she spat, her anger flashing. "In spite of what's happened, all is not lost. In spite of being hunted, the Outcast saw to it that *you* survived. The way is dimmer now, but it is still there. You shall have to reach deep inside yourself if you dare seek to embody it."

His resentment flared, causing the ugliness to stir. "Embody what?"

Keisella smile was sly. "The legend that is already told of you, of course."

"I know nothing of legends," he said, feigning ignorance. Was she goading him?

She stepped so close he could hear her breathe, her eyes hard. "It's in you, isn't it?"

His belly lurched and the ugliness roiled. She *was* goading him. "There's something in me?"

"I see it written upon you, same as your father. Like a raging stallion you keep penned, ever pressing and thumping at the stall gate. Even now you are tempted to mount and ride. But you know that would be too dangerous. Is it not so?"

'*I know what's inside you. Because it's inside me, too.*' He dropped his gaze, pushing it down. "There is an ugliness within me. I have learned to keep it at bay. I can continue to do so." The scalp in his belt caught his eye, and the ugliness shivered in complaint.

"Keep it at bay? Oh, that'll never do."

"My queen?"

She raised her chin. "Your father was a gifted warrior—the finest in the realm. You must see that it's unlikely you will ever live up to that. And it's doubtful you'll be as charismatic. Few in this life are." She raised a brow, appraising him for a reaction. He had no words. He sought for calm. "What I am telling you, Young Lion, is that if you wish to succeed—to find your way to the ascension that is foretold— you must embrace this... what did you call it? This *ugliness* within. You must harness it and learn to ride the angry stallion, for there are many just as deadly who ride against you. Can you do this, Vahldan son of Angavar?"

His mouth had gone dry. "I... I'm not certain."

She raised a brow. "It's well that you are uncertain. For you must

also know that should you embrace it, even if you learn to harness it"
—she leaned in—"it is likely to consume you."

As if in confirmation, the ugliness flared again, rising from his
belly to his chest.

"Now." Keisella started to pace, her voice commanding. "Heed
me as your father would not. Stay true to the old oaths, as they have
stood the test of time. All Dania is out of balance. The Gottari are
divided, and your family is not without blame in it. Without the
effort of those few who might unite it, the Gottari nation shall decay
from within and wither away."

His face grew hot. He both resented her words and feared she
was right.

"Well?" she demanded. "Will you heed me?"

He bowed his head, barely containing his outrage. "I will heed
your words, Queen Keisella," he said stiffly.

Her smile grew sly again. "I'm so glad you agree. Your effort must
begin straight away."

THE QUEEN TURNED from her doublespeak with Vahldan, her keen gaze
darting to Elan. "Blade-Wielder, you shall guide the Young Lion and
his family to Danihem."

"To Danihem, my queen?" Elan was stunned.

"Yes, Danihem. And when they have arrived safely, you will
request an audience with the Wolf Lord. Alone, if he is willing. You
will then escort young Vahldan to the longhouse to see him. Once
there, you'll ensure that Vahldan has an opportunity to make his
case. He will ask Lord Thadmeir for his leave, and perhaps his aid, in
seeking a safe haven for his family. Preferably in the home of an
Amalus Rekkr—one with a qeins or daughters who can aid in the
care of Vahldan's sisters. All of this you will do in my name."

Elan bowed her head. "My queen." She'd presumed she would
return to Hildeanna's host. She glanced at Anallya. The blood-bitch's

grin was as wicked as expected. Anallya's version of this would be the one shared among the Blade-Wielders. Elan would be cast as a nursemaid, assigned to hold the hands of orphans all the way to Danihem.

And yet... It sounded as though the queen sought some hidden agenda with Vahldan. Elan's grandmother certainly had grand expectations. Who could know? Perhaps this mission would be part of a legend in the making. If so, it seemed Elan would play a role in it.

The queen stepped closer and lowered her voice. "Seek to arrive in Danihem unheralded. Keep them unseen. Travel on seldom-used paths. Once there, report directly to the captain of the longhouse—a man named Urias. He is the foster-brother of the Great Wolf, and a man of honor."

"Urias. Yes, my queen."

"Once inside and with Urias, your charges should be safe—temporarily, at least. Should the Great Wolf cling to his grudge for their father, remove the family and return here by safe routes. Do not leave them without an Amalus Rekkr to vouch for them. If the Great Wolf does not cast them out, and yet you still fear for their safety, send word and stay with them till you hear from me."

"It shall be done, my queen." How was Elan to know when they'd be safe? She'd never set foot in Danihem. She cringed inwardly at the thought of being stuck in a stinking village full of oafish men for the gods knew how long.

Keisella turned to leave. "My queen, perhaps I should accompany them." Icannes boldly stepped forth.

The queen rounded on her daughter. Icannes at least had the sense to bow her head and brace herself for the slap that might have come. Since it didn't, Icannes went on, "What with the Spali abroad —particularly on the back paths they'll be traveling—another Blade-Wielder would better ensure their safety."

The thought was a relief, and yet Elan feared for her. Icannes had been harshly punished, even publicly tied and lashed, for outbursts her mother deemed insolent. To call their relationship contentious would be an understatement.

"You question my judgement, *Princess*?"

Icannes kept her head bowed. "No, my queen. I thought only to offer my service."

"*You* thought. Are you not a Blade-Wielder? Are you more than a tool at my disposal?"

"No more than that, my queen. But I also thought that during the journey there might be time for me to aid the Young Lion in his training. I thought it might be a boon to his pursuit of justice. I humbly offer it in your name, as it seems you deem his endeavors worthy."

The queen pursed her lips. Elan held her breath. Keisella turned to her horse and mounted. Elan glanced at Vahldan. His face glowed red. He looked flustered, perhaps even angry. How unsettling this all must be for him. No one had consulted him on where he should go, who he should see, or whether or not he wanted travel companions —let alone training.

Once in the saddle, the queen offered a hooded smile. "So be it. Princess Icannes shall lead your quest." Elan turned to share her relief with Icannes, only to find her facing Vahldan. And smiling. Elan's chest tightened. Icannes would be training him. Training with Icannes was something Elan recalled all too well.

Keisella nodded to the rider on her right. "Blade-Wielder Kukida shall ride as well, as the guardian of the princess." Elan silently thanked the gods she hadn't assigned Anallya. Kukida was an acclaimed warrior, but she wasn't as haughty as some of the other celebrated Blade-Wielders. Indeed, the woman rarely spoke.

Keisella added, "So too shall Alela ride along, as a nurse to the babe." This was a relief as well. Elan had no clue how they would've fed and cared for the newborn.

The queen started to rein away and stopped. "Blade-Wielder Elan, know that you alone shall be held accountable for the well-being of Vahldan and his kin. I am setting a Fulhsna-Utanni upon his head, and naming you as its assignee."

Vahldan's head snapped to Elan, his anger morphing to puzzlement. Icannes scowled.

"A Fulhsna-Utanni, my queen?" Elan's voice cracked.

"You heard me, Blade-Wielder. The Young Lion is the subject of your duty, from this day until he acquires sufficient status and means to protect himself and his family."

Elan bowed. "Yes, my queen. I shall protect him with my life." Her path had twisted yet again. There would be no returning to ride with her host. Not anytime soon. She was duty-bound to a strange trek with a young man and his orphaned siblings. And the words *status and means* were so nebulous. The gods only knew how long this would take.

She sensed Vahldan was beyond upset now. She glanced. Maybe seething was an apt description. The queen spoke of his family as if they were witless livestock. They'd lost both parents in a few days. They hadn't even had time to grieve, and they suddenly had a keeper and a set path. Their lives had been irrevocably altered by what seemed a hasty series of royal decrees. From a queen who'd just admitted she wasn't theirs.

Vahldan opened his mouth to speak. He was more likely to make things worse than better. Elan elbowed him and shook her head. His eyes flared. She smiled in response, and mouthed, *Trust me.* Thankfully he bowed his head, though she read a silent curse on his lips.

The queen wore the smile of a prankster. "Don't look so annoyed, Young Lion. It's been long years since the Blade-Wielders have so honored a scion of the Gottari. Nor should you be glum, Elan. At least he's aware of your duty. It should be easier than guarding an unknowing subject. You should count this a blessing, from what I hear of your initial success."

Elan gave Icannes a sidelong glare. She'd told her near-sister how he'd nearly caught her on the first night. Icannes offered a shrug that was hardly apologetic.

Keisella went on. "Heed my daughter well in training, Young

Lion. In spite of her willful streak, she has a gift with a blade. It might even save your life."

Vahldan bowed his head, still bristling. "I will, Queen Keisella." He should've thanked her, but at least he hadn't overtly offended her.

The queen reined and cantered back toward the Jabitka, her retinue in tow. Elan turned to find her new subjects gathered around their mother's body. The little ones still seemed to be in shock, and untold emotion wracked Vahldan's expression. She wanted to comfort him somehow, but could find no word or gesture. She went to Icannes, who was tightening the laces on her forearm guards. "What of the mother?"

Still working the laces, Icannes glanced up at the family. "Oh, yes. Good thinking, Elan. The boys will want to be involved in the burial. Fetch them shovels and help them. I'll see to our provisions for the journey." Icannes turned and mounted, leaving her alone to deal with the grief-stricken family. Not for the last time, Elan suspected.

CHAPTER 8—BY
SELDOM-USED PATHS

"Many singers tell a version of the role the Carpan priest Túkash played in Angavar's tale, and then in Vahldan's. The songs tell of how Angavar and Badagis hunted down and captured Túkash, how the pair coerced the Carpan to reveal the mine near which they built the compound that became Vahldan's childhood home. Few realize that Túkash deceived them, as Angavar's mine was not the true source of the famous Carpan gold trove. Fewer still have gleaned that Túkash came to be a tool of the usurping Amalus lord Desdrusan, who had spared Túkash's life during Angavar's campaigns against the Carpans.

What almost none knew, for long years to come, is that Túkash had his own secret schemes. The Carpan played a long game, pitting all sides against one another. In the process, Túkash changed the course of history, and not just for the Gottari."—Brin Bright Eyes, Saga of Dania

VAHLDAN RODE AHEAD of his siblings and Alela, following Elan into a clearing at dusk. Elan drew them to a halt at the crest of a steep drop into a ravine. They sat overlooking a mist-filled bowl of drooping evergreens that opened into a vale, revealing the twilit western horizon. It had stopped raining but Vahldan was soaked and stiff. They were sure to get even wetter down there.

Elan was staring into the space above the vale. He followed her gaze. A bird was soaring there, seemingly immobile. "What is it?" he asked.

"A kestrel."

"Looks like a small hawk."

"A falcon, actually."

"How is he staying up there like that? He looks like a leaf floating on the water."

"She." Elan glanced with a raised eyebrow. "Her instincts help her to find even the slightest air current. She's lifted by facing that which resists her."

"So she's just drifting?"

"Gods, no. She would never just drift. She's hunting. Kestrels hunt through stealth, fast and low to the ground. It's misty, so she's waiting for an opening. She's patient."

"How do you know it's a female?"

"Her size and her markings." Elan faced him. "The males are showier, but the females do the hunting. They're larger, more deadly to their prey." She grinned.

"You sure know a lot about kestrels."

She gazed at the bird again. "When I was a girl, I watched a kestrel chase a pair of eagles from her nest. The intruders were many times her size. She was so fearless, so determined. She hadn't even laid her eggs yet, but she would not be bullied." Elan offered a half-smile. "I've admired them ever since."

As if on cue, the kestrel cocked her wings and swooped, disappearing into the shadowy gloom. Vahldan scanned the fir-covered hills, unable to help but wonder what other hunters might be waiting to seize their chance to swoop down on their prey.

Elan pointed beyond where the bird had disappeared. "Rekkr Kohlsa's homestead is at the far edge of this vale." Green mountains loomed from the mist beyond. "If we hurry we can reach his pastures by nightfall."

The paths Icannes had been leading them on for days were narrow and muddy, often constricted by low-hanging limbs and fallen logs. They were routinely forced to dismount and lead their horses. Their plodding pace was punctuated with frequent stops for feeding and changing the babe. The closeness of the forest felt confining—like being an instant from being trapped. Worse, they were perpetually on hillside paths, offering a vague but constant sense of vertigo.

A distant rumble of thunder threatened yet another bout of bad weather. Vahldan felt torn. Shelter would be a welcome relief, even for a night. But it meant facing what he supposed would be an inevitable confrontation. He had to ask about it. "You're sure we're welcome here? This Kohlsa is a wolf, isn't he?"

"Kohlsa is one of the few Wulthus Rekkrs to live this far east. But he alone holds this land. He and his sons both farm and graze a herd. When the other landholders and guildsmen press him, Kohlsa presses back. These particular wolves are beholden to no one. I think it's why the queen is fond of him. She says Kohlsa reminds her of the days when the futhark held firm."

"You've met him?"

"No, but Icannes has, several times. She seems certain that he'll offer us a warm fire and a barn to sleep in." Elan urged Hrithvarra to the hillcrest.

Eldavar and Mara followed, Alela went next, and Vahldan took up the rear. A hooting owl called from behind and Elan halted them. They turned to find Icannes, beckoning them back.

"We're being followed," Icannes said as they met. "I had a feeling, so I sent Kukida to circle around behind. She confirmed it. They ghost our progress, watching from the heights."

"Who?" Elan asked.

"Carpans. Several of them—at least four."

"Carpans," Vahldan cried. "We have to hunt them—catch them." Surely they were minions of Túkash.

Icannes raised a brow. "You say that as if it's easy. The Carpans all but own the heights. They're mostly timid creatures, thank the gods. Hardly a warrior among them. Be grateful these who follow aren't Spali."

Her dismissiveness riled him. He opened his mouth to argue, but Elan interceded. "Vahldan, you have a duty to your brother and sisters. Just as I have to you. Leave the spies to Icannes and Kukida. The rest of us should hurry to Kohlsa's compound."

Elan reined to set out. "No," Icannes said, gazing down into the darkening vale. "I'm not sure what these Carpans are about, but I sense something is amiss. I'm taking you to Kohlsa's Roost instead. It's a shallow cave on a shelf of rock that overlooks the vale. It offers enough cover for a fire. It's nearby and all but impossible to approach without our knowing." Lightning flashed in the southern sky. "You'll be safe there."

"*We'll* be safe there? What about you?"

Icannes eyed Vahldan. "I can't say that we'll catch a Carpan. But I think it's worth trying to find out why they're following us." She raised a brow. "You wouldn't happen to have a guess about this, would you, Young Lion?"

Vahldan still didn't know how much the Skolani knew. But they knew the location of the mine. A mine built by Carpans. Certainly the queen had some idea about his father's ambitions. Did they know about Túkash? Or the gold Angavar sought? If he spoke of his suspicions, who else might hear of them? Whom might they tell? He shook his head. "None."

The princess narrowed her gaze. "Of course not. Why would you?" It sounded sardonic if not accusatory. He shrugged. Icannes mimicked it. "Ah, well, it's likely nothing. Carpans are superstitious. Perhaps they watch to ensure we don't trespass on one of their sacred places. But until they leave off, I won't have you roaming about in the dark."

Icannes reined and turned her mount, Starfire, then drew up. She looked back over her shoulder. "Carpans or Spali or come what may, I promise you this, Young Lion. I will see you and your family through to Danihem safely. Now come, I'll show you to the Roost." She kicked Starfire and led them uphill.

Vahldan looked to Elan. She forced a smile, looking like she was veiling annoyance, same as him. He doubted it was for the same reasons. Elan heeled Hrithvarra after Icannes. As it had been since the Skolani appeared in his life, he and his family had no real choice but to follow. And to blindly trust.

Túkash's old horse crested yet another hill. He gazed into the darkening woods of the next vale. One of his scouts stepped from the trees, signaling him with a wave. He was in the right place; he could even smell the woodsmoke, the cooking meat. His kinsman disappeared into the shadows again before Túkash could even make out his identity.

Túkash hated to face what was about to happen. "But I must," he affirmed aloud. He closed his eyes. "Zemele protect us all," he prayed to the goddess.

He knew it was best to be on foot as he approached—for the safety of the old stallion, first and foremost. At the base of the slope he found a grassy knoll and dismounted. He clipped the worn old hobble on the horse's front legs. As if he would have the energy to go anywhere.

Túkash felt like he'd been traveling for half of his life. He supposed that wasn't far off. He could hardly recall the last time he'd slept in a bed. Perhaps the last time he slept in the same bed for more than a night or two was while he was in captivity in Angavar's compound.

He felt a passing pang of regret. The woman, and her children— they didn't deserve what was happening. Túkash brushed it aside.

Angavar had brought it upon them. The Gottari would all get what they deserved, as a people. They'd been here for generations, but they were still invaders. Their cruelty as a nation far outweighed any virtue of any individual.

Túkash pulled his staff from its couch on his saddle and started on the path that he presumed would take him to a sentinel. His leg was soon throbbing, but he knew he would walk through it. Since the incident, pain was a constant in his life, his leg pain being of the type that could be endured. He'd become a widow on the same day he became a cripple. The pain of the loss of his beautiful soul-mate was far more difficult to bear.

It wasn't long before the sentinels appeared. Two Spali warriors were soon accompanying him, a javelin-length from either side of him. None of the three of them spoke. Túkash soon saw the firelight through the trees. He stopped to appraise Auchote's camp before entering. Every visible Spali was Paralatoe—the tattooed warrior sect, sanctioned by the Spali priests. They received the best food and had their pick of the women from any of the Spali subtribes. They did no labor other than martial training. The Paralatoe were said to be the instruments of the Spali gods. Túkash doubted this was true, but he was certain that they were brutal and cruel, as well as lethal.

To defeat the deadly, one must be just as deadly. And every Spali or Gottari death at the hands of one another was a small victory for the Carpans.

One of the sentinels flanking Túkash growled and prodded him into the torchlight with his javelin. Túkash winced and stutter-stepped, almost falling. The jab hurt, but seemed not to have pierced the skin, thankfully. Spali poison was not to be trifled with. He would wash and soak his robes afterward—if he survived the visit.

The camp's raucous atmosphere faded to a brooding silence as he shuffled through the throng of tattooed warriors lounging around several bonfires. He steeled himself for the inevitable and headed toward the tattooed chieftain. His objective sat fireside, gnawing the oversize joint of the gods knew what. Túkash could only hope it was from an animal.

He leaned heavily on his staff, seeking to project an aura of both mystery and feebleness. It was wise, he found, to remind the Spali that he was no warrior. It disgusted them, but that was better than openly inciting bravado. Everyone knew that the Paralatoe were comprised of only the biggest and most ferocious fighters. They should have nothing to prove. Still, central to their culture was the demonstration of their fearlessness.

The first came at a full run, a curved blade in hand. The warrior shrieked as he came, and only stopped when his bare, tattooed chest was a hand's width from Túkash's nose. It took all of Túkash's will to stand his ground. Elbows cocked back, the warrior shrieked and cursed. Túkash knew enough of the Spali tongue to get the crude gist.

With no assurance he'd survive it, he used his staff to gently nudge the menace aside and continued. The incident was replayed three more times, each battle cry all the more unnerving. The final man actually spit a wad of phlegm onto his robe before giving way.

Harrowing, and yet it was the expected welcome of those whose aid he'd sought. The gods only knew that they'd just as soon kill him as do his bidding, no matter the potential reward. Túkash had no guess how many Carpans had died at the hands of Spali assailants over the years. For generations, bands of young Spali warriors came to Dania to raid. They didn't care whether the sheep they stole or the families they sometimes burned out or murdered were Carpan or Gottari.

It was true, one was as bad as the other—Gottari or Spali. They both raised their sons as brutes. But Túkash's Duhadai—his people's divinely blessed spirit-guide—foresaw that he would successfully use the brutes against one another. Indeed, the Duhadai saw the role of these very Paralatoe in the fulfillment of Túkash's life's work. He'd made more progress in the last few months than in all the years since

Angavar's Gottari had killed his beautiful bride, leaving him with a lifelong limp and two motherless daughters.

He drew to a halt before the scowling chieftain. Túkash refused to bow.

The garishly tattooed chieftain ripped another mouthful from the bone and chewed. The black tattooing around his unblinking eyes made his glare all the more intense. Túkash forced himself to return it. The Spali leader's lips and chin shone with grease. The chewing made his tattooed skull façade look like the movement of a macabre puppet.

The fire crackled in the hush. Túkash waited, unsure whether he would be addressed or ordered hacked down.

"Well?" Auchote finally said.

"I came to speak of the fate of Long Shadow." It was the moniker for Angavar—one of the few things shared by the Spali and Carpan peoples.

Auchote's lip curled. "Long Shadow is dead." The Spali chieftain's Hellainic was clipped and guttural, but serviceable. "Now speak of the fate of the payment."

"The payment comes when the deed is done."

Auchote scowled. "I just said he is dead. I killed him myself."

"So I hear. But I hear differently of the family. Of the boy."

"Eh. The boy is a frightened rabbit. Surely even a fat one like your friend can run down the likes of him." Auchote grinned and spoke a few words in his own tongue. His men laughed.

It was as Túkash suspected. And as the Duhadai had foreseen.

Angavar's misguided faith in his son had turned out to be his greatest failing. Having Long Shadow's sullen scion both humiliated and left alive perfectly served the goals of the Carpan people. Now Túkash had but to stir the kettle. Better still, what served his aims was also what Desdrusan would bid of him. "Do you not wish to cease your enemy's line?"

"I have seen the likes of that boy," Auchote said with a sneer.

"He'll go nowhere far. Fear tethers him. The Paralatoe do not bother with frightened boys."

Túkash knew that if he proceeded, he would be in the greatest danger he'd yet encountered. "What if I told you that the Lion Lord will not pay you until Angavar's line has been snuffed."

"Bah!" Auchote slung his gnawed bone into the fire, spraying sparks into the night. The chieftain sat up, looking like a wildcat ready to spring. "You would have us chase a rabbit? For what? My people need to eat. Spali blood was shed in the killing of Long Shadow. And we came away with nothing—not even his scalp!"

Túkash kept himself from smiling at the opportunity. It seemed Zemele was indeed with him. "Perhaps you should take the payment that is owed." Auchote raised an eyebrow. "My spies, they follow Long Shadow's family. They seem to be fleeing to one of the Gottari's great homesteads. The homestead of a noble family. One with large stores of grain, and a sprawling herd. There are even wagons there, to haul the booty away. You could end Long Shadow's line and feed your people, all in one raid."

Túkash could think of no better way to stir things up in Dania.

Auchote's smile was incredulous. "Wagons. You make me laugh, little priest. How are we supposed to get wagons across the river?"

Túkash had an idea or two. In his travels east, he'd taken note of some unguarded barges at a ferry landing upstream. "Let me see to that."

Auchote looked away. "And what of the she-demons? All of the warbands our priests sent for those vicious bitches to chase hither and thither have fled back across the river. Many have bled to keep them from hounding us."

The savage was interested. Túkash saw it in his eager eyes. "I have more ideas about that. There are but two of the she-demons traveling with Long Shadow's family. My spies can guide you there by ways unknown, and then they can occupy these two Skolana." Two, four—he'd only rounded down slightly.

Auchote barked a laugh and beckoned a young warrior to him,

and spoke briskly in their tongue. The youth nodded and went off to another fire. Túkash suspected it was Auchote's son.

The chieftain turned to Túkash with a disdainful sneer. "Tell me, priest. Why do you do the fat man's bidding? What does he hold over you?"

"The fat lion believes I owe him a life-debt. The day he thinks he saved me was the day he cursed me. He believes I am pledged to him by my goddess. But Zemele has shown me otherwise. I do the fat man's bidding because he weakens his people. Which suits me. For now."

"Ha! We will let your little spies lead us. If we find the reward you promise, it will be you who suits me, priest." Auchote's real teeth shone against the tattooing of his jaw. "For now."

CHAPTER 14—AMONG WOLVES

"Though it could not compare to the stone cities of the Hellains, Danihem was even in those days a bustling center of commerce. As the Gottari spread across the breadth of the Danian River Valley, many settlements had evolved—homesteads clustered for mutual benefit and defense. Many even supported a smithy or a grain mill, but none could rightfully be called a village.

Danihem was not only the home of Dania's largest mill and marketplace, it also touted up to a dozen smithies—each claiming some specialty. Inside the walls there were two large stables: one for Wulthus horses, another for Amalus, lest the two interbreed—a tragic occurrence from the perspective of either of the ruling clans."—Brin Bright Eyes, Saga of Dania

ELAN FOUND the Wulthus captain's squinting stare disconcerting. The man was not tall but he was stout, his arms the size of thighs, his neck as wide as his head. The wolf kept looking from her to Vahldan and back again. Riding among the wolves, it wasn't entirely clear if they were captives or merely being escorted, but at least they were together and safe.

Escaping the mountain pass while also escaping the notice of a host of Wulthus Rekkrs headed in the same direction turned out to be impossible. And even if they'd managed, there was still the lingering danger of fleeing Spali, spying Carpans, and a trio of shadowy Gottari who seemed to master both groups.

Things could've been worse, but their company wasn't exactly pleasant.

Elan learned that suspicious staring wasn't the only unpleasant thing about wolves. They also stank. And they stank in so many ways! Some smelled of cooking cabbage or bad cheese, some of ale, some of horseshit. But overriding it all was the smell of unwashed bodies, made all the worse by their escorts' insistence on surrounding her party as they rode. She'd always heard that men stank, but she'd never really had a chance to verify it. Until Vahldan. With him, it hadn't crossed her mind. Seemed her subject was an exception. She was grateful.

When Vahldan was questioned by Ulfhamr, as the thick-necked captain had named himself, he'd said only that he was honored to be under the guardianship of Queen Keisella. Elan had to hide her smile. The poor wolf captain would never dare question the queen's intentions. In a single sentence, Vahldan had ended the interrogation.

The road emerged from the forest onto a hillside meadow, and Danihem came to view. The massive rectangle of the village squatted in a crook of the Danian River, its flow broad and protective to three sides of the village. The meadows gave way to tiered pastures south of the timbered walls. Within the walls were more roofs than Elan had imagined could exist so close together. Ribbons of gray smoke curled from scores of chimneys, mingling in a haze that hung over a swath of the valley. It had to be a dozen times larger than the Jabitka.

Elan heard Vahldan and his brother exclaim softly to one another. She silently prayed that Icannes was already there.

The thought of being inside, with the stink and the press of men, repelled her. It looked like an immense and elaborate trap. She reminded herself that she was in the queen's command. This was her duty. Her subject was far from safe here. She needed to remain vigilant.

Vahldan rode up beside her. "Well, there it is," she said.

"There it is," he repeated. The wolf captain glanced with a wry smile. Did Thick-Neck suspect whom Vahldan was?

Vahldan lowered his voice. "Let's get this over with. The sooner I get my family out of that rat's nest, the better."

Elan was all for it. "I agree. If no safe haven can be swiftly found, we'll leave. We can send word ahead as we make our way back to the Jabitka. The queen is sure to approve. The girls will be taken in for the winter, of course. And I'm sure we can find shelter for you and Eldavar nearby." Elan felt herself smiling at the thought.

But when she turned to Vahldan, his brows were knotted. "There'll be no need, Elan. I intend to regain the futhark sword. Once I do, there will be ample loyal Rekkrs to choose from for the safe-keeping of my family."

"You don't have to do this," she hissed.

"Do what?"

"Seek a trial."

"A trial? No need for that, either. You saw it, same as I did. That was him—the usurper. He has openly shown he's in league with savages. And Carpans, too. It names him a traitor. Not to mention a murderer."

A sudden ache pounded at her temples. "I saw three riders, all wearing helms."

"Who else could it have been?"

Thick-Neck tilted his head, obviously trying to listen. Elan put a finger to her lips. Vahldan bit his cheek. She wondered how he could possibly think it would be so easy. He'd grown since they met. He'd gained maturity, and was working on his impulsiveness. But, Horsella help her, he was still so naïve.

They moved onto a broad road of churned mud. Elan drew a breath and tasted the bitter tang of the smithies. One of the wolves' scouts reined in to speak to the Wulthus captain. Elan took the opportunity to speak. "I don't know much about Gottari politics, but I've heard enough to be wary. Let's just take it slowly, shall we?"

"What's there to know? Desdrusan has thrown in with the Spali. Everyone will agree about how wrong it is."

"In the stories I've heard, lords have a way of twisting things in their favor."

"This is no story, Elan."

"I fear it will be to them." Vahldan looked away, letting his frown speak for him. "We'll take it step by step," she suggested again. He offered a hasty nod but refused to look at her.

THADMEIR SIGHED as the longhouse door finally closed behind the departing daughter of Queen Keisella. He found Icannes to be impudent and exhausting. Unfortunately her departure was only a temporary reprieve. Not only would the princess be back, but with those she insisted on foisting upon him.

Thadmeir had repeatedly said no. How had she won out?

The longhouse was otherwise empty, at least. Only his brother would witness the absurdity of the audience she'd demanded. "Tell me again, Urias, why I am beholden to receive the children of my brother's murderer? Go and tell her I've changed my mind."

"I won't. You can't. It's the queen's request. You owe it to her to at least hear them out."

"So now I *owe* Keisella?" Thadmeir asked.

Urias tsked. "There is an oath called the Mithusstandan—I'm sure you've heard of it."

Thadmeir waved him off. "This has nothing to do with the alliance."

"Of course it does," Urias said. "Any Skolani request has everything to do with it. Surely you can agree that they ask very little in return for their diligence at the borders."

The truth of his assertion made it all the more annoying. "Keisella is meddling, and you know it."

Urias affected his tone in that patient, explanatory way. "Whether it's meddling or not, regardless of who their parents were, they are still Gottari orphans. They're victims of war, with nowhere to turn. Show some compassion."

Compassion? No one had any for him. Thadmeir hated the memories. He'd only recently been able to ignore them. It had been so long since the nightmare of watching his brother bleed out. Half a lifetime since Aomeir's murderer had been thrust out of Danihem. How galling it was that Angavar had stolen his victim's betrothed, taken her away with him, into exile. That the villain had fathered children with Thadmeir's brother's woman—it made his innards twist.

Today it was all too fresh again. Like it had just happened. If things were as they should be, Frisanna's children would be Thadmeir's nephews and nieces, not outlaw beggars.

It was only recently that Thadmeir had finally found a bit of real happiness again. Amaseila was a soothing balm to the political rancor that refused to fade away.

At the time of Aomeir's murder, Thadmeir's father had claimed the deal they had made was the only way to maintain balance, to avoid more bloodshed. Could what the council had with Desdrusan be called balance? The man's own clan was constantly railing against him. Desdrusan may as well openly declare himself a wool guildsman, so tightly was he ensnared in their thrall.

The entire Amalus situation was a disgrace! And now this.

Considering how long Thadmeir had wished for it, the news of Angavar's death was surprisingly unsatisfying. They were all gone now: his elder brother Aomeir, his brother's rival Angavar, and even Frisanna, the temptress who'd beguiled them both. And yet the ugly stain of scandal couldn't be washed away. In fact, what was happening seemed certain to reopen scarcely healed wounds.

"Why should I be troubled by the woes of exiles? Angavar brought this upon himself. By rights, they should never have set foot in Dania again, let alone in the longhouse. Yet here they come. And you scold me for lacking compassion?"

The longhouse door opened. Urias bent to his shoulder. "Remember, they are here with the Skolani. Please try not to insult the queen. And don't be so heartless."

Three Skolani entered—the princess, another harsh-looking young Blade-Wielder, and a third holding a babe—followed by a tall young man and two disheveled children. Thadmeir's lip curled at the sight of the eldest, with his chin high and his proud scowl. He carried himself with typical Amalus vainglory, oblivious to the disgrace he represented.

Once the motley gang was assembled, the princess bid them all to bow. "Rise. Come," he barked. Urias tsked again and Thadmeir shrugged. Curt was not the same as heartless.

Gods, the Outcast's firstborn looked just like the damned father. But for one thing: he was even more comely. The father's stern features were softened by the mother's beauty. There was symmetry to his face. And his shoulder-length hair was the same soft gold as Frisanna's.

Keisella's daughter lined them up in front of the dais. The eldest knocked one of the benches askew as he came to the line, and left it crooked. It made him even more irksome.

"Lord Thadmeir!" The cocky princess presumed to speak first, and loudly. "May I present Vahldan, son of Angavar. Here too are Eldavar, Mara, and the babe is called Kemella. Here with them is Elan, daughter of Ellasan, who has been named by the queen as the temporary guardian of the Young Lion. Beside her is Alela of the Skolani, who was kind enough to travel along as the nurse of the newborn." Each of them bowed their heads in turn.

The exhausting princess continued, "My lord, the queen bids us to seek your aid in securing shelter for the Young Lion and his siblings. The queen trusts in your wisdom and in your kindness. She hopes you might commend them to one of their kinsmen; preferably one with womenfolk under roof, in light of the care the babe shall require."

"I asked before and got no answer. Why would Queen Keisella not have him seek the lions themselves? Lord Desdrusan sent word that he is returning to Danihem even as we speak." Thadmeir caught a glimpse of the eldest son stiffening. Clearly even the mention of his father's betrayer pained him. No surprise. Of course Angavar would steep his children in his own hatred.

"It's not my place to question my queen, Lord Thadmeir. She bid us to seek you, and you alone. Her trust in you is implied." Icannes inclined her head and waited. The others cast their eyes to the floor as well; all but the eldest boy, who stared defiantly.

Thadmeir rose and stepped from the dais. He stopped before the son of his brother's killer. Damn, the boy was taller than him. Had it really been so long, that the product of that despicable union had grown so? Angavar's son looked down his nose.

"Do you grasp what's gone before, boy?"

"I do."

"You knew that banishment includes progeny?"

"I did."

"And still you came."

"Had I not been bidden by the queen, I would not have come. Not yet." His tone was brazen, utterly lacking remorse, let alone respect.

Thadmeir's gaze was drawn to the glaring presence at the son's shoulder. The boy's twitchy Blade-Wielder guardian loomed within arm's reach. "How fortunate, to have a Blade-Wielder as a protector," Thadmeir said. "Tell me, what merits such a gift?"

The man-child and his attack raptor both scowled, but the brash princess replied. "His status, as the scion of one of the ruling clans. He is still the blood of the Amalus kings of old." Had she really dared mention the Amalus kings? It was an old saw the boy's father had crudely employed in his pandering to the common herdsmen.

Thadmeir refused to look away first. Icannes added, "It's said that Blade-Wielder guardians were once commonplace." Was she connecting such guardianships to kingship? Were the Skolani now willfully undermining Gottari law? Maddening, but it didn't really matter. Banishment was irreversible, regardless of status or bloodline.

"It's a pity," Thadmeir said, "that my brother never received such a boon. If he had, it would've saved you the trouble of guarding this one. He'd have never been born."

The man-child nearly vibrated with restrained rage. Thadmeir had expected a bit of feigned groveling. But it was clear that this one would never be penitent.

Thadmeir had seen enough. He was about to reaffirm their sentence and throw them out when Urias spoke up. "My lord, if I may. There are many Amalus Rekkrs from the countryside in Dani-hem, making ready to ride east with young Arnegern. Perhaps he could help us determine if any of his clansmen have families willing to shelter them—at least till the Spali threat has been put down. I'm sure that in the meantime Vahldan and his brother would be willing to earn their keep. Wouldn't you, Vahldan?"

The insolent cub's eye was drawn from Thadmeir's at last. "Of course. We would be honor-bound to do so."

Thadmeir gave his brother a hard look. Urias nodded, assured he was in the right. His brother was always so concerned about appearances. Bickering with his captain in front of them was beneath Thadmeir, and Urias knew it.

Thadmeir returned to the dais chair and sat heavily. He just wanted them out of his sight. "I'll not be known for thrusting children into the arms of Spali raiders." The ragged group seemed to sigh in relief. "But I would not hold to hope," he hastened to add. "If Arnegern is wise, he'll want nothing to do with this."

"Thank you, my lord," the princess intoned. Gods ablaze, they thought they'd won.

He went on. "In any case, the raiding we have seen is sure to be temporary, same as all those Dania has already endured. Our laws stand firm. This family is beholden to their father's banishment. Do not become comfortable inside Dania's borders. Outlaws are not welcome to dwell here. Know that I will be appraised of your whereabouts. And I will see to your departure. In fact, you'd best be gone from Danihem's gates by nightfall, as well, if only to one of the hostels along the river road. There is a mustering going on, and I have a feeling your presence would not sit well with some of those who will attend their sendoff."

A familiar voice rang out from the far end of the hall. "With some? With every last law-abiding Gottari, more like."

Thadmeir slumped and groaned. Desdrusan marched up the center aisle, certain to make the situation uglier than it already was. And he'd been so close to having done with it.

CHAPTER 9—THE ECHO OF GLORY

" ' And a king shall rise from among the kingless, born of exile. In glory shall he rise, and glory shall be his song, calling to the faithful, echoing across the ages. And even in his doom shall he lead unto Urrinan. Such is the fate of the Bringer.' So say the hymns of the Dreamers of the Skolani."—Brin Bright Eyes, Saga of Dania*

By NIGHTFALL the children and Alela were settled in the cozy hollow of Kohlsa's Roost—a shallow cave at the back of a shelf of bare rock jutting from the mountainside overlooking the vale. They arrived just before a brief thundershower and had a nice fire going in the stone-lined firepit, thanks to the dry wood Kohlsa's sons kept stacked in the back of the cave.

Vahldan saw to it that Eldavar and Mara ate. He'd made a warm porridge of barley and carrots fortified with the meat of a partridge which Elan had shot earlier in the day. The satisfying meal and the wind through the pines lulled them to a calm silence.

Vahldan fed the fire and sat on his haunches, warming his hands.

Everyone sat staring at the fire. Including Elan. "Shall we set a watch?" he asked.

Elan shook her head. "No need. Icannes and Kukida have it in hand. There is only one approach. Icannes said she'd let us know when one of us needs to take up the watch."

The rain had ended, and a chill wind swept the night sky clear. Vahldan gazed out into the star-studded deep blue, rubbing his hands together.

"Have a seat," Elan said, and patted the spot beside her. He reluctantly sat. "Now try to relax," she added with mirth in her tone. He leaned against the log and stretched his legs out.

He tried to relax, as bidden, but his tapping toes seemed unwilling to cooperate. He wished he could be more like his siblings. Eldavar had fallen asleep with his unfinished bowl in his lap. Mara dozed with Kemella nestled in her arms. Even Alela curled up on her side and was instantly asleep. It seemed Alela could sleep whenever an opportunity arose, which Vahldan supposed was a useful trait for a wet-nurse.

He released a sigh. A deep restlessness filled his belly. Not like the fluttering that preceded the ugliness, but troubling just the same. He told himself that all was well. His family was safe for the moment. But the thought provided little relief.

He reached to run his fingertips over the wound on his cheek. It was scabbed over but still sore to the touch. The pain was a reminder. He had no right to feel relieved or content. His father was dead. And now his mother, too. His failure had been the start of all that had befallen his family. Now he was the eldest. He was responsible for all that befell them going forward. *"Gods, what will come of us if this falls to you."*

Anxiety clenched, like a constricting serpent, wrapping his chest. He sat up, drew another breath and blew it out. Elan was watching. He forced himself to lean back and faced her. The ledge fell away behind her, the star-filled sky framing her angular face, full of concern. "Tell me," she said.

"What would you have me tell?"

"Tell me about what twists you so."

He smiled. She'd sensed the same serpent. "There's much. Where would I begin?"

"Just tell me all of it, then. It always helps to tell a friend."

Maybe she was a friend. "Guess I didn't realize. I've never really had one."

"Well, you have one now."

It felt like pity. Being pitied only fed his anxiety. "I guess it's mainly that I can't believe that they're gone." He looked to the fire, swallowing back the emotion that chased the words to the top of his throat. "It's..." He swallowed hard. "A lot," he managed.

They sat in awkward silence a moment. "You heard Icannes," Elan said. "She promised that she'll get us all to Danihem safely. Trust me, Icannes says nothing lightly. She only makes promises she knows she can keep."

Vahldan softly laughed. "Getting there safely is just another beginning." He looked at her. "And to be honest, I'm not sure if it'll be the beginning of something better or worse." Her eyes filled with sympathy. Or was it more pity? He looked to the fire again.

"You're right," she said. "What you've been through: it's a lot. But you've taken every blow and kept on. You've faced each new step head on." She paused and sighed. "I know how hard..." He looked back to her. "Look, you went there and you won. You submitted to Thunar's Blessing and you found your way back. It's no easy thing, even for a seasoned warrior. But you've faced the worst. Knowing that means you don't need to fear facing it again."

His father's words sprang to mind. *'I know what's inside you because it's inside me, too.'*

"Exactly how much did you hear?" he asked her.

She looked away. "I'm sorry. I was sent to see to your fathers injuries, but I immediately saw that it was too late. You already had your father's sword, and..."

"And you stayed to eavesdrop."

"No!" She lurched to a sitting position. "I mean, yes. I did eavesdrop. But I'd been sent to see to your safety. I... I didn't want to intrude. My duty is to avoid interference. I felt I had to stay near but hidden, in order to adhere to that duty. I didn't mean to eavesdrop."

At least the pity was gone from her eyes. Sincerity had replaced it. He nodded. "I see."

"I'll say it again. I'm sorry, Vahldan."

"Apology accepted," he said. "I suppose since you heard it all, you really do know that it's a lot."

She settled back with a sigh. "Yes. It really is."

"Speaking of being twisted, I'd say you're one to talk," he turned it on her. "I saw your reaction when the queen brought up the Fulhsna-whatever-it-is."

Elan smiled. "The Fulhsna-Utanni. It's an honor, you know. For us both. Or so they say."

"This happens a lot?"

"No, not in generations. But the tales are still told. The guardian is always so heroic, the subject so grateful. And oh, how blessed are the times to follow, due to his having been saved." Her playful smile shone in the firelight. "And, of course, he often falls in love with her, only to have to bury his yearning away forever—a burden borne by both, to the end of their days."

"Sounds tragic."

"Oh, aye. It always was."

She was joking, of course. But it made him anxious in a whole new way. He had to admit, he found her fascinating. She kept catching him staring, in spite of her reminders. He'd rarely found anything so difficult to avoid. He'd never met anyone like her. Had she read something into his intrigue? Was she setting firmer boundaries by joking about it? "Well, I'm already grateful, but I'll try not to burden you with my buried yearning."

She laughed and looked away.

Gods, had his dumb addition made it worse? "I don't mean to

make light of it. Seriously, I don't know where we'd be if you hadn't come along. It feels like a gift from the gods."

"Ha. Didn't I tell you that the gods are fickle? We'll see if I still seem like a gift once we get to Danihem." She gazed skyward. "You're right, though. I was surprised when the queen assigned me. I thought I would return to my host. I'd be hunting Spali right now if..." She looked over at him sheepishly. "If the gods weren't so damned fickle." She winked.

"I'm starting to see your point," he said. Elan smiled but went back to stargazing. "So, hunting Spali? That's your dream?"

Her gaze snapped to him. "My dream? Why would you ask that?"

He shrugged. "Just seems important to you. Like what you are called to."

"Oh." Elan settled back. "Important, yes. But I wouldn't say it's a calling."

"Tell me," he said, imitating her.

Elan's smile was wry. "I suppose I owe you. After my accidental prying." The silence stretched and her smile faded. "They killed my mother. When I was eight."

"Oh gods." He'd done it again. "I'm sorry. I didn't mean to—"

"It's all right." She patted his arm. "It's important to me to talk about her. Her name was Ellasan. She was a healer not a Blade-Wielder. She ran out to help a wounded companion in battle. She wasn't even fighting them. But that didn't keep those savages from shooting her. The poison would've taken her, same as your father. And I wasn't there to see that it didn't. That was left to the hand of her patient. They both died there on the field, helpless and isolated. I suppose it's how I came to consider the gods fickle. And it's definitely why I'm driven to hunt Spali."

Did she really think his father's end was better? Was it?

She went on. "Some days I think I'd give anything to have been there with her, to offer her comfort, to hear her final words. To thank her. To tell her I love her. But thinking about what you had to do...

Well, I can't imagine how hard that must've been. How hard it must still be."

His feet started tapping again. He managed to nod. Had he squandered his opportunity? Why hadn't he thought to thank his father and tell him that he loved him? His fingers absently drifted to touch his face wound.

"It'll always hurt," she said, "but trust me, it gets better."

"It won't for me. Not until I make things right."

"I used to feel the same. But it's changed. It's not about vengeance anymore."

He meant much more than vengeance, but she'd made him curious. "What else?"

"Well... It's difficult to explain."

"I'm awake." And he preferred keeping the conversation about her.

"It's sort of why it startled me when you called it my dream." She shook her head and covered her eyes. "To explain, I guess I'd have to tell you of one particular dream."

He sat up. "Yes, tell me."

She glanced. "This isn't something I do. Only a few know of it."

"Oh come on. I guessed there was a dream, didn't I?" She pressed her lips tight. He gave her a little grin. "Like you said, you sort of owe me."

"Oh all right." Elan looked off into the sky. "Here goes. So I have this dream, again and again." She dropped her chin to her chest and fell silent.

"Always the same?" he prodded.

"Always."

"When did you first have it?"

"The first time was right after my mother's death. It's the clearest dream I've ever had—as easily recalled as waking life. It feels...different, like it's trying to tell me something."

"Which is?"

"You promise not to judge? Or laugh?" He nodded. "Well, it feels like it's trying to show me my future. Or maybe more like the future I should be striving for."

Vahldan stifled a smile and propped his head on an elbow. "Let's have it, then. What's your future?"

"You'll think it's silly. Or conceited."

"I said I wouldn't judge. And it always helps to tell a friend."

"So I've heard. All right, here it is. In the dream, I'm a renowned warrior. So acclaimed that crowds cheer me." He nodded. That seemed possible. "You should know that I started having this dream well before I won my blade. Even before they allowed me to train to become a Blade-Wielder."

"It already seems prophetic, then."

Elan squinted at him. "You said you wouldn't make fun."

Vahldan raised both hands. "I'm not. Promise."

"Anyway, in the dream I ride at the shoulder of a great leader. Together we've won great glory. This leader has gathered mighty armies, and tallies untold victories, against the Spali and others. All Dania sings our praise. Our enemies fear us, and the rest of the world respects us. I alone have the honor of riding at the great one's right hand. Together we parade through cheering throngs, sometimes in Dania, other times through the streets of stone cities. I see us surrounded by mountains and in view of the shore of the sea."

"The sea?" he said. "Have you seen it?"

Elan shook her head. "No, that's just it. These are all places I've never actually been. And yet, I can see them. And they're so real. Even the crowds. Glory shines on this warrior and me, and we both know we reflect it well on one another." She fell silent.

"Icannes?" he asked.

"Yes," Elan replied without hesitation. She sat up, hugging her knees and gazing into the fire. "At least I like to think so." She huffed a lone laugh. "As does she. But..."

"But what?"

"The truth?"

Vahldan cocked his head. "Among friends it's all that'll do."

She sighed. "I can't actually see the leader. There is only shadow when I seek for her identity. Besides that, the Skolani renounce fighting in foreign lands. I asked my grandmother, who is wise about such things, what it means. All she'll say is that it reveals my special purpose. Which she's said all along. She also admitted that she has this same dream of me. But she'll say no more." Elan shrugged. "At least nothing that makes sense. She tends to speak in riddles."

"Your grandmother has the same dream? That's got to mean something, right?"

"I thought so, too. And it's bigger than just hunting Spali. It's about...." She shook her head, evidently at a loss for words.

"About seizing your destiny?" he ventured, recalling Angavar's final words.

"Exactly!" she exclaimed, turning to him. "Oh," she said, her expression falling. She'd remembered.

"I guess we both have a lot on our shoulders."

Elan sat back with a sigh. "We do. And yet here we are, on our way to seizing destiny."

Gods, she made it sound easy. She seemed so sure of things, so in control. He'd made so many vows: to his father, to his mother, and to himself. *'Promise me you'll heed your legacy. Restore our honor. Claim your rightful title. Lead our clan to glory. Take it back. Glory is the way.'*

'Have patience. Trust your heart. Family first.'

'I won't let them win! They'll pay for what they've done.'

The ugliness stirred. Vahldan had already lost himself to rage once. What if Elan hadn't been there? He'd killed without hesitation, and his bloodlust had nearly gotten him killed in the process. How was he supposed to confront those he would face in Danihem? The wolves of the wool guild had been behind his father's downfall, and it seemed his clan's own chieftain—his father's cousin—was behind his father's murder. Not to mention that the killers were still hunting him and his family. Now he was being delivered right into their hands.

He felt her watching. "Here we are," he repeated. It sounded more sarcastic than he'd intended.

Elan squinted at him. "You don't see it, do you?"

"See what?"

"Yes, we're heading to Danihem. Yes, your father had enemies there. But there are others. Others who will support you. Others who believe."

"Believe in what?

Elan pointed at his chest. "In you."

"Me? Why would they?"

"Because of your father, for a start."

"Well, guess what—I'm not him."

Elan seemed to recoil. Was she annoyed? She pressed her lips tight and looked skyward, seeming more exasperated than annoyed.

He crossed his arms and they sat in silence. His brooding swiftly morphed into regret.

"And a king shall rise from among the kingless, born of exile. In glory shall he rise, and glory shall be his song." She'd spoken the words in a wistful, sing-song tone.

He slumped and closed his eyes. "What's that supposed to mean?"

"Just something the Skolani Dreamers have passed down. I'm told it's very old."

Vahldan turned to her. "Is this about the bedamned prophecy? Because that's got nothing to do with me. I don't want any part of it."

"You might not, but you can't change what others think. Plenty of herdsmen believe that you're the Bringer."

He sat up, feeling a little alarmed by the thought. Just how wide-spread was this? "I can't help that. I didn't ask them to." He had enough problems without having their fables laid on him.

"It doesn't matter if you asked. People believe. It could be useful. Seems like your father thought so."

Vahldan frowned. "How do you figure?"

"Glory is the way?" She gave a shrug. "Sounds like a mission for the Bringer to me."

He shook his head. "See? I don't even know what that's supposed to mean, and he was my father. And here you are, telling me he was talking about the prophecy."

Elan sat up beside him, face to face. "It seems pretty straightforward to me."

"Explain it, then."

She shrugged again. "For me, glory is about inspiring people to fight for justice. It's about giving people hope."

Vahldan drew his knees up and dropped his head, cradling his face in his crossed arms. "I... I don't know how. I hardly have enough hope for myself. Or for my family."

"Whether your father was talking about the prophecy or not, he clearly believed you could do this. And he's not alone. Apparently the queen believes it, too. I mean, she provided you with not just one, but three Blade-Wielders."

Gods, he hadn't thought of it that way. More expectation. More pressure.

Elan put a hand on his shoulder. "I know they're not the only ones. Want to know how?" She gave his shoulder a squeeze. He lifted his head. "I know because I believe in you, too." Had she come back around to pity? Her smile was warm, though.

"I don't deserve it," he said.

"You don't think you do, but there's a cure for that" Her smile grew lopsided, crinkling her nose. "You can start believing in yourself."

The fluttering rose from his belly to warm his chest. "You think so?" Gods, her hand was still on his shoulder, her gaze totally focused on him. Her eyelashes were red like her hair.

"I do. Trust me, it works wonders."

"What works wonders?" Vahldan jumped and Elan snatched her hand back.

They both twisted to face the speaker. "Welcome back," Elan said. "Any sign of the Carpans, my princess?"

"None." Icannes threw a thumb at Vahldan. "You're in my spot." Before he could move, she leaned on both their shoulders and sat, wedging herself between them. Icannes twisted her shoulders, squaring her back to Elan. "Undo me." Elan started unbuckled her harness and breastplate. A sly grin spread across Icannes's face and she put her hand on Elan's thigh.

They were way too close. Vahldan scooched away and stood, feeling taunted and awkward. Icannes kept an unsettling gaze fixed on him. "So. Have you two been chattering all this time? What was that when I came up? Something works wonders?"

"It was nothing," he said too quickly.

"We were just talking about believing. I told him the queen believed in him because she assigned three Blade-Wielders to this mission."

Icannes continued to grin, but her eyes hardened. "Makes sense. I believe in you too. I'll prove it by trusting you to take the watch till morning. In spite of the fact that you missed the opportunity to get some sleep when you had it."

Vahldan bowed with a flourish. "I am honored by your belief, Princess Icannes."

Elan finished her stays. Icannes tossed aside the gear, wrapped an arm around Elan, and laid back against the log, pulling Elan down with her. Vahldan stood there, still flustered. "On your way, then," Icannes said, flicking a dismissive hand.

He grabbed his sword belt and his bow and quiver, and started for the ledge-like path out. "Oh, and try not to shoot Kukida," Icannes called after him.

He waved without looking back, afraid the flushing he felt in his face might show.

CHAPTER 10—KOHLSA'S COMPOUND

" I t's true that Icannes began to win acclaim at a young age. The tale is oft told of her taking her first battle victim before her first moon-blood. Also before she'd earned her blade. Having overheard a messenger telling her mother of a nearby Spali raid, young Icannes snuck off alone before a tracking party could be gathered and sent. She trailed the Spali till nightfall, then killed not one but four raiders, with only a wood axe and a belt knife.

Upon her return, Icannes was severely punished, by lashes followed by a moon of imposed shunning. But she took it in stride, including famously receiving the lashes without uttering a sound. In the end she gained not just the whip scars, but scalps and esteem that served her ascent. It's said that Keisella privately admitted she had only herself to blame. For her daughter had inherited her own willfulness." –Brin Bright Eyes, Saga of Dania

ICANNES ROSE before dawn and left Elan and Kukida sleeping. After the night Kukida had had, her scouting partner deserved a break. She silently saddled Starfire and set out just as the sky began to gray.

She'd slept too little to be at her best, but it would have to do. There was something strange going on in these hills, and she hoped that Kohlsa could help her to figure out what it was. And she preferred to speak to him alone.

The last thing she needed was this odd game of chase and seek with Carpans. She needed to focus on getting the Outcast's son to Danihem. Seeing this mission through to success had become vital. She'd initially been shocked by how easily her mother had agreed to sending her along. But when she'd gone back to the Jabitka to gather her gear, Ursellya had laughed and chided her, saying, *"Oh, the elders are going to love you for this."*

By the time Icannes had grasped Keisella's clever tactic, it was too late to change course.

But no matter. Icannes could continue to play both sides of the conflict between Keisella and the Skolani elders. Their dispute often centered around the tribe's involvement with the outside world— particularly the queen's interest in Gottari politics. Keisella's interest only grew keener in light of the prophecies that Dreamers like Sael thought were coming to fruition, embroiling both tribes.

Icannes had long sensed that several of the elders wanted to coopt the queen's daughter. These wily women ever sought to groom her as a more compliant and less meddlesome future queen. It'd been simple enough for her to seem to take the side of her mother's rivals. And Icannes had enjoyed playing the part. It was an entertaining way both to frustrate her mother and to court future favor from those Icannes would one day have to outmaneuver herself.

Icannes's impulse to seek to come along had been rooted in a compulsion to see to Elan's devotion. Elan was hers. Icannes had marked that claim years ago. She'd heard the tales of the Fulhsna-Utanni, same as everyone. She recognized the dangers—certainly better than Elan seemed to. The Young Lion had already shown a tendency to sniff too closely to Icannes's prize, and Elan was clearly too naïve to notice. She hadn't been around males enough to learn that the hang of their loins weighed in nearly everything they said or did. The issue definitely called for closer oversight.

Clearly Elan's assignation went beyond Keisella's delight in meddling. It was also a slap to a defiant daughter. But now Icannes saw that the coupling had also been bait. As soon as Icannes had stepped into the noose, Keisella had snapped her up in it. Her mother was seeing to it that Icannes became firmly—and openly—entangled in Gottari politics. In addition, if things went ill with the Young Lion, Keisella could lay the blame on her. Icannes had been outwitted.

Icannes still saw the path to making the misstep work in her favor. The elders would be easy. There was no question that the old prudes would disapprove of Elan's assignation. The Fulhsna-Utanni had been abandoned generations ago, and with good reason. Hence, Icannes had merely come along to ensure that a fellow Blade-Wielder remained chaste—a slap back at her mother, and perfectly in sync with Icannes's goals. She'd since begun to glimpse that the mission might also offer a chance to win acclaim—both from the Gottari and the Blade-Wielders.

Although she was baffled by the behavior of the Carpans, she sensed it was related to the presence of the Young Lion. She'd become more convinced than ever that Vahldan was being hunted. The fact that someone wanted him dead demonstrated how much keeping him alive would stir things up. And by keeping him not only alive but thriving, she placed herself at the vortex. If there were Spali involved, all the better.

It made this an opportunity to harvest scalps even as she reclaimed Elan's affections.

Keisella may be the cleverer of them, but there was one thing about which Icannes had no doubt. As a warrior, she was unsurpassed. There was no need to qualify it. Everyone knew it. To deny it would be false modesty, which served no purpose.

Besides, staying close to the son of the Outcast was hardly a burden. He was a bit boyish yet, but handsome—certain to only improve. Sure, flirting with him might distract him from Elan, but it was fun, as well. And who could know? Perhaps by propping him into the right status, she might mold herself a fine candidate for mating someday.

She neared Kohlsa's compound as the first sunbeams shot through the leaves. She'd yet to be hailed by a sentry. She brought Starfire to a halt to listen. No songbirds. Worse, the distant scolding of crows. Icannes felt the first tingle of Thunar's Blessing. Danger and death were near.

She came to a trail of freshly hoof-churned soil and leapt from the saddle. Oddly, someone had driven a flock down the road that led to the river. The flock had been trailed by several wagons. Stranger still, the size of the hoof prints alongside suggested Spali ponies.

Realization struck, and cold dread washed over her. Could Carpans and Spali be acting in league? They were normally foes, but it would explain much. Kukida had complained all night of the Carpans' audacity. Her scouting partner had said that it seemed the hill-dwellers tactics had been designed to mock them.

If Icannes was right, it was much worse. She and Kukida had been baited in order to distract them.

She longed to give chase, but it wouldn't be right. Instead, she led her friend off the road. She hid Starfire in a copse of firs, munching on tufts of grass. She had to check on Kohlsa and his family. Protecting Danians was her duty, after all. As she drew nearer to the compound, the charnel reek of a sodden burn filled her nose. She crept to the tree line.

It was worse than she'd imagined. Kohlsa's cabin was a smoldering heap of black beams. The adjacent pastures, normally full of goats and sheep, were empty. She scanned the compound. There were several lumps in the grass. Her eye alighted on pale flesh. A human body sprawled between the main cabin and the open meadow gate. She drew her blade and ran.

Crows flapped away as she approached. The corpse was a

graying female. Icannes had only met the woman in passing, but she knew it was Kohlsa's qeins. The poor woman lay face down in the pasture with a Spali arrow protruding from between her shoulders. She'd been shot in flight. She'd been scalped. Flies crawled across rust-brown dried blood smears on her skull. Crows had already pecked the soft spots of the corpse.

Icannes moved on to the scorched but still standing stable. Bodies littered the ground in front of the open doors. This had been the site of a violent standoff. Kohlsa and his three sons were among the fallen males, as well a boy no more than ten years old. The boy's head was severed and lay several spans from his body. The men had been viciously mutilated. Kohlsa too had been scalped. One of the sons' bodies had been decapitated.

The ground surrounding the grain bins was littered with grain, the door swinging in the breeze. It was empty. The rutted ground revealed that the contents had been loaded on Kohlsa's own wagons.

How had she allowed this to happen? She'd been so near, concerned only about her own little fellowship. But why this? If these Spali were in league with the Carpans who shadowed her party, if they truly hunted Angavar's son, surely they'd known he wasn't here. They could've attacked her camp, but they spent all of their energies on raiding this homestead. What would a Spali raiding band do with so much booty, so far from home?

Were they really hunting Vahldan? Had they given up?

Icannes heard something inside the stable. She raised her blade and stole to the door, peering into the shadows. The horses had been stolen. A bit of light shone through the partially burned thatch. There were more bodies strewn inside. A low moan drew her on.

The first body within was one of Kohlsa's granddaughters, little more than a girl. Icannes felt for a pulse. Nothing. The homestead's females lay scattered like tossed sacks of grain. She heard it again—a wheezing sound. She moved past a stall and gleaned movement. One of the women was alive. She sprawled on a stack of hay, her hands bound and tied over her head, holding her up in a sitting position, leaning against the wall. It was one of the son's wives.

Icannes ran to her. Her face was bruised and her arms were covered in slashes and welts. Thunar's Blessing surged up from Icannes's belly to boil in her chest, leaving the burn of sick in her mouth.

Blood oozed from a cut on the woman's fat bottom lip. The hair on one side of her head was crusted with blood. Icannes cut the cords and lowered her arms. She gasped, and one of her swollen eyes popped opened. She recoiled in fright.

"I am Skolani. I'm here to help." Icannes held her hand.

"You're too late," she croaked.

"Shhh, stay still. I'll go for water."

The grip on her hand tightened. "No. Don't leave me."

"I won't," she assured her. "Who did this, Spali? Why did they come? What did they want?"

The woman's swollen lip curled. "They didn't say. They just *took*." Tears streamed from her eyes. "My babies... my daughters. They're gone. The youngest, I watched her die. I couldn't even hold her. The other..." She squeezed her eyes shut and sobbed.

"This is an affront to Horsella, to Freya."

The woman snorted a bitter laugh. "*They're* affronted?" Her voice became a breathy growl. "The gods stood by while those beasts killed our men. They tied me here, left me to watch while they hunted down my hidden girls, killed them one by one. They were laughing." A sob made her cough. "Affronted or not, the gods let those savages take everything. What can they offer me now?"

"They sent me," Icannes hissed. "And I am the blade of their wrath."

The woman settled back, and actually nodded. She closed her eyes. Icannes said, "Come. I will bear you to my sister. She's a healer, and she's near."

The woman's grip tightened again. "No. My lungs... they fill." She coughed again. "I drown even as we speak."

Icannes heard that it was true. "What comfort can I offer?"

"Only mercy. For me, for my daughter. My eldest—they took her. She ran to me, tried to untie me. They dragged her away. My darling girl. Find her. Promise me."

"I will, I promise. My companions will attend to your dead, this very day. Then I, Icannes daughter of Mighty Keisella, will track and find those who took your daughter. I will save her if I can. But know that I will not rest until you and your daughters are avenged."

The woman nodded again. She believed. "Come then, blade of the gods... Time is past. Deliver me." She laid back and pointed to the center of her chest.

Icannes stood square over her, brought her blade up, and placed the tip below her sternum. "You are ready?" The woman gave a final nod, the gaze from her swollen eyes unwavering. Icannes slid the blade in and up. She swiftly withdrew it and set it aside, and took up the woman's hand again. The woman gripped her fiercely.

Icannes prayed as she gasped her final breaths. "Hel, great goddess —She who guards over the spirits of the dead—this woman comes to you now. As she kneels before you, know that she loved and was loved in this life. She brings an honorable soul, for she was brave beyond compare. Watch over her, Hel, as she crosses the bridge, from this life to the next. Welcome her with glory, and let her never be forgotten."

The woman's grip went slack and her stare lost focus. Icannes crossed her arms over her chest wound. "I'm sorry I failed you."

She found a horse blanket and covered her, pausing before she covered her staring eyes. "I promise," she whispered, "I will not forget you." And she covered the woman's broken face.

ELAN ROSE from her knees after she and Vahldan lowered the woman's corpse into the long grave they had dug together in the soft soil at the edge of Kohlsa's pasture. Elan stretched her back. She surveyed the pit. Gods, so many. The hard work had imparted a sort of numbness, but seeing them together jarred her from it.

"Is that it?" Vahldan asked.

She'd been wrapping the female bodies inside the partially burned stable in saddle blankets and dragging them to the doorway before having Vahldan come and help her carry them to the grave. She considered going for the final corpse, but an idea lingered. She shook her head. "No. There's one more inside."

Vahldan stood staring, his face slack. They'd been at it all day. The grim duty had taken a toll on the whole group. He had to be exhausted, having spent much of the prior night on watch. Right after their arrival here, Icannes and Kukida had left to hunt the savages who'd done this. Elan had sent Eldavar to help Alela with the evening meal prep and Mara to hold the babe.

Elan gave the final nudge. "Would you mind? Back corner, behind the stable wall."

Vahldan frowned but started for the open doorway. He'd only been inside a moment when it came—a guttural roar and a crash. Then another. Elan drew a deep breath and followed him in. She found him on his hands and knees, retching. She edged by him and went to the girl. She lifted the girl's slender form till her weight rested on her shoulder. Holding the body with one arm, Elan drew her belt knife and cut the rope to the loft from which they'd hung her. She lowered the poor girl's body to the blood-splattered straw below.

Vahldan stood, grunting and spitting. She took the final horse blanket and laid it out beside the body. She lay the girl on the blanket, sensing Vahldan behind her. She took the far edge of the blanket to wrap her.

"No," Vahldan grunted. "Leave it." She leaned back, squatting on her haunches. Coagulated blood had dried in the girl's hair surrounding the bashed crown of her skull. Vahldan knelt to gently brush blond curls from the purpling face, and then pushed down the lids over bugging green eyes. In spite of the bruises, mud, and gore, the resemblance was even stronger than Elan had realized.

Vahldan squeezed his eyes shut, and murmured in prayer to Hel. He carefully wrapped her, scooped her into his arms as if she were sleeping, and carried her out. Elan followed.

He got to his knees at the graveside, and slowly lowered her in next to one of the elder females. Elan grabbed both shovels and came up beside him, holding them at either side, ready to draw them up defensively if necessary.

After a long moment on his knees, he stood, glowering at her. "You did that on purpose."

Elan stared back, facing his anger. "I felt you should see her."

"It was cruel. You saw that she looked like Mara." Elan conceded with a single nod. "Why?" he barked. He was close to giving in to his rage, trembling, fists clenched.

"Because I need you to fully understand what we're up against."

He turned and spat on the ground. "Don't you know how hard this is for me?"

"It's hard for all of us."

Vahldan shook his head. "When I go there, I lose myself."

"You can learn not to."

He growled and kicked a fence rail, knocking it down. "I've tried! It's different for me."

"It's not. What's different is, you're a highly trained, highly skilled fighter. You own a sword. If you learn to accept Thunar's Blessing, and maintain control, you will be an asset to your people. And a threat to those who inflict such horror as this." Elan pointed a shovel handle at the open mass grave.

"You're asking me to accept that I'm a killer, same as them. Same as my father."

"I am."

Vahldan rounded on her. "Why?" His shout startled a crow into flight from the pasture.

"Because you'll be good at it. Because I trust you will use your gift wisely. Because being a killer doesn't necessarily make you a monster. Because Dania needs you."

He started pacing and muttering. The flight of the startled crow drew Elan's eye, and she saw something else in the evening sky. "Look." Elan pointed to the soaring raptors.

Vahldan begrudgingly did as she'd bidden. "The birds?"

"They're kestrels. Remember when we saw the female, last night?" He didn't answer but at least he was looking. And calming down. "She's the one with the brown wings, hovering above. The lower one, with the blue wings, is her mate."

He sighed. He was coming back from the brink. "All right. What of it?"

"He's hunting. When he dives, and as he takes his prey, he is lost in what he's doing. He becomes helpless, utterly vulnerable to attack by a larger raptor or a ground predator. She's there to watch over him —to keep him safe."

Vahldan finally looked at her. "Seriously, how can you know this much about kestrels?" He almost smiled.

"I just do," she said, allowing herself a slight smile. Elan tipped one of the shovel handles toward him. He took it. She shoved hers into the pile and started filling the grave. He joined her.

"Remember," she said as she worked. "You are my duty. I am your guardian. I understand how difficult this is for you." Elan stuck her shovel in and leaned on the handle. He paused and met her gaze. "I will always be here for you. Understood?"

Vahldan sighed and nodded. "Understood," he said, and they both continued shoveling.

CHAPTER II—THE TRIALS OF TRAVEL

"No one can be sure when the Fulhsna-Utanni came to be. Some say the guardianships were a part of the Mithus-standan from its inception—a show of good faith on the part of the Skolani, who better knew the land and its dangers. I imagine it was offered as a gift rather than to meet a demand—a way to ensure the thriving of the Gottari royal clans in a new and often hostile landscape.

Based upon the number of the old songs that mention it, the custom seems to have faded largely due to the frequency of tragic entanglements between guardian and subject. It would seem Freya has a hand in such links, and enjoys toying with those placed in Her thrall."—Brin Bright Eyes, Saga of Dania

VAHLDAN SCOLDED himself and turned away from his distraction. It was time to face his duty. He'd spent most of his watch period not watching. Well, not watching the way he was supposed to be. Rather than patrolling the perimeter, he'd been watching Elan sleep.

She'd fallen asleep reclining by the fire. Thunder rumbled in the distance again. It had looked like rain since before the sun set. The western sky was black as bottom soil, but the moon remained overhead. They'd set up one of the pavilions the Skolani had packed. He kept thinking he should wake Elan and send her inside. But he hadn't. Not yet.

Alela and his siblings were asleep inside the only undamaged building left in Kohlsa's compound—a small food storage shed with barely enough floor space for the four of them.

Vahldan added fuel to the fire and slowly backed to the edge of the firelight. He told himself he wanted to keep Elan warm, but the flaring light compelled him to take another long look at her. During the days he worked hard to avoid staring at her. Which made looking at her now feel illicit, if oddly satisfying.

The wind rustled in the brush. It startled him more than it should've. He looked around, felt himself blushing. For no one. Why was he feeling so guilty?

He told himself he wasn't ogling her. It wasn't like some animal attraction. She was just so strong, so resolute. But as he got to know her he saw more. At first she'd seemed harsh. In sleep it was easier to see that her hardness was a façade—like a personal shield. With the shield down, there was softness to be found.

Yes, he found her fascinating. Yes, he was naïve, and yes, he was attracted. But it was attraction rooted in admiration. Maybe even in friendship. He couldn't be sure—he'd never experienced any of these feelings before.

When he'd been very angry with her earlier—on the verge of losing himself to the ugliness—he'd noticed something strange. He'd remained conscious that he shouldn't, or perhaps couldn't, release his anger on her. Or even in her presence. It was as though she willed him to stay grounded, in control. At the very brink of his outrage, in the depths of despair, she somehow tethered him to his true self.

After all that had happened, all that they'd seen and done, Elan's guidance, her commitment to their safety, felt like one of the few things he could depend on. She kept them all going, held them all together. In just a few short days, this fierce Skolani warrior had somehow come to embody his will to persist. And he knew she provided a similar lifeline for his siblings.

But really, this had to stop. How could he allow himself to think about such things, after all that had happened? When Túkash or his minions could be lurking nearby, perhaps watching him at this very moment?

Vahldan felt guilty about watching her sleep. But he also felt guilty whenever he allowed his grief to lapse. He even felt guilty for setting aside his guilt. It seemed like his responsibility to his family somehow relied on it. Like setting it aside was a betrayal.

A horse snorted in the adjacent corral. It jolted him again. This time he sensed movement in the trees above the meadow. Then he heard hoofbeats. He nocked his bow and crept into the trees, heading toward the sound.

"So now you're the bold one, eh?" Icannes appeared from the pines, startlingly close. She walked past him, giving his bow a tap. "Best put that away. Kukida will be along momentarily. Be a shame if you shot at her." He bristled but returned the arrow to the quiver.

A shroud-wrapped body was slung over the rear of Icannes's chestnut mare. Kukida appeared from the shadows, slowing from a trot to a walk. They dismounted and led their horses to the adjacent corral. Vahldan followed, scanning their reins. It was too dark to tell if any of the scalps that hung on either horse were new. "You found the girl?"

"The bloody savages made damn sure of it. The bastards used her as bait, to get us chasing again. When we finally closed on them, two Spali appeared atop a rocky ridge holding her. They pushed her down to us, bound hand and foot. The little pricks pulled the sack from her head right before, to make sure she experienced every bit of the terror of her execution." Icannes shook her head. "I still can't get her screams out of my head. Thankfully the fall put a swift end to her misery."

Icannes lifted the body from her horse and Vahldan moved too late to help as she laid the girl alongside the corral gateway. "We'll bury her with her family come morning."

The pair began unsaddling their horses. "They escaped?" Icannes's glare made him wish he hadn't asked. And yet he couldn't keep himself from asking another question. "Were they with Carpans?"

"If they hadn't been, we would've caught them." She slung her saddle from Starfire's back. "That's what's still bothering me. I've never seen Carpans and Spali working together like this. It makes them almost ghostlike. Every time we think we have them, they melt away."

"What became of the wagons?"

Icannes shook her head. "We don't know. The trail ends at the river. There's no sign of them, nor of the stolen sheep."

"Damned Carpans and their devilry," Kukida said, and spat on the ground. "Their mystics practice dark magic. It's said they command the very rock of the mountains to open and swallow them away, the very trees to lift them to impossible heights. It seems they command the very waters of the river, as well. The little shits dare not face us, so they delight in tricking us." Kukida spoke so rarely that her vehemence startled him.

"They can't elude us forever, my friend," Icannes said to her. "First we see to the delivery of Vahldan's family. If we haven't by then, you and I will see to these devils. Get some sleep. You've had little these past few days."

"As have you, my princess," Kukida scolded.

"This awful day has left me restless. Sleep won't come to me yet. But you have no such problem. Go and sleep. The Young Lion will help me with our tack. Won't you, Vahldan?"

"Of course."

Kukida nodded and strode to the fire. She wrapped herself in her cloak and slumped against the side of the shed without even removing her breastplate or sheathed sword. She seemed to be asleep the moment she settled.

Vahldan greeted Kukida's mount before removing her harness. He bent to set the head gear on Kukida's saddle and turned to find Icannes watching him. "Have you slept?" she asked.

"For a bit. Elan took the first watch."

"Good," she said. "Let's walk the perimeter of the homestead together. Stretching my legs would do me well, I think." He nodded, feeling relieved by the shift in her mood. "Help me off with my armor, would you?"

She turned her back to him and held her braids aside. The rippled muscle of her arms and the tops of her shoulders shone in the moonlight. With clumsy fingers, he unbuckled and released first her broadsword holster, then her breastplate. She slid from the two sets of shoulder straps as he held them, pressing against him as she extricated herself.

Vahldan stood holding her gear, unsure what to do with it. In a flash, Icannes first slipped her tunic off, then the leather thong holding her breasts. He tried not to look as she bent to wash her arms, face, and neck in the watering trough. The moonlight revealed ridges running in stripes across her back. Were those scars? He wondered who could've done that to someone like her.

Distant thunder rumbled. Damn, he was staring again.

He stepped off, pointedly facing away, and sat on his haunches. He took a moment laying out her armor with her saddle. Before he knew it, she was crouched beside him, shoulders touching again. She opened her saddlebag. He stood and she mirrored him. Gods, it was difficult averting his eyes from all of that bare skin. She handed him a bundle. "Hold that, please." It was the softest doeskin he'd ever touched. He held it low to hide his increasing arousal.

Without a hint of modesty, she eyed him as she wiped herself dry. She dropped her arms to her sides as she finished and tossed the cloth aside. She held out her hand. Dumbstruck, he realized what she wanted. He focused his gaze over her shoulder as he handed the bundle over, then clasped his hands before him.

Icannes stepped closer and made a show of glancing down. Her lopsided grin grew as she sedately unfolded her shift and pulled it on, smoothing it over her hips. "You are pleased by the sight of my flesh, Young Lion?"

Vahldan looked down, silently cursing his instincts, searching a tactful reply.

She huffed a laugh. "Never mind. You don't have to say it."

"I mean no disrespect."

"I certainly wouldn't call it a lack of respect. There is no shame in it. I'm pleased by you, too. We are both human, after all."

"It's just... I feel like such an oaf. After all that's happened."

"Perhaps it's nature's way. Sometimes I think lust is a byproduct of death. Could be it's the gods' way of leveling things." She stepped closer. "I suppose you're right, though—that the timing is off." Her voice dropped to a husky whisper. "But who knows? Perhaps the day will come when we can act on..." She glanced down again. "Our mutual response."

He swallowed and Icannes grinned again. "First things first," she chirped. "I suppose for now we'll have to distract ourselves with our duty. Agreed?"

"Agreed," he blurted, perhaps too quickly. But she nodded, as if they'd agreed that the rain would hold off. "Thank you..." He trailed off. What on this side of Hel's bridge was he thanking her for? The possibility of a future fuck? Gods, he was hopeless.

Her only reply was an amused smile. She hefted her bow and quiver and set out. "Come," she commanded, slapping her leg as if he were a pet. He supposed he deserved it, and set out across the moonlit meadow after her.

They walked in silence for a time. His thoughts drifted back to the Carpans. "Tomorrow I'd like to accompany your hunt, Princess," he ventured.

"Oh Vahldan. We both know that's impossible." She glanced, and he tried not to look disappointed. "Come now. We've spoken of this before."

"I know. My duty is to my family."

"There's that. And what about Elan? You realize you're her duty, don't you? What would she say to the queen if anything happened to you? You wouldn't wish that on her, would you?"

"No. It's just that..."

"You feel like helpless bait. You're angry. You want answers. You want to take action."

"Yes, all of those," he said.

"They killed your father and forced you to flee, which led to the death of your mother. And still they hunt you. You want to turn it on them, to make them pay."

"It's not that simple."

"Seems pretty straightforward."

Vahldan shook his head. "I need to figure out who's behind this, to bring it to an end for good. Only then can I make those who are responsible pay."

"I'd say it's a good bet you'll eventually face them," Icannes said.

At the base of his belly, the ugliness stirred. "You think so?"

Icannes glanced. "Seems likely, since whoever it is seems intent on having you murdered. All you need do is stay alive. Which is why I've decided to forgo pursing your assassins."

"What do you mean forgo? And how can you be sure it's me they're after?"

She rounded on him. "You have a better guess?"

'You're my son! It's got everything to do with you. What will you do when they come for you?' He looked down, unable to hold her gaze. "No."

She smirked and walked on. "As I thought. Anyway, what I mean by forgoing hunting them is that we'll focus on speeding our progress to Danihem instead. If the hunters catch up, we'll face them. But I prefer to evade them. For now."

The idea of rushing to Danihem made his belly roil and his hands tingle.

Again, Icannes read him. "Facing Danihem worries you."

"By law, we're forbidden to be here. So yes, it worries me." Not to mention that he was fairly sure those who were trying to kill him were there. "If we showed up in Danihem without you, we'd either be turned away at the gates or slapped in chains. We're outlaws by birth."

"Regardless, you are the blood of one of the ruling clans. You go to declare what is rightfully yours. The Skolani intercede only because it is clearly so."

"It'll be clear to the wolves, too—clear that we have no rights."

"Perhaps so. But I suspect it's in Danihem that we will find the answers you seek. May as well face up to it."

Face up to it? "We could rightfully be hauled away to the border. And if my father's enemies are allowed to take us there, how long do you think we'd survive in their company?"

Icannes grabbed his wrist, stopping him. "You seem fairly attached to that." She nodded down and he realized he was clutching his sword hilt.

"Forgive me," he said. He released it and pressed down the flutter of the ugliness.

"No need. In fact, I've been meaning to discuss it. Elan tells me you've been trained?"

"I have."

"By your father?"

"Of course." Who else?

She nodded. "I still have much to learn about the customs of your people. But I have heard of this *Ananth-jahn*." She raised a brow. "You know of it?"

His laugh was a bitter bark. "Know of it? My father spoke of the Ananth-jahn most every day, up to his last in this world. We sparred in mock versions of it since before I can recall."

"As I suspected." Icannes strolled on. "Such trials are granted to a rightful petitioner on the longhouse floor, are they not?"

"Yes."

"And your father—he'd planned to seek one?"

"Yes."

"Soon, I take it?"

Vahldan wondered how she'd gleaned that. "He wanted to arrive riding at the front of an Amalus host. I suspect he had friends secretly working on gathering one. I also suspect it wasn't going as well as he'd hoped."

"A host?"

"He wanted to ensure he retained some advantage. Without a show of strength he feared he too might be slapped in chains. As I say, these things are not so simple."

"I see." She looked skyward. "Do you believe that he would've wanted you to take his place? Assuming your safe arrival there and the safety of your family were ensured."

"Maybe. But my mother bid me to see to family first. I don't see how I can do that if—"

Icannes stopped. "Tell me this, Vahldan. You say your father spent long years and much effort on training you to fight this very sort of trial, right?"

"Yes, but..." He couldn't admit that both he and Angavar knew he was still unready.

"No buts. Would he have worked you so long and hard if he hadn't anticipated the possibility of this outcome—that you might well end up in this exact circumstance?"

"I suppose—"

"Do you believe you're ready for the trial?"

He made himself say it: "My father didn't consider me ready."

"I didn't ask what your father thought."

The ugliness in his belly flared, reminding him. "I... I'm not like him. I—"

"I didn't ask if you were like him. I asked if you were ready. You've yet to answer."

"I said it's not so simple." He'd all but shouted, his inner flames rising.

Icannes's eyes narrowed, studying him. "Explain it, then."

Vahldan wrung his hands, avoiding the impulse to grab the hilt, tamping down the ugliness. "I... I get angry."

"Good. All capable warriors do."

"Sometimes I lose myself. When it happens, I don't even know who I am, or what I'm doing. I just want to kill."

"Hmmm. I see." She started walking again and he followed. "Let us lay out our kits and count our arrows, shall we? Your parents are dead. Your home, burnt; everything you ever owned, gone. Someone hunts you. They want you dead. All you have left is that." She reached to tap the hilt of his father's sword. "It's the only means left to you to provide for them."

Icannes brought them to another halt. "Even if you regain your father's status, those who hunt you may still want you dead. Indeed, it may strengthen their wish. Of course it's complicated. But can you honestly think of a better way to seek wellbeing for your family than to reclaim your honor? What else can you do? Flee? Where would you then find shelter? Safety?"

Vahldan's gaze drifted to the dark sky. Lightning flashed far off.

She said, "While you consider your answer, you might also consider what your siblings have to lose versus what they might gain. As it stands now, with or without you, they are beholden to the charity of strangers. Without you, they'd likely no longer have killers hounding their every step. But the brother and sisters of the Lion Lord would want for nothing, be beholden to no one."

Easy enough for her. "I'm not so sure," he said, bitterness seeping into his voice.

"No need to decide now. But perhaps you could turn that anger of yours toward something useful." She tilted her head, eyeing him. He wasn't sure what she was hinting at, but he didn't dare ask. Instead he suppressed the ugliness, composing his face. "Come," she said, spinning away. "Escort me back to camp."

Vahldan found himself vibrating in the aftermath of his flare as he followed her to the edge of their camp. Icannes stopped outside the firelight and said, "I told my mother I would train you along the way. We start tomorrow."

"But I—"

She put her fingers on his lips and leaned in. "Do you trust me, Vahldan?" With her fingers still there, he was forced to nod. "Good. Then trust me when I tell you how delicious it will be once you learn how to harness that anger of yours."

She ran her fingers down through his beard and let them graze over his chest and down his arm. He shivered. "You're good to continue the watch?"

"I doubt I'll be sleepy anytime soon," he admitted.

Icannes gave his arm a jab that he presumed was meant to be chummy but was actually painful. "I wish you the peace of man seeking self-possession. Good night, Vahldan."

She sauntered to Elan and bent, whispering to wake her. Elan smiled and stretched, and Icannes pulled her up and into a lingering hug. Icannes looked over Elan's shoulder, seeming to make sure he was looking. Finally, with an arm slung low around Elan's waist, Icannes led her to the pavilion. She held the flap for Elan, ducked in behind her, then looked again. This time he was sure of it. She was looking right at him, wearing a sly smile as the flap fell closed.

Pain shot through the arm Icannes had punched. He realized it was because he had absently reached to squeeze his hilt. She'd hit his arm in the exact spot to cause it.

ICANNES AWOKE to the sounds and smells of cooking. She was alone in the pavilion. She stretched as she donned her tunic and stepped out, blinking against the sun, which had risen above the rim of the vale. The air was clean and fresh after the predawn rain. She'd overslept. It was the most rested she'd felt in days. She shaded her eyes and scanned the grounds.

She turned back to find Elan had sidled close. Her near-sister held out a steaming bowl of porridge. Icannes sat by the fire and accepted the bowl. She dug into the mash of boiled barley, nuts, and dried berries with a hunger born of being well-rested and more certain of the future.

"Sorry about the girl," Elan said. "You didn't say."

Icannes shrugged. "Didn't want to trouble you." She swallowed warm porridge. "Horrible as her end was, at least she's with Hel now." She looked back toward the corral. "Speaking of which, she needs to be buried."

"Vahldan and his brother saw to it at dawn. We said the words together."

She sighed. It was a relief. Icannes had prayed to Hel too often of late. And doing so this time would've felt like admitting to a failing. "She's back with her family then."

Elan folded her lips. Icannes recognized the look. "Something troubles you, Elan?"

"Vahldan tells me you wish to hurry on to Danihem, to leave off your pursuit of the Spali who did this." She indicated their burned out surroundings.

"I do. For now. Seems to me pursuing the pursuers had us chasing our tail. It's time to change the game."

"What of your oath to the girl's mother?"

Icannes stared into her bowl. No, she wouldn't let Elan change her resolve. "I admit, it weighed on me during the ride back. But Horsella has since whispered to me. She assures me I will meet these Paralatoe again. I will yet avenge these women. I know my oath is secure."

"All right then, what of the babe?"

"Which babe?"

"Vahldan's sister," Elan snipped.

"We'll have to risk her distress to gain some distance."

Elan frowned. "Risk her life, you mean."

"I'd say all of our lives are at risk out here, Elan. Is hers worth more than any other?"

Elan shook her head, but still seemed disgruntled as she handed Icannes a cup of hot bitterroot tea to wash down the porridge.

Icannes scanned the compound over the rim of the steaming cup. Alela and Eldavar were packing up remnant foodstuffs while Mara held her little sister. Icannes shielded her eyes to search the surrounding meadows. Elan said, "Vahldan went with Kukida on a quick ride of the perimeter. If it's one of them you seek." Elan's tone had been nonchalant, and she focused on her cleaning of the cook-pot. She'd ever been perceptive of Icannes's thoughts.

"You allowed your subject from your sight?"

Elan still didn't look up. "He seemed to need to go. And I thought he'd be safe enough with Kukida. What, it worries you?"

"I'll leave the worrying to you, Elan. I have other things in mind."

"So I gathered." Elan's brows were knitting.

Icannes almost laughed. "You've gathered something?"

"I presume what's on your mind has to do with the long talk you two had last night?"

He'd told her. Interesting. "You gather well. I thought Vahldan and I could begin the day with a training session before we leave."

"You really think that's wise?"

"I do. I need to assess his skills, to see how much there is to be done."

"I thought you intended to make haste," Elan said.

"That too. This won't take long. He has to be ready when we arrive in Danihem. We can't know when he'll get a chance to fight his trial."

"His trial? The queen bid us to seek an audience with the Great Wolf. She said nothing of a trial."

"Who can guess what will happen? It's obvious that the queen is sending us to the Wulthus lord because she doesn't trust the Amalus leadership. What becomes of our charges if our petition is denied? What if Thadmeir decides to hold Vahldan to the terms of his father's banishment? If it comes to that, do you really think there's a lion who will vouch for them?"

Elan frowned up at her. "Meaning?"

"Meaning Vahldan needs to keep his options open." Icannes slurped her tea, watching Elan's eyebrows twitch as she went back to scrubbing the pot. "He's your subject, Elan. It's a burden you'll bear until he finds the means to protect himself. What better means to that end could there be than his regaining his rightful status?"

"My duty is to see to his safety. I'd hardly call a trial with swords a safe option."

"But it's *his* option, not ours. Perhaps it's a risk he'll be willing to take, depending. Obviously, if it comes to it, you couldn't be held responsible for his safety inside a trial ring."

The pot looked as clean as it'd ever been, but Elan kept scrubbing. "You recall that he has trouble imbuing himself, right?"

"I do. It's one of the things I need to assess."

Elan's frown deepened. "It's an issue of the mind. He resists going there. And not without reason. He loses himself to rage."

Icannes shrugged and hid a smirk. "Most good killers do."

Elan finally looked up. "That's just it. He doesn't want to be a killer. He seeks balance."

"I'm kidding. I intend to teach him control. Which, in turn, will offer him balance."

Elan went back to her scrubbing. "And if he loses himself in a trial? What if he's defeated? What will come of his family?"

"If he loses, he'll have lost with honor. His siblings will be beholden to others—same as they are now. But what if he wins? As an Amalus chieftain, he would have a home and a loyal host. And best of all, your duty would be fulfilled. You'd be free to go back and ride with Hildeanna's host. That *is* what you want, isn't it?"

Elan finally rinsed the scrubbing sand from the pot with a swish. She stood and dumped the rinse water. Icannes was relieved it hadn't been over her head. "Of course it is. But I'd prefer to gain my freedom of him with honor. I don't see how that's possible if he has to die for it." She turned and strode to stow the pot on a pack horse.

Icannes called after her, "Which is why I'm going to begin our training. Today."

Elan nodded but kept her gaze focused on adjusting the straps on the pack horse. "Yes, my princess." Her tone made it anything but concession.

ELAN KNEW Icannes was goading Vahldan to attack. It worried her. She feared Icannes was purposely pushing him to see him fall to rage. But instead of losing himself, he stood almost flat-footed as Icannes danced into one vulnerable position after another.

Elan suspected Vahldan was solely fixated on resisting his impulses, which would provide little benefit. He'd stalled for an almost embarrassing period, during which he mostly whined about the size of Kukida's buckler that Icannes had insisted he use.

He dragged his boots as they circled, his head clearly not in it. Elan just wanted to have done with it. "Wake up, Vahldan. This is meant to help you."

He frowned and Icannes grinned. "No use stalling," Icannes said. "Show me what you've got."

Vahldan's behavior reminded Elan of his confrontation with Auchote. She wondered if his fear had seized him. Vahldan grimaced and sunk into a deeper crouch, but his feet stayed flat. Icannes danced within his reach and offered yet another opening. Still he resisted. The babe started crying. Vahldan glanced away. Icannes sharply clacked his practice sword, almost knocking it from his hand. Elan knew the lesson could've been worse.

At least Icannes had gained his attention. He swung the buckler around to block her next blow, but it was slow, his feet still leaden. He should've countered, but he hadn't. Which offered Icannes a new opportunity. Her backhanded counter-stoke soundly thumped his shoulder with the flat of her wooden blade. He winced, but still resisted using the skills and instincts Elan knew he possessed. He had to find his way to commanding rather than resisting them. Icannes had made his reluctance sting, and it would only get worse.

Vahldan's defenses remained up as he regained his position, but his feet finally lifted properly. Icannes curled her lip. "I heard you were trained. Perhaps I heard wrong."

"Time," Elan called. "Come here, Vahldan." He shuffled toward her, fussing with the buckler straps, looking like he'd tasted sour milk. She felt ashamed for him. "Look at me," she hissed. He did. "Hear me?" He nodded. "Good. Because you are better than this. I know it, and you'd better know it, too. I've seen what's inside. You have to learn to access it, use it. And you can! Do you believe me?" He nodded, but she saw the doubt in his eyes. "If you're satisfied with who you are, don't waste our time. If you're ready to grow, you must reveal who you are before we can help you become who you aspire to be. Understood?"

Vahldan scowled but nodded. She glimpsed a growing wildness in his eyes. Good. Better than this moping. "Now, go find your instincts. No more dallying. Devote yourself through the entire training session, then leave it in that sparring circle till you get to the next. We need to get moving in order to keep your family safe."

"Come now," Icannes called. "Show me the lion you keep caged." Vahldan stepped into the ring glaring. Now he was moving as she knew he could. Icannes feigned an attack, and he danced into a proper counter maneuver. "Ah, that's better," Icannes said. "You're awake."

Elan smiled... until she saw his darkening expression.

Icannes came at him again. She gauged his hand speed now. Her series of blows all went shield-blocked or parried, but he continually yielded space. Only her relenting kept him in the circle. "Watch your position," Icannes scolded. "You're allowed to step out twice, but the third is as good as spilled blood. Worse—it names you craven."

Vahldan got back into position. Elan called, "Stay lively, Vahldan! Make your own space. Keep her off balance."

Vahldan wore a savage expression, but he seemed to hear her. It was a good sign. His movements were still sharp. Icannes came on wearing a wicked smile. Elan called, "Take in every step and gesture. Sense her countermoves even as you make yours. Find the flow of the fight!" He passed up Icannes's feint and counterattacked as she retreated, surprising his opponent with a solid thump to her shield —a blow she was barely able to block.

Icannes squared up again, no longer smiling. Their sparring quickened, each combatant's intensity all the more apparent. Vahldan's blade and buckler snapped into proper position for each strike and block as they danced the circle. His instincts were good. His basic skills—both learned and inherited from his renowned father—began to shine.

But the dangerous flare in his eyes only grew. It was as if success fueled darkness.

Icannes lowered her shoulder, placing her foot in an awkward position. It looked accidental, but Elan knew she was baiting again. This time he bit, but with stunning speed. Icannes parried but wasn't able to retreat. She hadn't quite led him to the misstep she'd sought. In close quarters now, the pair traded a blistering series of blows, all parried or blocked. He was actually, slowly, beating Mighty Icannes back. It was stunning. The veiled confidence Icannes naturally wore faded. For a moment, the two huffed and grunted with equally fierce effort. Until Icannes did an empty fade. Her stunningly swift riposte set Vahldan on his heels. On his countering chop, she turned her blade just so, shedding his parry, her tip flicking his ear.

Vahldan snarled and staggered in response. Elan knew from experience that she'd purposefully inflicted the sort of pain that pierced even deep imbuement. But rather than waking him, Icannes had tipped him to fury. He bellowed and lunged, barreling into Icannes and pushing with both buckler and blade.

The sparring match suddenly became something else. Something dangerous.

No longer were these the actions of opponents on the tarp. This looked like a blood-match on the field. On Vahldan's part, there was no thought or control, only blind rage.

Elan stepped in the circle and cried out, "Enough." He relentlessly roared and pushed, boots digging. They were out of the circle now, Icannes laboring to avoid hurting him.

Elan's adrenaline surged. "I said enough. Vahldan!"

Out of nowhere, Kukida flew into the melee, slamming a shoulder into Icannes's attacker, knocking him clear of the princess. Vahldan hit the ground hard, with the huge Blade-Wielder on top of him. Kukida held a naked blade—a real one—and she'd landed straddling his backside, a knee on his buckler, one hand pressing his head to the ground, and the tip of her sword at the back of his neck. His roar became a frustrated howl.

"Vahldan!" Elan ran to him. He bucked and pushed off from the ground, still fighting.

Kukida managed to hold him down, but kept her blade in striking position. "Be still, Young Lion," Kukida said. "I don't want to hurt you." Her voice was low but commanding.

Elan's heart trilled. She had to get him to lie still. She dropped to her hands and knees, positioning her face to fill his view. "I'm here," she called. "See me? Come back to me." His struggling slowed and then ceased. His eyes cleared. "Like the kestrels. Remember?"

Vahldan fell to stillness. He took a deep breath and blew it out. He finally nodded.

"Let him up," Elan said. Kukida looked to Icannes, who nodded. Kukida drew herself up slowly, but held her blade ready. Elan stayed on her knees, stayed in his line of sight. "It's hard, I know. But you'll find the way. You were there for a moment, in control. It was amazing." She smiled. "You'll find it. There and back. I'll help. I'll be there for you."

He sat up, stretching his back, grunting in pain, gathering himself. His hand drifted to his bright red ear. He checked his fingers. It wasn't bleeding, at least.

Icannes held her hand out to him. Vahldan glowered at her.

Elan jumped up and got behind Icannes, putting herself back into his field of vision. "He was doing well for a moment there, wasn't he, my princess?" she said brightly. His eyes found focus on Elan. The glower faded and he took Icannes's hand.

Icannes yanked him to his feet. "For a moment," she conceded. She glanced to Elan, and Elan saw her concern. Icannes recognized the extent of the challenge ahead.

"We'll help him find it, won't we?" Elan prompted.

Still gripping his hand, Icannes said, "Elan's right. I can see there is promise, Young Lion. But we must find our way to your self-control."

Vahldan flushed, shaking his head as he regained his wind. "I'm sorry. I can't—"

Icannes pulled him close, forcing him to face her. "First, don't apologize. Second, never say you can't. Understood?" He nodded, his brow furrowed. "Trust me on this. Your skills are there. Your instincts are good. We will find our way to control. And you will be among the finest in the realm. Do you believe?"

"I'll do my best."

Elan knew it wasn't the answer Icannes sought, but she released him with a nod. Vahldan limped in circles, hands on hips and panting, walking it off.

Kukida came to retrieve her buckler. "May I?" she asked. He held out his arm. As Kukida unbuckled it, she asked, "Are you unhurt?" He nodded. "Keep at it. I've seen very few match my princess like that, even for a few moments. It's why I feared for her. If you can manage to last a few moments longer each try, I'll begin to like your odds— even against an Amalus champion." Vahldan's head snapped up, and Kukida demurred, "No offense."

Elan didn't think he'd taken offense. She suspected he'd yet to consider the use of a champion against him.

As the shield came free, Kukida leaned in. "Also, know that if I sense she is in danger again, I will not hesitate." What she wouldn't hesitate to do was clearly implied. He bowed his head to her and then bent to retrieve his practice sword.

As his guardian, Elan bristled. But it swiftly dawned on her that the warning might actually help to keep him tethered during imbuement. Kukida was not a foe, but she knew Vahldan grasped how dangerous the big Blade-Wielder could be.

He straightened with a wry grin. "Let's see if I've got this. All I have to do is manage a few moments more before she beats me? All while being goaded to lose control so that I can learn to maintain it? Again and again until I'm either killed or get it right?"

Kukida actually smiled. "Sounds about right."

His smile brightened. "Ah, good. Something to look forward to." He went to Icannes and bowed. "I eagerly await being goaded and beaten again, Princess. Thank you."

Looking like her mother, Icannes inclined her head and strolled to the waiting horses with a hooded smile.

Elan stepped lively to catch up, pitching her voice so only Icannes could hear. "So this assessment of yours required humiliating him? Not to mention risking his life?"

Icannes shrugged. "I had to find out where we stand. The risk to his life will only grow—especially if he doesn't find the control we need to seek. And humility will only serve the goal. The ear will be fine. You ought to know that."

"Can you just be careful, please?"

Icannes continued to stow her gear, but glanced with a raised eyebrow. "You, of all people, wish to question my teaching methods?"

No one had believed in Elan when Icannes had started working with her. "I'm still responsible for his wellbeing."

"Ease yourself, Elan. You recall our sessions, don't you? Look how well you turned out."

She sighed. "I remember. All too well."

Icannes's grin grew wicked. "Ah, so that's it. You also remember the passion that eventually came of our sessions. They ended up providing the spark that lit the flame for us."

Elan felt herself flushing and shook her head. "It's not that."

"Fear not, my love. This one's all yours. I'll get his blood hot then return him so you can enjoy the warmth."

"Don't bother. I don't intend to enjoy any of this. I'm his guardian, remember."

"I do remember," Icannes said. "I'm glad you do, too." She cupped and squeezed Elan's bottom. "Hot cheeks."

Elan leapt away, spinning to see if Vahldan was watching, grateful to find he wasn't.

CHAPTER 12—DRAWN BY FREYA'S PULL

"*It's difficult for those who haven't witnessed banishment to comprehend it. The banished are dead and yet alive, a ghost to everyone they ever knew, to all who'd named them family, to all who loved them. They no longer exist to those who gave them the very concept of who they are.*

For what are we without those we love? The loss brings grief and resentment and frustration. But worse is the resignation. The grasping of meaninglessness."—*Brin Bright Eyes, Saga of Dania*

ELAN HAD HOPED that getting away from Kohlsa's burned-out farmstead would raise the company's spirits. It didn't. Hers least of all.

Their food stores were replenished, but fear continued to stalk them, and death to haunt them. Particularly the children. Even at the faster pace Icannes set, Elan found the tedium of traveling with an infant made the journey all the more exhausting. Alela was a gift from the gods, riding on whether the babe in her arms was squirming, crying, or sleeping. She now fed the babe while riding on. The days seemed unending, and the nights scarcely replenishing.

Danihem was normally only a three or four-day ride from the Jabitka's current position in the eastern valley, but their chosen route —on winding and hilly side-trails—would make it twice that or more. Elan found herself longing to gallop. Which made her envious of Icannes, who rode out each day to scout with Kukida, leaving Elan with two irritable children and a squalling infant. Even Vahldan was mostly a brooding presence these days.

Elan had ventured to ask Icannes if she'd be willing to switch roles, even for an afternoon. Icannes had smiled, at least, and said, "Surely you can see how our duty prevents it."

She did, but it still stung. There'd been a time when Icannes strived to please her, even if it required breaking rules. Icannes had doted on Elan even before they were protégés, when Elan had been a wisp of a child. Icannes was only two years older, but even then she'd dwarfed Elan. Icannes had carried her about like an infant as they played at mother-daughter.

Even when the elders had relented to allow Elan to be trained, she was still the smallest among her peers. Her early days as a protégé were brutal. She was taunted and battered—and often bloodied. Elan knew the elders had given in to her being trained out of respect for her grandmother. The problem was, her fellow trainees knew it, too. And resented it. Most pushed for her to quit, and the trainers turned a blind eye to their abuse. It seemed everyone thought Elan's failure would be for the best. Elan's dogged refusal to be ousted had only made the bullying worse. No few of her mother's friends tried to convince her to quit, and no few admitted to fearing for her life. But Elan had resigned herself to fulfil the dream or to die trying.

During one harsh training session, Elan launched herself at her opponent—a particularly nasty protégé named Anallya. She surprised Anallya, knocking her to the ground, punching and kicking. A jeering gang gathered 'round them. Anallya easily reversed the momentum, pinning Elan. Anallya's cohorts grabbed Elan's wrists and ankles while Anallya brutally beat her. The only nearby trainer simply walked away, pretending not to notice.

Elan was certain they would kill her, and in her torment and pain she welcomed it. She had only a vague memory of her savior, thrashing her attackers with a practice sword. Elan remained certain that no one else would've, or could've, interceded. No other protégé could have stood up to Anallya and her brutes. Undeniably, Icannes saved her life.

From that day forward, Icannes had claimed Elan, and taken her under her wing.

Elan eventually hit a growth spurt and filled out. Under Icannes's dedicated tutelage, her skills swiftly improved. Through it all, they'd only grown closer. After they both ascended to the ranks of the Blade-Wielders, they chose to become near-sisters. They both realized that they loved one another, and they wanted to commit to a lifetime of love. It was that simple.

And that complicated.

Although Elan recognized from the start who they were as a couple, sisterhood could never provide them with equal status within the tribe, or even within their personal relationship. The complications were bound to cause friction. When Elan was invited to join the vaunted scouting host of Hildeanna, it seemed that she was finally emerging from Icannes's shadow. And Icannes had seemed supportive. Right up until her Fulhsna-Utanni assignation to Vahldan.

Elan felt well-shaded once again. But it wasn't just Icannes's ability to ride away from the slower pace with a cranky infant. The situation rankled because Icannes seemed to be pressing it home— to imprint her dominance, to ensure Elan was back in her proper place.

Each evening Icannes always managed to arrive from scouting

just after the camp was set up and the meal prepared. Then, rather than helping out with the chores of the camp, Icannes insisted on training with Vahldan till sundown. Which kept him from helping, as well.

The one bright spot should've been Vahldan's improvement in the ring, including his growing control. He was becoming much less prone to losing himself to rage. Icannes was careful about pushing him, and he still needed to work on both accepting and releasing Thunar's Blessing, but the progress was undeniable.

Elan knew his growth should please her, and she pretended it did. But secretly she felt conflicted. She had to admit, at times she resented its cost and she feared the outcome. She hated to admit it, even to herself, but she sort of liked the thought of him relying on her.

At the end of the fourth day's ride since leaving Kohlsa's, Elan asked Vahldan and Eldavar to gather firewood while she began tending the horses. Surprisingly, Icannes arrived early, before the meal was ready. Her near-sister nodded to Elan and scanned the site from Starfire's back. Elan knew what she was looking for, but she said nothing. Icannes finally dismounted and surprised Elan again by unsaddling her own horse.

Vahldan came into the clearing as Icannes removed the harness. Elan continued brushing the burrs from Hrithvarra's tail, and prosaically asked, "Kukida is still scouting?"

"She wanted to check the southern rim. But I wanted to get back. We won't have many more opportunities to train. His counter-stroke still needs work, but I think we need to move on to the inside tricks and footwork."

Icannes watched Vahldan and his brother stacking their collected firewood and starting a fire. Finally, she delivered what Elan expected. "Would you mind, Elan? Starfire has had a long day." She held out the chamois with which she'd only just begun to rub down her friend.

Elan sighed. At least she'd made it a request. "Go. I'll finish up here."

Icannes strode off without thanking her, calling to Vahldan to mark out the circle as she went to fetch the practice swords.

Alela had Eldavar unloading the pack horses. Once the wet-nurse had the carrots, onions and dried strips of goat in the pot and over the fire, she sat alongside the training circle to watch as she fed the babe. Mara sat beside her. Once Eldavar had the pack horses unloaded he joined the audience. Elan was the last one working.

The resonant thwacks of practice swords echoed across the campsite. Elan furtively watched as she worked. The speed of Vahldan's hands and lightness on his feet were impressive. He'd gained decisiveness. Icannes had worked on building a foundation of skills he could call upon under duress. Most importantly, he was gaining confidence. It would all help with his willingness and ability to imbue without losing himself.

Elan remembered the growth of her own confidence; how she'd glowed in the approval of her tutor. She remembered the warmth of Icannes's body, her strong arms enfolding her after a good training session, their sweaty skin slippery. She looked up to see Icannes wrapping Vahldan in one arm, squeezing him to her before playfully pushing him back. Both of them resumed their defensive stances. Vahldan was grinning, his gaze rapt.

She didn't care. Or at least she didn't want to. Icannes was a powerful presence, but Vahldan was becoming his own man. He was the head of his family now. It was beyond her to direct or even to advise either of them.

And yet she'd allowed the situation to make her heartsick. How had this happened?

Elan attempted to refocus on her work. Their laughter rang out. She raised up from cleaning one of Starfire's hooves. Icannes stood close to him, demonstrating how to push off a closing opponent. He tried to mimic her technique, but she slipped inside his shield arm.

Vahldan responded by wrapping her in a bear-hug and lifting her. They digressed into wrestling. Icannes tripped him by wrapping his leg in hers. They tumbled to the ground entwined, laughing and rolling. Body to body.

Elan dropped the mare's foot. "You call that training?" she muttered. A white static filled her head. Her heart was racing. She reminded herself to breathe. She strode toward the ring. "That's enough of that, you two. You're training for a trial by swords, not a wrestling match!"

Vahldan released Icannes in response and got to a knee to stand. Eldavar leapt on his back. Then Mara hopped onto Icannes with a joyful squeal. The four of them fell into a pile of wriggling otters.

Alela laughed and looked up at Elan. She forced herself to smile.

But she still didn't feel like smiling.

It ached, knowing she should want to laugh. Disgusted, she went back to finish the horses. She stooped, grabbed the hoof-pick, and lifted Starfire's foot again. Even scraping shit didn't banish her swirling emotions. The worst part was, she couldn't decide whether it was Icannes or Vahldan that made her feel this way.

A nudge at the back of her shoulder made her spin to face whoever had dared intrude on her sulking. Hrithvarra lifted her long snout, nudging Elan's arm. The mare snorted and bobbed her head, expressing her solidarity. Elan couldn't help but smile. She dropped Starfire's foot to turn and give her dearest friend some loving. "I know," Elan softly admitted, cradling her head. "You're always the loyal one. I do appreciate you, dear heart."

ELAN HEARD her approach and feigned sleep. Icannes settled down behind her, sliding beneath their blankets. Elan had yet to sleep at all since awakening Icannes to take the second watch. The night had grown cold and damp. Icannes snuggled up to her backside, wrapping an arm over her waist. Rather than offering comfort, Elan felt chilled. And small.

Icannes had awoken Vahldan to take the next watch. Elan heard his steps recede, heading out to walk the perimeter. She listened to ensure the others were asleep. "I know why you're pushing him so hard."

Icannes raised her head. "Sorry, did I wake you?"

"No. I was awake."

"Oh. What did you say before?"

Elan rolled. "I said I know why you want him to ascend."

Icannes scrunched her nose. "Who, Vahldan? I said why, to you and to him. So he can take care of his family." Icannes's gaze darkened, scrutinizing. Elan tried to keep her face blank. Icannes laid back with a huff. "We can talk in the morning. Go to sleep." Her near-sister pulled the blanket tight as she settled again, this time not touching her.

Elan wanted to let it go, to roll over and go to sleep. But the bitterness she'd gathered and stored sought release. "A newly risen lion lord would certainly make a fine selection for my princess to invite to the rites. I'm sure you'd be the envy of every young Blade-Wielder. Perhaps a daughter would come of it. How fitting that would be."

Icannes raised up on an elbow. "It says much that you're making this about me, Elan. I only want what's best for Vahldan and his family."

"Do you deny having thought of it?"

A sly smile crept to the corners of Icannes's mouth. "Of course not. But that doesn't mean that I'm ruled by my loins. Or my ambitions. I'm doing this for the right reasons." Her brows rose. "What about you? Are you thinking selfish thoughts about your subject?"

"Me? I was assigned to him, remember?"

"I remember. But would you hold him back, even when he decides to seize an opportunity to restore his status? After all, once he ascends, he'll no longer be your concern. Will his infatuation for his guardian linger on after she's left his life, I wonder?"

Elan felt every muscle tighten. She wanted to lash back, but the proper words wouldn't come. She suddenly wanted the conversation to end. How had she allowed herself to start it? She pulled the blanket close and clenched, staving off the shivers. She wanted Icannes to press against her again, to warm her. But she knew she couldn't ask for warmth.

Icannes clucked in victorious mirth and settled in again, leaving a windy chasm between them. "I hope you don't think I can't see."

"See what?" Elan asked.

"How you look at him, for a start. I also see how convenient it is that the subject of your admiration is also the subject of your duty."

"The way *I* look at him?"

"Yes you. Oh, I readily admit to a bit of lusty attraction." Her grin grew lopsided. "He's turning into a real chunk of manliness, after all. But at least I'm not dancing in Freya's entangling arms."

Elan had heard that the Gottari called it Freya's Blessing: the longing between a man and woman. But to the Skolani, falling to Freya's lure was a curse. Submission was a shameful weakness. And dangerous. For Freya's grip often led to banishment—a fate worse than death. It was death with dishonor. "That's ridiculous," she said, rolling away.

"Is it? I see the way you've been mooning around. If you can't be honest with me, at least be honest with yourself."

"Please, stop," Elan whispered.

"Oh, now I should stop? You remember who started it, I hope."

"I know." Tears filled Elan's eyes. "I... I don't want this. I want it to stop."

"Then stop it!"

If only it were so easy. Elan blinked her eyes clear, anger replacing frustration. Everything was always so easy for Icannes. Everyone wanted her approval, needed her aid. She could never know how it felt to be uncertain, about anything. "All right. I will."

"Good. Now, may I get some sleep?"

"Don't let me stop you. I'm sure your conscience won't."

"Good night, Elan," Icannes said with finality. She draped an arm over Elan's side. Elan had longed for it, but it felt heavy now, like she was a child being placated.

Or was she being reclaimed?

CHAPTER 13—A FINAL HURDLE

"*M*ost *agree that the Carpan people dwelt in Dania long before the Gottari arrived. Although they coexisted with the Skolani, the timid Carpans have ever feared and reviled the warrior women. It was only upon the coming of the Gottari that the Carpans were driven from their farming settlements in the fertile valley up into the mountains. Forced to eke survival by growing crops between rocks and raising climbing goats, their numbers dwindled. And yet, they survive as a people.*

Later generations of Gottari named the Carpans High Hill Dwellers, most unknowing that their own forbearers had made them so. For those willing to reflect, it is not difficult to imagine the accruing resentment of the displaced." –Brin Bright Eyes, Saga of Dania

VAHLDAN REINED in to watch a raptor, soaring above their progress. The graceful bird swooped ahead and disappeared behind the crest of bare rock, jutting above green foothills that rose before them. He briefly wondered whether it was a hawk, or maybe a kestrel. It also made him wonder how far away the sea was. The rocky ridge before them blocked their way west, but the peaks grew even steeper to the south.

"Looks like we're in for another climb," he observed.

"It'll be the last, though," Elan said, pulling up beside him. "Kukida says the pass is narrow and a bit twisty going up, but that the road down is an easy descent. She also said that once we're over the top we'll be able to see Danihem. We're almost there."

"For better or worse," he said.

"Don't worry. Icannes will make things right for our arrival."

Vahldan wasn't convinced that was possible. Icannes had left the company to head north in order to take the more direct road along the river to Danihem. Taking the faster route would give her time to seek an audience with the wolf lord. Kukida had argued for accompanying her, but Icannes wouldn't allow it. The royal guardian was to scout the way for the remaining group rather than the lone royal. And Kukida was far from pleased about it.

Kukida had begged Icannes to reconsider, to keep them together until they were all inside Danihem's walls. Icannes had laughed and said, "If you believe our charges will be safe once we're there, you will never understand why I have to arrive ahead of them."

He could only assume Kukida was somewhere in the heights ahead. Elan led them into a narrowing canyon single-file. Vahldan brought up the rear, pulling the tethered pack ponies behind. They emerged from the trees onto a rising shelf-like trail that dropped off more steeply to their right and rose higher to the left as they went. The afternoon grew hot, making the cooling shade of the canyon welcome.

Elan turned in her saddle. "I think we'll see the crest just around the next bend. We should be able to find a level spot to camp by nightfall."

An eerie whooping shriek echoed through the canyon. "What was that!" Eldavar cried.

"Kukida. It's her battle cry." Elan drew her blade and reined to a halt.

Vahldan drew his sword as the first arrows fell. An arrow hit the hindquarters of the last pack horse, and the beast bucked and bolted, charging past the column along the narrow path. The children wailed and their mounts reared and stomped. Vahldan had no choice but to release the tether, and the frantic animal pulled his counterpart away with him.

"To that outcrop!" Elan pointed ahead. "Get the children to cover!"

The bare rock just ahead projected nearly vertically from the path's edge. Struggling to control the jittery horses, they managed to line up and halt alongside the steep rock. Elan dismounted and then helped the children down, directing them to kneel together up against the base. Vahldan dismounted, sheathed his blade, and took the bawling babe from Alela. The nurse leapt from the saddle, scooped the babe to her abdomen and crouched beside the siblings.

They were sheltered, but arrows continued to clatter on the stone around them. He'd been so worried about arriving in Danihem he'd all but forgotten that they were still being hunted.

The arrows ceased. Vahldan and Elan raised up to look. Elan pointed. "There." A flash of metal and a blur of movement atop a tree-topped ridge. Vahldan saw how they'd avoided being hit. The shot required a long, arching lob—an attack with a low probability for success.

"Spali?" he asked.

Elan frowned. "Seems unlike them. Spali would've charged us. For them there's no status gained in killing from afar."

"Who, then?"

"I can't guess. Carpans, maybe."

Vahldan shook his head. "I don't think so." He looked back down the trail and then ahead. "It's a poor site for a charge. Someone wants us to rush ahead." The trail curved from sight, but he suspected it only grew narrower until the crest. "Maybe Kukida forced their hand. I'm guessing they're trying to drive us into a blind." He pointed up the trail.

Elan looked uphill. "Seems a good guess." She surveyed the area. His family stared at them, huddled and terrified. "We can't stay here," she said softly. "They'll eventually surround us. And going back only takes us back into range."

Vahldan studied the ridge. An image sprang to mind of his skull-faced nemesis, ordering a feint attack on the gate to distract his father. If Auchote was behind this, he mustn't hesitate again. He couldn't let it play out the way the foe wanted it. "I'm going to climb after them."

"Kukida is probably on her way."

"We can't be sure. And we can't wait. If I draw off the shooters, the rest of you can flee back the way we came. Who knows? Maybe I can even take them out."

Elan frowned. "Vahldan—"

"My father always said the best way to fight the Spali is to go straight at them, to cut one quickly. Boldness and bloodshed spooks them. Besides, it's me Auchote wants. Even if I fail, once they have me they might not bother with the rest of you. It's all we've got. I'm going."

He started to climb, but she grabbed his shoulder, forcing his eyes to meet hers, and gazing into them. He realized she wanted to be sure he hadn't lost himself. "I'm clear on this. It's the only way."

"I can't just let you go alone. You're my subject. I won't abandon my duty."

"We can't just wait."

"No," she finally agreed. Elan hand-signaled Alela. The nurse replied with a stoic nod. She turned back to him. "We're going together." He looked past her at Mara's frightened face. Elan gripped his shoulder. "You're right. Going straight at them is all we have. We must be swift, and deadly."

Vahldan nodded and started to climb. Using her hands, Elan quickly outpaced him. He did his best to imitate her. He was amazed they were able to move across the steepest and smoothest sections. He never would've tried it without Elan's example.

They cleared the bare rock and gained the cover of the vegetation near the crest. He scanned the spot the archers had fired from and saw nothing. "Gone," he said. "Now what?"

"This way." Elan drew her blade and ran west along the mountaintop. She glided through the trees like a breeze, her footfalls light as pattering summer raindrops. He followed, feeling more like a boar than a bird.

Ahead, nestled in the pines just below the crest, he spotted black hair and tattooed torsos. The Spali lined the flat of the hilltop above the crest of the ravine path, hidden among the ferns and boughs with arrow-nocked bows and javelins.

Elan sped up, careening toward them, blade and buckler raised. He stayed with her, wondering if he should seek imbuement. But it was too late for that. A pair of Spali on the near end of the line heard them. One exclaimed and the other turned to aim. The Spali shot and Elan wove. The arrow whizzed past his head.

Elan hit the nearest one, her sword stroke powered by their downhill momentum. Her victim fell heavily. The second Spali turned his bow and drew. Vahldan had no choice but to swing. The blade reverberated with the impact on the man's skull, sending a sickening shiver through him. His belly roiled.

Without a pause, Elan ran on. Filled with disgust and anger, he roared, and the next two Spali along the firing line fled. The realization that these men had been waiting to kill him and his family caused the flame of Thunar's Blessing to flare. He ran after Elan, energized.

Their attack sowed disarray along the entire Spali line. He and Elan split to pursue the next two they encountered. Commands were called and horns blew. The foe was regrouping. His quarry disappeared. He stopped, winded and worried about Elan. She crashed from the trees beside him. "Run!" she cried as she flew past.

Her urgency pierced his imbuement. He sped after her. "They don't seem spooked," he huffed.

"No," she called back. "But at least we're drawing them away from the others."

DESDRUSAN FELT LIKE PACING, but he couldn't summon the energy to stand. Especially from this chair. It was his favorite—deeply cushioned. Instead he snatched up the knife and sawed a hunk from the smoked shank on the table before him. He'd no sooner stuffed the chewy lamb into his mouth when he heard Jhannas's qeins at the drapes to his chambers. "My lord?"

"Bring it in, Glismoda." He grabbed the chamois and started polishing the knife.

The woman pushed through the drapes carrying a tray. "Set it over here." He nodded at the table, keeping his hands busy.

Her expression revealed that she knew what he was up to, but so be it. He'd sufficiently cluttered the table, leaving the perfect spot free to make her stoop and reach. As she did, the low, loose front of the frock hung perfectly, offering a glorious view of the tops of her plump breasts.

"I'm so glad you wore the frock I bought you." He reached for the bread she'd brought and broke a chunk, smearing it with the mashed berries. Waiting always made him crave bread. And the sight of her cleavage had only made him more ravenous.

Glismoda forced a tight smile. "As you bid, my lord." It was worth every bit of the expense. Not just the cost of the frock, but settling all of Jhannas's gaming debts in exchange for her... *their*, indentured service. "Oh, and the fuller Hloed is in the main hall," she added.

"Gods, why didn't you say so?" he said, spewing crumbs. "Show him in, right away." Great breasts, but a bit dim. Ah well. All the easier to manipulate, he supposed.

She glanced at his bed, still rumpled from his nap. "In here, my lord?"

"Yes, yes. And bring some of the Illyrican wine and another cup, would you?"

She held the top of her frock to her chest and bowed before hurrying out.

Hloed came in, his good eye scanning the chamber. "My lord." He bowed, still gawking. "It's a grand place you have here. More spacious than I'd imagined."

"Please, sit." He pointed to the adjacent chair. "Your first time inside, is it?"

"It is." The fuller pointed at one of the cornices. They'd been carved into roaring lion heads. "That's finer work than anything in the longhouse."

Glismoda slipped in with a flagon and poured for him before handing a cup to Slant.

Regarding the carving, Desdrusan hardly noticed such details anymore. To him the Amalus residence felt like a set of empty, echoing boxes. "My mother always loved this place." Desdrusan only stayed because of the status it projected. "She was raised here, you know." An upbringing of the sort he'd been deprived.

"Of course," Slant said.

"It's a shame she never got to move back in." Winning back the prestige his mother deserved was one of the driving forces in Desdrusan's climb to the chieftainship. How he wished that she were still this side of Hel's bridge to witness his ascent. Only she could've make the cavernous place feel like home.

"Ah yes." Hloed smiled knowingly. "Her brother had taken over the residence. And her nephew after him."

"The nephew only briefly." Desdrusan smiled, still savoring his victory over Angavar. "I always found it amusing that the Outcast resented how the residence in the longhouse traditionally went to the Wulthus chieftains. My malcontented cousin complained that it wasn't always so. It was one of the few things about which he was correct. The Amalus, too, once had a residence space allotted within the longhouse. It was our grandmother who put an end to it. She insisting that our grandfather build this place. She hated the long-house. Not just because it was drafty and noisy, mind you. They say she hated living in such close quarters with Thadmeir's grandparents." He laughed. "Perhaps they too were sticklers."

"I see." Slant looked into his cup. "Say, this is delicious wine."

Hloed was willing to spy on his own lord for profit, but apparently joking about the comically fussy man was taking things too far. Which reminded him. "So? What have you learned?"

Hloed instantly brightened. The slinker loved to gossip. "There was indeed a reason that compelled the Wulthus host to ride out this morning. Seems a herdsman—a Wulthus bannerman, mind you—came rushing to the longhouse late last night to see Lord Thadmeir. As you can imagine, Lord Thadmeir was none too pleased, but the man insisted it was urgent."

"And was it?" Desdrusan prodded.

"Well, I suppose that depends on whether what he claims is true or not. Seems Lord Thadmeir has his doubts."

"He doubts because...?" Desdrusan took a drink to keep from screaming.

Hloed's smile pulled at the scar tissue over his bad eye. "Seems this bannerman claims he saw Spali. Within a day's ride of Danihem. In the pass above the green lake. It seems so farfetched."

It was Desdrusan's worst fear. "Spali? That close? Farfetched indeed." Could the cursed boy have possibly come so near to Danihem? Could the rumors be true—that he was being aided by the Skolani? If so, this was getting serious.

"Of course, Lord Thadmeir was leery of letting word get around. Can you imagine the panic? Particularly out in the pastureland."

"Very prudent." The boy was one thing, but tidings like these could spur an even larger mustering than the one being planned. Exactly what the wool guild had been pressuring Desdrusan to prevent. Too many guildsmen knew too much for Desdrusan to dismiss their veiled threats. They'd only grown more restless since Thadmeir had taken up with his little witch.

"Unlikely or not, my lord thought it best to discretely send a small Wulthus host. He of course selected his cousin Ulfhamr to lead it, so as to keep tongues from wagging."

Tongues like this man's. "Also prudent," Desdrusan intoned.

The tower bell clanged, and Hloed pitched upright, nearly spilling his wine. "Could that already be the host returning?"

"Could it?" It could if the gods were kind, and they'd hardly looked and found nothing.

Glismoda appeared at the drapes. "Forgive me, my lord, but there's a lad here for Master Hloed. Says it's urgent."

Hloed stood. "I'd better go see, my lord." He made to leave, but paused to gulp the rest of his wine and hand the cup to Glismoda.

Desdrusan grunted and lunged, then sat back with a sigh. There was no way around it. "Wait. Help me up. I'm coming, too." He held out a hand to the startled fuller, whose good eye went wide with the effort it took to lift him.

Hloed clearly wanted to hurry ahead of him, but forced himself to hold the drapes open for Desdrusan to pass through first. Desdrusan recognized the boy as one of the Wulthus grooms from the longhouse stables. Probably only one of dozens of Hloed's gossip sources.

"What is it, boy?" Hloed asked. "Has Ulfhamr returned?"

"No. Skolani! A Blade-Wielder no less."

"Skolani?" The boy bobbed a nod and rocked, clearly anxious to go and watch.

"A Blade-Wielder? Just one?"

The boy nodded again. "Yes, my lord."

Heartburn clenched the right side of Desdrusan's chest. He pressed under the flap of his breast, pushing out a burp. This didn't bode well. Skolani rarely traveled alone. And Blade-Wielders were no ordinary messengers.

"Are you well, my lord?" Slant asked.

"Fine," he said, another burp slipping out with the word.

"They'll likely need you in the longhouse, my lord," Slant said. Both he and the boy stared, waiting.

Gods, what could this mean? What did the Skolani know? "Lead the way, then," he said, still pressing his chest.

The lane was full of folk heading for the commons. Hloed walked ahead of him, pushing people aside. "Make way for the Lion Lord." Desdrusan wished he'd shut up. The boy vanished among the mulling crowd. Desdrusan scanned the entrance to the Amalus stables as they passed, wondering where in the nine worlds Teavar and Jhannas had gotten to. He almost felt naked without having at least one of them within arm's length.

Just as they gained a clear view of the commons, the arriving rider entered the gate. Murmured awe rippled through the onlookers as they gave way before the visitor's progress. The Skolani's scowl herded the crowd like a prize hound compelling a flock. Desdrusan found himself backing away, too.

This Blade-Wielder was one of the most striking individuals he'd ever seen. She was large and muscular, and her braids were long and fair. She seemed young, but youth didn't detract from her commanding presence. Desdrusan had seen dozens of Blade-Wielders, but he'd never seen so many Spali scalps hanging from one of their warhorse's reins.

She halted in front of the longhouse and dismounted.

Hloed rushed to come around behind her, beckoning Desdrusan to follow. The reticence of the crowd made it easy for them to stay close. The woman twisted to look behind her, causing even Hloed to stop short. Desdrusan was glad for it. Hloed looked to Desdrusan. He shook his head and subtly signaled him to leave off.

Urias emerged from the longhouse alone, and was clearly startled. As often as Thadmeir and his brother hid things from Desdrusan, it was obvious they were not expecting this unusual visitor. Desdrusan side-stepped so that Hloed blocked him from view. Well, partially, at least.

The Wulthus captain dropped to a knee before the visitor, his head bowed. Slant gasped audibly at the deference, and a renewed murmur swept the crowd. Urias said, "Danihem is honored by your presence, Princess Icannes."

So this was Keisella's daughter. He should've known. It all fit—large, beautiful, and a Blade-Wielder. But it made it all the odder that she was traveling alone. Which made Desdrusan all the more fretful.

The princess's resonant voice fit her station. "Arise, Young Wolf. I come at the bidding of my queen. I bring her words to your lord—and, somewhat else." She offered the Wulthus captain a sly smile. "It is well to see you again, old friend."

Urias smiled, too. Seemed the pair was well-acquainted. How had this come to be? Desdrusan couldn't recall ever having seen the woman. Urias held the longhouse door for her, and they disappeared inside.

Hloed turned to him, brimming with nosey joy. "You'll want to get in there, I'm sure, my lord. Come."

Desdrusan grabbed his shoulder, halting him. "I think not. I'm sure they'll send for me in due course. In the meantime, I have business to attend to." He reached into the pouch on his belt, and pressed a gold skatt into the puzzled fuller's hand. "For your trouble."

Desdrusan spun and hurried toward the Amalus stables. He had to find Teavar and Jhannas. And then he had to find one of Túkash's slithering Carpans. It was imperative he find out what was going on out there. Besides that, it suddenly felt like a wise time to get himself gone from the village.

Vahldan's lungs burned as he tried to keep pace with Elan. She ran uphill as if it were downhill. Thunar's Blessing had abandoned him, but the roar and crash of their pursuers spurred him on. Hoofbeats among the noise behind signaled that some Spali had mounted for the chase.

He and Elan emerged from the pines at the lip of a treeless gorge with a dry rocky streambed at its base. Elan slowed to consider their course. He glanced back to find a score of the tattooed warriors coming. The three in the lead were mounted. If they ran into the gorge they'd make themselves easy targets.

"Up!" Elan said. They ran uphill along the rim, back toward the plateau they started on. It occurred to him they were leading the Spali back toward his siblings. For the first time since the arrows of the initial ambush ceased, fear surged into his pounding heart.

The gorge grew shallower as they went. He scanned the top. Three men sat ahorse in the shade of the trees at the top, watching their approach. "You see them?" he managed to call.

"I see," Elan replied, but kept running toward them.

They looked like warriors but they weren't Spali. "Gottari?"

"We can only hope. It's either them or the Spali." The path along the edge narrowed, forcing them into the streambed.

The three at the top wore chainmail, and their helms covered their faces to their beards, with slots to see. The two on either side held arrow-nocked bows. The center rider sat squat in the saddle. A heavy man. Vahldan had never laid eyes on his father's nemesis, but he instantly had a guess who this was. His rage flared to life at the thought, filling his limbs with vigor.

"Desdrusan," he said between breaths. "The usurper."

The top of the streambed became a crag, and its rock sides sprang up before them. "It's too steep," she said. "We'll have to fight." They beat to a halt, raised their swords and shields. Elan turned to face the Spali.

"What about him?" Vahldan said, still looking at the heavy rider at the top.

"No," Elan said. "Got to face the sure threat." He realized he was growling. "Stay with me," she hissed. "We'll have to hope those three shoot at the Spali instead of our backs." Anger thrummed within him, so tantalizing. He felt so sure. His father's rival was so close. "Vahldan," she called. "Hear me?"

"I hear." He made himself turn to stand with her and face the Spali.

They both panted for breath, Vahldan's coming through gritted teeth. The Spali had slowed and spread out, forming a tightening arc, closing around them. They were indeed Paralatoe, some with curved blades, others brandishing nocked bows or javelins. Vahldan scanned their ranks and found him. Riding behind the foe's line was none other than Death's Grin. The inner flame flared anew. "He's here." He pointed with his blade.

"So he is," Elan said, scowling.

"We both go for Auchote. It's our last hope."

Elan nodded. "Before the flanks close." They both raised their shields, and his head filled with a blind yearning. All he could see was Auchote, and his entire body pulsed with lethal energy. "Ready?" she said. He was beyond ready. He started to go, heading for his target.

"Hold!" The word came in Gottari from behind, echoing in the canyon. Elan threw out an arm, keeping him in place. Vahldan looked over his shoulder. The squat center rider held up a gloved halting fist. Amazingly, Auchote grunted a command, and the Spali froze in place. For Vahldan, everything came clear. They were in league—always had been. Gods, Vahldan wanted to go after both of them—his father's killer and the murderous schemer behind it.

Vahldan noticed that the pair flanking the usurper were now aiming their bows. At Elan and him rather than the Spali. "Stand down, Blade-Wielder!" the usurper shouted. "Your companion is an outlaw!"

He started uphill, and Elan wrapped her shield arm around him, pulling him back behind her. "I won't! Queen Keisella of the Skolani sends him forth. She has named me his guardian."

As the trio spoke together, low but inaudible, a fourth figure scurried into view. At first Vahldan thought it was a boy, but the belted woolen tunic and cropped dark hair suggested another likelihood. "Carpan," he hissed. Elan nodded. The final party in the murderous scheme.

The Carpan hurried to the squat man's side. Even as the smaller man gestured and prattled, a rumbling sound grew, coming from behind them.

He presumed the Spali were renewing their attack, and he and Elan spun to face them. But the Spali were doing the same, turning to face the growing thunder.

The trees along the ridge behind the Spali burst forth with riders. Horns blew and arrows arced down onto the Spali in the gorge. Rather than face the arriving riders, the Spali turned and fled. But the newcomers had the momentum. They rode into and among the fleeing Spali, blades hewing and hacking. Green banners flew from standards over the arrivals, and Vahldan instantly recognized the device on them. It was the snarling wolf of the Wulthus clan.

Unable to find Auchote in the chaos, Vahldan spun back to the hilltop, anxious to give chase to at least one of his father's murderers, but the three Gottari and the Carpan were gone. A roar of frustrated rage escaped him. He raised his blade and started for the nearest fleeing Spali.

"Vahldan, no!" Elan grabbed him again. He yanked free. "Your family!" Her words penetrated the roaring rage that filled his head. Gods, they were all getting away. He had his sword up, his hand gripping the hilt, his body coiled to swing, to chop. How could he not? He felt like a starving man being held from the feast table. Elan's face filled his vision. "See me?"

He resented her interference, knew he was snarling. She raised her brows, eyes imploring. He realized he'd been halfway gone, and fought for release. "I see," he said.

"Come. Quickly!" She grabbed his right wrist and ran, pulling him uphill, heading back over the ridge. He scanned the scene a final time, and followed her. Fear for his family won through, flooding him, drenching the flames of rage.

Vahldan's thoughts began to clear. His hatred for his father's killers faded and was instantly replaced by appreciation and gratitude for his guardian. Elan had not only proved herself brave and loyal, but a clear thinker, even while imbued.

Even more importantly, she'd kept him from losing himself throughout, even with his inner forge glowing red hot.

CHAPTER 15—OF TRIALS & TRIBULATIONS

"*It would seem that it was not in the service of prophecy alone that Keisella favored Angavar and his son. True, the queen considered herself an advocate of the futhark and of balance. But so too did she pride herself as a champion of justice, and it would seem she was privy to confidences regarding the Outcast's case.*

The queen made no great secret of her fondness for the Rekkr Badagis. So too do many who knew him attest to Badagis's certitude of Angavar's innocent intentions on the night of the Young Wolf's demise. For Badagis alone saw Desdrusan speaking to Aomeir along the road that day. And when the Wulthus heir arrived back in Danihem to challenge Angavar for sullying his betrothed's honor, Badagis alone knew it could not have been so. He alone had sat with Angavar drinking that evening, a session during which Angavar lamented that he loved and longed for a woman he had not, and could never, have."—Brin Bright Eyes, Saga of Dania*

VAHLDAN'S BELLY ROILED. The ugliness imbued him as the man who'd plotted to destroy his world and had left sorrow in its place strode

directly toward his family. Vahldan had been waiting for the opportunity to tell this mule of a Wulthus lord the whereabouts of his
counterpart on the prior day, and here was the Amalus traitor
himself. Vahldan's whole body felt like a drawn bowstring.

Elan stepped into his line of sight. She shook her head, her eyes
hard. She was anchoring him in place, keeping him from losing
himself. Vahldan knew she was right. He had to tamp down the
growing fire within.

"Forgive the intrusion, Lord Thadmeir," Desdrusan said. His
rolling gait and ruddy cheeks were almost comical. "If I'd known, I'd
have put a halt to it." The two hulks who shadowed Desdrusan were
the largest men Vahldan had ever seen, each towering over their
preposterous master. They wore mail hauberks and sweeping gray
cloaks. None of the arrivals had left their swords outside, as
Icannes's party had. Vahldan's gaze was drawn to the hilt of Desdrusan's sword. He instantly recognized it as Bairtah-Urrin, the Amalus
clan's most sacred relic. The futhark sword's pommel was fashioned
into a snarling lion, just as his father described.

Vahldan's sword hand flexed, yearning for a hilt to grasp. He
fought the impulse to rush the thief and snatch what had been
stolen. Elan touched his arm and whispered, "All in time."

Vahldan drew a breath and released it, pressing the ugliness
down.

Desdrusan kept his beady eyes on Vahldan all the way to the
dais. The man gripped the hilt of Vahldan's father's sword as he
rushed past them to the dais. Had he sped his step? Vahldan sensed
the man's fear now. It called to him, begging him to seize the
advantage.

"Patience. Your family," Elan whispered. She was right. The
usurper had already stooped to soliciting the aid of savages. Many
had already died because of this villain's recklessness. Desdrusan
would do anything to see him and his family dead.

Desdrusan's two guardians took up positions to either side of

Vahldan's family. His father's cousin squared himself to stand before his dais chair, the lesser of the two carved seats of Dania's lords. Once the false lord could look down on Vahldan, he spoke. "This is an affront, and should never have happened."

"What's done is done," Thadmeir said.

"Nevertheless, this is an Amalus issue," Desdrusan said. "These pariahs should never have been allowed to trouble you."

Thadmeir's expression darkened. "The Skolani brought them, hence it's a Gottari issue. And I am troubled no more. We just discussed their leaving Danihem." The Wolf Lord seemed annoyed, defensive. Of course there would be tension between these two. Seeing it offered Vahldan a glimmer of hope.

"Danihem? The Skolani have nothing to do with our laws. And by Gottari law, they must be expelled from all of Dania. Immediately!" Desdrusan's rising voice caused the babe to cry. Alela rocked and shushed Kemella as she stepped to the back of the longhouse.

Vahldan focused on Desdrusan's raised voice, certain it was the same as the helmed man in the canyon. Vahldan looked to Elan, drawing her gaze and raising his brows. Surely she heard it, too. She didn't seem to catch on.

Icannes said, "Lord of lions, we mean not to intrude. My queen bid us to seek aid for the Young Lion and his family upon our arrival, and Lord Thadmeir was kind enough to see us."

"Young Lion, you say? I see only outcasts here. Seeking aid for Gottari outcasts hardly seems like avoiding intrusion."

Icannes scowled, causing Desdrusan's tone to become obsequious. "Please respectfully inform Queen Keisella that our law is clear on this. The progeny of the banished suffer the sires' penalty—forever forward. Perhaps you and your queen were unaware, but these you brought are the offspring of a convicted murderer. They must be expelled from Dania without delay."

"No matter," Desdrusan said. He turned to Thadmeir. "Now that I'm here, I shall take the matter to hand. My men shall swiftly escort the family of your brother's murderer from your sight, straight to Dania's borders."

Vahldan glanced back at the door, considering the possibility of flight. His eye fell on Alela with the babe. He dismissed the idea.

He looked back to Thadmeir, whose brow was furrowed. Desdrusan continued before Thadmeir could reply. "They shall be taken to Thrakius, and sold to the slavers. As slaves, Angavar's children would be fed and sheltered, and the bargain would ensure their complete and final banishment. Your father was a merciful man, my lord. But mercy has led to this rude reminder of your loss. Rest assured, I won't let it happen again."

Thadmeir slumped, putting a hand to his temple. Was he conceding? Vahldan couldn't tell. As alarmed as he was by the threat of slavery, it wasn't the real issue. If Desdrusan gained custody of his family, none of them would make the Danian border alive.

The ugliness thrummed through him. The murderer was about to win. He had to act.

Vahldan pointed at Desdrusan. "This man is a traitor. He is in league with the Spali."

Desdrusan actually smiled. "What in the gods' names are you yammering about, boy?"

"It's true," Vahldan said. "He is able to command the savages. The gods only know what he's promised them in return. It's he who deserves banishment."

"My lord," Desdrusan began wearily. "I realize this flagrant deceit is like salt to a wound. We shall see that you are troubled no longer. Jhannas, Teavar, seize him." The thugs stepped toward Vahldan. Elan stepped to block them, an arm keeping him in place behind her.

"Hold!" The Wolf Lord stood and raised hands. Desdrusan's guards halted.

"This is absurd, my lord." Desdrusan smiled and tsked, but Vahldan saw a flicker of fear. "Surely we cannot let this criminal defile our house of law with such desperate lies?"

"Hold, Desdrusan," Thadmeir repeated. "However absurd or desperate, I will hear his claims. Uninterrupted." The Wulthus lord stepped to the edge of the dais. "You make a serious charge, boy. What evidence do you bring?"

"We saw him; Elan and I both. All three of them were there, when we were attacked by the Spali." Vahldan glanced at the thugs. Desdrusan's face went from red to white, his lips pressed tight.

"When and where?"

"Just yesterday, on the ridge above the Green Lake pass. We were set upon by the Spali in the narrows near the crest. We fled to the heights, to draw them away from my kin. These three sat watching from above as we were pursued and fired upon. *He*"—Vahldan jabbed a finger at Desdrusan—"bid the Spali to hold, same as you just did. And the savages obeyed."

Everyone stood silent, most everyone bristling. Even Icannes. She'd advised him to wait until his charges could be heard by more of the Amalus Rekkrs, in the hopes that his father still had some allies in the council. But waiting was no longer an option.

"A very fanciful imagination, at least," Desdrusan said, clearly feigning amusement.

Thadmeir eyed Vahldan coldly. "Why would he halt them? To protect you?"

"Well, no. I mean, I'm not sure why."

Thadmeir rolled his eyes. "I see." His tone was patronizing.

"No, you don't see!" Elan laid her hand on his arm again. He sought for calm. "Forgive me, my lord. I'm not certain, but I'd guess it's because he feared being linked to the death of a Skolani. But the rest is so clear. He wanted my father dead, and Auchote killed him. He wants me and my family dead. And again, Auchote's warriors appear, many days' ride from the borderlands. These same Spali attacked the homestead of Rekkr Kohlsa, killing everyone there on the very night we were supposed to arrive. Only Princess Icannes's instincts saved us."

"Ha. Such a tale! Clearly this one's not right in the head."

Desdrusan pointed at his own head and imitated a crazed expression. "All the more reason to make sure he stays gone."

Thadmeir turned to Icannes. "This is true? Auchote's warband killed Kohlsa's family?"

Icannes nodded once. "All of them perished. I am all but certain Auchote was behind it."

Thadmeir looked back to Vahldan with hooded eyes. "What happened next? In the pass."

"Just as the Spali halted on his command, a Carpan rushed to Desdrusan, obviously to warn him, because this came just before your captain's host arrived to scatter the foe. I turned away, and when I looked back, these three had vanished. Surely if nothing else proves them false, it's the fact that they fled their fellow Gottari rather than joining the fight."

Desdrusan actually laughed. "Oh my! It'd be funny if it weren't so poisonous."

Vahldan's nails dug into his palms. "See there, when he raises his voice? It sounds exactly the same as in the pass." It was all so obvious. He looked to Elan, who frowned.

"Well, he's creative and persistent," Desdrusan began solemnly, "but he's also devious. Which makes him dangerous. To concoct such an elaborate hoax! Clearly, the son is worse than the father. Thank the gods he's within our grasp, my lord. Seeing to this villain's banishment will rid Dania of a clever liar with a killer's blood in his veins."

Only Elan's tightening grip on his arm made Vahldan's realize he was leaning in, poised to attack.

Thadmeir held up another silencing hand. "Princess Icannes. They say that a Blade-Wielder's word is her honor, do they not?"

"A Blade-Wielder's word is her sacred bond, to her people, her queen, her goddess."

Thadmeir turned to Elan. "So, Blade-Wielder. What say you of this tale? Was Lord Desdrusan there when you were attacked? Was he in league with the Spali?"

Elan looked stricken. She glanced at Vahldan and released his arm. He raised his brows. This was it. With a word she could end the shameful mockery that was Desdrusan's lordship. His guardian held justice in her hands.

"Just tell us what you saw," Thadmeir encouraged her.

"I saw three riders—Gottari, by the look of their garb and armor. It was as Vahldan said, they sat watching as we were pursued by the Spali. At a word from one of them, the Spali halted. One of them asked me to stand down, to leave Vahldan to them. I refused. A moment later, a host of wolves attacked. During the fighting, the three riders disappeared."

It seemed no one was breathing. Thadmeir's voice rent the quiet. "Can you say, as Vahldan asserts, that the three you saw were these men here: Lord Desdrusan and his guardians, Jhannas and Teavar?"

She appraised them and turned to Thadmeir. "It could have been. But I can't be certain."

"Ah, there you have it," Desdrusan said, his smile reappearing.

Thadmeir frowned. "You said you saw them."

"So I did. But they sat in shadow, wearing helms that covered their faces."

Vahldan was stunned. "What about the voice?" he pled to her.

Elan shook her head. "It's similar. Many men's voices are similar."

"It's true," Desdrusan agreed, unable to mask his delight.

Vahldan slumped. Elan hurried to add, "I am sure that Vahldan believes it was them, Lord Thadmeir. And I've come to trust his judgement."

Desdrusan shook his head. "How sad. The boy even seeks to deceive his Skolani guardian, to use her honor against me. He mocks us all, Skolani and Gottari alike. Allow me to see to a fitting sentence, my lord."

Thadmeir slouched into his chair. "Silence. Let me think about how to proceed, for just a moment." He rubbed his face. Desdrusan ceased speaking, but continued to flaunt his sly grin.

Vahldan's anger and shock were swiftly replaced by panic. Could this really be happening? He'd promised his father that those who set him up would not get away with what they'd done—up to and including Angavar's murder. Here before him was the spider at the center of the web, and it seemed he was getting away with all that he'd devised. Vahldan couldn't even fight or flee without putting his family at risk.

The silence was broken by a surprise voice. "There is a simple answer, Lord Thadmeir." Icannes strode to the edge of the dais. "The Lion Lord demands justice, as does the son of Angavar. The solution seems all but ordained. Vahldan claims a blood-debt, against his father's honor. His first concern in coming was for his family's welfare. But he also came to claim his right to the Ananth-jahn."

At the mention of the word, Vahldan's flames began to rise again. The flames were swiftly quenched by fear. A trial was what he'd both longed for and dreaded since before they left the mine. What if the ugliness seized him during a trial? His family would be left helpless.

"Oh come now," Desdrusan interjected. "Convicted outlaws have no right to trial."

Thadmeir's frown deepened. "Is this true, boy? You also presume to demand trial?"

Vahldan paused, gathering his scattered thoughts, pushing aside his fear. He could not let this situation stand. He glanced to Elan. She stood stalwart, eyes hard. He'd been stunned and was still disappointed by her answer to Thadmeir, but he knew she could only speak truth. She was still his anchor. With her alongside, he would not lose himself. It was time for him to speak his truth. He would fight. Fight for justice.

"Yes, Lord Thadmeir." The long-rehearsed words spilled out: "Since my father's guilt was never proven, I am owed trial. Angavar vowed it was an accident, as did Frisanna—a witness who, at the time, was forbidden to speak. His hearing was rushed, pushed to a vote in the heat of outrage. The verdict was rendered with very few

Amalus Rekkrs present. A true consensus was never reached. These things are beyond refute."

Thadmeir rocked back, looking stricken. "You understand that my father was his accuser and presided over his hearing, do you not? Do you seek honor against the accusation or the method?"

"No, my lord. I know what was done was born of great passion. This was understood and accepted even by my father." He turned to face Desdrusan. "It's the deceit and betrayal of our own kin which I find at fault. I cite the lag of the Arrivals in demanding that I, as Angavar's son, be granted an Ananth-jahn—to regain his honor, as well as my rightful status."

Desdrusan's amused air was gone, replaced by a hateful glare. The feeling was mutual. "Yours is a false choice, my lord. The convicted have no rights. The simple solution is as I first suggested. This exile is trespassing. Allow me to see that he serves his rightful sentence. Please, Lord Thadmeir, I beg you to end this mummery."

Icannes spoke up. "If the interpretation of your law is at issue, perhaps a majority should decide it. Did you not say that your Rekkrs were mustering? Simply call for a hearing and put it to a vote. This time with both sides present. Surely no few Rekkrs would appreciate having a say. Some might even be bitter if they are once again kept from it. Vahldan is, after all, the blood of the Amalus kings."

Desdrusan's glare swiveled to the princess. He seemed unable to find a retort for this unusual adversary. His jaw worked behind pressed lips, causing his gelatinous jowls to quiver.

The Wolf Lord stroked his beard, his eyes never leaving Vahldan. Just as Vahldan had sensed fear behind Desdrusan's feigned calm, he now sensed fear in Thadmeir's reluctance. Both lords feared the truth, but he suspected there was more to it for the Wolf Lord. He guessed that Thadmeir actually wanted some version of justice. Vahldan knew the Wolf Lord considered himself a man of the law. In Angavar's planning, his father had relied on three things in regard to Lord Thadmeir: the man's reverence for Gottari law, his fear for

Dania's divisiveness and crumbling values, and his strong sense of honor.

Thadmeir turned to his brother. Urias nodded slightly. Without a word exchanged, it seemed the lord and his captain had reached consensus.

"So be it," Thadmeir said. "The matter shall be put to a hearing before the full council of Rekkrs and elders, three nights hence the full moon. Surely then there will be enough Amalus Rekkrs present to put an old contention to rest once and for all. Now begone from my sight, all of you."

Icannes gestured briskly. She was right—it was time to go. Vahldan and the others followed her toward Alela, who sat nursing the babe near the exit. It wasn't the victory Vahldan had thought foregone. At least they'd averted being dragged off to slavery or death. For the moment. Desdrusan's huge guards glowered as his party rushed into the aisle.

"One last item, if I may, my lord." Desdrusan's voice echoed. Icannes halted them.

"What is it?" Thadmeir's tone made it clear he was beyond annoyance.

"As I recall the old lag, since the boy is the challenger, he must represent himself on the tarp. But, as I was unwittingly challenged, I am accorded the right to name a champion, am I not?"

Thadmeir sighed. Again he turned to consult his captain. Again, Urias nodded. "Yes, that sounds right. The Elli-Frodei can confirm it before the council meets. Now go!"

Desdrusan hastened from the dais, boots thumping toward the door. Alela stood, gathering the babe's swaddling. Icannes beckoned the group out of the way. Desdrusan halted adjacent to them. "Well done, Vahldan. This is even better than I'd hoped for. Now please meet Teavar, son of Skaldan—your opponent, should you gain your ludicrous trial." If there was a larger and meaner-looking of the two giants, it was the man who grinned and bowed mockingly. The ugliness flopped in the base of Vahldan's belly, as if to remind him of the added danger of losing himself while facing this imposing menace.

"But fear not," Desdrusan said. He lowered his voice, "Trial or no, Teavar here shall deliver you to your rightful fate—same as your father's." The usurper's laughter rang until it was silenced by the closing thump of the wooden door behind him.

CHAPTER 16—THE ANANTH-JAHN

"*I*t must be remembered that the Ananth-jahn trials in Angavar's day were not the same as today's, which have become little more than ceremonial contests in which boys vie to prove their manhood and claim their name. In those days steel swords rather than wood ones clashed, and real blood was oft shed. And not just from bashed noses and split lips. After all, the Ananth-jahn was born to contain bloodshed between the riving clans, reining it into a four-span ring, limiting the lethal danger to the pair at the center of contention."—*Brin Bright Eyes, Saga of Dania*

ELAN HAD NEVER SEEN SO many Gottari in one place. Danihem's commons was a swarming mass of humanity. Men lined the walkways of the wall-tops overlooking the fighting ring and children rode on their parents' shoulders to see. Several mead-makers doled from barrels, and wandering hawkers sold meat on skewers, steaming honey cakes, and drams of spirits.

Elan's eye was drawn back to Desdrusan's champion. She spoke to Icannes under her breath. "Did you consider *this* when you convinced Vahldan to seek a trial? Gods, that man-beast is the tallest being I've ever seen. And his shield is ridiculous. It's as thick as my fist. The shield alone must weigh almost as much as Vahldan does."

Icannes continued to wax her buckler for Vahldan's use. "I considered neither his opponent's size nor his shield. I was too busy getting Vahldan ready for the opportunity of a lifetime."

Elan harrumphed. "The opportunity to cut it short, maybe."

Icannes scowled. "At least it's a fighting chance. Don't forget, he was about to be hauled off to the Pontean slave docks."

Elan scanned the growing press. The front was lined by Rekkrs, well dressed and wearing various bits of their finest armor. No few wore the crimson armbands or neckerchiefs of the Amalus. "Now he's got to face this behemoth in front of the very men he'd hoped to win over. Even if he survives, he'll lose."

Icannes stopped polishing and faced her. "I also failed to consider who would show up to watch. But I did consider his growth and increasing boldness in the ring."

"Boldness, ha. You mean the blood-rage you goad that he can barely control?"

"That's exactly what I mean. What I *goad* from him is the very thing that made his father the finest fighter the realm has ever known. And along the way to helping him tap into it, I made him believe he can face anything and come out on top. I gave him a winning attitude. At the moment his is a damn sight better than yours, Elan. It's a pity. He could really use your belief in him today."

Elan fidgeted. "I do believe in him." Icannes raised an eyebrow. "Well, I'm trying to."

"Whether you believe or not, you should be relieved. One way or the other, your duty to him will end today. That's still what you want, right? To get back to your host?" Icannes rose and took the shield to Vahldan.

Elan's tunic suddenly felt too tight, like she was tied up in it rather than wearing it. The champion's glower was fixed on Vahldan as he swung the futhark blade. She saw the gleam in Teavar's eye.

She knew that look. It was bloodlust. The man was a killer. Not a reluctant one, or one who'd kill under the right circumstance. Just a killer. "Not like this," she hissed.

The crowd suddenly felt too close. She wished they'd all back up a few steps. She'd been dreading this day. It had come so slowly, but now that it was here she wished there were more time. It couldn't be denied that the extra days had been a boon. She was glad that Icannes had moved them to the camp downriver.

Vahldan's improvement in the ring really was astonishing. It was clear he'd inherited his father's instincts. Even the change in his physique was impressive. But it still begged the question: was it enough? Had his practiced skills become second nature? Could he find his way to Thunar's Blessing and maintain his control? Sure, he'd gained some control in practice. But practice could never replicate actually having someone trying to end your life.

Seeing Vahldan improve had helped Elan to mostly get over her resentment of Icannes. She'd distracted herself by entertaining the children and finding unique food for them to cook together. She'd even allowed Eldavar to teach her to fish—a skill for which she secretly had more experience than he. In return, she'd shown him the finer points of the hunt. They did well. They ate well. But the blood of the kill, even the gutting of the fish, all brought this reality back to her. Through it all, the dread inside her grew. And now the day had come.

Icannes helped Vahldan with his buckler straps. Elan tugged her too-tight tunic and scanned the crowd. Their staring felt like the hot sun beating on her. It really was getting warm. Did they all have to stand so damn close?

She focused on Icannes and Vahldan. "Remember all we worked on," Icannes said to him. "Keep those feet moving. His reach is long, so you'll have to stay back and pick your moments. No dallying once you're inside, or when you retreat. Just get out of range. You'll have the speed advantage. Use it. Be bold, but patient. Submit to Thunar and trust your instincts."

She saw Vahldan's anxiety at the mention of imbuement. He swung his arm, checking the shield straps. It made Elan anxious, too. As did his lack of body armor. Icannes insisted he didn't need it. She said it would only slow him down. But the Amalus hulk wore a chain hauberk over leather. They'd learned that armor could be loaned to the challenger, but no one from his clan had offered to lend. It seemed even those who'd supported his father were unwilling or afraid to help. Elan supposed the reprisal that would follow his defeat seemed too likely.

Vahldan faced Elan as Icannes laced his right forearm guard. Elan smiled, trying to believe. Their eyes locked. He was reading her. They both knew they couldn't hide from one another. The connection had only grown over the weeks of training. She looked away. Better to spurn him than to reveal her fear. She looked up at the bright blue morning sky, trying to breathe.

Then she saw him. She searched higher and spotted her. A tingling sensation ran over her scalp and down her neck and arms.

The kestrel mates soared over the hillside meadows outside the village. Same as last time, the larger female hovered above the male, watching over him while he hunted. Her role was vital. She was there to ensure his success. Knowing of her presence allowed him to focus.

Serenity washed through her.

Elan realized she was resisting playing her vital role. Their certainty of her part in his success had only grown during the days of training since they'd seen the kestrels at Kohlsa's cove. Vahldan immersed in and emerged from Thunar's Blessing in connection to her. She anchored him to his true self. He found and trusted his instincts through his link with her. If he began to stray too close to his dark edges, seeing her and hearing her voice pulled him back.

She could help him as no other could. He needed her certitude. She could give it.

Elan turned to face Vahldan. He had already followed her gaze. He looked from the raptors in the sky to her. She opened herself to him, grateful to share what he would find. He nodded and smiled.

She blinked away the wetness that sprang to her eyes and nodded back.

She was his kestrel guardian, and he knew it. They both believed.

ARNEGERN HAD BEEN among the first to arrive on Danihem's commons, just after dawn. He was there even before the venders. And he was rewarded with a ringside spot, which included the chance to observe the dashing challenger and his illustrious companions up close.

As they always seemed to, Angavar's heir and his Skolani companions had caused quite a stir upon their arrival. The gate-house bell rang and the commons swiftly filled. The crowd gaped and pointed. They were such a sensation! And yet no one dared speak to them, including him.

But no one was willing to miss out. The fierce daughter of a Skolani queen, trainer to the handsome son of a banished lord; not to overlook his striking Blade-Wielder guardian. And they'd come to restore the honor of an ancient bloodline, from an undeniably corrupt usurper. It was the stuff of legends.

Thus far they did not disappoint. Arnegern was riveted. The trio seemed so assured, as if it were a routine occurrence to fight in a perilous trial against a giant.

The sun grew high. The lords of Dania would arrive soon, to sanction the event. The commons was overflowing as the sun cleared the east village wall. Arnegern had no doubt that many came just for the thrill of likely bloodshed. But to Arnegern this was about much more. He couldn't help but wonder about the appearance of Angavar's heir at a time like this.

For months, Arnegern and his allies among the eastern herdsmen had fought to gain some sort of a unified response to the alarming increase in Spali raids. They'd been the ones to bring the Priestess Amaseila to Danihem. And change finally seemed nigh.

Arnegern sensed it was more than simply an impending

mustering of his nation's warriors. Something auspicious was coming. He could feel it. He kept going back to the spring equinox session, and the lines Amaseila had spoken while in the trance of the goddess. *'And a king shall return to the kingless, born of exile.'*

Her words had caused an uproar. Yes, she'd incited accusations of treason. But she'd also stirred renewed rumors of how the Outcast's son seemed to fit the prophecy. And now, just before the solstice, that very son had appeared in Danihem. Could it mean that Urrinan was actually approaching? Arnegern found he couldn't dismiss the notion.

Arnegern had actually seen Lord Angavar when he was a boy. The Lion Lord had come to visit Arnegern's father, drawing a host of followers and admirers to their homestead in the eastern marches. Even then Arnegern had felt the power of the man's presence. Angavar's charm had put the women of the house aflutter, all smiles and blushing cheeks. His quips to the men brought swelling chests and raised chins. The Amalus had seen the best of themselves in him. And for those who'd believed, Angavar's downfall had broken their hearts.

Now Arnegern saw the father in the son. The same fire burned within him. Prophecies aside, this young man's radiance drew every eye.

But for most, Vahldan's success was a thing too perfect to dare to hope for.

Who could doubt that the youth would fall to Teavar's might? The giant had never lost. The gods knew how often even Teavar's practice sessions resulted in the injury of opponents. In battle Teavar was accorded the same respect as a small host. Arnegern had once watched Teavar wrap an arm around the neck of an Illyrican merchant's bodyguard, strangling the twisting and kicking man to unconsciousness as he guzzled an entire cup of mead, simply because he'd disliked something the man had said to him in passing.

Arnegern saw his cousins Belgar and Herodes making their way through the crowd, and waved them over. "Gods, he's so thin," Belgar said as he arrived.

"And yet there is strength," Arnegern said "He's lean but well proportioned, much as the father was."

"Lean strength won't be enough," Herodes replied. "Teavar's reach with that blade—there'll be nowhere to hide."

Belgar sighed. "How sad for us. I hope you've placed your bets accordingly, cousins."

Arnegern watched as the Skolani guardian nodded in some unspoken message to Vahldan. There was something special going on. It was in his eyes. The auburn-haired warrior seemed to have awoken him to his bloodline, and it pulsed through him. "No. I haven't. In fact... I'm starting to wonder. Maybe it doesn't need to be sad. Perhaps I *should* risk a wager."

Belgar laid a hand on his shoulder. "You can't be thinking he has a chance. He isn't even wearing armor. And does he consider that little disc on his arm a shield?"

Arnegern had to admit, those were concerning issues. "But what if he did have armor? And a better shield?"

Belgar hissed and shook his head.

Everything had been all wrong for so long. But what if their fortunes were changing? What if the gods were speaking to Arnegern now? If the son of the Outcast won... "It'd change everything," Arnegern said aloud.

"What, a bit of armor and a shield? You're mad. That's Teavar he's about to face, remember?"

"Maybe I am mad. But what if I'm meant to act? What if I'm to be a part of his destiny?"

"No. You wouldn't." Belgar sounded alarmed.

"I think I might. My armor and shield are right over there, just inside those doors." He nodded toward the Amalus stables.

"Arnegern, no. You can't. You've heard the warnings Desdrusan's thugs have been spreading. Anyone who openly supports him will face the fat man's wrath."

Arnegern smiled. "Maybe that's why it falls to me. What more can Desdrusan do to us?"

"Plenty."

"Such as?"

"For starters, he can have the wool guild ban your family from the shearing market."

"They already pay us a pittance. And they overcharge us for grazing, too. Since my censure over the incident with the Hellain buyer, we'd do better to corral the herd for milk, cheese, and meat." Belgar frowned, but didn't argue. "If I do nothing, we'll lose the chance to find out if he might become whom we hope he will."

Belgar started to say something, but Arnegern didn't wait to hear it. He weaved and shoved his way to the stable. His biggest worry suddenly became making it back in time.

Arnegern burst through the stable doors and rushed to his kit. His leathers uncoiled along with his chain hauberk. He left the leathers in a pile and put the hauberk over his shoulder. He snatched up the shield that had been his father's, freshly painted with his family's red and gold roaring lion crest. He hesitated. Was he really willing to risk his father's faltering estate? Not just his inheritance, but his family's reputation?

But what would he gain by avoiding risk? More of the same. Corruption and injustice.

He drew a deep breath and headed back. Again he was forced to push and weave his way back to the ring. A cheer rose to his right. Thadmeir emerged from the longhouse. Urias parted the crowd to lead the lords' procession to the ring. Thadmeir's young priestess qeins, rumored to be expecting his child, walked beside him wearing a fine white robe, a hand laid daintily on his arm. She'd been the milkmaid daughter of one of his father's bannermen, and now look at her.

Several prominent Wulthus Rekkrs trailed the esteemed couple. Once again, he silently thanked Freya that he'd given in and brought Amaseila to Danihem. Amaseila had insisted and he'd resisted. She kept insisting it was her destiny to come here. Arnegern had remained skeptical. He hadn't dreamed where it might lead. In looking back on it, he had to consider that perhaps Amaseila had foretold destiny. Now he wondered about his own role in it.

Arnegern was closer than the lords, but his way was more obstructed. Desdrusan exited the longhouse behind the wolves, a handful of his Amalus old-guard allies behind him. Everyone in the crowd was turned to face the procession. Arnegern put his shoulder to his shield and unapologetically shoved the final distance.

Arriving ringside just ahead of the lords, his bright red shield suddenly seemed frightfully obvious. He handed the shield off to Belgar, rolled the hauberk, and slipped it under his arm. With all of the attention on the lords, he was able to skirt the ring and sidle up to the challenger. "Vahldan, son of Angavar, I have a gift I wish to offer you."

Vahldan turned to him with curious eyes. Arnegern put his back to the lords and proffered the hauberk. The young man studied Arnegern's face but made no move to take it. Time was running out. The cheering crested. "Please, take it. My father and yours were friends. I wish to honor that friendship." Vahldan's eyes narrowed, considering. Arnegern added, "It's only fitting. For a trial to be just, it must be fought on equal terms. Teavar wears one of these."

Vahldan's guardian appeared at his shoulder, scowling. "Should I?" he asked the Skolani. She too studied Arnegern a moment, and finally gave a single nod. Vahldan accepted the gift with a bow. But it was too late. It'd taken too long. The Lion Lord was ringside with Teavar, glaring across the tarp. Arnegern turned back to Vahldan, who was studying the lion pendant at the collar of the hauberk. "Your father, he fought with mine." It wasn't a question.

"Yes. And now you must win, or my father and I shall face a great deal of trouble."

Vahldan inclined his head. "Thank you. I understand. Better now than before."

Lord Thadmeir was the first to step out onto the pristine hide. The Priestess followed, her pale eyes sweeping the crowd.

The Wolf Lord raised his hands for quiet. "The son of Angavar the Outcast has called for his right to the Ananth-jahn. He seeks the restoration of his father's honor, and his rightful status." Thadmeir turned to Vahldan. "You swear that the victor of the match will decide the outcome of the issue, and that you and your kin will forever abide by it?"

"I swear," Vahldan said.

Thadmeir turned around. "Who stands for the challenged?"

"Teavar, son of Skaidan." Gods, that voice—deep as Wodin's curse.

"Do you, Teavar, swear to seek the rightful outcome of this dispute in your clan's name, and that, once settled, you and those you represent will forever abide by the outcome?"

"I do."

Thadmeir turned to his qeins. "Priestess Amaseila will say the prayers, that those whose death finds them here may pass to the Banquet."

The Priestess moved first to Teavar and took his hand. She tilted her head back, murmuring in prayer. The whole crowd leaned in, trying to hear. She released the champion then turned to the challenger. Arnegern had ended up right behind Vahldan. Even as a child, Amaseila had always seemed like a crone in a girl's body. She'd become something more. If he'd ever doubted she was divinely imbued, seeing her now banished it.

Vahldan knelt and placed his hand in both of hers. At the moment of their contact, Amaseila convulsed, eyes bulging and knees buckling. The audience gasped. Thadmeir swept to his qeins' side, holding her upright. "What is it, my darling?" Thadmeir asked.

Vahldan seemed to be trying to pull his hand free, but she clung to him, in spite of the shock or pain it seemed to cause her. "*You,*" she breathed. "In glory shall he rise, and glory shall be his song."

Vahldan's face went white. "What did you say?" The young man's voice was tremulous.

Amaseila's voice rose, "The Bringer. You are he. You will cause great pain. But also glory shall you bring. What is to come through you will change us all— Gottari and Skolani alike—forever. For you shall be the start of it. Upon your doom, the Urrinan shall ride."

A murmur ran through the crowd. She continued, "In knowing that the daughter who grows in my womb shall also be entangled with it, I can't help but feel both elation and sorrow. It weighs heavily upon me."

Amaseila bent over his hand, drawing and releasing several deep breaths. When she looked up at him again, she wore a weary smile. "And yet... I am glad to have met the man with whose my blood shall mingle. Take heart, Vahldan son of Angavar. For from the bloodshed you will sow, greatness shall be reaped."

Vahldan stared at her, his jaw working behind closed lips. Princess Icannes broke the silence. "I presume, Priestess, that you foresee the Young Lion's survival of today's trial."

Amaseila smiled. "Yes, brave princess, he will survive this day. And again and again, he will face what will seem certain death. And again and again he will survive. Indeed, he shall thrive. His doom he will bring upon himself. He will know it, and face it with no regrets. For in his upheaval, the world shall be made anew. Through all the long ages to come, songs will be sung of what shall be wreaked."

Amaseila looked back to Vahldan. "Ah, but let me still say the prayers for you. There are times when Freya's visions are laden with trickery. Alas, I am a mere mortal." She tilted her head back and murmured in prayer as she had with Teavar.

Amaseila finally released Vahldan's hand, but stood gazing fondly at him. "He'll be beautiful," she said musingly.

"Who?" Vahldan asked.

"My grandson." She turned and strode off the mat.

Whispers turned to murmurs, then to a rising drone of voice. The entire crowd seemed to be waking from a spell. Arnegern turned to

Belgar. His cousin's eyes were wide. "You just mentioned the prophecy."

Arnegern held up his hand to show that he was trembling. "I told you something strange was happening."

Herodes pursed his lips and whistled softly. "And I thought she was spooky before."

Arnegern ventured a glance at Desdrusan. The Lion Lord mopped his brow with a cloth. Teavar, however, stood on the tarp's edge looking bored.

VAHLDAN COULDN'T BELIEVE IT. The priestess's words were so close to what Elan claimed was from a hymn of the Skolani Wise Ones. And she mentioned glory, just as his father had.

Everyone knew his father was Dania's best—as a warrior and a leader. Vahldan knew he could never live up to it. But this? Someone saw something special in him. He could become something his father never could have.

No, damn it. His mother had warned him not to get caught up in such nonsense. He certainly couldn't rely on the bedamned prophecy to get him through this trial. If anything, it was a distraction.

He had to get past it. Frisanna's words came to him. *Let it go. Focus on what you know to be true. Don't ever let anyone convince you that anything is ordained.*

"Let it go," he said aloud. He focused on his breathing to calm his hammering heart.

Thadmeir stood center tarp. "May the gods be with you both. Let the Ananth-jahn begin."

Vahldan danced forward. Teavar strolled out like he was browsing the market. Vahldan's belly churned. It felt more like fear than Thunar's Blessing. Submitting to the ugliness was the path to disaster. He pressed it down rather than reaching for it and stayed alert, lifting onto the balls of his feet, side-stepping the perimeter, keeping his distance. He had to banish his jitters. Teavar followed Vahldan's progress by swiveling his head, his feet planted until it was necessary to turn a step to square up again.

Icannes called, "Patience, Vahldan. Find your way there."

Vahldan's eye flicked to her. It was the slightest lapse. Teavar swooped, the whir of futhark blade flashing in the sunlight. Vahldan threw up the buckler just in time. *Thwack!* The resound of splitting wood came even as the giant moved into his follow-through. Vahldan fell back, unsteady as he fled. Someone called, "Step out!"

Vahldan followed his momentum off the tarp. The raised hands of the crowd kept him upright as their booing and jeers rained down on him.

His shield arm stung. "Seems this giant can fly," Elan said as she released the straps of the cracked shield and checked his arm with trembling fingers. "It's not broken," he reassured her. He hated how shaken she looked. The jitters crawled across his skin and the churn flowed up and out, making his limbs floppy.

Elan raised her gaze to meet his. They both knew it had slipped away. Neither of them could find the belief he needed.

Thadmeir raised a finger to him. "One fall is charged to the challenger. One more is allowed. A third is defeat. Flight to a third, disgrace."

Vahldan nodded. Gods, why was he already out of breath?

The crowd began to cheer again. "Here, take my shield, as well." It was the lanky young man who'd given him the hauberk.

This time Vahldan didn't hesitate. He accepted with a tilt of his head.

The young man held it while Vahldan put his arm through the straps. He said, "It may survive such a blow. But I wouldn't advise you to allow another." Vahldan didn't disagree.

Icannes blocked his return. "Find your instincts. If you react, you're already too late. *See* what is to come—feel it, know it." Vahldan's belly churn became a boil. Gods, it was still fear.

Thadmeir called, "Let the match continue."

Icannes ignored the Wolf Lord and moved nose to nose with him. "You and I know your victory is rightful. It's already there. Find your way to it." She stepped aside, her voice commanding, "You know it's true, Vahldan. Go there. Find it!"

He nodded and clanked his sword against his borrowed shield. It was substantial—more like those he'd trained with since boyhood. Teavar waited. The giant wasn't even winded.

Vahldan turned to Elan. She smiled, veiling concern. "Kestrel," she said. He nodded. He could let go. She would keep him from getting lost.

He turned to face his rivals. Teavar grinned across the tarp, and Desdrusan chuckled as he gloated to his companions. Rage whispered at the edges of fear. *'They won't get away with it. I won't let them win!'*

Vahldan danced again, letting the molten rage flow up and through him. The roar in his ears became a monotone, the multihued crowd a backing blur. *'I know what's inside you, because it's inside me, too.'*

Teavar raised his sword and shield but was still flat-footed. Vahldan's rage protested the insult. It was time. He cast aside the fear and reached for the anger. He darted a step, feigning a charge. Teavar readied to counter. He sidestepped and chopped. He was retreating even as he heard the knock on Teavar's shield. The big man had barely made the block.

"Yes!" It was Elan. "Hear me?" Without looking he gave a nod. "Go, then. Go!"

'This is where I end and you begin.' These men killed his father. They were behind all of it—his family's banishment, his mother's death, all of it. The hatred and violence of Thunar's Blessing thrummed through him, out into his limbs, and yet he still hadn't lost himself.

'Seize... your... destiny.'

He'd shocked the giant from complacency. Teavar took a defensive pose, but Vahldan dashed left for another attack. This rush became a series of blows. He blocked everything the man threw. And although Vahldan hadn't drawn blood, he'd occupied the giant and was burning his energy. The big man's feet were leaden, and his hand speed slowed. Vahldan smelled blood, and he wanted to spill it.

This man was a part of all that had befallen his family. He was a tool of the usurper, of the guild. Teavar was a hired killer. For Vahldan it was kill or be killed.

He growled and stepped up swinging. Teavar backpedaled, blocking and parrying.

Elan's voice pierced the crowd. "Yes! Go there. I've got you!" His spirit flared. His chest became a crucible for his fury, burning off the slag of clumsiness and fog of the old ugliness. It was forging him anew, leaving him clear and clean, lithe and sharp—hardened. And lethal.

Channeling Icannes's teaching, he stayed in close, rendering the larger man's power and reach useless. He kept the giant on the defensive but had yet to get past it. His fury grew. So did Teavar's. The giant bellowed and lunged, slamming his shield into Vahldan's, throwing him back. Vahldan's feet skittered to the hide's edge. Teavar lowered his left shoulder and drove. Vahldan gathered his balance and sprang from Teavar's push. Growling, he landed a blow on Teavar's helm as he slipped into open space, sending the giant staggering, barely able to catch himself from going out.

Before the giant could recover, Vahldan pressed again, beating his rival back, his footwork and swordsmanship coming naturally. The forge flared and the heat of the crucible built, delivering power and speed he'd never before realized. Teavar looked dazed. He seemed to be tiring.

"That's it, Vahldan. You're seeing it!" Icannes called. As he parried and blocked, Teavar's eye glanced to the edge of the tarp. "There! Now!" Icannes cried.

Vahldan's arm was already swinging. He shed Teavar's parry, audibly gashing the giant's armored shoulder. Teavar staggered from the tarp to avoid the next blow. "Out!" The crowd erupted. Thadmeir stepped between them with hands raised. "One fall charged to the champion."

Vahldan barely restrained himself from shoving aside this man who'd dared interrupt him from harvesting his reward. The bellows blew, flaring the forge, and his fury flowed to the crucible—molten hot. He laughed to banish a roar of frustration and bloodlust.

Fear had lost its power over him. He was both present and filled with the surging power of Thunar's Blessing. Elan had his back—she believed. It felt like a focused delirium; a vengeful, ravenous joy. He wanted nothing but to make his enemies pay for what they'd done— to harvest the blood debt they owed him. Perhaps the spooky priestess had delivered some sort of divine touch. She said he was doomed, and indeed, he no longer feared death.

Which meant he need not fear the ugliness. For it was in the fear that he grew lost.

He was free. He saw death for what it was—an inevitable gateway. But death was also a tool, a weapon at his disposal. Vahldan knew he could, and would, use it before he met his own.

Teavar no longer looked bored.

Arnegern was stunned. The Outcast's son was a wonder! The crowd cheered feverishly. The performance was beyond his wildest hopes. No one had ever lasted this long against Teavar. The champion had actually been forced out of the ring! And the young challenger's last hit seemed particularly close to scoring a blood wound. The champion's chainmail shone like new where Vahldan's blade had gouged it. Teavar rotated his shoulder, checking it.

Best of all was the look in the challenger's eye. He believed he would win. Vahldan had never resembled his father more.

"No more toying with this pariah, Teavar," Desdrusan called. "Finish him!"

Teavar marched on Vahldan, glowering. The big man immediately initiated a blistering exchange of colossal blows, the clangs and thuds resounding through the commons.

Somehow Vahldan was able to parry, block, or slip away from each colossal strike. The younger man's eyes remained hard, but he was losing ground. Just as Arnegern's cousins had feared, the size difference between them began taking a toll. The challenger was quickly out of space, his back foot very near the tarp's edge as he labored to keep Teavar at bay.

As Vahldan absorbed yet another massive blow, the back edge of his heel slid off the mat. Desdrusan flung himself, pointing. "He's out! That's a fall!"

Teavar and Vahldan ignored him, their battle raging on. Vahldan managed to duck and slide to safety as the Lion Lord and his supporters railed over the infraction. Arnegern sensed Thadmeir's reluctance. It was such a minor slip. But the Wolf Lord stepped onto the tarp with hands high. "A second fall is charged to the challenger." The crowd booed.

The opponents halted and backed from one another, both glaring at Thadmeir. Teavar seemed as peeved as Vahldan over the petty call.

Angavar's son growled as he huffed for breath. "Put it aside, Vahldan," Icannes called. "Nothing has changed." He scowled her way in response. For the first time since the opening moments of the match, he looked rattled.

"Hear me?" It was the guardian. Vahldan's gaze snapped to her, his expression softening. "Good. This is it. Go all the way. I'm here!" He nodded, looking more assured again.

The opponents squared off again. Teavar tipped his head before raising his weapons. The Young Lion drew himself up and bowed his head in reply. Their expressions were still hard, but clearly they'd gained respect for one another.

Teavar leapt to the attack again. The result was similar. Vahldan was forced back to defense. More cautious of the edge now, he dancing laterally as he parried and shield-blocked. Teavar bellowed and stomped sideways to cut him off. Both competitors were winded, and Teavar's size and strength loomed as the decisive factor. Vahldan stumbled as he cross-blocked a roundhouse stroke. He barely deflected the blade as his right arm buckled, sending him to a knee.

Teavar was instantly over him, bringing the futhark blade down in a mighty chop. Still kneeling, Vahldan brandished Arnegern's shield. The impact's resound was the loudest yet. Arnegern cringed, hoping; the crowd gasped, expecting the shield to break.

But it didn't.

Teavar paused, and then yanked on his hilt. The deeply imbedded blade wouldn't budge. Vahldan roared and threw all of his weight against the shield and into a roll. The move surprised Teavar, wrenching the hilt from his grip.

Vahldan leapt to his feet and danced away. With his opponent's sword.

The challenger knocked the hilt on the ground to jar the blade loose. It fell to the tarp and Vahldan put his foot on it. All he had to do was kick it to his supporters. The crowd was in hysterics. The blood drained from Teavar's face. The big Rekkr grimly raised his shield, ready for the inevitable.

Vahldan stood scowling savagely, grunting as he caught his breath, calculating the finish.

"Come back to me." It was his guardian again. Vahldan glanced. The savage expression faded. "Hear me?" He nodded once. "Use it wisely. Stay above them. Be the better man. That's how you win. I'm with you." Vahldan's transformation was swift. In a few blinks, he seemed to have pulled himself from bloodthirsty wrath. He nodded again.

Then rather than kicking the weapon away, Vahldan called over the raucous crowd, "Step out and I'll return the blade!" The crowd quieted.

Teavar's brow furrowed. "I ask for no pity. I'll fight without it!"

"I came seeking honor. Would you deny me an honorable

victory? Take the fall. We can decide this as the gods intend. One fall or the blood of one of us on the tarp ends it, fairly."

Teavar squared his shoulders, raised his chin, and strode off the mat.

Desdrusan bellowed in unintelligible outrage, stalking the sidelines, waving his arms like a madman. Teavar stepped back on the tarp. Vahldan picked up the futhark blade. He paused, feeling the famous weapon's weight and balance. It had been in his family for generations, Angavar realized. Vahldan tossed it, hilt first, and Teavar deftly caught it. Before bringing his returned weapon to the ready, the giant solemnly bowed at the waist to his rival. Vahldan replied by dropping his chin to his chest, arms at his sides—a show of trust as well as respect.

They began again, both moving slowly. Vahldan managed to slide away from Teavar's sporadic lunges, and the giant shed the brunt of the few blows the younger man scored. Finally, Teavar unleashed another blistering attack. Vahldan was forced to the edge of the tarp again.

"Move! Clear out!" Icannes shouted. Her pupil was too busy fighting for his life to obey.

From behind Arnegern, a child's voice shrieked. He turned to find Vahldan's young sister in the arms of the younger brother. "Vahldan!" the girl cried. "Don't hurt him!" Their brother was trying to haul her away, but the girl wiggled and bawled. Arnegern had no idea where they'd come from. They hadn't been among the spectators before. The Skolani guardian ran to help.

It was too late. Vahldan's distraction was apparent. Teavar kept the blows coming. Vahldan tried to slip away, but he tripped on a crease in the hide and fell on his back. He had no choice but to shield-block the blow everyone knew was coming. *Thwack!*

Arnegern's shield could take no more. It fell into two.

"Now! End this!" Desdrusan shrieked.

Vahldan rolled, but Teavar was over him now, kicking him and trapping him between his massive legs. Teavar's next sword blow came down just as Vahldan's blade rose to cross-block. Metal clashed. Vahldan, flat on his back, just barely held the futhark blade from his grimacing face. It was all but over. The crowd went silent but for the weeping of the girl. Vahldan's guardian held her, but stood gaping in horror.

Both fighters grunted and hissed. Desdrusan shouted, "Finish him, you lummox!" Teavar pressed on the blade, but Arnegern sensed his rage had faded. It should've been over by now.

Abruptly Teavar leapt back, releasing his downed opponent from the mat. Vahldan scrambled to his feet, shaking the broken shield straps from his arm. Teavar retreated to the edge of the tarp. Desdrusan howled and ranted.

Lord Thadmeir stepped out between them, silencing the crowd. The opponents stood panting. Thadmeir turned to Teavar. "What's this, Teavar? Will you not strive to settle the trial?"

Teavar shook his head. "He lost his shield out of concern for the girl. It's clear to me that he is blessed by the gods. He's fought better than any man I have ever faced. He has shown me his honor, and the man who has me fighting in his place has shown that he has none. I no longer wish to fight the son of Angavar."

Thadmeir frowned and glanced at his qeins. Amaseila gave a single nod. "You wish to forfeit the match?" Thadmeir asked.

Teavar nodded. "I do."

"Even should it dishonor you?"

"I am dishonored already. I am left with only one worthy course."

"Not so!" Vahldan called. "You've done only as you were bidden. You've proven yourself more honorable than he who bid you. What if we both stepped out at once?" Vahldan turned to Thadmeir. "It would make it three falls apiece. That would be a draw, wouldn't it? Teavar can retain his honor, and I can seek another trial." Vahldan craned to glare at the far side of the tarp. "Maybe then my father's cousin would be forced to fight his own battles."

Thadmeir raised a hand to quiet the crowd and Desdrusan. "This has no precedent. If you both choose this path, the result would require deliberation. I cannot promise you another trial. You'd be placing your fate into the hands of the Rekkrs' council once again."

Vahldan turned to the Skolani. The princess's face was impassive but his guardian's face lit up. Arnegern was surprised when Vahldan next turned to the Priestess Amaseila.

Amaseila smiled slyly and gave him the slightest tilt of her head. She looked as if she'd known the outcome all along. Perhaps she had.

Vahldan moved to where his opponent could see his foot raised over the edge. Teavar did the same. At Vahldan's nod, they both stepped off the tarp. The crowd roared, a few in resentment but the vast majority in wild acclaim. Everyone there knew they'd witnessed the unfolding of a tale they would tell for the rest of their days.

The Skolani and his family rushed to Vahldan, with Arnegern, Belgar, and Herodes just behind. The first to get to Vahldan was his guardian. She took his sword and held his hand, and spoke softly to him, nose to nose. The young man actually smiled. He looked wholly transformed, like a new man. Clearly a special bond existed between them.

Teavar pushed his way to his opponent and the pair clasped forearms and bowed their heads together. Teavar also spoke softly to his rival. Vahldan nodded.

Arnegern felt eyes on him. He turned to find Desdrusan glowering. He looked away and sighed. Ah, so be it. This was a victory, for Arnegern and for Vahldan, as well as for the Amalus. Even the fat man couldn't spoil it. Vahldan had won a great deal of support.

And yet, Desdrusan could not be dismissed. He was still the lord of Arnegern's clan, and was still dangerous. And powerfully connected. Those who controlled the wool trade and grazing were unlikely to allow this upstart another opportunity to change the status quo.

Arnegern was finally able to step in to congratulate the victor. Vahldan turned to him and grinned, clasping his shoulder. Arnegern instantly felt a warm connection. The young man indeed had his father's magnetism. "It seems I owe you a shield... my friend."

He'd ended awkwardly, and Arnegern realized Vahldan didn't even know his name. "Think nothing of it, Vahldan, son of Angavar. Perhaps one day you'll come to see that it is I who owes you." He bowed his head. "Until that day, know that Arnegern, son of Vildigern of the Amalus, remains at your service."

CHAPTER 17—TOGETHER ALONE

"Many claims have been made regarding the two futhark swords of the Gottari. No few believe the blades magical, and that their magic can be wielded only by a rightful and worthy bearer. Claims of magic aside, it cannot be denied they are ancient and beautiful weapons. But their true worth lies in how they are revered by all.

All Gottari recognize them as the sacred symbols of their tribe's oldest oath, which is carved into the matching rings on their two hilts. No Gottari disputes that without the futhark inscribed upon them, their nation would not have survived, let alone thrived.

Nor would any Gottari dispute that forsaking the futhark is perilous, and likely a path to tragedy. This is the futhark's augur. Therein lies both the power of the swords and the inherent limit of that power."—Brin Bright Eyes, Saga of Dania

ELAN STOOD BACK from the family, trying not to interfere in their farewell. Eldavar stared sullenly as Vahldan lifted Mara over the backboard to set her on the bed of the loaded wagon. Alela then handed Mara her swaddled baby sister. Vahldan turned to face his little brother. The brothers stood staring at one another a long moment. It was clear neither of them knew what to say. Eldavar had wheedled and whined well into the prior evening, trying to avoid being sent away, to no avail.

Elan broke the tension by stepping up to slap Eldavar's shoulder. She moved to the back of the wagon, stooped, and laced her fingers, cradling her hands to offer his little brother a boost into the wagon. He and she had perfected the move while picking plums in the weeks before Vahldan's trial. Eldavar didn't move. "Ready, El?" she prompted with more cheer than she felt.

Rather than lifting his foot or calling her Eel in response to her nickname for him, as he'd come to do (which he usually thought to be hilarious), Eldavar shook his head. "It's not fair. You said we'd always stay together."

Gods, it made her heart hurt.

"We're still a family," Vahldan said. "I keep telling you that you're the man of the family now." Eldavar looked away, scowling. "I'm serious. I need you to do this. I need you to watch over our sisters. Can you do that for me? Please?"

Eldavar hung his head, but he finally nodded.

Elan dropped to a knee, took Eldavar's hand in hers, and gazed into his sad eyes. "Remember when I told you about my mother? How I carry a piece of her inside me, and how you will always do the same with yours?" He nodded. "Well, there's something else inside me now. I never had a brother—never really had any family since my mother. But now I feel like I have two. And two more sisters, too. There may be times when we're not in the same place, but we'll still have a piece of one another, here." She put her hand on his chest, and held his hand to hers. "So, in a way, we will stay together. Always." She smiled wryly. "Understood, El?"

The corners of Eldavar's mouth curled up. "Understood... Eel."

Elan huffed a laugh. "Good. In the meantime, I'll watch over him for you"—she jerked her head toward Vahldan—"if you watch over them for me." She nodded toward Mara, who was cradling Kemella. "Deal?"

"I guess so," he said, but his small smile faded as the reality of the bargain sank in.

She got to her feet and laced her fingers again. Eldavar stepped in her hands and she boosted him up to scramble into place next to Mara.

Elan felt torn, seeing her subjects split apart. And she resented that Icannes had left them here. Letting the children go left her unable to see to their safety, but leaving Vahldan was out of the question. She alone could see this through. The queen left no doubt: Vahldan was the core of her duty. There really wasn't a choice.

She stepped back to give Vahldan room to embrace his little sisters. He kissed Mara's cheek and then the top of Kemella's fuzzy head. Ever the quiet one, Mara looked sullen, too.

Gods, they looked so helpless, so young. Particularly Mara, who sat holding both her baby sister and her own baby doll. The juxtaposition said so much about how wrong things had gone. The image jarred a realization. "Oh, Horsella help me, I nearly forgot. Mara, you have to wait for me." The girl's face lit with curiosity. Elan dashed to the Amalus stables, found her gear and dug through her saddlebag.

She ran back along the mounted column of Amalus warriors, lined up ahead of the wagon. Elan proffered the stuffed horse doll to Mara. "I almost forgot about Neeha."

The girl accepted the horse reverently. It was clear that Mara held back tears. Elan put her hand to her chest. "You too. We'll always be together, right?"

"Always," Mara said, trying to sound brave.

Elan wanted to hug her, to stop the world, to try to talk Vahldan into changing his mind. How had it come to this? How had she come to feel so attached? What had happened to her? This wasn't supposed to happen to a warrior. She was acting like the nursemaid she'd sworn she would never become. She offered a stoic nod, but couldn't take her hand from her chest.

Arnegern's horse stepped up, and he reined in beside them. "Don't worry, they're in good hands. My parents will welcome them gladly. And my father has a dozen bannermen that answer to his call. Trust that they're safe at our homestead, come what may."

Vahldan suddenly looked as conflicted as Elan felt. "You're sure about this? Delivering them won't interfere with your orders?"

Arnegern glanced toward the longhouse, where Desdrusan's spies lurked in the shadows under the broad eaves. The young Rekkr lowered his voice. "We all know what my orders are about. He seeks to make you feel friendless and alone. Know that it isn't so. They can order us to ride, but they can't keep me from getting your family clear of the fat one's clutches."

Although the mustering Thadmeir had sanctioned was incomplete, Desdrusan had ordered Arnegern to lead the Amalus who were ready to ride to patrol the foothills southeast of Danihem. A wool guildsman had conveniently reported sighting yet another Spali raiding party. The order was clearly in retaliation for Arnegern's aid to Vahldan in the trial, but it was well-played, as no one could dispute the need to respond. Since the alleged sighting had occurred in a region not far beyond Arnegern's homestead, it offered an opportunity to secure Vahldan's family. Desdrusan had argued against the added stop, but Thadmeir had overruled his protests.

The Rekkrs' council that would decide Vahldan's fate would be without his new friend and many of the youngest and most ardent among his potential Amalus supporters. Many of the lions who remained had more to lose if they opposed the guild. From what Elan could tell, it seemed Vahldan would face a jury that was nearly as biased as the one his father had faced.

Arnegern leaned from the saddle. "Be careful tonight. I sense that the snares are set."

Vahldan frowned. "You'd think he'd watch his step. Desdrusan may have dodged our accusation, but he still hasn't offered an alibi."

"Desdrusan will do everything he can to make sure this remains about you rather than him. And he'll have support in that effort.

Don't underestimate him, Vahldan. He has powerful friends—friends who can reap favor from the beholden. The worst part of it is, our rotund lord fears you. Which makes him all the more dangerous." Arnegern reined his mount. "Until we meet again, my friend. Hopefully alongside the tarp for your next trial—this time facing the real villain. Farewell."

As Arnegern rode back to the head of the column, Alela stepped to the wagon bed. The nurse offered a pensive wave. It broke Elan's already fractured heart. Elan lunged to embrace her. Alela was taken aback, her arms trapped. Skolani normally refrained from such displays, but the impulse couldn't be denied. Elan simply had to hug someone.

Alela finally returned the embrace. "Be strong," the nurse said. "Your mother would be proud."

Elan released her and stepped back, banishing the threatening tears. Alela climbed into the wagon. Vahldan signaled, and a horn blew. The tower bell clanged in refrain as the procession set out. The ponies they'd won from the Spali trotted on a string behind the wagon.

Mara wouldn't look, kept her focus on Kemella. Eldavar's lips were pressed tight, but he managed a wave as they cleared the village gates. Within moments, they disappeared from view.

It was done. They were gone. She and Vahldan stood in silence, absorbing the shock of it.

Vahldan sighed and turned to the longhouse. "Well, tonight's the night," he said with exaggerated bravado. "An outcast lion forced to face a den of wolves."

"I don't mind wolves," Elan said, "but I hate snakes."

He forced a smile. "We'll just have to watch our step."

Although no one was near, Elan's words came as a whisper. "Don't do it."

"What?"

"Don't go tonight. You heard Arnegern. It's a trap."

Vahldan shook his head. "You know I have to."

"No, you don't. We could leave. We'd catch up with the kids. You already tried it their way. They'll do whatever it takes to be rid of you and your family. If we disappeared, they'd have it their way. And we'd be alive, and free."

"No. I have to try. I can't just run."

"You can. Many would say you've already restored your father's honor."

"It's about more than that."

"What, then? The sword?"

Vahldan shook his head. "The sword is part of it, but—"

"Another chance will come to win it back." He raised a brow. "Or you could just..."

"Just what?"

Elan looked off toward the southern mountains. "Just let it go."

His mouth smiled but his eyes frowned. "What's gotten into you?"

"Nothing. What do you mean?"

"A Blade-Wielder advising me to run from a fight? It's not like you."

It stung, made her flinch inwardly. But she instantly recognized that he had a point. Everything was changing. For so long they'd prepared for the trial. They'd gotten past it, but they still hadn't won. And sending the siblings away felt like a failure. He was all that was left of her duty, and she had no idea how to help him now. "I guess I'm not sure how to fight this way. A Blade-Wielder is honor-bound to duty. I'm not sure exactly what my duty is anymore."

Vahldan joined her in staring into the mountains. "It's funny." She glanced. "Wasn't that long ago that I wanted to leave. To let it all go, and run away. I didn't care about the sword. Or any of it." He gestured to indicate all of Danihem. "I wanted to go to the sea."

"The sea? Really?"

Vahldan shrugged. "Seemed like sailing away was the route to freedom."

"But...?" she prompted.

He faced her. "I've always been afraid of myself. Afraid of what was inside me. Afraid of becoming what I thought my father had become before me."

"Which was?"

"Angry. Full of hate. Not just willing to kill but wanting to." He looked off again. Elan waited. "I've wanted to kill. In the trial, and before. When we killed those Spali—I don't know whether I was more afraid of them or of what I would become. And it happened. I went to a place where all that mattered was killing. I lost myself in it, and almost got killed because of it. Hatred and bloodlust, they come too easy to me. Even though I didn't lose myself like that in the trial, I still wanted to kill Teavar when he lost his sword." He turned back to her. "But I didn't. And I know it was because of you. I faced what was inside me—used it, even. But I never completely lost myself, and I found my way back. Because of you, I took the most honorable path left to me."

Elan sensed it was true. Or at least that he believed it. "You asked what's gotten into me. Maybe that's it. I was terrified of the trial. But we made it through, and I felt like I helped—even if only a tiny bit. Maybe I'm hoping I can help find the way to get us clear of danger, and to keep our honor in the process. Maybe I'm kidding myself."

"I get it. I spent years avoiding facing up to this stuff." Vahldan looked back at the longhouse. "But I made a promise to my father. Told him I'd stay true to him, that I wouldn't let them get away with what they'd done. It fed my hatred. Which made me more afraid of myself, of what I might become. But I've come to see that leaving would be more than letting them get away with my father's murder. They'd be getting away with what they've done to my clan, what they've done to balance, to the futhark. I'd be letting them get away with what they're still doing to my people. The Gottari have been robbed of justice, same as my family has. We deserve better. And I'm at the center of it now. My people need me."

Elan knew he still blamed himself for his father's death. He thought that facing the council would make it right—that, even if he didn't prevail, standing up to them would somehow take away the guilt and the pain. That either dispensing vengeance or absorbing unjust punishment would provide relief. She had her doubts, but who was she to judge? She'd spent years telling everyone who'd listen that she wanted to become a Blade-Wielder to honor her mother. She knew she'd absorb plenty of unjust punishment. In hindsight, she had to admit that it was as much about proving herself worthy, and proving her detractors wrong, as it was about honor. She'd been seeking relief at any cost, same as he was now. "I see," was all she said.

Vahldan looked into her eyes, reading her. He sighed. "I see, too. You think there's more to it. And I suppose there is." He chuckled. "Funny, but you know all of the talk about my role in the prophecy?"

"That you're the Bringer?"

"Yeah, that." He hung his head. "Even if it's superstitious nonsense, none of it matters if I run. If I run, I throw away their belief. All I've ever done is disappoint everyone who believed in me. I feel like I finally earned the chance to change that."

That caught her. Elan thought of Hildeanna's host, how they all presumed her a fraud, that she had been selected as a healer and hadn't earned her spot. Elan had gone along with a shaky premise, just to earn a chance. She was still taking risks. Risks she'd hoped would change things for her, same as he was doing. And when she'd taken her most recent one, in the ravine with the Spali, he'd followed her. Without hesitation. In spite of the fears about himself that he'd just confessed.

"Well, I believe in you. And I'm far from disappointed."

Head still bowed, he peered up at her. "I know that. I do. And I stand corrected."

"I guess that settles it. If you're going, I'm going. You'll never stand alone. It's the only thing I can truly promise you." Elan extended her arm to him.

He rose into his shoulders, smiled, and they grasped forearms. "Together, then."

Vahldan paused at the longhouse door. He nodded and Elan pulled it open. Two Amalus thugs awaited him just inside the torch-lit chamber. Jhannas was one, but Teavar was no longer his counterpart. The new one was only slightly less intimidating. The crowded chamber fell to silence. "Blade," Jhannas said. Vahldan released the buckle to his sword belt and handed it to Elan. At the top of the aisle, Jhannas held up a halting hand to Elan. She could come no further. The pair escorted him, one at either elbow, through the parting sea of solemn faces.

He felt so alone. The thought made him look back over his shoulder. Elan nodded again. She had his back. Just as she had since before they actually met.

They headed up the aisle between the Rekkr's benches. Most of those seated on the sparsely filled Amalus side were solemn graybeards. The Wulthus side was packed to overflow. Younger wolves were lined up along the sidewall. At the front sat a trio of bored and ancient looking Elli-Frodeis—the Wise Ones who would ensure that this time whatever was decreed would be final.

They reached the dais and halted. As Elan had so aptly suggested, Desdrusan resembled a coiled snake, waiting to strike. The Lion Lord hefted himself from the dais chair, but the Wolf Lord remained seated. It seemed Thadmeir was ceding control of the hearing to Desdrusan.

Not good.

The reality of the situation shook him as never before. Vahldan was likely to have his banishment confirmed—this time with the very real threat of enslavement. His stomach flopped, and his hand sought the missing hilt. The fear he thought he'd left behind returned, swelling like a rising gorge. Vahldan scanned the crowd, searching for a bit of hope.

And he found it. In his guardian. His friend.

Elan had found a spot along the wall, alongside the back Amalus benches. She mouthed the word: *Kestrel*. Same as she had at his trial. He nodded in reply and reined in the fear.

Desdrusan's voice boomed. "This man makes a mockery of Gottari justice."

The Lion Lord looked out over the packed chamber. "This pariah dares to come before us yet again. I keep wondering, how is it that this... *outlaw* continues to elude justice? I assure you, my brothers, it's a flagrancy I intend to end this very night.

"I'm sure you all recall that this man is the son of a murderer. But I feel I must remind you that this was no commonplace killing. No, this was the murder of a fellow Rekkr, a brother in arms. But it was even worse than that.

"Our Wulthus brothers well remember how this murder stole away their rightful heir—a brilliant young warrior with a bright future ahead of him. Worse, it was committed by an Amalus chieftain—a heinous insult to the futhark itself. And for what? Ambition, greed, lust. By his monstrous act, this man's father spat on our laws."

The onlookers murmured. To Vahldan it sounded like mass concurrence. He hated hearing his parents slandered, but it was worse hearing such lies so willingly accepted. The churn in his belly began, and heat rose to his face—the ugliness making its presence known.

Desdrusan looked down on Vahldan. "Now the murderer's son shows himself to be as power-hungry as the father. Worse, he willfully embraces killing as a means to seizing it. Our laws are clear. The progeny of such weakness and savagery must be cut away, cleansing our bloodlines of their poison." Desdrusan drew the Amalus futhark sword. Bairtah-Urrin's blade flashed in the torchlight. "The Wulthus and Amalus are the two halves that complete the whole of our people. There can be no tolerance for bloodshed between us."

Vahldan almost laughed at the irony. The gods only knew the extent of the bloodletting this man had set in motion.

Desdrusan pointed the famous blade at Vahldan. "Behold, here stands the progeny of the murderer who stained this precious relic, thereby staining our most sacred oath!" The words echoed in his pause. Any amusement Vahldan had felt fled, and the heat in his belly rose to his cheeks. "The Outcast's son has already been granted a trial, against the wishes of many. By manipulating the outcome he not only spat upon our customs, he insulted the gods. Now he comes begging again. His bloodthirst cannot be quenched. For the sake of our laws—indeed, for the sake of all we hold sacred, we must join our voices. Tell him nay! The gods are already displeased. We cannot afford to insult Them again."

The Lion Lord raised the blade. "What say you, my brothers?"

Vahldan tensed, waiting for the overwhelming verdict against him. Instead, only a few distinct voices rang out in agreement amongst a tepid chorus of discontent.

A deep voice boomed over the crowd noise. "Let us hear from the accused if we are to judge him." Vahldan glanced back. There among the Amalus Rekkrs sat Teavar. The crowd grew silent. "Does not the law you claim to hold so dear demand it?"

Desdrusan swung his razor glare to his former guardian. Someone from the crowd shouted, "Yes, let him speak." A furor erupted in response, even among the Wulthus.

Lord Thadmeir stood and the chamber fell silent. The Wolf Lord indicated the Elli-Frodeis. "I bid the Wise Ones to address the right of the accused to speak."

The one in the center looked as if he'd just awoken. The other two bent their wizened faces in triad, occasionally shooting Vahldan an irritated glance as they spoke.

The youngest looking of the three stood. His hair and beard were white, but he stood bolt upright. "It matters not whether his trial was an affront or a clever tactic. It cannot be altered that he was offered the chance to petition the council. It's not only in accordance with the law to hear him, it's absurd to imagine holding a hearing that refuses to hear the petitioner." The man smiled wryly. "Having said that, I believe it would behoove you, Young Lion, to explain why you sought to manipulate the Ananth-jahn. And why, having done so, you think yourself deserving of yet another. It's said that you held the victory in your hands, and yet you cast aside the gods-given favor."

Vahldan turned to face the chamber. He paused to collect himself, to push down the fluttering ugliness. "It wasn't favor I sought, but honor. I meant not to cast aside the gods' grace, but to embrace it. For isn't it by Their grace that we are able to sort honor from disgrace? Isn't that what separates men from beasts? I rejected the impulse to spill the blood of a weaponless man. To me, it seemed the most honorable course."

"If only the father had chosen such a course!"

Vahldan didn't see who called out, but the quip came from the Wulthus side, initiating a chorus of acclaim and jeering in response.

He shouted over the din, "Teavar granted me what no one granted my father!" The statement caught the curious ear of enough of them that the uproar faded.

The Elli-Frodei said, "Pray tell, Young Lion, what was that?"

"A fair and honorable chance. Teavar offered me the sort of justice that is still withheld from my family. He offered me a choice. For my father's course of action was not chosen by him that fateful night. It was cleverly devised by another, manipulating his actions. The scheme to steal away my father's choice also stole justice away that night—from him and from his victim."

"From his victim?" The Elli-Frodei frowned in puzzlement.

"That's right. Justice has been stolen from Aomeir, too. For the real villain behind his death was never unmasked, and remains unpunished."

The furor rose anew. Vahldan had incited more wolves than ever. Again Vahldan shouted over them. "I was not there that night. Nor were most of you. Indeed, the only one I'm certain about is him!" He pointed at Desdrusan. "Besides my parents, only Desdrusan and his allies witnessed Aomeir's death. How convenient, that tragedy turned out to be so rewarding to those few who witnessed it. And one particular witness has since reaped the greatest reward of all."

The crowd quieted to low grumbling. He went on, "Most of you know that my father claimed that Aomeir was stabbed by accident. He claimed Aomeir was in a drunken rage, and as far as my parents could ever discover, no one has disputed that the Young Wolf had been drinking all that day. At his so-called trial, my mother was not allowed to speak. It was left to others to tell of how she and Aomeir had argued that day, right here in this very longhouse. Others were willing to say that my mother had confessed her shame to her betrothed. If she had been allowed to speak, she would have admitted to her confession, and told of its nature—that she and my father had fallen in love. She also would have told of her forceful denial of Aomeir's accusations of infidelity. She would've told of Aomeir's threat—that if she could not make an end of her feelings, he would.

"No one even bothered to dispute that my father had been attacked. Angavar had been left with no choice but to defend himself. Many hold to a belief that what happened was no accident. I agree. How can something so perfectly schemed be called an accident? One thing I can tell you that you may not know is that to his dying day, my father regretted that he'd been duped. He regretted it not just because he was banished, but because of the loss of Aomeir's life. He regretted it because of the harm, the division and decay, that came of it for our people."

Vahldan turned to Thadmeir. "And yet, he was never given the chance to express his regret to you or to your father. He was sentenced, bound, and hauled away before Aomeir's body had even lost its warmth. All I ask this day is the honorable chance Angavar never received."

He looked to the giant, sitting in the crowd. "And I believe that Teavar, in his gods-given ability to sort honor from disgrace, offered justice in giving me that chance. I can only pray that there are others who share that ability." Teavar solemnly inclined his head.

Vahldan fell to his knees before the Wolf Lord. "Lord Thadmeir, as I am accorded the right to speak, I would use my words to appeal to you—to extend my father's regret, and my family's condolences." He hurried on before Desdrusan could intervene. "For I have been made to better understand. I now share your father's and your grief, having had my parents snatched away too soon. Grief's shadow has laid between our families for too long. The dead are still dead, and the past cannot be undone. The futhark has been cast aside, but not by us. We have been deceived and used. Let us find our way back to the honor for which the futhark stands."

Thadmeir stroked his beard, eyes staring but distant. Desdrusan looked like a boil on the verge of bursting. "My lord," Desdrusan began. "This is beyond—"

"There can be no balance," Vahldan interjected. "Not with him. Surely you can see how wrong it's gone. The power to restore it can be yours, Lord Thadmeir. Take it back."

"Oh please!" Desdrusan sharply intoned.

The ugliness and the fear had been swept aside. The forge flared but his head was clear. Thunar's Blessing thrummed through him. His voice rose. "You know the good men of Dania will follow your lead." Cheers of support now rang out. Vahldan stood and pointed to Desdrusan. "Grant me a trial against the source of our shared grievance. Bid this man to fight his own battles, and let the gods resolve it, as our forefathers intended." *'I won't let them get away with it!'*

"You see?" Desdrusan whined. "Look at him. His bloodlust is in full view. He not only seeks to supplant me, he wants to murder me, too. I implore you to remove this poisonous evil from our midst."

Vahldan banked the fire within and forced a smile. "You, of all people, dare name me the source of evil here? How about we let the gods decide that?"

"Stop it, both of you," Thadmeir scolded. Vahldan bowed his head, fearing he'd pushed too far. He glanced to find what could only be hatred in the Wolf Lord's eyes, hard upon him. "I grant you this, Vahldan, son of Angavar. Grief has long weighed upon my feelings for your family. And time has only made grief fester—moldering it to rancor."

Gods, he really had pushed too far.

The Wolf Lord drew a deep breath and sat back, staring. His gaze lost its intensity. He began to look more sad than angry. Unfortunately, his sadness didn't seem like a basis for hope.

This was it. Either Vahldan would get a chance to make things right, or—more likely—he'd fail his parents yet again. He looked to Elan. She gestured with her hand on his sword belt, slung over her shoulder, her brows raised. He discretely shook his head. He wouldn't allow her to risk herself. In spite of the thrum of Thunar's Blessing, any bloodshed that came of an attempt to escape would only prove Desdrusan's point. Undoubtedly it would make things worse. He had to let things play out, maintain his honor and hold to hope.

Just as the Wolf Lord opened his mouth, the muffled clang of the gatehouse bell intervened. The councilmen stirred. Paired tolls followed by a lone one. "A messenger. At this time of night?" Thadmeir almost sounded relieved to be interrupted.

"It can have no bearing on this," Desdrusan growled. "The boy has had his chance to speak. He used it to insult us both. He's not just an outlaw, he's a stain on the futhark. You have but to wipe it away, my lord. Make a decree. Call for a vote. Let's have done with this."

In the expectant silence of the chamber, galloping hooves and excited calls could be heard from outside. Everyone turned as the door burst open and a guard appeared. "The Skolani princess, my lord. She wishes to—"

"It's war!" Icannes shouldered past the guard, boots thumping as she strode toward the dais. "It can be avoided no longer, my brothers. The time to stand and fight for Dania has come!"

CHAPTER 18—THE MAKINGS OF WAR

" Strong the Gottari and Skolani alliance may be. But it has been and remains a rarity for the two tribes to march to war together. The Skolani have mostly spurned foreign warfare. The Blade-Wielders' focus has ever been upon securing the borders and safeguarding the realm. But when the warhorn blows, ever have both peoples ridden to the other's side.

Such has it long been. May it ever be so."—Brin Bright Eyes, Saga of Dania

ELAN STARTED MOVING, taking small, furtive steps toward the dais, every muscle tense. She hated feeling helpless. She refused to be. She refused to plead to the gods, too. Any solution the gods might bestow would only provide another opportunity to toy with her.

Before she and Vahldan had set foot in the longhouse, she'd made her decision. She would not abandon him. She would take action. She would rescue him, or die trying.

If he died, she died. That was the essence of her duty. He'd waved her off, but she would not accept merely waiting or hoping. She scanned the longhouse, planning what she'd do if Desdrusan's giants seized him or bound him, or... Gods, it was looking as though taking action would be the only way. The time to decide was upon her.

At the height of her increasingly frantic planning, the gatehouse bell rang. And Icannes appeared. Elan flopped back against the wall, sighing.

Icannes swept down the aisle, scanning the audience. Many bowed their heads. Her near-sister always made the most of an entrance. Elan's gaze alighted on the guardians striding at Icannes's shoulders. One was Kukida, as expected. The other instantly flipped her relief to ire.

Anallya wore a satisfied smirk. How could Icannes bring the blood-bitch here?

Icannes arrived before the dais. Thadmeir spoke up. "War, you say? How is it you've come upon such dire tidings and brought them back so soon?"

"My lords, my guardian and I met our kinswomen on our return journey—Blade-Wielders sent with a warning and a plea from the queen herself to her Gottari brothers. And knowing of your gathering here this night, I chose to hurry back with them, riding through much of last night and on through the day."

"You have our thanks. Please, share all you bring." The Wolf Lord seemed suspicious.

Icannes faced the chamber. "What many long feared has been confirmed. Skolani scouts report from beyond the border. The whole of the Spali nation masses in the east. The Paralatoe gather their people's warriors in Afletam Forest. Behind them, their women, children and elders form an ever growing encampment, strewn across the plains of Oium. Day by day, the warriors' numbers surge. It can mean only one thing. They intend to strike west. They seek to claim a foothold in our homeland. The movement of their entire nation makes their purpose clear. The Spali intend to claim all of Dania as their own. This, my brothers, is an invasion."

The murmur was anxious. Icannes raised her voice. "Even as I speak, the queen moves to counter them. My mother has established a camp on the Danian side of the ford at the confluence. She gathers her Blade-Wielders there, but knows we are not enough. She beseeches our brothers to ride out to join her. The foe must be kept from crossing the river. Every Danian warrior is needed—indeed, every able body that can stand and hold a spear or release a bowshot should join us. Come east that we Danians might be the first to strike. With a mighty Gottari army beside us, the queen is confident we can deliver the blow that will save our homeland."

Desdrusan stammered, "She...the queen intends to march forth from Dania? Into those haunted forests and swamps?"

One brow raised, Icannes offered the Lion Lord a curt nod.

Hloed, a man Elan had come to know as not just a wool guildsman but a meddler, cried, "But what of the Seven Sons? Long have their spirits stood vigil. Crossing over to that accursed shore is forbidden. It is a matter of faith!"

Icannes huffed a belittling laugh. "You speak of ghost tales at a time like this? If you wish to speak of faith, you may have faith in the fact that Spali savagery is no tale. Have faith that more than ghosts will be needed to keep this evil at bay. It will require keen blades and stout hearts. But you may also have faith as I do, that marching together, the Skolani and Gottari cannot be made to know defeat!"

The longhouse roared in support. Her voice rose above them. "Now, my brave brothers, how will you answer the queen's call?"

Those still seated leapt to their feet, fists pumping and boots stomping. The ovation made Elan's ears ring and her heart sing. The Gottari had been roused to war. Elan cheered, too, although she was unsure what it meant for Vahldan. She craned to find Desdrusan glaring at him.

The cheering receded to excited cross talk. The Lion Lord banged an empty cup on the arm of his chair until he could be heard. Desdrusan turned to Thadmeir. "It is rightful that we are resolved to defend Dania. But it's no excuse to leave tonight's business to fester as it long has with the Outcast. I demand resolution, my lord. Will you not make a decree, and call for a vote? Should we not put a lance to this swelling boil before we march to war?"

Thadmeir looked down on Vahldan, his eyes filling with an unreadable hollowness. Everyone around Elan remained standing. She slung his sword belt over her shoulder and discreetly threaded her way through the benches. It was time to stand at his side.

Icannes boldly spoke up. "In light of what's come, Lord Thadmeir, it goes without saying that every sword will be needed in the days ahead. Nor can it be denied that young Vahldan is talented with a blade. I suggest putting him at the fore of the fighting, where the gods are sure to be pleased by the chance to judge him. For myself, I would gladly have him at my side in battle. Turn him over to me and I assure you he'll face the worst the foe has to offer. Should he survive, his judgement will have only been delayed."

Elan arrived at his side. Vahldan glanced, then looked again. She read his relief. And that he teetered on the edge of imbuement. She slipped her hand into his and he gripped it. Her presence would keep him grounded. She felt Anallya's glare on her back. She didn't care. He needed her, and she was here for him.

Thadmeir's face was stern. He seemed to have aged years in mere moments. "So be it. Vahldan, son of Angavar, you are remitted to the service of your clan for the coming war. If you choose to disobey, or to flee, your banishment is confirmed." Thadmeir rounded on his counterpart. "Until Dania prevails, I'm certain you'll offer him the chance to serve his people."

Desdrusan puckered like he'd bitten a sour cherry. Then suddenly his eyes brightened. "Perhaps the princess has the right of it. Put him at the fore, chained in the Penance Line."

Thadmeir shook his head. "No, he will fight beside us, unfettered. His fate will await our victorious return to Danihem." The fat man glowered but did not argue.

The Wolf Lord turned back to Vahldan. "Till then, Lord

Desdrusan will leave aside his contentions, as you must, too. Do you swear to it?"

Vahldan bowed his head. "In the name of Dania's safety, I swear it."

Thadmeir narrowed his eyes. "This is your chance, boy. Prove me wrong."

"Wrong?"

"Prove that you've risen above the depths your father sank to. That you're above vainglory and ambition. You say you want what's rightful, that you sincerely seek balance. Prove it. Prove that there is still honor and valor in the blood of our Gottari lions."

Vahldan grimaced and looked down. "Thank you for the chance," he managed.

Thadmeir's expression softened. "Serve our people well, Vahldan. With the gods' guidance, a just end will come of this."

Elan beamed. To her it sounded like concession. The Wolf Lord allowed for the possibility of Vahldan's return to his rightful status. He'd all but said it.

The Lion Lord ranted and the excited Rekkrs blustered, but Elan didn't hear a word of it. The commotion around her became a blur. They'd been offered a chance. It was all they needed. She gave his hand a squeeze, and he smiled.

A strong hand gripped her shoulder. Icannes's voice was in her ear. "Follow me out, both of you." She held Vahldan's shoulder as well.

"Out? Where?" he asked.

Icannes eyed the arguing lords. "No time to explain. Quickly now, before we're noticed."

VAHLDAN WALKED in a daze behind Icannes, her fierce companions parting the crowd, swiftly leading them to the longhouse exit. Everything felt so unsettled. At least Elan was with him. The tidings of war had captivated the Rekkrs, and few took notice of their leaving. Until Teavar appeared before them, grinning. "This time we fight together, my brother. Side by side."

Vahldan couldn't keep from grinning back. "Pretty sure I'll like it better that way."

The giant laughed and Icannes snatched Vahldan's wrist and pulled him on. A moment later they were out. The cool air offered reprieve. "Put this on," Elan said, handing him his sword belt. "Pretty sure I'll like it better that way."

He buckled it on as they hurried after the Blade-Wielders, briskly striding toward the Amalus stables. A Blade-Wielder he didn't recognize stood guard at the doorway. Icannes swept past the sentinel, her two companions peeling off to join the guard. Vahldan and Elan followed Icannes down the lamp-lit corridor. A cloaked and hooded figure leaned on a saddle atop a bale, sharpening a naked blade.

The figure turned to their approach, face in shadow, fist gripping the blade. "By the gods." The voice was deep but warm, smooth as honey. And familiar. "Look at you, Vahldan. A man grown." A chuckle issued from the hood as the man sheathed the blade.

"There won't be much time," Icannes said. "The fat one was still wheedling and whining, but it won't be long before he notices Vahldan's disappearance."

"Do you know me, boy?" The man drew back his hood, revealing the great golden beard, as wavy as his gray-streaked mop of hair and split by a grin.

Relief flowed through him. "Of course."

"Master Badagis!" Elan sounded as surprised as Vahldan felt. "We were worried, what with all of the Spali, and hearing that you weren't at your homestead."

"Not to fret, Blade-Wielder. The Spali had nothing to do with it. I merely moved to a new homestead, and had yet to inform my queen of it. Did we arrive in time, my princess?"

"We did," Icannes replied. "Vahldan's judgement has been deferred. He's free to fight."

"Ah, perfect. Just as we hoped." Badagis's delight was evident.

Vahldan tried to make sense of it all. "In time? What's happening?"

Badagis gripped Vahldan's shoulder. "When your father didn't show by the solstice, I went to the queen. I heard. I'm sorry, son."

Vahldan nodded, swallowing back the sorrow that instantly resurfaced.

"Your father was a great man. And my truest friend. Trust that my loyalty now falls to you." Angavar's voice rang in memory. *'Gods, what will come of us if us if this falls to you?'*

"I'm honored." But Vahldan still didn't understand what was happening. Or what good Badagis's loyalty was to him now.

Badagis's brow furrowed. "Why didn't you come to me, son? Surely your father bid you to, didn't he?"

"My mother," Vahldan began. He swallowed past the lump in his throat. Badagis expression grew pained. He knew of her death, too. And likely knew of her distrust of him. Best leave that alone. "And then the queen said you'd left. And, well, it all happened so fast."

Badagis squeezed his shoulder. "No matter, then. We're together now. And just in time. You must come with me."

"Come with you? I just swore to serve my clan in war."

"You'll do just that. But first we must leave. You too, Blade-Wielder." Badagis nodded at Elan. "Quickly. Before that blusterous barrel of lord-lard learns I was here, or that you're gone."

"Where? Why?" Vahldan wondered if he could trust the man. Would doing so make things worse?

"You're coming to my new homestead. I have something to show you." Badagis grinned again. "Believe me, son. It'll change everything."

THADMEIR SLUMPED in the dais chair, staring at the disheveled longhouse chamber floor—as annoyingly jumbled as his thoughts.

Benches were askew, and disgusting half-empty cups were abandoned everywhere. The longhouse smelled of mead, sweat, and bad breath.

Thankfully Desdrusan had ceased his whining about the Outcast's son and left. And yet disorder still reined. A handful of warmongers still toasted and sang at the center hearth. It didn't seem to bother the dozens who'd already bedded down for the night. At least the plans for a full mustering had been laid. Riders would set out at dawn to spread the word. Indeed, several had left already. The nation would rally to this cause, he knew. There was nothing left to say or do.

Still Thadmeir sat, rehashing it. The world had tilted. The night was supposed to have come to a simple decree and call for consensus. How had Desdrusan muffed it? How had the boy's fate ended up back in Thadmeir's hands? When it came back to him, why hadn't he simply reaffirmed Vahldan's banishment? Had he betrayed his father, his brother's memory? Why did Angavar continue to haunt his life? Now he'd be riding to war beside the Outcast's son. The son who supposedly fit the prophecy that foretold the coming war. Damn the man's ghost!

Thadmeir longed to set things straight—the disheveled chamber and so much more. Freya's grace, it was well past time to let it go. At least for the night. He rose and shuffled to the residence.

He parted the drapes, and there she stood, smiling. Thadmeir briefly wondered how she could've known when he would come to her. He quickly dismissed it. He'd sworn off wondering over her mysteries.

Amaseila beamed, as carefree as a herdsman's wife welcoming him home from the pasture for supper. Her hands rested on the swell of her belly. Her pallid face glowed with the light of the new life inside her. She offered such comfort. He couldn't have imagined it when he first saw her oddly pale eyes, but he found tranquility in them.

She was his home now.

Amaseila enveloped him in warmth. Her touch, her scent, eased the fret from his mind. She guided him down onto the cushions, put a warm cup in his hand, and slid behind him as he sipped her mulled wine. She massaged his shoulders with healing fingertips.

"You heard?"

"I heard," she said. "But I needn't have. The session only confirmed what we already knew. Surely you weren't surprised?"

Thadmeir took a long pull, swallowed, and sighed. She wanted him to believe in her. He believed that she believed, at least. And he was coming to accept that some things couldn't be explained. Or controlled. "Believing in the seer does not make the prophecy's fruition any less alarming, my love. Knowing of war beforehand hasn't made me less terrified by its arrival. Let alone the rest of it, with the boy."

"Oh, it's not so gloomy as that. There is glory and joy to come, as well."

He smiled over his shoulder and grasped a massaging hand. "Never mind me. I'm just tired. And disappointed."

"Disappointed? What about our daughter? What about your grandson's ascent?"

His innards twisted. Freya's mercy, he found it unsettling when she mentioned the unborn children—both his and Vahldan's. He simply would not accept her foretelling of Angavar's offspring being destined to defile his own. As always, he batted it away. "I'm just disappointed that it must come to this. People will suffer. Many will die."

"As they always do." She leaned to kiss his cheek. "I know it hurts you. You have a kind heart, darling. But even you must set kindness aside. Destiny beckons. Tomorrow the Urrinan begins its ride, at last."

Thadmeir shook his head. "The Urrinan. All my life, the wise and the holy who came to the longhouse spoke of the prophecy bringing glorious exultation. The Urrinan was supposed to raise the Gottari people up, not sully and slaughter us. It's almost impossible to imagine that glory could come of these sordid affairs."

"All the more glorious, for its humble and human beginnings." Amaseila twirled a finger in his hair, sending a shiver through him. "Come now. Let it trouble you no more. Rest your weary mind, my love."

"Ah, but if only it were so easy. My mind won't stop, no matter how weary I am. I can't stop wondering if I should've condemned him, had him taken away. If doing so even now might change things."

His qeins shook her head. "I think you know the answer. You have done as it has been ordained. A decision about his trial is moot. For the Spali have arrived. The Fierce Daughter is right: Dania needs him. He is the true lion, the Bringer. Sending him away would only serve to steal hope. Worse, it might rob Urrinan of its steed. There really never was much choice."

Gods have mercy, the bedamned prophecy. Thadmeir sometimes felt as if the Urrinan had been devised merely to steal their freewill. "Perhaps that's why I'm so tired. Tired of having fate thrust upon me again and again. Tired of accepting the meddling advice of a brash Skolani princess. Tired of being made to remember. Tired of having it all dragged back into the light of day, reeking and foul, for all to reexamine. Tired of—"

"Of finally sensing the truth of what comes? Of being made to see that your brother's death was not in vain? Of finding you have sympathy for the Young Lion?"

Thadmeir dropped his chin to his chest. He'd known it on the day that Amaseila had come before him. He felt it in the air, in his heart. Something special was happening, and Amaseila was central to it. And yet Thadmeir resisted giving himself over to belief. Wasn't she simply clever and perceptive? Didn't she simply imagine her divine connection? But here they were, bound in Freya's Blessing, just as she'd said they would be. War had come, just as she'd said. And Angavar's son had not only arrived in Danihem, he'd survived nigh impossible odds to ride and fight among his people. Just as she'd said.

Thadmeir wasn't sure how to keep his denial alive, but he knew he still needed it.

He gave her a nod of surrender. "Tired of my qeins always being right."

Still stroking his shoulders, his qeins pressed her soft breasts and the taut swell of her belly against his back. He closed his eyes, relishing the warmth of the contact. Her voice fell to a soothing hum. "You are tired now. But you are also honorable and wise. You, my mighty lord and husband, will always do what's best for your people, even should it pain you to do so. You are their tower of stone. Everything that was done this night was rightful. Most will openly say it's so. And the rest know it, or will come to know it—and soon. This is it. The time has come."

Thadmeir drained the cup, set it aside, and laid back. Amaseila nestled into the crook of his arm, curling against him. He chuckled. "How can I have been so blessed? I feel like we've known each other a lifetime."

Her voice fell to a whisper. "Even longer. Our souls have dwelt together since time immortal, and will do so long after these bodies are returned to the soil. Now rest, my lord, my love. Rest." He closed his eyes, and felt himself drifting. "Dream of our daughter, as I do."

His eyes sprang wide. Sleep suddenly lost its appeal. The night was half gone. Perhaps he'd just stay awake until the dawn. For if he slept, he might dream. If he dreamt, it would now likely be of his daughter.

And his dreams of his daughter were always troubling, full of bright fire and red blood. In them, his fierce daughter bound him to a terrible and inexorable fate.

CHAPTER 19—
REVELATIONS OF THE
BLOOD

"**M**any who knew her say that Angavar's Aunt Hanalda ever resented Angavar's ascent. After Lord Beremund had three daughters, the Amalus chieftain's first and only son, Angavar, finally arrived. But Angavar had been a sickly infant, and few thought he would survive. That Beremund's younger sister Hanalda then chose to bond with a first cousin—their uncle's first-born son Desamund—betrays her desire to produce a prince of the blood who could supplant her weak nephew. Many say her son Desdrusan was coddled so that he might be the healthier of the two boys when the time came for an Amalus heir to ascend.

Yet Angavar surprised them all, swiftly growing not only hale but fit and tall, renowned as a warrior by the summer he claimed his name. Some say Hanalda nourished not only her son's hearty appetite, but his bitterness and insatiable craving for power."—Brin Bright Eyes, Saga of Dania

They crested the last ridge, and Vahldan whispered, "Gods be good."

When Vahldan was a boy, he'd visited Badagis's previous homestead. That place was nothing like this. It'd been little more than a decrepit cabin and a slumping stable.

This place was more than a homestead. It was a bustling settlement, sprawling across an entire valley. It had a series of fenced meadows, dotted with oaks and scattered with shaggy goats. Cabins lined the eastern edge, sheltered by tall pines. Down the wide lane from the cabins to the base of the valley stood wooden structures, surrounded by at least a dozen pavilions.

The log structure at the center seemed nearly as large as the longhouse of Danihem. A crimson banner flew from the projecting ridgepole, adorned with the roaring lion of the Amalus.

Even more astonishing, the entire vale was filled with people! Women at cookfires, men stitching leather, and boys sparring. There was even a pair of smiths working over a forge.

"Who in the nine realms...?" Vahldan muttered.

"They're your kinfolk," Badagis said, reining to his side.

"My kinfolk?"

"Well, they're mostly kin. Some are only distantly related. Many take great pains to trace the lineage. Ah, but it doesn't matter if they're truly of the blood. Those who stretch to claim an Amalus pedigree are no less welcome here."

Of the blood? "But how did this happen? Why are they here?"

"They're here because they believe in you," Badagis said.

"In me? They don't even know me?"

Badagis laughed. "Maybe it's better to say they believed in your father. But the reasons that they came, and that they stay and work, go beyond belief in one man. They believe in the Amalus clan. They believe in our cause. Yes, many of them hope there is truth to the prophecy. But whether they think the Urrinan is upon us or not, they're each certain Dania's leaders have lost their way. All of us here want to make things right, same as your father wanted." Badagis raised a brow. "As you shall."

"Me?" Vahldan squeaked. "How can I make things right? It hasn't been decided whether I'm still an exile or not."

"That's not for anyone else to decide, son," Badagis said.

"Tell that to the current lords and the guild they serve."

"Believe me, we intend to." Badagis grinned. "Or maybe I should say that we'll show them."

Elan shaded her eyes, scanning the vale. "I see why you claimed this will change things." She almost sounded perturbed. She'd been in a foul mood since setting out from Danihem. Vahldan suspected it had to do with Anallya, who left their party with Icannes the prior day, heading directly to the queen's mustering.

Badagis laughed again. "Oh-ho! You think you see, do you? There is more than what meets even your keen eye, Blade-Wielder. Much more. Come and see."

The big man kicked his mount to a downhill gallop. The others followed. A bell clanged in greeting and faces turned to their arrival. Vahldan had never seen so many smiles. Children ran and called in excited voices. "He's come! He's here, he's here!"

Elan rode beside him though the growing commotion. He felt her watching him. "You know they're talking about you, right?"

It startled him. He'd presumed they were excited to see Badagis, just as he himself always had been as a boy. "Oh," was all he managed, heat rushing to his cheeks.

Elan smiled. It seemed like the first time in days. "Must feel odd. Strangers and yet kin."

"Odd is putting it mildly."

Badagis led them to the largest building. Expectant faces lined the path, with more coming. Some hailed Vahldan like an old friend while others bowed their heads reverently.

It was disconcerting. Their anticipation was palpable. They were expecting a younger version of his father. How could he live up to that? At the base of the hill, he waved and they cheered. Gods, it was worse than he thought.

Badagis dismounted outside the closed double door. From the corner of his eye, Vahldan was startled to glimpse his father's disappointed expression. Again, his head snapped around, this time to find a more wizened version of Angavar's stern face framed by graying hair and beard. Instinctively Vahldan straightened in the saddle. The man offered a solemn nod and took the reins of Badagis's mount, caressing the stallion's nose and making shushing sounds.

"Vahldan, this is your father's uncle, Lefric."

Vahldan dismounted and bowed. "Greetings, Uncle."

Lefric replied with a slight tilt of the head. "Well met," he offered stiffly.

Badagis went to the doors and thumped a pattern. "Lefric is your grandfather's youngest brother. For many years he was the Amalus stable master in Danihem. He's played a vital role in what you're about to see."

With a clank and a whoosh, the doors opened. At either door stood two grinning young men. "Behold the Bringer," one exclaimed. "Welcome to your host's cache, my lord," said the other, and they both bowed.

"He's not our lord quite yet," Badagis said, stepping past the pair and beckoning the group to follow. "Best not get used to saying it too early. It's bound to rile the wrong ears." Badagis put a hand on the shoulder of the one who'd spoken. "Vahldan, meet your cousin Belgar. He is the eldest son of your Aunt Jovanna."

"I'm eager to serve you, Cousin," Belgar said with another quick bow.

"And this is your cousin Herodes, who is the only son of your Aunt Brunella."

"Eager to serve, Cousin."

"I have seen you both before," Vahldan said.

"You have," Belgar confirmed. "At your trial. We were with Arnegern, who gifted you the hauberk." He pointed at Vahldan's mail armor. "As well as the shield that trapped Teavar's blade. Arnegern is also my cousin; his father is the brother of mine."

"They were fine gifts. I owe him my life. But I fear he's paying a price for giving them."

"It's true, Arnegern suffers the wrath of the usurper. But we've gotten word that he rides to meet us here. He and his host will join us on the ride to the mustering."

"Enough of this cousin talk," Badagis bellowed, moving farther inside. "My head spins. Well enough to know we're all of common cause. Now, come and see."

Badagis led them down a partitioned corridor. Vahldan's eyes continued to adjust. The space smelled of horses and leather. There was straw underfoot. "A stable?"

"In part," Badagis said.

"Master Lefric has delivered some of the finest warhorse stock I've seen," Belgar added.

"But there's also this." Badagis threw back a roughspun drape, revealing a long chamber lined with racks. The racks were filled with scores of spears, bows and quivers, and dozens of swords. Belgar strode past the chamber to yank open another drape. "And this." The next chamber was filled with chests and shelves full of warriors' gear of every sort. Hauberks and helms, grieves and gauntlets, saddles and tack.

"By Horsella's blade," Elan murmured beside Vahldan.

He was still trying to process it all when Badagis slapped his back. "Your host will be the best equipped in the whole of the Danian army. And we have your father to thank for it."

"My father?"

"Of course! It's all his doing. He even helped Lefric and I to raise this barn. Did you think all of your years of toil in the mine went for naught?"

"I did, actually. All we found were little nuggets. Nothing like the veins of gold that Carpan bastard promised. Father said it was only enough for supplies."

"Well, here are the supplies those little nuggets bought. Shows how things add up for those who practice patience, eh?"

"But... he never said a word." The weight of it pushed down on him, causing a slight stirring of the ugliness. His father had planned that far ahead? Hadn't he trusted Vahldan enough to tell him?

"Of course not. Not even to your mother. He knew she'd worry. And it was all so fragile, such a risk. Very few knew, and those few were sworn to secrecy. We only started to spread the word after we heard that Desdrusan had initiated his hunt. Your father knew facing his enemies could be put off no longer. It was time to put all of our plans into action. He was going to ride to the solstice session of the council at the head of his host, to claim his right to trial. Most of us thought we'd missed that chance. I'm sure Desdrusan thought he'd won, the murderous snake. But as it turns out, the usurper only won a partial—and temporary—victory. All thanks to you and Princess Icannes."

"Let's introduce him." Lefric wore what could almost be called a smile.

"Good idea." Badagis put a hand on Vahldan's back and steered him down the corridor. Stalls lined the way on either side. "Your uncle bred and trained Samwë for this very purpose—for your father to ride at the head of his host. And now that honor falls to you."

His father's voice echoed in his mind: *'What will come of us if this falls to you?'*

Angavar had kept this from him. His father had done all this for himself, not for his son. Vahldan felt like a stand-in—someone his father's loyal supporters were resorting to.

Lefric hurried ahead and opened a stall. He led one of the largest stallions Vahldan had ever seen out into the corridor—snow-white with golden mane. The horse yanked his head and shied when Vahldan reached to pet him, one eye fiercely staring.

Lefric said, "He's of the blood of your great-grandfather's vaunted stock."

A thump from the stall behind startled Vahldan. It was closely followed by a loud, long neigh. "Don't mind her," Herodes said. "That mare is always cross."

"Especially when the attention's not on her," Belgar added.

Elan peered over the gate. A large silver-gray head with charcoal mane loomed out to greet her. Elan held out her hand and the mare didn't hesitate to stick her nose against it. "He's right, she's cross. But for good reason. She knows she's better than him."

"Careful, Blade-Wielder," Lefric said. "That nag's known to bite."

Elan petted her nose. "Perhaps she only bites those who consider her a nag." She looked to Vahldan. "This is a fine horse. If it's yours to choose, you should consider her."

Elan opened the gate and stooped to feel her legs. Vahldan went to her and raised his hand. The mare reared and stomped, snorting as she backed away.

"You see?" his uncle said. "Best stay clear. If she dislikes you, she may even kick."

Elan harrumphed. "Dislikes him? She's only just met us." She stroked the gray's neck, instantly settling her. Elan beckoned him. "Slowly this time. Show her that you're worth knowing, and let her decide if she's up to it."

With one hand on the horse, Elan extended the other to Vahldan. He took it, and she guided him over. He resisted the urge to reach and pet her. The mare extended to breathe him in, nuzzling his hair. "That's better," Elan said soothingly to the gray. "See? He's not so bad. He doesn't stink like most of them. He's from good stock, just like you."

"She may be well-bred, but she sure is headstrong," Lefric grumbled.

"That doesn't mean she wouldn't serve you well. It only means bonding would take patience. Headstrong mares often become the most loyal friends. She may not have the strength of the stallion, but I'd wager that she's as fleet. And that she won't tire as quickly."

"I suppose I've fared well with headstrong females." Vahldan gave Elan an arch glance.

Elan offered an exaggerated smile. "Hilarious."

"What's her name?"

"She is Ardua," Lefric offered.

"Hello, Ardua," Vahldan said as he carefully began petting her.

She snorted rather than pulling away. Elan was right, he'd been too hasty, was all.

"Sa Vaskr Ardua," Elan said. "It's from the old tongue of the Skolani. It means she's of the valiant hearted."

Lefric nodded. "You know your horse stock, Blade-Wielder. This one's his doing." He threw a thumb at Badagis.

Badagis grinned. "Indeed. Her sires are from the queen's own string—a gift from Keisella's mother to my father. I see the Blade-Wielder's meaning, Vahldan—she suits you. A Skolani guardian, plus a Skolani mare for good measure. It would make the tale all the richer."

Elan smiled. "I should've guessed she was from the royal string. She's certainly a far leap from that old Spali pony you've been riding."

Vahldan turned to his father's uncle and raised his brows. He sort of liked the idea that he had an inside track with her through Elan.

Lefric scowled. "Don't look at me. She'd be your problem, not mine."

Badagis clapped his back again. "It's settled then. Our captain shall lead us from Ardua's back. Now we're ready for war." Vahldan's stomach flopped and his hand drifted to his hilt.

"Come!" Badagis barked. "We need food and drink, to mark the occasion." The big man started back toward the doors.

Vahldan turned to Elan. This talk of war had shaken him. The ugliness lurked within, and Elan looked sullen again. "Go," she said. "I want to see to Hrithvarra." She hadn't even bothered to try to read him. Or perhaps she had, and wanted to stay clear.

He was on his own.

Belgar beckoned him. "Stick with Herodes and me. We'll introduce you to the others." Vahldan reluctantly turned from Elan and went with his cousins. "So, Captain, how does it feel?"

What was Vahldan supposed to say? How could he even pretend he thought he was worthy of this? He would never be the warrior or leader his father had been; he'd never been in a real battle; and he was prone to getting lost in his rage. Gods, the man these kinfolk had planned and labored for was dead because of him. "If you only knew," he said.

Herodes smiled. "It's a lot to take in, I suppose."

They emerged into sunshine, and Vahldan stopped. At least two score of mostly young men had gathered along the lane to the cabins, all staring at him, grinning. Badagis was already halfway up the hill. "A bit much," Vahldan agreed.

Belgar laughed. "Come now. It's not so bad as that. All has been made ready. The only thing left is to ride to war. And here one has come, just as it's been foretold."

Vahldan scanned the eager faces, their hopeful gazes, their bowing heads. Just as it had the day he met the Skolani queen, everything had changed again. All without his choosing. "Only that, eh? Just ride to war." It was far from being so simple. These... *strangers* had placed their faith in him. Living up to their expectation would be like living up to a legend. Not just his father, but the stories told of Mighty Angavar. All in Vahldan's very first battle. Simple as that.

All his life Vahldan had been told that he was born to lead. He'd never believed it. Or maybe he'd just resisted accepting what his parents knew would befall him.

It seemed he had no choice but to don their weapons and armor, mount their warhorse, ride at the head of a host of strangers, and lead them to war.

CHAPTER 20--
MUSTERING
CONVICTION

"*D*ania's borders are born of nature, and greatly enhance the realm's safekeeping. The valley spreads out from either side of the Danian River, which runs eastward through it. To the north stand the high Carpan Mountains, rocky and new, nigh unpassable by a host; To the south, the Pontean Mountains, round and green, with but a few easily patrolled passes out to the rugged Pontean seacoast.*

At either end, the Danian's banks are swallowed by mountains, and the river flows in and out through canyons of rock. At the eastern edge of the valley, where the Danian is joined by the Tala Vatna River, there is only one crossing fit for a force of any size, not far downstream of the confluence. The Skolani know the ford and its surrounds well—better than any foreigner could hope to."—Brin Bright Eyes, Saga of Dania*

THE TIME HAD COME! Elan would soon be with her people again. Better still, she would no longer be a lone female in a host of men. Finally. Exactly what she needed.

After months of being the outsider, Elan could embrace being

Skolani again. Rather than being held apart, as a necessary but dangerous presence, like an unpredictable guard dog.

Eager for the change, Elan cantered out ahead of the column alone. Her excitement lured her beyond the normal distance she was willing to stray from her subject, knowing that Skolani sentinels monitored their approach. She crested the last hill and the queen's camp came to view, spreading across the high vale. Scores of pavilions were scattered across a bowl of waving grass in the setting sunlight. It looked like a miniature version of the Jabitka.

Nearly half of her tribe must have come. The sprawling camp was divided by a gap marking a separate parcel for the men. Which suited her fine. Elan was tired of being gawped at, preached to, and judged by men. It was beyond exhausting.

The evening shadows deepened. A breeze carried the smell of cooking meat. Groups of warriors gathered in clumps around a score of fires. On the Gottari side, banners fluttered over each cluster of pavilions, half featuring the howling wolf of the Wulthus on green and half the snarling lion of the Amalus on red.

Elan turned in the saddle to find Vahldan absorbed in his cadre of maleness, all of them so boisterous and cocky. As usual, he was flanked by Arnegern and his cousins Belgar and Herodes. Their days in the saddle were filled with suggestive jokes, teasing and mocking, burping and farting—all accompanied by insufferable laughter.

Before meeting his host, Vahldan had been such a thoughtful, occasionally witty, but mostly solemn presence. Together they proved what a terrible influence males had on one another.

Elan reined Hrithvarra toward the Skolani corrals at a brisk trot, hoping her departure from Vahldan's column would escape notice. Skolani sentinels greeted her as she dismounted. Her spirits lifted. A protégé came and offered to attend to her friend, but Elan waved the girl off. Unsaddling and grooming Hrithvarra would soothe both horse and rider.

As she worked, Elan mused that during their flight to Danihem, both she and Vahldan had grown a bit too reliant on one another. Vahldan seemed willing to break free of it. Which left her wondering about her own tendencies. Before Vahldan, Elan had relied on Icannes. Too much so, she suspected. Icannes certainly didn't depend on anyone. Certainly not Elan. If she hadn't made it clear before, Icannes proved it by blithely riding away with the blood-bitch.

Elan was done with it. She could rely on herself. She was a Blade-Wielder, after all.

She tried to focus on brushing her friend's mane and tail. She allowed herself to peek. She instantly spotted him. Vahldan was being welcomed to an Amalus Rekkr's fire. She doubted he even noticed her absence.

Like lazy lions to a fresh kill, Rekkrs and young bannermen made their way to him. The legendary Badagis was himself a rare sight. But his arrival alongside the Outcast's heir, at the head of a well-equipped host—well, it was bound to create a stir.

Elan had to admit, Vahldan possessed a magnetism that only grew. To the young, he was a legend in the making, and they wanted to be a part of it. For older Rekkrs, although most didn't dare openly support him, Angavar's heir was a fresh breeze blowing across their banked coals of hope. He'd yet to stoke a flame, but they couldn't help but glow in his presence.

The giddy hope of the lions only caused the tales of Vahldan to grow in the retelling. His performance in his trial, his judicious handling of its outcome, the Spali scalp hanging from his reins, and even her own presence at his side, were all fodder for embellishment. To top it off, the tales were so easily tied to the prophecy. To many it seemed the Urrinan was surely fast approaching now, here in such turbulent times.

As if to match his ascendancy, his physique had undeniably responded well to Icannes's rigorous training. Vahldan had always been handsome, and he'd only grown more manly. But there was more to it. When he wanted to be, Vahldan was charismatic. He could be fiery, but he could also be kind. He'd become the perfect raw material for the fabrication of a hero.

Watching Vahldan with his hangers-on brought Badagis's secret to mind. For years, Vahldan's father and his inner circle had kept their schemes and efforts from Vahldan. Seemed that they all plotted to mold him into what they wanted him to become. Something they surely realized he did not want. Had they always planned for him to spring the trap of his legacy?

And their scheming had changed Elan's life, too. She'd dedicated a sizeable chunk of her new life as a warrior to him. Now that Vahldan had his own host, Elan presumed that the queen would declare her duty concluded. Why did that thought make her insides twist?

She told herself it was because it seemed premature. Vahldan had yet to fight a battle, and still she would be discarded. She'd been nothing more than a tool, or a weapon. A temporary one, like the blade Vahldan's father had left him to use until he regained the futhark blade.

Elan reminded herself that their impending separation was for the best. For both of them. Why should she let it twist her? She laughed at herself and turned back to her work. She had to admit it, if only to herself: she'd somehow allowed herself to occasionally fantasize that *he* might be the leader from her dreams. Preposterous! He was such a man-child. She felt herself blush at the admission. Of course the dream had to be about Icannes. It made so much more sense.

In any case, Elan was done fretting over him, done caring what he thought or how he felt.

Elan carried her gear to the storage pavilion alongside the corral. She looked again. Vahldan was smiling. She could even make out the dimples under his beard. The crowd around him had thickened. A lad scurried up to deliver a drinking horn. Such service!

She went into the tack pavilion and found a spot for her saddle. She bent to stow her gear. It smelled like home. She stood, stiff after a day in the saddle. She stretched and pushed a loose strand from her face. Her hair needed to be rebraided. She'd been putting it off, waiting for help.

The time for that had come, too.

She headed to the Skolani royal pavilion. Elan spotted Icannes, reclining beside Keisella's fire. She had scarcely spoken to Icannes since her near-sister had appeared in Danihem with Anallya. What stung was that Icannes hardly seemed to notice. Elan sought to banish her resentment. She didn't want to start this reunion on the wrong foot.

The queen sat bolt upright, focused on the current speaker. Keisella was always gathering and processing. The daughter laughed, causing the mother to scowl.

Elan suddenly didn't feel up to facing either of them. She'd rather wait to be summoned.

Elan scanned the other pavilions. Hildeanna's pavilion was in the place of honor beside the queen's. Elan's captain sat centered before her fire, her leathery face contorted into a wrinkly grin, delighted to regale her followers. Hildeanna looked fit as ever, in spite of her graying braids and the paunch above her belt. Elan strolled over to sit among her fellows.

Hildeanna was, of course, the featured hero of the tale she was telling. Elan had heard it before. She dropped to her knees near the back. The captain's cheeks were rosy with drink.

The first to notice Elan's arrival was Sochana, sitting off to her right. "Elan?" Ursellya's sister seemed surprised by her presence.

"Hey there," she whispered. "How's the back?" Sochana had thrown out her back during their last patrol together. Up until their separation, Elan had massaged it mornings and evenings.

"Much better, thanks." Sochana seemed uneasy. "Stopping by to visit the old host?"

"Old host? I've only been gone since the solstice. I hope to rejoin you soon."

The Blade-Wielder frowned. "But I thought—"

"Well, if it isn't the little lion keeper." Elan's heart sank. Anallya rose from among Hildeanna's warriors, pointing with a slosh of her cup. "Where's your naughty little cub, Elan?" The blood-bitch smirked and swayed. It clearly wasn't her first cup.

"What's she doing here?" Elan hadn't meant to say it aloud.

Sochana spoke behind her hand. "The queen requested it. As a reward for the swiftness of her ride to Danihem. Sorry, I was going to warn you."

Everyone turned to the disruption. "Something of note?" Hildeanna asked.

Old Gaerteh leaned to their leader. "It's Ellasan's daughter. She's been living among Gottari men, you know."

Elan stood and bowed. "I have. I'm sure you'll recall assigning me to watch over the family of the Outcast. It seems my duty is all but complete. I'd be honored to serve you once again, if it pleases you, my Captain."

Hildeanna took a drink, eyeing her over the cup's rim. "So, the young healer finally tires of the poor souls she fretted over so? Ruined a perfectly good attack, this one." Sycophantic laughter ran through her audience. "Yes, yes, it pleases me fine. Come back as you will. Never hurts to have a healer trotting along behind. Even one who's a fretful meddler." Hildeanna smirked. "Damned healers and their lost causes. If they're not getting themselves shot over dying victims, they're flying off to coddle battle orphans."

The laughter rang louder. Elan's scalp prickled and her cheeks burned. Were they really laughing that her mother had been shot while trying to save their comrade?

As the laughter faded, Hildeanna went back to her tale. "Where was I? Oh yes, the sneaks hiding in the trees above us. Afletam is full of the little tree weasels—the gods only know from what race they're spawned..."

Elan turned and fled.

~

VAHLDAN WASN'T LISTENING to the young man talking at him. He nodded or laughed when it seemed appropriate, all the while scanning the Skolani camp. He'd yet to spot her auburn braids, and it was getting more difficult as it grew darker. He'd hoped that here in this larger camp he'd have a chance to get past Elan's shield of sullenness. Damned if she hadn't slipped away before Vahldan had even dismounted.

He shouldn't be surprised. Vahldan should've known the camp would be divided, and that Elan would choose the Skolani side. It still stung, even though he knew it shouldn't.

Another thought occurred to him like a bolt from a clear sky. What if her assignment was complete? What if the queen ended Elan's guardianship? The ugliness stirred, deep within. Gods, how would he navigate this craziness without her?

"Vahldan!" He was startled back. "This is Attasar. His father Halasar is your father's cousin." Badagis had an arm around a slim young man. The newcomer bowed. How was Vahldan ever going to remember all of these names? He'd already forgotten this one. The new cousin was well-dressed, beardless and wore his combed hair tied back. He was tall but boyish.

"Attasar is fresh back from the imperial academy at Efusium. He's the one I spoke to you about." Vahldan smiled and nodded but had no idea what Badagis was referencing. Since his trial, Vahldan had met and briefly conversed with scores of relatives and supporters. "Attasar's schooling will one day serve a leader well." Badagis winked.

Vahldan was tired of the cryptic talk. "How's that?"

The young man—Attasar, was it?—blushed. "To start, I fluently speak and can read and write both Hellainic and Tiberian. I can also read the runes of the Tutona. In addition, I speak four other tongues well enough to be understood, including Carpan and Spali. I also studied the strategies of war under General Caliesus. I spent six years devoted to learning how I might best serve a Gottari lord. And I have your father to thank for it all."

"My father?" Another surprise from Angavar's secret past?

"Of course," the young man said. "It was all Lord Angavar's doing. He bid me to seek out the very best tutors, whatever the cost. Your father was quite generous. He will be missed. I'm sorry for your loss." Attasar leaned in and lowered his voice. "Since your father has passed, my pledge of service now falls to you, of course." The scholar bowed again, flush with pride.

The others had all grown silent. They were waiting for Vahldan's reaction. "I... I don't know what to say." What did they want from him? He wasn't his father, dammit.

Badagis gripped Vahldan's shoulder. "Best not to say anything. Not yet. Just accept his support, same as you do with the rest of us."

"Aye. We're all here to follow you," Belgar said, and others murmured in consensus. The ugliness stirred again, pushing upward into his chest. For the hundredth time, he contemplated telling them what a bad idea following him was.

"Well, well—the legendary Badagis." Everyone turned as Desdrusan strode into the firelight, Jhannas and Ermanaric towering over his shoulders. "It's been so long, I wondered if you still had your tongue stuck up the ass of your fallen hero when they buried him."

Vahldan found himself squeezing his hilt. His cousins and Desdrusan's giant guards all had their hands on hilts, as well. They all stood poised at the edge of violence until Badagis barked in laughter. "Guess I lost my focus." The tension eased.

"Guess he should've taken lessons," Lefric said. "Perhaps from one who managed to keep the asses of an entire pack clean." Several cousins were unable to suppress muffled laughter. Vahldan found the situation disorienting to absorb. Of course all of these strangers knew one another.

Desdrusan rounded on Lefric with a smirk. "Ah, good of you to turn up, as well, Uncle. I feared you were as dead as your favorite nephew. It's a shame you stormed off. The Amalus could've used your breeding skills while you were out here soused and sulking. It's said you had a delicate touch that both stallions and mares found oh-so-satisfying."

Lefric sneered. "I can't imagine keeping any horse in the Amalus stables satisfied now, what with the irksome burden required of them." As the ugliness stirred in Vahldan's belly, he recognized it in his great uncle's flaring glare. *'I know what's inside you, because it's in me, too.'*

Desdrusan's laugh was forced. "Perhaps you've lost your touch, then. And I would've thought trembling hands to be a boon." Desdrusan's glare swept the circle. "Speaking of the irksome, did I hear someone mention *following* this son of a murder into battle?"

Vahldan wondered how could it be that the lifelong conflicts of men he'd just met were now his to navigate. The ugliness became a twitch in his arm and in one eye. He perfectly saw his blade skewering the protruding belly before him.

Still smiling, Badagis put a hand on Vahldan's shoulder and squeezed. "You must've misheard. They were speaking of following *me*. This is my host, you see."

Desdrusan tilted his head. "Oh? That's surprising. You've only ever been a follower. But it's hard to figure what scent will lure this rogue pride. Anyway, it works out well because this criminal has been placed under my watch until his trial. Vahldan is to serve in my host."

Desdrusan scowled at Vahldan. "And don't think to slip away from me again, boy. Your next misstep will be the first on your way to the Thrakian slave markets." Vahldan bristled, longing to simply submit to the impulses of the ugliness. Gods, it would be satisfying to punch the man's face. "As for the rest of you," Desdrusan said. "I'd reconsider following this man." He nodded at Badagis. "He's more likely to lead you to a Skolani fertility ceremony than a battle."

Badagis scratched his beard. "Sounds about right, actually." Vahldan hid a smile that helped the ugliness to fade slightly.

Desdrusan ignored Badagis. "Still, it's wiser than following an exile, which is forbidden by law. I'd hate for any of you to choose poorly. As would the wool guild, from what I hear. It'd be a shame if any of you lost your access to the fleece market, or found your flocks have nowhere to graze."

"Baaaaaa." One of the cousins mimicked a dismayed sheep. Laughter rang throughout the circle. A snort escaped Vahldan.

Desdrusan's lip curled. "Ah, such an amusing host, Badagis. Perhaps their jokes will help when they're begging for food." He stepped between Badagis and Vahldan. "The queen has insisted that you and the boy come to her parley." The Lion Lord leaned toward Vahldan, wearing a squint. "Best watch your tongue over there, snot nose. Don't you dare embarrass me."

If Badagis was as shocked as Vahldan, he hid it well. "When shall we arrive?"

"Now. Why else would I subject myself to this stench?"

Desdrusan stalked off into the darkness toward the Skolani side of the camp, his thugs in tow. The tension melted, Vahldan's muscles eased, and the cousinly banter resumed.

IT WAS GETTING DARK QUICKLY. Elan dashed the tears from her eyes, angry to have shed them. She stumbled through tall grass, tripping several times on the tufts. She stopped and surveyed the camp. She hadn't a clue where to go. She set out again, heading vaguely through the empty area between the Gottari and Skolani sides. She checked the queen's fire as she passed. Icannes was smiling, deep in conversation with several prominent Gottari Rekkrs. A war parley, no doubt. Going there was out of the question.

Elan stopped and stood in the center of the camp, feeling alone. Laughter rang from the crowd around Badagis's pavilion fire. No way she'd go back to the bedamned cadre of maleness. Icannes's laugh rose above the hum to echo in Elan's hollow core.

So much cheer. Elan couldn't stand it. She had to get away. She decided on the corral. Elan would find her gear, retrieve her saddle blanket, and find a spot to sleep in the nearby hills.

She spun to set out. And ran into him.

She knocked his cup and spilled mead on both of them. Elan grabbed his shoulder to regain her balance. Vahldan's free arm swung around her. She let go and tried to retreat, but he held her there. She leaned back. He smiled and wiped the sticky liquid from her forearm with his tunic sleeve. "Don't bother," she said, pulling away.

It was dim, but his eyes were shining. "Sorry," Vahldan offered brightly.

Elan looked away. "My fault. Didn't see you." She knew she sounded snappish.

"I didn't mean to sneak up on you."

"If you didn't mean it, how did it happen?" How *had* he managed that? When had she gotten so careless?

"It just did. Mainly because you were in my way."

"It's an open field, not a path."

Vahldan looked away. "Actually, I stopped when I spotted you. I've been standing here, trying to think of how to say something."

"Say what?" He shook his head. Elan wasn't sure she wanted to know. He was still too close, damn him. She took a step back. His arm fell away. He looked deflated. She summoned her anger back. "Where are all your little friends?" she asked.

"My friends?"

"You know, the gaggle of penises that follow you around."

He huffed in laughter. "Well, I'll give you that they seem like a gaggle. But I'd hardly call them friends. I don't know them, and they don't know me. To them I'm like a white skunk— worth seeing for the tale to tell, but not to be gotten too close to."

"Oh, come now." Elan rolled her eyes. "What about your cousins?"

"It's weird, isn't it—to have never met your cousins? It's like I was kept hidden away. Like I wasn't fit to be presented. Then I cause my father's death, and surprise! Here they are. It feels so strange."

"Well, I won't argue that it's strange."

Vahldan took a drink and glanced at the queen's pavilion. "As for a friend, I was thinking about my only real one. You know, the one without a penis." He grinned. "What I wanted to say was that I need her."

"I don't think that's true."

"It is. I need her because I've been summoned to a queen's parley. Which makes me jumpy as a spooked colt. We've faced a lot together, this friend and me. And I can't imagine facing this without her."

Elan frowned but her hollow core was aflutter with a startled flock. How could he do this to her? "I wasn't summoned."

"*I'm* summoning you."

"It's not your place."

"Alright then, I'm begging you."

"Don't," she snapped. "It's you they want."

"Whatever they want, it's not me. They only want what they think I am. A living version of my father."

"Then show them that you're not him."

"How?" Vahldan's voice grew whiny. "I've tried, but no matter what I do they treat me like I'm some sort of good luck charm. Or like a banner they can wave to rouse their followers. All except Desdrusan, of course. He wants me too, but only to keep me away from them. And once it's over, even if the war goes well, not a one of them will stand up to the wool guild on my behalf. Remember? If I survive, I still have to face banishment."

"Oh stop." Elan was sick of it. How could he not see that he had everything going for him? That his tale was just beginning while hers was ending? "Most war leaders are little more than good luck charms, or banners. What does that matter? Once a battle begins, a warrior has to make their own luck. This is your chance to prove you're something more—even more than your father was. They want to name you the Bringer? Wear it. Win them. Find your way. Step up and take your place." The queen stood to greet the arriving Wolf Lord. "But whatever you do, you'd better hurry. They're about to begin without you."

Vahldan grabbed her arm. "Let them," he said, low but urgent. "It doesn't matter. I keep trying to tell you that I need you. Don't you understand? None of it matters without you." She couldn't look away, trapped in his fierce gaze. "I get lost without you."

Elan swallowed. "You'll learn how to find your way. You already have. You can do this. Without me." Her voice dropped to a whisper. "You'll have to. Accept it." The thought made her chest hurt.

They'd drifted together until their faces were a hand's width apart. Gods, it hit her—how much her duty meant. How much he meant. He'd given her purpose. How could it just disappear? His arm was behind her again. How had that happened? Elan was conscious of her own breathing. She tried to swallow but couldn't. She feared he was about to kiss her. She feared he wouldn't.

"Vahldan, we're waiting!" Badagis called from the gathering. The spell was broken.

"Coming!" he called without looking. "Sorry, I refuse to accept it. You're coming too," he said to her, and pulled her by the arm.

She resisted. "They'll send me away."

"Then they'll be sending us both away." He continued pulling her.

Elan gave in, allowing him to compel her. Had she chosen this? Had he?

Then it struck her. Why shouldn't she attend with him? There was nothing else; nothing left. They'd given Elan to this young man, and no one seemed to care to have her back. How could they blame her for what they'd imposed upon her?

With or without him, she was caught between worlds. Her dreams were merely dreams—they'd made sure of that.

Maybe Elan was the one who needed to accept it: that nothing remained but to follow Vahldan's lead. There was no path, only an open field between camps. And he was the only one left who wanted or needed her alongside. Why shouldn't she chose him?

AFTER THE PARLEY ELAN stayed back, watching as Rekkrs laughed and slapped each other's backs. The attendees swiftly dispersed into the night. The plans were set, and things had gone surprisingly well. She kept her eyes on the Lion Lord, whose own glare was locked onto Vahldan's back. Badagis wrapped an arm around Vahldan, bear-like, guiding him back to their pavilion. Desdrusan seethed, his hatred radiating as he followed. Things had not gone the Lion Lord's way. It made him all the more dangerous.

Icannes patted Elan's shoulder, startling her. "Mother wants you."

"My subject." She pointed at the departing men.

"He's in good hands. Come. You know she hates to be kept waiting."

Icannes led Elan into the queen's pavilion. Keisella sat on crossed legs, alone. "I have words for Elan," the queen said.

Icannes plopped down and helped herself to a handful of berries from a bowl. "And I brought her," Icannes said, her mouth full.

"Hence, my need of you is fulfilled." The queen waved a dismissive hand.

"She's my near-sister."

"As Annakha was your wet-nurse. Shall I summon her so you can suckle as you butt in?"

Icannes's lip curled. She stared at her mother as she rose, grabbed another handful of berries, and then slowly sauntered out the pavilion flap.

Keisella's toothy smile didn't reach her eyes, making Elan all the more certain she was about to be scolded. Surely this was what she'd been dreading. She was about to be relieved of her duty to Vahldan. "Your grandmother is on her way," Keisella said.

"My queen?"

"Sael. She's coming."

"Here? To a war camp?"

"Yes, as I've said. Twice now, actually."

Elan shook her head. "I'm sorry, my queen. It's just that I'm surprised."

"Oh, you know how she is. Seems she believes there's some dire piece of the prophecy she must bear witness to. The woman has the patience of a protégé." Keisella's fondness for Sael was clear in her tone, but Elan must've made a face. "Don't look so worried, Elan. I know she's all but blind, but she's not helpless. I'm assigning two Blade-Wielders to guard her. It'll keep her away from the fighting, if nothing else."

Now things were beginning to make sense. "Ah. And you're making me one of them."

"By Horsella's Blade, no! Were you asleep through the parley, Elan?"

"My queen?"

"Did you miss what's about to transpire—what your subject volunteered for?"

"Yes, my queen... I mean no. I mean, I did hear. But I thought—"

"I'm shocked, Elan. By the time the moon sets, your subject will face the greatest trial of his life. Are you telling me you would abandon him at a time like this?"

Elan tried to suppress a grin. "No, my queen."

"Really? That's it? Where is your fervor, Blade-Wielder? After all, the turnings of the Urrinan itself lie in the balance."

Elan raised her chin and all but shouted. "I am eager to serve, my queen!"

"That's better."

"Is there anything else you would have of me?"

Keisella smirked. "Go. Do you duty. Your grandmother will be here to greet you afterward. Make us proud."

"Yes, my queen." She was being used again, but at least it was a worthy use. Elan tried not to hurry as she swept through the exit flap.

CHAPTER 21
—STEPPING UP

"The Spali invaders who led the attack in Queen Keisella's War were not the herdsmen of an untested militia. It's said the elite warriors of the Paralatoe are selected as they grow from babe to boy, trained to fight from the time they are taught to speak—often pitted against one another, often to the death, so that only the strongest survived to reinforce the brotherhood.

Those who survive the brutal upbringing are rewarded at puberty with ritual facial scars. They earn their tattoos through theft, rape, and murder. Once they are marked, they are encouraged to go into their own people's camps, to take whatever young maiden pleases them. Most girls are taken against their will, but their fathers reckon it an honor. All Spali warriors consider women to be beneath them. They are wrong. The Skolani, on the other hand, know exactly what the Paralatoe are: savage beasts wrought from innocent boys, no longer recognizable as men.

Our mothers' mothers long ago learned that which remains true— that there can be only one means of dealing with the Spali. Which goes far toward explaining the training of the Blade-Wielders." –Brin Bright Eyes, Saga of Dania

· · ·

GRAY TINGED THE PREDAWN SKY. Vahldan heard the water before he saw the river—the dull rush and gurgle of the current swallowing the sound of his companions as they crested the last ridge. The queen's words ran through his head. *'The time has come.'* Gods, it really had. He was about to be tested, as never before.

Vahldan still marveled that the Skolani queen maneuvered him into this. The uproar at the parley still haunted him. Keisella had merely suggested his name for the mission. So many had doubted him. Most of them still did. The queen stood and raised her hands for quiet. "Prior to Aomeir's death, whom would we have picked to lead this mission?" she'd asked. They'd all stayed silent. "Can any of you deny the choice would have been Angavar, son of Beremund?" Again, silence. She'd strode to loom over Vahldan. "Who trained you?"

"Angavar, son of Beremund," Vahldan had managed, knowing he also owed much to both Icannes and Elan. Indeed, he knew he would be even further from ready without them.

With a hand on his shoulder, Keisella had faced the parley. "Vahldan is the blood of Dania's most vaunted warrior. If he is but half as daring and skilled as the sire, surely he is worthy of being chosen for this moment."

Keisella had smirked then, narrow eyes scanning the wolves in attendance. "And for those who still consider him an exile, his failure upon this attempt would deliver a fitting sentence, would it not?" Again, they'd all remained silent.

The queen's fierce gaze had dropped to meet his. "Are you, Young Lion?" she'd asked.

Stunned, Vahldan had idiotically murmured, "Am I what?"

"Are you at least half as daring and skilled as your father was?" Still stunned, he'd simply stared, his innards flopping. She'd bent to him and lowered her voice. "The time has come, Vahldan. It falls to you. Are you ready to step up? Can you prove the strength of your bloodline remains?"

Vahldan had agreed to step up and lead the mission, but he'd never answered the second question. He had his doubts, but he couldn't dwell on those.

"I am ready," he affirmed aloud. He hoped saying it would provide certitude, but his current view swiftly stole it away.

His crew gathered around him. "Not with those clothes on, you're not," Elan said. Vahldan nodded and began to strip, handing off his garments to her, straining to make out the features of the far bank. All he saw was dark, dense forest.

He gazed at the dark swirling water. "By Thunar's nuts, what have I gotten myself into?"

"You're about to wish your nuts were in Thunar's divine sack." Teavar's smile shone.

"Yours seem to have disappeared, my Captain." Belgar stooped to examine his man parts.

He covered himself with his hands. "Hey, it's cold out here."

"Not half as cold as in there." Arnegern nodded toward the churn of the Tala Vatna.

"His nuts are wise then, to nestle themselves so," Herodes offered.

"Enough," Elan said, and Vahldan was grateful. She looped the rope around Vahldan's waist. "Focus on the far bank and keeping yourself moving," she said as she tied the knot. "Get yourself out of the wind as soon as you tie off. We'll be right behind you." Her deliberate manner was almost enough to make him forget his nudity. Almost.

Once she finished, Elan rose to face him. "*Now* you're ready," she asserted with a nod.

He wanted to tell her how grateful he was; that she was the source of what little courage he felt; that he wouldn't have made it this far without her. Instead he said, "As I'll ever be."

Elan pulled her bow from her shoulder and nocked an arrow. "Kestrel," she said. It meant that she had his back while he swam.

Vahldan sat on the bank. Time to perform. Or face what came of revealing what a poor substitute he was for Angavar.

He slid till his legs were in, then swiftly submerged his body. The shock was unavoidable, but he hoped speed would lessen the agony. It didn't. The cold stole his breath and needled his skin. Numbness creeped into his limbs even as the current's pull took him. The steep banks of the far shore loomed, and the spot he'd targeted quickly became impossible in the swift flow.

As a young boy, Vahldan had swam in the current of the mighty Danian River, but that had been languid compared to the powerful sweep of the Tala Vatna here.

That he would be the one to swim, setting the draw-line for the rafts to follow, had been beyond debate. Others had offered, but he'd considered this the only way to lead. It's what Angavar would've done.

He must've been mad. There was no way he was the strongest swimmer.

Their success or failure relied on his capabilities alone—including his mediocre swimming skills. Too late to reconsider, though. Whether the spooky vision of the priestess was superstitious nonsense or truly divine, one thing kept coming clearer to him: the gods favored the bold. Hesitancy had forced him to become the hand of his father's death. But boldness had brought Elan into his life. What more proof did he need?

He quickly started to tire. The other bank was so far. Vahldan tried not to think about the scouting reports, about how they would face the fiercest of the foe. The Paralatoe manned the defensive positions that oversaw the ford. They were well-hidden and strung out along the ridge. A surge of energy ran through his numb limbs in realizing he was about to face the very clansmen that killed his father—perhaps even Auchote himself.

Vahldan would soon have his chance to redeem himself—to get past his failure.

But it was also another chance to lose himself. Or to freeze again.

The current slackened. He'd made it through the center sweep. But he'd been pulled so far south, closer to the rocky rapids. Not to mention the foe. His arms flopped on by rote, no longer seeming like his own. His lungs burned.

The alarms of instinct screamed. He'd drifted too far. Just as he was about to signal his mates to pull him back his foot struck the riverbed. With leaden limbs he flopped and lumbered up and over the slippery rocks, unable to even care about the sloshing noise he made.

Vahldan climbed out of the water using the exposed roots of cedars. The cold wind lashed his wet skin. With trembling fingers, he untied the rope. Moving upstream to tie off was a slow process, as he was forced to navigate the tree-lined shore, dragging the rope in the current.

Across the river, he saw the glint of a blade, signaling he had reached the correct spot. He knotted the rope on a stout cedar's curved trunk and gave the line two tugs. The rope went taut, rising from the current. He dropped down between an outcrop and the broad base of the tree, hugging himself and shivering. The rope creaked with the rhythm of strong arms tugging in unison. The increasingly lighter sky warned of dawn's swift approach.

The moment the raft struck rock, Elan sprang from the bow. She swiftly enfolded him in a blanket and wrapped strong arms around him, rubbing him with her hands. Vahldan couldn't help but shudder. She brought each of his hands up to warm them with blown breaths.

Once all were ashore, Teavar and Badagis cast off to go back for the others. Vahldan smiled at Elan, nodding that he'd be fine. Arnegern proffered his pack and Elan snatched it, handing over his clothing piece by piece. She corded his leggings as he laced his forearm guards. Then they each tied one of his boots. Last, she slung his sword belt and shield from over her shoulder. Badagis was to return to let the queen know they'd crossed successfully.

The second half of the group arrived as Elan strapped on his buckler. He'd come to appreciate the Skolani shield. It was particularly suited to this mission—light and portable. He was dressed and armed by the time his full team gathered around him.

Arnegern said, "We are yours to command, oh mighty scion of kings."

'Your father held such lofty aspirations for you.'

Everyone grinned at Arnegern's quip. "I live but to serve," he replied with the same levity. "Remember, slight as the breeze until we're the storm." Realizing nothing came of delay, he set out, picking the course southward, stealing over slick boulders and between trees. His instincts for path-finding, honed in a youth spent in a mountain vale, served him well.

They crossed a small stream, and along the next rise he spotted the Spali among the pines, hunched in the shadows. His squad's targeted victims faced away, watching the ford. Vahldan raised a fist and gathered them. The west end of the foe's lines was most heavily manned. The Skolani scouts reported a series of small Paralatoe sleeping camps, arrayed in a semi-circle on the crest north of the ford, running southeast. The main Paralatoe camp was deeper in the forest, on the backside of the crescent of watch posts. The first watch post was just east of his team's position. Their mission was to take out these sentinels, then move to take as many of the small camps as possible, minimizing the threat to the crossing Danians.

The better they disrupted the foe's warning system and response, the better the chances the allies had for gaining a foothold on the eastern bank.

With blood pounding in his ears and his belly starting to boil, Vahldan directed them into position with hand signals. He stayed at the left end, so that he could lead them from the initial strike to the attack on the camps. He looked down the line as they took their places. Their lives depended on him. So far, Thunar's Blessing eluded him. If he lost himself to rage, things could swiftly go awry.

Elan stepped close, filling his view with her face. "See me?" she asked. He nodded. "Good. Hear me, too. You can do this. Go there. I am here. Understood?"

Vahldan nodded again and sought for the flames. Instead, all he felt was fear. He couldn't quite catch his breath and his limbs still felt floppy. He shook the tingle from his arms, slowly drew a breath, and sighed it out.

The sky began to blue as they gained their positions. Time was up. The queen would attack at sunup. Vahldan targeted the Spali who seemed the last on their left flank, and raised his sword to signal. Elan's bending bow creaked beside him.

He dropped his arm. Elan's bow snapped. He ran, crashing through the brush, charging uphill. The swelling roar of the attack came as he spotted his first victim. He could not hesitate. He forced himself on, raising his blade. The gods favored the bold. The blanket-wrapped Spali sentinel slumped even as Vahldan's arm chopped by rote. Elan's arrow protruded from the back of his neck. Not his victim. Why was he relieved?

A Spali he hadn't seen beforehand dashed into the pines to his left.

He paused, surveying the fight, fretting about his team. "Let's go!" Elan said. "They have this." Gods, he'd momentarily frozen.

She slung her bow over her shoulder and drew her blade. Vahldan set out after the fleeing Spali and sensed Elan right behind. The way was little more than a deer path, but their quarry knew it well. Vahldan's feet were heavy. He pushed himself on, slogging toward stirring branches and boughs as his target repeatedly vanished into the shadows.

He pushed through a curtain of spruce branches, and a snarling tattooed face appeared. He halted just as the Spali threw. The tumbling projectile bounced from the rocky turf, ricocheting up to glance his thigh. The throwing axe ripped his leggings and scraped his flesh. The burst of pain in his leg finally ignited the flame within. His rage flared from his belly to his limbs and head. Elan scooped up the axe and threw it back just as the Spali fled.

"You all right?" she asked.

Vahldan nodded and dashed after the thrower, squeezing his

hilt. The longing to spill the blood of his prey began to energize him. Dense pines turned to sparse hardwoods as they ran downhill through knee-high ferns. Their quarry came to view just as the first campsite did. The man called as he passed through, rousing a sleeping trio of Paralatoe around a smoldering fire.

Vahldan charged the camp. All three waking Spali scrambled to unwrap and arm themselves, even as their initial quarry disappeared in the trees beyond. The first Spali he reached snatched up an arrowless bow, raising it with both hands in an attempt to block his sword stroke. His blade snapped the bow like a twig. The man fell to his back and crossed both pieces to block the next blow. A guttural roar erupted from Vahldan's lungs as the blade sliced the fingers off his victim's hand on the way to crunching into his skull.

The second Spali growled, brandished a dagger, and set himself to spring. Elan crashed into him with a Skolani battle cry and a roundhouse blow. Her well-aimed swipe sliced the Spali's neck and he fell back holding his neck. The third freed himself of his bedding and fled in the same direction as their original quarry. This one was not only fast but large. He was heavily tattooed and his hair was tufted.

Thunar's Blessing thrummed through Vahldan now. His gaze met Elan's, and they were one. Without a word, they ran on, chasing their new quarry.

He lost sight of the Spali giant among the gray beech trunks and slowed, scanning the forest. Another Paralatoe darted snake-like from behind a massive oak's trunk, swinging a curved blade at Vahldan's head. Vahldan raised his blade and skidded to a halt, slipping on the mossy rock and thudding onto his backside. He attempted to roll, but the Spali was instantly atop him, one foot pinning his sword to the ground. The attacker snarled and raised his blade.

Elan shrieked as she leapt, flying downhill and slamming feet first into the Spali, sending him sprawling. Vahldan lunged, jabbing the Spali's thigh. The man howled and contorted, opening himself to

Elan's thrust. Her blade plunged halfway in, just behind his ribcage. They scrambled to their feet, and Vahldan stabbed downward, silencing their wailing victim.

He raised his blade again. Elan pulled his shoulder. "He's done. Still with me?" Vahldan felt the same clean burn as he had in the trial. He nodded. "Good. We need to stop him." She pointed after the fleeing giant. They ran again, clearing the ridge and pounding downhill.

Voices and horse sounds echoed through the valley. The main camp was near, and was roused. The big Spali had already warned them. It made Vahldan angrier.

Elan led him through the boughs of hemlocks till a clearing opened at the base of the hill. The camp sprawled before them. He spotted the big man and started for him. Elan blocked his progress. "See me?" Only as he nodded did he notice the dozens of scrambling Spali beyond her. The big man was shouting orders and directing them. Elan had saved him from losing himself. She pointed down the treeline, and led him along the hillside at a trot.

The forest thinned, and Elan turned into the hemlocks that skirted the camp. They'd come around to the camp's backside. They halted and crouched in the boughs to survey from their new position. They were behind a half-dozen pavilions. Beyond the camp's center was a makeshift corral. Every Spali was in motion. A score had already mounted, and the riders streamed from the corral to gather in the clearing.

"They're forming up for a counterattack," Elan whispered.

"How do we stop them?"

Elan shook her head. "We don't. Too many. It's suicide."

Vahldan spotted an opportunity. "Maybe not." He pointed, the inner forge flaring.

Auchote sat on his mount alongside the entrance to the corral, bellowing commands. Vahldan had never felt a stronger impulse to kill. Besides, taking down their leader was a sound move.

"The gods favor the bold," he said. He tapped her bow. "Cover me."

He started out, but Elan grabbed his arm. "No way. Too dangerous. We need you."

Vahldan rounded on her. "Getting Auchote is worth any risk. Just get me to that last pavilion." He pointed with his blade. "From there I can strike. Then we run."

"It can't be done. You won't make it."

"I have to try. He killed my father because I didn't act. I can't let it happen again."

Elan leaned to his ear, annunciating her words. "I will not let you go. Hear me?"

She thought he was lost to rage. His head was clear, though the flames roared. He still might lose himself. Perhaps he should. "I'm clear," he insisted. "And I'm going."

Elan pulled him back again, more forcefully. She moved in, nose to nose. "See me?" He nodded. She looked deeply imbued, too. "I am your guardian," she hissed. "If you go, I'm coming."

There was no use arguing. "Together then," he said. She'd tamped down the flames. Vahldan's head was clearer, but his hatred remained hot. He was doomed. He did not fear death.

She nodded. "Our destinies are one. We go in fast and silent."

He touched his blade to hers. "The gods favor the bold," he said, and set out toward the back of the first pavilion. He sensed her just behind and drew strength from it.

Vahldan surveyed the gathering swarm of riders as he ran. The Spali all faced away, toward the river. They just might make it to the initial strike. From there, they'd figure a way forward. As they approached, Auchote bent from the saddle to speak to a warrior. It was the big man, their quarry.

The big man turned to point as he spoke, and his eyes locked on Vahldan. The tattooed warrior sprouted a grin, which was enunciated by two long scars, one rising from each corner of his mouth.

The big Spali exclaimed and Auchote's eyes found him. The chieftain barked out commands and three Spali footmen ran to follow the giant, already running toward him. The one they'd chased brandished a curved sword in one hand and a long dagger in the other. The three in his wake were armed with javelins and woven wicker shields.

Nothing mattered except acting. He would seize his destiny, whatever the cost. Vahldan raised his shield and blade and ran straight at them, trusting that Elan was right behind.

It was clear to Elan that Vahldan was deeply imbued in Thunar's Blessing. The sight of the Paralatoe chieftain pushed him to recklessness. He wanted to take what seemed an incredibly dangerous risk. But his eyes were clear, as they had been during his trial. This wasn't an unthinking blood-rage.

Elan had made a vow. She had his back, same as she had during the trial.

The huge Spali they'd pursued came on with a blade in each hand. Auchote held a javelin over his shoulder, riding slowly to stay behind his three shield-bearers on foot. Death's Grin baited Vahldan. "Come, little rabbit," he called in accented Gottari.

Elan stayed behind Vahldan's shoulder, minimizing the target they presented.

Before they met the foe, the forest echoed with the mournful blare of Gottari warhorns. The queen's attack was underway.

Death's Grin gave a frustrated bark and reined around to canter away, shouting commands to his waiting column. Auchote pulled up again, calling to Vahldan, "No worry, little rabbit—they stay to kill you!" The murderous chieftain laughed and kicked his mount to ride out alongside his host. The ground rumbled with the Paralatoe's departure.

Their chance to take out Auchote or to delay the counterattack was over. In spite of their lost cause, they still had four Spali warriors to contend with.

The gods were fickle, indeed.

Vahldan veered as he ran, turning to cut down the alley between the pavilions to their right, away from the oncoming foursome. Elan knew that it wasn't an evasive maneuver. He was still chasing Auchote, without a thought to tactics. She followed him and cried, "Vahldan, no! It's too late!"

In a mere moment, the departing Spali disappeared over the ridge. Vahldan beat to a halt and turned to her, red-faced and furious. One of the javelin-bearing Spali dashed into view from the end of the nearest pavilion, arm poised to throw. "Get down!" she cried as the Spali released.

Without looking, Vahldan threw himself to the turf and she lunged, diverting the missile with a glance of her shield as she charged the thrower, who fled. Elan easily ran him down. Her lunging chop to a shoulder felled him to a tumble. Another spearman came around the far corner. She careened past her victim to plow into his surprised companion, shield first, knocking him over. The spearman landed on his back, hiding behind his wicker shield, his spear useless. Elan leapt onto his shield and plunged down with her sword. Her blade punched through the wicker and the man screeched. He convulsed as she pressed down, all of her weight on the man's shield and her hilt. Once he stilled, she braced with a boot and yanked back her blade.

She spun, searching for Vahldan. He was out of view, but she heard his growl rising above a growing commotion. She ran toward the sound.

Elan cleared the corner of the pavilion to find Vahldan dancing with the third spearman. Rather than attacking, the Spali played defense, backpedaling and seeking an angle to jab with a tip that was likely poisoned. Vahldan lurched, chopped, and leapt from the man's thrusts.

Elan ran to help him... and never saw the body blow coming.

She hit the ground hard, her attacker landing atop her, jarring the breath from her lungs.

Her attacker's bulk pressed against her, trapping her blade against her ribcage. She managed to turn her head enough to see the scarred Spali face grinning down at her. The giant was enjoying this. Cocky bastard.

Her shield arm was pinned high, but she managed to swing her elbow to hit the Spali in the throat. The jab wasn't hard enough to take his breath, but it caused him to momentarily ease up. She threw her weight into a roll just as his dagger rang against the rock where her head had been. She scissor-kicked, pivoting on her hip and knocking his knee out from under him. He scrambled to regain his position, pushing her back down. Cocky, fast, and a slippery bastard.

He brought his long blade down, and she freed her own just in time to parry. Their blades gnashed and their feet churned. He finally pushed off, pulling the long blade back to swing again. There wasn't time to lunge again. She was forced down, flat on her back in order to parry. The blades rang and locked again. They struggled on, blade to blade and buckler to dagger. A cocky and relentless bastard.

He outweighed her. And damn, he was strong, like fighting a horse with arms. She still hadn't quite regained her wind. Panic crept into the periphery of her thoughts.

The Spali let up to try another attack. Elan twisted and her opponent let her, then swiftly regained his position atop her, pressing down. This time his foot landed on her blade, pinning her hand to the ground. His grin grew. They both knew Elan had made herself even more vulnerable. He had her now.

The villain laughed. His tone was taunting. "Mar, zura sampas. Now you die."

The Spali was free to raise the curved blade. It came swishing down. Her only choice was to release the knife to block with her shield. Just as he'd planned. Even as she absorbed the blow, his dagger flashed. She managed to save her face by throwing up her elbow. The dagger sliced into the triceps of her shield arm. A current of pain jolted her, and her arm flailed.

Elan lurched, trying another roll. She was too winded and poorly leveraged to gain any momentum. The giant used the space she created to knee her in the midsection. Now she really couldn't breathe. Her body naturally sought to curl into the fetal position, but couldn't. Her sword was still pinned. She was utterly vulnerable to the strike of his choosing.

She waited for him to let up in order to stab or slash. Instead, the brute kneed her again. A third kick jammed the edge of her buckler into her chin, knocking her head on the rocky turf.

Elan's last thought as she swam toward oblivion was that her dream had betrayed her. This was it. Dead before any of it came true. So stupid of her to have believed she was special.

THE CLANG of metal on metal jarred Elan to consciousness. Her cheek was pressed to the cold rocky turf. She sucked in a breath. Pain flared, first in her abdomen, then in her upper arm, and on through her body. She tried to lift her head and fought for another breath. The blurriness was clearing. A hand's width from her face was the backside of Vahldan's boot. He was fighting over her, straddling her body. The Spali giant's sandaled feet were just beyond. They fought toe to toe. She didn't dare try to move for fear of tripping her protector. It occurred to her that Icannes's training of him, something she'd once resented, just might save her life.

Vahldan bellowed and the blades rang again. He took a step forward and she was free of his straddle. She lurched upright. Too quickly, it turned out. Her head swam. She pushed to her knees, then to her feet, staggering clear of the fight. Her legs were weak and her senses whirled.

Elan feigned readiness by raising her blade and buckler. The Spali giant recognized his lost advantage, turned and fled. For a tall man, he was remarkably fleet. She took a step in chase, but immediately dropped to her haunches, wheezing. Running was impossible. "Go," she said.

"No way. You're bleeding." Vahldan took a defensive stance, surveying the scene.

A galloping horse drew their attention to their quarry riding off. "I'll kill that bastard," she said. Her bravado was rewarded by a spate of coughing.

Vahldan sheathed his sword and knelt beside her. "Never mind him. I'm just..."

He sounded fraught. "What?" He shook his head. Vahldan stood and held out a hand. Elan let him pull her up. She was still wobbly, but he kept her upright. He was definitely clear of Thunar's Blessing. It was normally a difficult transition for him.

"Let's have a look at that arm." She allowed him to guide her to an outcrop between the back corners of two of the pavilions. She leaned heavily on it. Vahldan peeled her sword hilt from her hand, sticky with blood, and set it aside. He took his dagger and cut a strip from the hem of his tunic. He carefully wiped her wound. She hissed. "It's not that deep. It'll heal well." Elan remembered thinking the same about his face wound, and she'd been correct.

He carefully wrapped her arm. Neither of them spoke of the possibility of poison. She finally caught her breath, and the dizziness was passing. They had to be good signs. Partly to avoid thinking about poison, she wondered what he was going to say earlier. "So, you're just...?" Elan prompted him.

"I don't know." Vahldan's eyebrows nearly met as he focused on tying her bandage.

"Yes you do," she said. "Tell me."

"I guess I was going to say I'm...glad." He finished tying, but wouldn't look at her.

"You're glad? I get sliced open and bashed down, and you're glad?"

Vahldan shrugged. "Maybe more like relieved. I don't know...I thought I'd lost you. It... gutted me. I'd rather die myself. I know that now. I can't do this without you."

A shiver momentarily seized her. "You don't have to. Neither of us does." She shook her head. "Some guardian I was, though."

Vahldan's eyes met hers. He smiled. "Guess it's about time I saved you."

Elan smiled back. "Sort of a switch, isn't it?" He started to laugh and she joined him.

As their laughter faded, she glanced down at his thigh. "You're one to talk."

"What?"

"You're bleeding, too." She pointed at his torn and blood-soaked legging.

"It was that bedamned throwing axe."

Elan dropped to her knees and unwrapped the cording and pulled down the legging to take a look. The entire area was purple. The impact had scraped off a palm-size chunk of skin. Blood and pus oozed from it. "Ouch, that's ugly. Does it hurt much, my love?"

Vahldan didn't answer. Elan looked up into his smoldering gaze. She realized what she'd said and looked away. She slumped against the outcrop, eyes averted, lips tight, hoping they could simply move past it. But the blaring silence said otherwise. "I'm sorry. I only meant—"

He slid down to his knees, took her by the shoulders and drew her into his arms. His intent was clear. Elan's head swam again, but this was different. There was no time to think, only to act. She opened her mouth to his oncoming lips. Their noses bumped, but they adjusted the tilt of their heads and their kiss gained intensity. They clung to one another, their hands groping. He drew them up and pulled her tight, till they were pressed together from their chests to their thighs. She felt the swell of his excitement.

Her insides felt liquid. She broke from the kiss, and their eyes met as they both drew a breath. Gods, they were galloping blind, and she had to find the reins.

Vahldan's eyes widened. "What? I'm sorry. Did I—"

"No, it's not you," Elan said. "It's just... I'm afraid."

"It's all right. I think the Spali are all gone now." He scanned the camp.

Elan shook her head. "That's not what I'm afraid of."

His gaze returned to hers. "I've longed for this, for you. Nothing else matters."

Elan knew then. It couldn't be stopped. "You're right, nothing else. One of us could die." She nearly had. "Before that happens, we deserve to have it all. I deserve to have you."

She snaked her hand down to grasp his member through his tunic, pressing her pelvis on his hip bone. Having dressed him, she well knew he wore no small clothes. She lifted his tunic, ran her hand over the ripples of his stomach muscles. She kept kissing him as he reached under her tunic to tug her leggings down and cup her butt cheeks.

Elan pushed him back against the outcrop. "Straighten your legs." Vahldan sat on his butt with his tunic bunched up and his cock arcing toward his belly. She straddled and kissed him again, pulling her underpants aside and guiding him into position.

They fumbled together, unable to find the right angle for entry. She knew their contact wasn't wet enough. She broke their kiss. "Hold on." She spit in her hand, realizing it was smeared with dirt and gore. Her spit only made reddish mud.

Elan wiped her hand on her legging. "Hold still. We need to get things wet." She crawled down to sit on his feet and took the head of his cock in her mouth. He gasped. She slid her lips up and down a few times and his hips started to undulate. Vahldan was trembling; getting close fast. She slowed, focused on the task, to reduce the friction of what came next. As soon as it was slick, she hurried to position herself over him, kissing him and using her hand to guide him into place again. And...

"I always knew you were humping him, Elan. It never mattered what the others said."

Elan leapt up and spun, yanking up her leggings, hoping it was just a nightmare. But it wasn't. Anallya stood smirking at the end of the alley between the pavilions. "But even I never would've guessed you two would go at it in the middle of a battle."

Vahldan scrambled to his feet beside her, both of them pulling together their garments. Anallya raised a brow and called, "Over here, my princess! I told you I'd find them. It helped that they stopped off for..." The blood-bitch smirked. "*A little breather.*"

A host of riders emerged from the hemlocks on the ridge. Icannes and a half-dozen Blade-Wielders sat looking down on the scene, their face paint in no way camouflaging their disdain. Shame came to her like black smoke, filling her lungs, stinging her eyes, and burning her throat.

Anallya emoted her glee. The blood-bitch would spread word of this far and wide.

Teavar and Arnegern appeared, running on foot behind the mounted Skolani. Then came the rest of Vahldan's attack squad. Teavar's deep voice boomed back to the others. "I knew it!" The giant grinned. "By Thunar, they're both alive. Covered in blood, but alive."

Elan didn't want to know what he'd been sure of. She looked down at herself. Blood from Vahldan's leg wound was smeared over her leggings. She looked to Vahldan to find she'd gotten blood from her soaked arm bandage all over his arms, chest, and neck.

Elan couldn't bring herself to look at them. Icannes and the Skolani sat in silent judgement while Vahldan's men hurried to surround their leader. His cousins shook his hand and slapped him on the back. They grinned and giggled like a pack of naughty boys.

How was it that Vahldan was being lauded while she was scorned? Everything they'd done this day, they'd done together.

Elan was tempted to just turn and run, but she knew that would only make it worse. She had to face Icannes. Head hanging, she went to stand before Starfire. "My princess, how is it that you're here?" Horsella help her, she sounded like a frightened little girl.

"We came for the two of you, Elan. The queen was concerned, as was I. Seems we shouldn't have been."

Elan forced herself to look. "My princess, I'd fallen. He drove off my attacker, and... Well, we were relieved, and—"

"Relieved! So it seems." Icannes glanced at him. "He's injured?"

Not as severely as Elan was. "Just a flesh wound. But I can explain."

"I've heard enough. There's still a battle to be won." Icannes finally looked away, and shouted to the combined force. "It's hardly the time to celebrate! The foe's lines are broken, but the battle continues. What say we finish it?"

The lions and Blade-Wielders roared their approval. Icannes led the Skolani away on the path the Spali had taken to the ford, with Vahldan's squad trotting in their wake.

Vahldan stood waiting for her. She started to run. "I'm sorry," he said as Elan ran past him. He didn't look it, though. He seemed almost giddy, all but oblivious to her humiliation.

"Don't be," she called over her shoulder. Elan sped her step, staying ahead of him. "I brought this on myself," she muttered.

CHAPTER 22—SOWING DIVISION

" I , for one, do not believe Afletam Forest is haunted, in spite of the many tales that claim it's so. The forest is, however, ancient. Its oaks and beeches stand apart, their massive trunks like gray columns for a high, dark canopy that keeps all but the hardiest of ferns from scattering across an otherwise barren forest floor. In contrast to the lively green pines and maples of Dania's hillsides, Afletam has a decrepit look and smells of decay. Spending time there reminds one of the inevitability of decline. And so, whether or not I believe Afletam haunted, when there I am haunted by it. Given the choice, I prefer to dwell elsewhere."—Brin Bright Eyes, Saga of Dania

AT DUSK Thadmeir finally made his way through the Danians' first camp in Afletam, heading for the pavilions of the Wulthus vanguard. He was one of the last to arrive. He felt ill and exhausted. It was the end of the first day of combat, but it already felt like this war had been going on for weeks.

The mud on Thadmeir's boots, from the banks at ford's landing, was rust-red with the blood of the fallen. The dead had been laid out between the Skolani and Gottari sides of the camp, and scores of wounded were being treated in a series of open pavilions nearby. Every healer, Skolani and Gottari, was still working to save lives. As Thadmeir walked among the wounded, offering his well-wishes and gratitude, the somber scene had been jarringly overridden by the raucous laughter and song drifting from the Gottari side of the camp.

The Gottari portion sprawled in disorder. Clearly no thought had been given to its defensibility. The wagons were yet to be unloaded, but the mead barrels had been tapped.

The situation was beyond disrespectful, beyond undisciplined. Thadmeir's bloated stomach complained audibly. He'd started the day fighting Spali, and had been battling a nigh-crippling case of indigestion since.

He spotted the Wulthus banners. Urias had set up the vanguard's pavilions at the center of the site. It was the only precise setting in the camp. Most of the merriment came from a branch that shot off to the southeast. Even from a distance this offshoot looked slovenly. Lamps hung at various heights from the sweeping low branches of the oaks, illuminating the red banner with the golden snarling lion's head.

No surprise—this noisiest, messiest quarter belonged to Badagis's host.

Thadmeir entered the circle of his own fire, his chair perfectly placed, facing east toward the foe, squared with his back to the entryway to his Pavilion. He nodded to the somber Wulthus Rekkrs awaiting him around the fire. An Elli-Frodei was rewrapping Hjal-falm's wounded shoulder across from Thadmeir's seat. He bowed his head to the aging warrior before sitting. The prominent landowner and guildsman inclined his head in reply.

Just as Thadmeir sat, raucous singing echoed through the trees from Badagis's camp, the voices drenched in drink and mirth. His Rekkrs all stared at the fire. Reluctantly, he pitched his ears to the lions' song.

"...And tho' they faced a mounted score, They slew until they saw no more,

Yon their way the fight did flare, Skolani cry and trumpet's blare,
They pushed the foe unto the fore, Set in flight to shirk his roar,

LITTLE DID YOUNG LION CARE, *He took his rest in Spali's lair,*
While battle's rage and tempers burn, In lion other ardors yearn,
For there he stole a thing so rare, Skolani lips, a kiss so fair,

ARRIVED *the host to save his skin, Hearts made light upon their ken,*
Beheld by those with eyes once sore, Fierce the thirst bespoke by lore,
Young Lion roused and rested then, Took up his sword to fight again!"

THEY DISSOLVED into laughter followed by shouted toasts. Urias appeared and sat at Thadmeir's right. His brother handed him a brimming horn. "They sing of Vahldan. He and his Skolani guardian are the talk of the camp."

Thadmeir felt his lip curl. "I know of whom they sing."

"The makings of a memorable song. Though I doubt the subjects will appreciate it."

"It's a disgrace," Thadmeir said before releasing a soft belch. "They should be ashamed."

"If you're speaking of the song's subjects," Urias replied, "from what I've heard, it seems they are. No one's seen Elan since the queen called a halt to the pursuit of the Spali's retreat. And they say Vahldan is little more than a prisoner in Desdrusan's camp. He hasn't shown his face since his pavilion was raised."

"If only the rest of their lot could find their way to decency. They should be honoring those who sacrificed. While the Outcast's son humped his Skolani wench, brave warriors died to gain our foothold here." Urias said nothing, but Thadmeir sensed his discontent. "I suppose you disagree?"

Urias shrugged. "Is it really so unusual for young soldiers to celebrate a victory? Or to tease one another over a romantic conquest? I'd say after a day like today, a song or two is to be expected."

Rather than argue, Thadmeir belched. The departing air seemed to provide space, so he drank. It was typical for Urias to offer a different viewpoint—which was part of what made him a fine first captain. But it often rankled. He knew his brother thought himself less gloomy, more open-minded. But these men were behaving without respect or humility.

Thadmeir relished the burn of the mead flowing to his sore limbs. "At least this will seal his fate, once this war is over."

Urias frowned. "How do you mean?"

"I mean, after today's disgraceful showing, Vahldan's banishment is all but foregone. The Rekkrs I've spoken to are disgusted by his antics."

"That's an odd take. By all the accounts I've heard, if Vahldan's attack squad hadn't taken the heights, the casualties at the ford would've been far greater. And Vahldan and Elan also seem to have delayed the Paralatoe's counterattack. I think you're relying on a tainted sample. The old guard will scoff, but I suspect others will see it differently."

Thadmeir nodded to indicate the wounded captain. "Hjalfalm's footmen suffered the highest casualty rates. Can you imagine any of them applauding Vahldan's spectacle?"

Urias shrugged. "Oh, I don't know. It's hard to resent two warriors willing to storm a Spali camp, risking their lives to buy those very men every possible moment before they faced Spali arrows." His brother lowered his voice. "As the man who sits on the dais chair, you might consider embracing the efforts of all. It would set an example for our unity."

Thadmeir took another sip. Debating Urias could be trying. "I feel I must point out, Brother, that the ones embracing Vahldan's debauchery are the louts—young and vainglorious."

"Ah, but a farsighted commander might consider *young and vainglorious* to be a fitting description of tomorrow's victorious warriors."

Yes, bickering with Urias was about as pleasant as it had been crouching over the sewage trench, trying to pass the turd that had been hardening inside him since the day he left Danihem. In either case, Thadmeir knew there were times when it was best to just try again later. He drank deeper, emitting an involuntary grunt as the liquid hit his bloated gut.

Urias sat back with a soft chuckle. "May as well admit it, Brother. You're getting ornery with age. Which of these fires would you have been drawn to when you were young?" Thadmeir raised his brows, frowning toward the mess of Badagis's camp. "Never mind. I forgot. You were never young." Thadmeir opened his mouth to retort, but Urias cut him off. "Think of it this way: keeping morale up in war is a commander's biggest challenge. You should be grateful."

"Grateful? It's also a commander's goal to avoid the bloodshed of those he leads. Drunkenness and bluster among them rarely lead to that end." Urias rolled his eyes. Thadmeir went on. "Have you considered that the Spali allowed us to win through? That they're leading us to the spot of their choosing, likely from which retreat will be difficult if not impossible? What good will their ribald songs do us then?"

Thadmeir realized he was all but shouting. All of the Wulthus highborn had turned to him with stern expressions.

Urias smiled his damn buoyant smile, raising his cup in salute to the onlookers. "If that turns out to be the case, I say it's all the more reason to enjoy tonight. To the bottom with the rest in your beard, Brother." He drained his cup. With so many watching, Thadmeir could only hoist his own cup and drink.

As Thadmeir forced himself to swallow more than he wanted, young Arnegern appeared. "Ah good," Arnegern said, raising his cup. "Glad to see you all have plenty to drink. But I've been sent with an invitation, if it pleases you, Lord Thadmeir." Thadmeir nodded, holding back a burp, and the young lion continued. "The Amalus Rekkr Myric has sent a gift to honor Badagis's host for their part in today's victory—in particular Vahldan's successful raid on the ridge. It's a barrel of fine Hellainic grape, distilled to the point that drinking it steals a man's breath. Ask me, it's a bit like swallowing lit lamp fuel. But it leaves a lingering warmth, at least. In any case, Badagis wishes to share this gift with our Wulthus leadership, that our two ruling clans might drink to victory together—in tribute to the futhark."

No one spoke. Arnegern fidgeted, then stared at his feet. "So... come as you will. The barrel is tapped but far from empty."

Urias made a scolding face and gestured. Thadmeir realized his brother was probably right. About this, anyway. "Thank you for your kind offer, Rekkr. Please convey my gratitude to Badagis, as well." Arnegern nodded, backed up a few steps, turned and fled.

Again, they all sullenly stared Thadmeir's way. He felt compelled to say, "Any of you wishing to sample the lions' strong drink may do so. I will content myself with mead, and hope for a clear head and a settled belly come dawn."

Thadmeir was chagrinned when several of the younger men rose and hurried off.

Urias stood, too. "I'd best see they find their way back." Thadmeir frowned up at him. His brother smiled. "I still say Vahldan and Elan are heroes worthy of toasting. Might seem like a grudge if at least one of us doesn't partake." Urias shrugged. "Besides, it's not every day a man gets a chance to sample lit lamp fuel. Sleep well, my lord."

Elan hated this. She'd rather go back into battle than sit here alone, waiting. She'd been told nothing. Indeed, beyond being ordered to wait in Icannes's pavilion, Elan had scarcely been spoken to.

The silence was bad enough, but it was worse knowing they all whispered behind her back. And this was just the beginning—a pittance compared to what was surely coming. Elan had broken one of the primary tenets of the Blade-Wielder oath, and everyone knew it.

A young protégé healer had cleaned and bandaged her arm wound. Annakha had been in momentarily. Keisella's near-sister and most trusted healer had given Elan's wound a cursory look, and left. Annakha's appearance meant that the queen knew everything. The only words Annakha spoke were to insist Elan drink a foul-smelling concoction. At least they were actually worried about the possibility of Spali poison. Or maybe they hoped she'd been poisoned—as though it might explain her behavior.

Elan really couldn't blame them. She was being as hard on herself as the queen and the elders were. She'd been weak. As if she was wanton, or needy. She loathed those qualities.

She sat and hugged her knees, staring out the narrow gap in the entrance flap. Her heart lurched with every passerby. The yellowing beech and alder leaves filtered the setting sun, creating an eerie glow that infused the torch-lit camp. Under another circumstance she might consider it pretty, but tonight it seemed ominous.

By now the fallen had been attended to, the horses cared for, and the wagons unloaded. The evening meal preparations were well underway. It was the time of day when the battle participants would pair off to celebrate the cleansing ceremony.

But of course there was no cleansing to remedy Elan's soiling.

Any moment now the queen or one of the elders would come to impose Elan's punishment—likely a tribal confession. Such events were little more than public humiliation. Elan tried to imagine standing before the entire tribe to confess what she'd done. The last confession she'd attended had seemed harsh, and she had hardly known the confessor. The elders had taken turns haranguing the woman. The confessor had stood mute through the verbal lashing, chin high. The woman had only broken down when the entire tribe filed by, hurling insults and spit-wads and even dirt clumps. Elan clearly recalled the woman's tears, the scornful glee of the younger warriors, and the palpable disgust of the older women. Not to mention the hollow stares of shame displayed by the woman's relatives.

At least Elan would have it done and over. And yet, would it be? The punishment for breaking the Blade-Wielder's oath could be much more serious. She knew the verdict rested on intent. Was it an accident, a misjudgment? Or were there deeper forces at work? Would the elders be able to see inside her, to read her heart? If they could, would what they saw aid Elan's case? Was she burying her feelings for Vahldan—hiding a pathetic weakness, even from herself?

Could she actually face the ultimate punishment? She stood and paced.

Elan had never seen an actual banishment take place. She'd heard the horror stories, though. As a little girl she'd witnessed a banished Blade-Wielder's attempt to return to the Jabitka. She'd been told the woman had willingly left, to be with a Gottari man she'd claimed to love more than her life among her people. The offender had run off with her man in the spring. By autumn she was back. The wretched woman wandered the camp blubbering, begging for someone—anyone—to acknowledge her presence. But no one did. Everyone simply ignored her.

Elan's mother had caught Elan staring at the wretch. Elan had been weak then, too. She'd felt pity, and Ellasan had recognized it and taken her to task. The woman was a ghost, a curse who brought ill luck to those who acknowledged her, or even secretly pitied her. Elan had later learned the ghost had finally gotten the attention she sought. A gang of Blade-Wielders had beaten her bloody and dragged her off at the end of a rope. No one seemed to know, or to care, whether or not the woman survived. The pathetic victim was merely a ghost, after all.

What if it came to that for her? Could Elan really leave her people? She couldn't be certain, but she imagined Vahldan might join her. Vahldan had mentioned seeing the wider world. It shamed her to recall, waking in the night and imagining them living alone, in the wild. She'd imagined them wandering to the sea together, and sailing away. Elan shook her head and scolded herself, even for the memory. Besides, Vahldan had his own issues to contend with. As the hours apart passed, even the idea of some sort of shared life with him felt more and more ludicrous. Gods, half of the time he seemed intent on driving her to new heights of annoyance.

Best not to think about Vahldan at all. Allowing him to dwell in her thoughts was how she'd gotten into this mess. She poked at the fire in the brazier and fed it.

Darkness overcame the twilight. Elan found herself pacing again. The camp settled into the deep quiet of the cleansing ritual. The Wise Ones would be performing the ceremony for the queen and those who'd won honor in the field. If they hadn't yet, it would be some time before anyone could be bothered with deciding Elan's fate. Let alone inform her of her fate.

Elan resigned herself and sat again. She jumped back up when the flap opened. In strode Icannes. Alone. More surprisingly, Icannes carried a steaming pot of cleansing paste.

"You first," Icannes said. "Off with your things. I want to check that arm beforehand."

"Me?" The word squeaked out.

"Yes, you. Clothes off. You've already been disarmed. You shouldn't need my help." Icannes set the paste pot on the hook over the brazier and scrubbed her hands in the wash bowl.

In all their years together, they'd never been paired for the cleansing.

Elan's eyes stung. She'd been expecting humiliation. Instead she was being honored. By someone she loved. By someone she knew she'd disappointed.

With nervous fingers, Elan unlaced her boots and leggings. Icannes removed her own boots and all but her sleeveless doeskin under-tunic. Elan worked awkwardly on the laces of her remaining arm guard with the tingling hand of the wounded arm.

Icannes beckoned her. "Come, let me."

Elan obeyed, feeling childlike. Icannes finished removing the arm guard and pulled Elan's blood-stiffened tunic over her head. Elan stood dwarfed by her, in her breast strap and underpants.

Icannes gently pulled back the bandage without removing it, scrutinizing the wound. "The bleeding has stopped and the puss runs clear. Good signs."

Icannes's gaze rose to Elan's face, her expression solemn. She unwrapped Elan's breasts and bent to pull off her underpants. Elan stepped out of them, feeling utterly exposed. Icannes appraised Elan from the feet up. Her voice came soft and husky, "A few bruises. But beautiful as ever, dear one." Elan shivered. She didn't feel beautiful.

Icannes sighed and abruptly embraced her. "I know how hard this is." Her breath was warm in Elan's hair, one hand stroking the small of her back.

Elan drew a breath and flung her arms around Icannes. She shuddered, emotion seeping from her seals. Icannes tightened her grip. Whatever the consequences, they wouldn't be as bad after this affirmation of shared love.

Icannes broke the hold and patted the bench. Elan sat. Icannes knelt and began applying the warm paste, starting at her ankles. She focused her massaging efforts on Elan's calves and thighs. The warmth of human touch radiated from Icannes's strong hands. The strokes seemed to slough away her anxiety. For the first time since the battle, she became aware of her exhaustion.

Icannes broke the silence. "You've purged his seed?"

Elan's anxiety reasserted itself. "No. There's no need." Icannes looked up, both brows raised. "We... we didn't actually manage to do it."

"Not for lack of trying, from what I heard."

"It was a surprise, you know," Elan blurted.

"Indeed! I was certainly surprised."

"For him and me, I mean." She felt herself blushing. "What I mean is, what happened, it came out of nowhere—out of relief, I think. We were both so raw from battle, so full of..."

"Lust?"

"I don't know. I suppose, but..." Elan certainly couldn't explain that it was deeper—something born of their connection, of kestrels, and of shared trust. She suddenly worried that Icannes might be jealous. Elan had been jealous, too, after all. "It's not just that I'm horny. I mean, not for him. Not exactly. I understand that's an itch you and I can scratch."

"I should hope so." Icannes smiled archly, but still seemed to be veiling something.

Elan knew when Icannes was upset and hiding it. If it wasn't jealousy, what was it? Did she already know Elan's punishment? "So, they'll impose confession?"

Icannes's eyes flicked to hers. "No. Mother seems oddly resolved to this. It's troubling."

"What, then? Not banishment, I hope." Elan made it sound like a jest.

Icannes huffed a laugh. It lacked assurance. She worked her way up Elan's sword arm, massaging her forearm and bicep. Elan tried to relax. Icannes went on. "I won't hide it from you, Elan. I argued for confession. It would put it all firmly behind you. I even suggested that I would advise you to publicly confess anyway. I was told that it wouldn't be allowed."

Elan didn't know what to think of that. "What will they do, then?

Icannes looked up, her eyes hard. "Nothing. They mean to leave you dangling."

"Oh." It meant their disapproval had no ending.

Her disquiet must've been apparent. Icannes forced a smile. "We'll figure it out."

The paste all applied, Icannes rinsed her hands and bid Elan to lean back. Icannes began to unbraid Elan's hair. It felt nice. It should've been a peaceful moment, but anxiety held its grip. She realized why. Another unresolved issue still lay between them. In the moment, broaching it seemed better than enduring it.

"Why did it have to be *her*?" It came as a whisper. A moment passed. Elan kept her eyes closed and found herself hoping that Icannes hadn't heard. Or that she'd let it pass.

Icannes sighed. "You shouldn't need to ask. It's part of your problem."

"What?"

"Your heart. Your tender feelings."

It stung. "Spare me the sermon, and just tell me. How could you take her in?"

"I took her because she's the best. The best scout, the best hunter, the best shield-mate, you name it. She's relentless."

"She's a blood-bitch."

"True. But sometimes that's a good thing."

"I can't see how," Elan said, her voice tremulous.

"I think you can. You just don't want to. Yes, Anallya is cruel. And bloodthirsty. But when you're up against Paralatoe, a blood-bitch makes for a good companion."

Elan squeezed her eyes tighter, making them burn. "It hurts."

She sensed Icannes moving around to face her. She opened her eyes to a much softened countenance. "I'm sorry, dear one. But it's time to put all of that behind us—at least during wartime. We were all just girls then. Anallya has won the queen's favor. She fought well today—fearlessly as well as skillfully. Yes, she's a blood-bitch. But, in the midst of battle, she's *our* blood-bitch. Surely you know this. We are Blade-Wielders. We were taught to be merciless, pushed to be ruthless. Those things are rewarded, not scorned."

Elan stopped herself from saying how well Icannes had taken to her training.

Icannes went on. "You do know that Anallya was pushed harder than any of us, don't you? Her mother beat her, you know. Even before she was a protégé, she was shoved, slapped and battered into what she's become. I remember once, at a feast my mother gave to honor one of her mother's victories, Anallya threw a bowl of hot food that displeased her at the server. The bowl broke and cut the woman's head. Anallya's mother laughed and praised her. She was six."

Icannes returned to untangling Elan's hair.

Elan tried to stay quiet. "That only makes her all the more loathsome," she blurted.

"I'm not asking you to stop hating her. Only to accept reality."

Elan's sulkiness would not abate. "I had battle victims, too. At least four. Not that I had a chance to claim a trophy."

"That's just it. What incited such passionate effort? For whom were you fighting today?"

It felt unfair. "Whom else have you ever asked to confess their motivations for fighting?"

"No one," Icannes exclaimed. "But no one else's choices have begged the question."

"Because I had a moment of weakness and tried to fuck him, now everything I do is suspect?"

"Oh, you better know this is about *so* much more than fucking. This is about *all* of your choices."

"All what choices? His protection is my sworn duty!"

"Come on, Elan. You know you've made choices. And one of the first was when you chose to swear to Horsella, remember? It was long before you swore to Vahldan's protection."

This was all striking too close to the bone. "Protecting him was tasked to me by my queen. Just last night she asked me how I could even suggest abandoning him. If I've made any sort of choice, your mother certainly seems to support it?"

"Let's leave Keisella out of this. The gods know she's enjoying her little game."

"See? This isn't fair."

"Unfair? Ha! Welcome to my life. Besides, you're not so innocent yourself."

"I am so," Elan said.

Icannes stopped combing and loomed over her. "You're telling me you're completely helpless in all that's happened. Since the beginning."

"Yes! Vahldan is my assigned duty. What else could I have done?"

"Answer me this, Elan. Who was it that demanded that the Outcast's family be saved? When Angavar was wounded, it seemed clear by all accounts that it was mortal, and yet you urged your captain to rush the attack. You did it in order to save his son, didn't you?"

It felt like Icannes had slapped her. This had been discussed? By whom? The queen? The elders? Elan's head spun. "It's true, Angavar was likely dying. But the others... They're Gottari."

"Many Gottari lives could've been saved by wiping out Auchote's host that day."

"How could I have...? I mean, Vahldan was right there. I couldn't just let him be..."

"Left alone? Like you were when Ellasan was killed? Or maybe you were thinking about how Sael whispered hints that Vahldan could be the Bringer? Maybe you liked the idea of sharing in a bit of that renown? Maybe it would make you special—someone they wouldn't be able to mock and push around anymore. Did any of those things occur to you that day?"

Elan felt defeated. She wanted to rub her eyes but her hands were smeared with paste. Icannes's tone softened. "Don't you see, Elan? You sacrificed certain victory over one of Dania's most murderous foes in order to save him. You *chose* to be his guardian. You chose to take him down the mountain; chose to allow him to fight beside you; chose to bring a male to the Jabitka. And last night you chose to show up uninvited to the battle parley at his side. You chose to stand with him, to publicly support the dangerous attack he volunteered to lead. At the least, you've chosen to behave recklessly. Can't you see why some of us are concerned?"

Elan swallowed back the sob she felt building. No sobbing now, not after being scolded like a child. She wouldn't give Icannes the satisfaction.

Icannes wasn't done, though. After allowing her scolding to sink in, her supposed dearest friend added: "Can you imagine Anallya making those same choices?"

She choked on the sob she'd been holding in. "How? If you really care for me, how can you throw *her* in my face right now?" Tears dripped from Elan's jaw, unwiped.

"I can because I'm afraid! I'm afraid for the next choice. In case you hadn't noticed, your so-called subject is a legend in the making. They're already singing songs about him. Vahldan is a star on the rise. Even if you still believe he's your duty, it's a duty that's bound to end. And I'd like it to end now."

"What? You can't do that."

"I can advise for it, fight for it," Icannes said.

"I can't leave him. Not now."

"All right—I'll take the bait. Why not?"

Elan pressed her lips tight. She knew she shouldn't talk about it. No matter what she said, it would be misconstrued. "It's not my place to decide."

"Are you sure? You could try it. Even present it as a request. See what happens." Elan glared. She hated how unfair this was. Icannes's laugh was sardonic. "I thought not."

"Why are you doing this to me?"

"I'll tell you why. Because it's so clear! At least it is to everyone but you. You've chosen him—even over your sisters. Even over your-self. I'm afraid that the next misguided choice will be your ruin. And you know the one I'm talking about. If I see what might come next, and do nothing, what sort of sister or friend would I be?"

Elan's galloping heartbeat flushed her prickling skin. Icannes leaned in to scrutinize her. "You've already considered it. Haven't you? You've already thought of running off with him."

Elan turned away. Icannes took her chin and forced her to look. "Elan, you *must* listen to me. Banishment is not so simple as merely being dead to your people. It's death with dishonor! At the very best, it's a sentence to an eternity among strangers."

She twisted her chin out of Icannes's hand. She wasn't planning on going anywhere, but Vahldan was the farthest thing from a stranger. He was the only one who actually needed her.

Icannes's expression flared. "You think I'm exaggerating? Just what do you think we are to them, Elan? We are warriors, and damn fine ones, which they admire. But what about beyond that? What are we to the Gottari once we're no longer Blade-Wielders? I'll tell you what—we're freaks! Their women scorn us, and their men are intimidated by us. Or worse, they think us a challenge, sure to offer a good tussle before a fuck. We'll always be foreign to them. And even if you think Vahldan would be different, are you so sure he'd even be allowed to protect you? As a chieftain, he'll be expected to marry well —for advantage." Icannes paused and lowered her voice. "A banished Skolani is an advantage to no one, Elan."

Elan felt cold again. And exposed. Goose-flesh covered her and she trembled all over. She shot to her feet. She wanted to radiate furious contempt, but her fierce façade melted. She turned and fled, snatching up her cloak as she rushed to the exit.

"Please don't," Icannes pleaded. Elan stopped and wrapped herself, facing the exit. "I had to. Please, Elan. Come back."

Elan turned partway, but still couldn't look.

"Come on," Icannes's voice was honey again. "Let me take care of you. Haven't I always taken care of you, dear heart?"

Elan turned back, her chin to her chest. She was so damn tired. The fighting had just begun, but she already felt beaten.

In spite of the paste, Icannes wrapped her in her arms and rocked her. "I'm sorry, but you have to face it. He may not intend to, but he *will* forsake you. Know that I never will. I promise you that. Besides, there's still glory to be won. I'll see that you share in it. Do you believe me?"

Icannes drew back to face her. Elan wanted to believe. Maybe this *was* all her own fault, all due to her poor choices. But she was still a warrior. And the battlefield was where warriors atoned. She needed to stay in the fight. She nodded.

Icannes kissed her forehead. "There, you see? You belong to me. And I'll always be here for you." Icannes wrapped her tight again. "After all, I'm the woman of your dreams, aren't I?"

Elan hated that she'd never really been sure. Worse yet, today made her even less so.

CHAPTER 23—LURED TO ACTION

"Much is made of the sameness of the visions of the Skolani Dreamers, the Gottari Seeresses, and even the Carpan mystics, who – to my knowledge – never met face to face. For those who believe, the similarity of their foretelling of Urrinan offers proof of its verity. The unbelieving deride their mystic connectivity, and account the resemblances to happenstance and proximity. But for those who've known a Gottari Seeress or a Skolani Dreamer, as I have, no proof is required. Once the power of their presence has been felt, belief is foregone. Doubters can but deprive themselves of the gift."—Brin Bright Eyes, Saga of Dania*

THE GROUND WAS spongy under Túkash's feet. The musty odor of decay had a sulfurous undernote. It was chilly enough to keep the bugs away, but nightfall's chorus of frogs covered the sound of the horses' approach until they were almost upon him. Somehow, the fat lion had pulled it off. Desdrusan brought forth the she-devil, just as Kochia had assured Túkash he would.

The unlikely duo appeared to be alone, but he knew the witches had the area surrounded. No doubt a half-dozen or more drawn bows were trained on him. Vicious creatures.

The pair dismounted. Túkash had never been so terrified. He'd originally selected this meeting time and place—sunset at the edge of the swamps—thinking that if things went awry he might have a chance at escape. He realized now how ludicrous that was. Hidden archers aside, simply appraising the awful spawn of the Skolana queen told him there could be no such escape. The she-devil's limbs rippled with muscle, and her sword was as long as Túkash's good leg.

If she had so much as a whim of annoyance, he was dead.

The Skolana radiated malevolence, waiting for him to speak. "It is good of you to come," Túkash said in Hellainic. "It bodes well for turning back this dangerous horde from our borders, a goal as vital to the Carpans as to your two tribes."

"He's a pitiful little toad, isn't he?" the woman said in Gottari. Túkash understood the language better than he spoke it, but during his captivity with Angavar, he'd learned enough to make himself understood. Still, he cocked his head inquiringly.

Desdrusan laughed. "If you can believe, Princess, he thinks to put himself in the same category as us. But the toad has a point. Without our victory over the Spali, his people are doomed."

The beastly woman bent to appraise him eye to eye. Túkash gripped his staff, holding himself in place. His every instinct screamed to flee, but he was resigned to what came. His life was but to serve his people.

"It would be wise for you to bow to Princess Icannes, priest," Desdrusan said in Hellainic. "Or at least look away."

Túkash smiled but kept his eyes on her. "No. I will honor our agreement, but I will not bow. This woman and her ilk have murdered scores of my people. Let her do as she will." Brave talk. Too bad the quaver in his voice made it laughable.

"Ask him what he wants. Let's have done with this," the she-devil spat in Gottari.

In Hellainic, Desdrusan said, "If you so much as offer her a hand signal seeking to reveal we are connected in any way, I swear, I'll tell her you're planning to kill her mother in her sleep. She'd sooner slice you from throat to prick than pull the burs from her hair. Now, talk about how certain you are that you can bring the Paralatoe into the trap, and I'll take care of the rest." Desdrusan's false smile grew to farcical proportion. "You *have* figured out how to lure the Paralatoe into a trap, haven't you? For your sake, I hope so."

"It's as I've said—Auchote is no fool. I will do as I can. But I have faith in our Duhadai, and in her communion with the goddess Zemele. All things are possible through Her guidance."

Desdrusan rolled his eyes. "Yes, she's clearly a boon to your people." Túkash couldn't wait until the fat man received his justice. He drew in a calming breath, contenting himself that the day would soon come. "Well, keep talking. Tell me something worthwhile that I can share with this woman. She's far from the most patient person I know."

"Tell her that our spirit-guide has foreseen that this ambush will alter the course of the war." If not necessarily for the better for the Danian side. "Tell her that the Paralatoe will soon cease to exist as we know them." Even if it won't be at the hand of the Skolani. "Tell her that Lord Desdrusan will win a victory he has long desired." Though it will be short-lived. "Tell her that the days to come will change everything for the Gottari and Skolani—that brighter days are on the horizon for Danaae due to what is about to happen." Even if they'll be brighter for the Carpan people, not for these two and their savage tribes.

Desdrusan began relaying his forecasts to the horse-witch, but her expression only grew more cross. She abruptly interrupted. "Carpans led Auchote to the mine," she said in clipped, accented Carpan. "Why?"

Túkash appraised her a moment. He decided it was time. In

Gottari, he said, "We led Auchote so as to kill Angavar, him who Carpans name Long Shadow. Long Shadow killed many Carpans. Always he looks to rob my goddess, to take all from us—our gold, our land. Our lives. I led Auchote to have him gone. Praise Zemele, he is dead. So our great foe now is the Spali."

Desdrusan's shock swiftly morphed to anger. "Damn you. You've been able to—"

The she-devil held up a halting hand to the fat lion. She narrowed her eyes on Túkash. Continuing in Carpan, she said, "Then why him?" Her eyes darted to Desdrusan. "For a trick?"

Túkash stayed with Gottari. This bit he particularly wanted Desdrusan to hear. "I owe this lion a blood-debt." A debt that would only be paid by his death. "Long ago, he saved this man's life." Túkash pointed to himself. "Desdrusan kept his brothers from coming against me. If not, I am dead." Although it was merely convenient. The pig did nothing beforehand to save Túkash's wife from being murdered for the crime of aiding her daughters in flight. "Also, I serve the lion to defeat Spali." For they were perhaps an even worse plague than the one that already infested his homeland. "I serve you and him with no tricks." None that would be evident for some time. "I serve you and him to save Danaae. I serve to make the blood-debt even." Which would be when their infestation of his homeland had faded from memory.

The she-devil scowled for a long moment before she pivoted and started back to her horse. "Bring them," she spat. "Tomorrow night. When the moon rises."

Desdrusan scurried to follow. Once ahorse, the murderous she-devil steered her huge beast to loom over him. In Carpan, she said, "Cross me, then I and you have blood-debt. Much blood will spill." She reined to leave. "All yours." She heeled the beast to canter off.

Desdrusan glared and muttered a curse and rode after her. Túkash sighed audibly and released a bit of urine in the bargain. In spite of accidentally relieving his bladder, he was indeed relieved. Not just to be momentarily out of danger, but relieved to finally be sure. He now knew he could face his death as befitted a man of the gods.

Auchote glared at Túkash, a low growl rumbling in his throat. Túkash had never felt closer to death. He simply had to trust in Zemele. Finally, the brute spoke. "Tell me, priest. Why should the Paralatoe risk such a venture?"

Túkash sought to ignore the pain the two Spali brutes twisting his arms were inflicting. "Without their leaders, the Gotar's attack will wither. They will fully turn on one another, wolf against lion. And the Skolani are vastly outnumbered without the Gotar brutes."

Auchote squinted. "How can you know this?"

Túkash shrugged. "I am but a humble messenger. It has been foreseen."

"Who has foreseen this?"

Túkash firmed himself, raising his chin. "Our Duhadai, who is blessed with foresight by Zemele, the earth goddess who created my homeland."

Auchote chuckled. "Where is this Doo-whacky?"

"Our Duhadai is a conduit. She receives her goddess from alongside our sacred lake, from which only she can drink. It is hidden deep in the mountains. She bids me to warn you: only if the Paralatoe undertake this attack can the future Zemele has shown her be assured."

Indeed, the Duhadai had foretold everything that had come to pass. She'd also foreseen that Túkash's own death would play a vital role in the cleansing of Danaae of savages like these. If this were the moment Zemele took him, it would serve to liberate his oppressed kinfolk. But he sensed it was not to be. Not yet.

Auchote snarled, revealing wine-stained teeth. "We should risk our lives on the say-so of a skulking Carpan bitch?" He spoke mockingly in the Spali tongue and his men laughed. "Perhaps this lake water is tainted, and has poisoned her mind."

As the laughter faded, Túkash solemnly shook his head. "It is blessed, not tainted. Our Duhadai has seen much that already has come to pass. She knew that Long Shadow would fall if you attacked his compound. She knew you would escape the Skolana with grain for your people. She knew that the fat man's ascent would begin to divide his people. And she knows this attack will alter the course of this war. If you want your people to survive, you will listen."

Auchote's smile faded. "Bah! Survive? The Gotar dogs are as the clinging leaves of autumn." The chieftain indicated the forest's dwindling canopy. "The Spali are as the wind that shall hasten their fall. I would suggest you fret less over our survival and more over your own."

Túkash raised his chin. "And yet these dogs drove you from the banks of the ford. You flee before them as if you are the leaves and they the wind."

Auchote moved to where Túkash's nose almost touched his chest. The chieftain took him by the chin and forced him to look up. "Where and when we meet them is *my* choice, little cripple. Know that I have five warriors waiting for each one of theirs. Know that each step their warriors make in pursuit takes them farther from their mothers and children—those who will soon become our slaves. Do not believe we are blown by any wind. Do not believe I care whether the Gotars are divided or whole. *We* shall divide them. Into the dead and the slaves." Auchote released his chin with a painful flick.

Túkash was trembling all over, but he refused to look away. "I said this attack would alter the course of this war. I wonder, how many of those five Spali warriors might bleed to stop these who march against you? I also wonder how many fewer they would face should you eliminate their leaders in but a night's work. There is little risk by the ways I shall lead, through the swamps. The Gotars are superstitious, and believe the swamps haunted. They will neither suspect our approach, nor guard against it. If they somehow do, we simply retreat. Even the horse-witches will not dare follow. I offer you little risk for a great advantage."

Túkash took his eyes from Auchote for the first time, scanning the men around them. He knew only bits of the Spali tongue, but ventured, "These of heart to love take of Gotar scalps. Hair of foe chieftains sure to prove bravest of these ones."

Auchote laughed. The chieftain turned to speak rapidly to a young man at his shoulder. The youth's torso had few tattoos, but he wore the tufted hair and scarred cheeks of a warrior tested and proven. The beginnings of a tattoo on his jaw resembled Auchote's skull teeth. The young warrior tilted his head back to emit a piercing battle shriek.

"My eldest son shall lead this attack," Auchote said, grabbing the young man's shoulder. "His eyes shall stay on you, little priest. Know that if your plan fails, or if some treachery is revealed, that you will be the first to die."

Auchote spoke to his son. The young man swiveled into a martial dance, his blade swishing once, twice, three times—the last halting just a finger's width from Túkash's throat.

Túkash had to admit, the deft display left no reason to doubt that Auchote spoke true.

VAHLDAN SUSPECTED she was outside his pavilion again. He closed his eyes and listened. Long moments later, he heard her sigh. He longed to see her—to regain their old connection.

Elan was just a few spans away, but Vahldan couldn't reach her.

He'd tried, but Elan had firmly resisted. If she heard him awake, she'd be gone. Everything had changed. During the day, if he called to her or approached, she fled.

Vahldan didn't regret what they had done. Rather what they'd tried to do. He'd heard the mocking songs. He knew this was a joke, even to his supporters. None of it bothered him. What bothered him —what pierced his heart—was that his actions had hurt his one true friend.

It bothered him nearly to the point of constant panic. He feared he'd lost his anchor to his true self. Elan showed him the way to Thunar's Blessing and kept him from losing himself. How would he navigate the future—any future—without her?

Vahldan feared he'd ruined the best thing that had happened to him since the Spali attack on his home. He went over and over it. How had it gone so wrong? How could he fix it? Especially if Elan was unwilling to let him try. She wouldn't even see him or speak to him.

He heard it again—movement. Maybe an exhaled breath. Vahldan suspected only he and the Amalus sentinels knew of Elan's afterhours routine. The fact that Desdrusan had made him all but a prisoner in his own camp was irksome enough. Enduring her night vigils, knowing how close she was but never actually seeing or speaking to her, made his detainment a torment.

Vahldan stared at the pavilion ceiling. If he could only find a way to get past it. To make her listen. If he had the chance to apologize, to find out how he could regain her trust.

He had to try. He slid from his bedroll, hardly daring to breathe. He took a step, waited, another, waited again. He ghosted to the flap and nudged it open a crack. Elan sat just a span away, facing away, wrapped in her cloak. He drew a breath and slipped out. In two long strides he reached her. She shot to her feet, but straight into his arms.

"Please, tell me how I can fix this," Vahldan said, his tone soft but urgent.

"No, there's nothing you can do." Elan twisted but he kept his grip. She looked away.

"I've got to try. I need your help."

"This has nothing to do with you," Elan said. "It was my mistake."

"Please, don't say that. It wasn't a mistake. It was just—"

"Stop it," she spat and twisted again. "You have to let me go."

"No, I won't. You can't just abandon me."

Elan lifted her face to his, eyes blazing. "Abandon you? I was assigned to you. We both knew it would end."

"What am I supposed to do?" Gods, he sounded pathetic, even to himself.

Elan's lip curled. "Here's a suggestion: Grow up!" She grabbed his hand and wrenched his thumb, breaking his hold. "And let go." She backed away, her pose defensive. "If you're going to become a leader, you'll have to step up and be a man."

Vahldan moved his thumb and the pain in his hand shot up his forearm. The ugliness roiled in his belly. "Become a man? You mean become my father."

Elan harrumphed. "Or maybe you could try becoming the man he hoped you'd be."

He was stunned. No words would come. The bitterness of the accusation, the pain in his hand. Her words became a bellows, stoking the inner forge.

A female voice called softly in the night. "Elan." It came from the direction of the brush that lined the top of the slope that dipped down to the swamps.

"Yes?" Elan replied curtly.

A young Blade-Wielder Vahldan had seen but didn't know by name stepped from the brush and approached. The woman appraised him, glanced around, and said, "The Carpan has been spotted. He's leading a band of Paralatoe. They'll be in position soon. It's nearly time."

"The Carpan? Paralatoe?" Vahldan said. "Nearly time for what?"

Elan rounded on him. "This has nothing to do with you."

"It's got everything to do with me. You're talking about my father's killers. It's me they're coming for." Gods, how could she have kept this from him?

Elan shook her head. "It won't come to that. And you're staying clear of it. If the Spali scouts sense anything amiss, it's all ruined. I won't let that happen. Not again."

It suddenly all made sense. "So this redeems you, but I'm just the bait." The boiling crucible overflowed, the molten ugliness filling him, flowing beneath his skin to his face and head, pulsing up from his chest to his neck, and down his arms to his fists.

"You're not going to spoil this," Elan said. "Guard!" she called into the night.

He and Elan stood glaring. The sting of her betrayal stunned him. He wanted to lash out, but how? Even with the ugliness filling him, he could never hurt her. A pair of Desdrusan's thugs strode toward them. "You would really do this to me?" he asked.

The change in Elan was instant. Her demeanor softened. She realized that she'd hurt him. She looked away to guards. "He's done nothing wrong," she said. "Just make sure he stays inside." Then she turned to the Blade-Wielder. "Lead on, Sochana." The woman nodded and the pair set out.

"Elan, please." She stopped but did not turn.

"It wasn't your sword hand," Elan said. "When the time comes, you'll still be able to fight." The second Blade-Wielder had stopped at the hillcrest to wait.

Vahldan flexed his left fist, causing the pain to flare, heating the ugliness to a boil.

"Back inside with you." Something blunt struck Vahldan's shoulder from behind. He rounded on the guards, snatching the end of the staff that one of them had jabbed him with. He yanked, almost pulling it from the startled guard's hands.

The companion's sword came out, its tip hovering beneath Vahldan's chin. "Let it go." Vahldan released the staff and held out his open hands to either side.

"Back inside, lover boy," the first guard said. "Or you'll find yourself in chains."

The molten heat roared back through him, pressing against the backs of his eyes, and hovering at the top of his throat. He was trembling but not with fright.

In spite of the roiling of the ugliness, Vahldan's head was clear enough to recognize that this wasn't the right fight. In order to get to it, he had to be rid of Desdrusan's guards, gain his freedom. Without a word, he strode to his pavilion flap, glaring at them until he ducked inside.

CHAPTER 24—PRISONER
TO PROPHECY

"Icannes almost never spoke of Urias. Which is perhaps why I find this story of their shared childhood so memorable. And revealing. Before Icannes began her training, her mother took her to the longhouse to be presented to the lords of Dania. Once formally introduced, the chamber digressed into adult discourse which young Icannes found tedious. Always a bold child, she slipped away to explore. She found her way to the drapes at the door leading to the longhouse residence. Thinking to peek, she reached out. The moment she touched the cloth a hand gripped her wrist, pulling her through. She found herself face to face with a golden-haired boy of about her age. He put a finger to his sly smile and beckoned her.

Icannes followed the boy up a ladder to a smoky loft in the rafters above the residence. The far end formed a cubby, faced with wooden slats to keep the stray birds and bats from the sausages and haunches that hung there to cure. The boy knelt in the straw and patted the spot beside him. Once there, Icannes could perfectly see and hear all that went on at the dais just below. The boy had shown her his secret hideaway. Together they spied in secluded coziness, until they heard the adults realize that the princess had gone missing. The boy then took her by secret ways to reap-

pear from behind the visiting delegation. It was only then that the two were introduced by name.

In their parting, Icannes recalled punching Urias in the arm. She said he'd looked puzzled, almost hurt. Only when she'd smiled had he understood it as a gesture of appreciation for their adventure." –Brin Bright Eyes, Saga of Dania

VAHLDAN KNELT IN A DAMP RUT, peering through the sumac on the hillside overlooking the swamp. His two companions crouched in silence behind him. As expected, they hadn't bothered to ask for much explanation. Which was why he'd picked Arnegern and Teavar in the first place.

He strained to hear or see something—anything—but the inner forge still flared within him, filling his head with white noise. Vahldan squeezed his hilt, seeking beyond the pulse and thrum of the ugliness, wishing his head would clear. Every nerve twitched, begging him to run down and find a target. The only thing holding him still was knowing that stillness would deliver the opportunity to kill. The moon had risen, but the swamp was obscured by mist and shadow.

Again and again Vahldan made a fist with his shield hand, reviving the ache Elan had given him. The pain kept the forge hot, his anger fresh. The Skolani had tried to keep him from this chance. It wasn't right. This vengeance belonged to him. *'I won't let them get away with it!'*

The moon cleared the canopy to reflect in the still water below. Vahldan's patience was rewarded. Two shapes emerged from mists of the island and waded into the swamp water. The pair split up as they slipped from the water and started to climb the bank below his position. Spali scouts. They were sneaking toward the Danian camp. He perceived the row of warriors creeping behind. The forge flared and the crucible filled, molten hot. Surely Auchote was at the fore. A man as vain as Death's Grin would never let another take his place to lead an attack.

Vahldan beckoned his companions close and whispered, "Take these two out. I'm going after Auchote." Arnegern's eyes widened, but Teavar merely nodded.

The ugliness pulsed through him as the scouts slowly approached. The climb slowed them. Vahldan focused on finding a clear path to run between them. They spread out even farther as they came. His opportunity arrived, and he launched himself in a downhill sprint. The scout to the left raised a bow and drew aim. Vahldan raised his shield and blindly ran on, gaze fixed on those moving from the island to wade into the swamp.

The scout's arrow thunked into the shield, followed by a warning call. Vahldan kept running, leaving the stir behind. He didn't look back. Several figures were in the water and more were still on the island. The warning cry stopped the column short. The Spali on the island scurried to form up, calling in alarm. He kept going, scanning the scene, looking for Auchote.

Vahldan splashed through the water until he couldn't pull his feet clear of the surface, then trudged on with mud sucking at his boots. He didn't see the skull-like face he hoped to, but he spotted his first target. His fury was fueled by a surge of deranged joy. At last! One of those responsible was about to pay.

Túkash struggled through the water, fleeing to the island. The cripple was making slow progress, his long heavy robes dragging behind him. Vahldan powered through water that rose to his waist, the pulsing heat within driving him.

Túkash slipped as he parted the cattails skirting the island. Vahldan yearned for his first taste of vengeance. In spite of the ugliness that filled his head, he sensed a presence off to his left. He didn't think, he just spun into a roundhouse sword stroke, growling. His stealthy attacker's shrill battle cry was cut short when the blow dashed a tufted Spali's head, dropping him with a splash. The joy of it pushed a raucous shout from him as he followed the stroke with a plunging jab to the bobbing body, pressing into flesh, holding the gasping Spali under the dark, churning water. Delirium fed the flare of the forge as his victim went still.

He wanted more. He'd dealt death but hadn't reaped the vengeance he craved.

He stepped on the corpse, pulled his blade free, and flung his shield off his arm to speed him after the Carpan, floundering in the mud. Flaming arrows arced overhead, a few hitting the island and bursting to ignite the trees and leaves. The scene became queerly lit with a flickering orange glow, illuminating his next victim. High-pitched battle cries echoed through the valley before giving way to the thudding of hooves. He quailed to see the Spali on the island fleeing into the darkness, a few of them carrying their wounded. Their flight fueled the red-hot forge.

He would still get Túkash, dammit. He raised his blade and lunged through the water, each powerful step bringing him closer to being able to swing. The swamp became shallower, speeding his step. The Carpan looked back and fell. His pathetic victim scrambled to rise, but too late. Vahldan was over him, poised to strike.

"No, no!" Túkash cried in accented Gottari. "I'm with you! I led the Spali to the trap!"

Vahldan didn't listen, didn't care. He swung, yearning to hack the liar to pieces. The bastard rolled and slipped under the surface of the churning water. Vahldan slid in the mud as he chopped again, his blade splashing the water. Túkash broke the surface, gasping for air.

"You led them to my house!" he bellowed as he regained his footing and raised the blade again. His head swam. The ugliness compelled and energized him. He fought for focus, unwilling to miss again.

"They made me!" Túkash flopped and pushed, crawling backward, one hand up, as if he could stop razor-sharp steel. Vahldan stayed in striking distance, arms aching to swing.

A voice called. "Vahldan, hold!" He barely heard. Didn't matter. He wouldn't be denied.

Túkash looked beyond him and actually smiled. "Ah, my allies are here. You ruined it again, eh boy?" The liar thought he'd been saved. He hadn't. Vahldan trudged on, staying over him. "The trap. You sprang it too early," Túkash yammered. Vahldan grunted, squared up, letting the smug Carpan's lies fuel him.

More urgent calling echoed around him. He growled, hating the distraction. The priest rolled over to flee again. Vahldan kicked, taking out his good leg. Túkash splashed in the shallows, face first. Vahldan straddled him, and the worm rolled to face him, quailing. His target knew he could go no further. He finally had him.

The priest's eyes bulged as Vahldan aligned his sword with the center of his forehead, as a woodsman would to seek perfect strike to split a log. Vahldan raised the blade. Oddly, the priest suddenly became rapturous. "Ah, Duhadai—now I see!"

It startled Vahldan, and he paused. "Not another word!" he bellowed.

"But I now see. It is you." The priest pointed at him, grinning. "You are the curse."

"I said, no more!"

"Ha. Your father was such a fool. That he died for the likes of you! You are the most savage of them all. You shall lead the Gotars to their bloody end. Praise Zemele!"

Everything blurred. He cursed himself for listening. No—he wouldn't let the liar deceive him again. His body was coiled, ready. "Come, killer!" Túkash taunted. "Show us who you are." A roar erupted as Vahldan brought the blade crashing down.

Túkash's skull cracked and parted like a boiled egg. The liar's limp body flopped like a netted fish in the shallows. Why was this creature still alive? It enraged Vahldan. He kicked the disgusting thing and raised the blade again, aiming for another strike.

Strong hands gripped his arms from behind. Vahldan howled in complaint, struggling to fight off whoever dared touch him. He twisted to find Teavar's face, filling his vision. "It's done. He's dead. Leave off, my friend." The resonant voice penetrated Vahldan's fury.

His blade hand was forcefully pulled down and a huge arm encircled his waist, holding him in place. "Easy now. It's over." The big man spoke as if to a spooked yearling.

Still vibrating with frustration and unused energy, the forge cooling, he finally nodded, panting to catch his breath. Teavar released him and stepped back. His blurred vision was clearing. He found focus on a line of riders, arrayed along the shore. A host of mounted Skolani, all scowling at him. Arnegern stood in knee-deep water before them, his sword and shield hanging limp at his sides.

Vahldan's gaze was drawn up. Torches winked through the trees at the top of the hillock. A column of Gottari in full battle gear marched toward the scene.

Vahldan spotted Elan among the Skolani, sitting on Hrithvarra's back. He started for her. "Stay where you are," a deep female voice commanded.

He stopped but kept his eyes on Elan. Disapproval radiated from her like heatwaves from a fire. Her gaze darted to the floating body. "It's him," Vahldan said. "This is Túkash. The Carpan priest. He's been behind all of it. He led them to the compound, to kill my father. And they hunted us, because of him." Elan said nothing. The ugliness was fading. Yes, he'd lost himself. But what had come of it was rightful. "This man was a murderer—just like the Paralatoe you all hunt." Elan looked away.

The voice boomed again. "We know who he was. A deal was made. The Carpan was leading the foe to us. He'd been promised mercy."

The speaker was Elan's captain, Hildeanna. Vahldan shook his head. This couldn't be happening. "Túkash didn't deserve mercy." The torch-bearing Gottari column drew nearer. Hildeanna said nothing. He turned to Elan. "Elan, please. Tell them." She wouldn't look.

How could it have come to this? Elan had walked away. She'd told him to step up, to be more like his father. Surely Angavar would've dealt the same justice. Would these warriors have condemned his father like this?

The Skolani disdain closed around him like a rolling fog. He blurted, "The Skolani broke no vow. Túkash had yet to deliver."

"No, he hadn't." Hildeanna's anger grew more apparent "Once again, our victory was snatched away by a blundering man-child. Twice the Paralatoe have been moments from their destruction. Twice they have escaped because of you." The Gottari column was less than a bowshot away.

"Twice?" Vahldan asked.

Hildeanna's lip curled. "The savages were all but trapped at the Outcast's mine, same as here. Your father, he understood. We'd signaled him. He had but to hold them off—to bide time. Then you came along. We'd yet to encircle them. The charge was called early to keep them from you and your wounded father. Although I now question the price of what was bought that day."

Vahldan turned to Elan. She dropped her chin to her chest. "Elan? You knew this?"

"Of course she did," Hildeanna scoffed. "It was Elan who insisted on it. For her impudence, she was given the chore of watching over the survivors." The grizzled captain turned to Elan wearing a cruel smirk. "I suspect even she now questions the bargain she struck."

Elan met his gaze. He took a step toward her. She shook her head and reined away.

"Blade-Wielders, we're done here," Hildeanna cried. "Scouts to the chase, but keep your distance. Fleeing Paralatoe have left archers in the trees before. Assume that they will again. The rest of you form up in squads to patrol the camp's perimeter." The Skolani all went into motion.

Elan disappeared into the shadows as the torches of the Gottari approached and the Skolani departed to make way for them.

VAHLDAN'S FEET sloshed through the muddy shallows, his thoughts churning.

Marching Gottari soldiers fanned out along the shoreline, many bearing torches. Behind them came a mounted column, filling the gap those on foot left for them. The two lords of Dania led the riders, flanked by Desdrusan's two thug guardians and the Wolf Lord's brother Urias. The riders behind were high-ranking Rekkrs—mostly landowners and guild members.

"Sheath that blade, villain," Desdrusan demanded.

Vahldan scanned their faces and found the only one that wasn't glowering. Although he looked concerned, Urias nodded for him to obey. Vahldan sighed and reluctantly did as bidden.

"Do you now see?" Desdrusan said to Thadmeir. "It's not merely that he disobeyed again. Nor that he ruined an attack that could've ended this war and saved many Danian lives. Beyond all of that, he's revealed himself as the worst kind of killer. As it was with the father, the son cannot control his savage impulses." Thadmeir gazed past him at Túkash's floating body, red tentacles blooming from it in the black water. The Wolf Lord's lip curled.

Desdrusan tsked and shook his head. "The Carpan was an ally. An unarmed holy man. We are at peace with his people. We'd given Túkash our word. Certainly you now see what should've been done the moment this pariah showed himself in Dania. Angavar's spawn simply cannot be trusted, my lord. His bloodlust can only curse us, even in wartime."

Thadmeir raised a silencing hand. "Peace, Desdrusan." The usurper actually managed to shut up. Thadmeir frowned down. "Do you recall what I said that last night in the longhouse?"

Vahldan shrugged. "There was much. Which part?" The ugliness, still roiling his belly, would not abate.

Thadmeir's face clouded. "Gods afire, boy! All I asked in return for giving you this chance was that you prove you could rise above the past. Your reprieve was a concession to my qeins—to what she claimed she foresaw in you. But even Amaseila admits that the best ideals of the gods are a man's to throw away. And you have, Vahldan. You've thrown it all away. And for what?"

"The man was a snake. He was behind my father's murder." Vahldan pointed at his clan's false lord. "And Túkash has long been in Desdrusan's command, just as he was tonight."

"Enough!" Thadmeir roared. "Your accusations are worthless. Nothing you say matters anymore. You vowed to *me*. I risked much for you. I thought to act for the good of our people. For the good of the futhark. I offered you a chance to redeem your honor. But you've shown me the value of your word." The Wolf Lord shook his head. "You leave me with no choice."

Thadmeir turned to Desdrusan. "Vahldan, son of Angavar is remitted to the custody of his chieftain. His fate is Lord Desdrusan's alone to determine, without constraint or condition."

Thadmeir reined and rode uphill. The Wulthus Rekkrs followed in procession.

The Wulthus lord claimed he had no choice, but he'd obviously made one. Now it was Vahldan's turn. The ugliness flared at the thought. Elan wanted him to be like his father? Fine. He would take what vengeance he could. His last act would be to kill, to avenge the murder that was the start of all of his woes—the murder that initiated this entire gods forsaken war.

Vahldan's hand went to his hilt and squeezed. He had only to manage it before they killed him.

Desdrusan didn't bother veiling his glee. "Look at him. Even now he longs to kill again. Jhannas, Ermanaric, disarm him. The rest of you, see that he's escorted safely back to camp."

The Lion Lord's giants dismounted, blades drawn, and strode toward him, closing on angles to prevent flight. A half-dozen more thugs formed an array behind the pair, blocking Vahldan from his target. Tall odds. "Stand down, Rekkr Arnegern," Ermanaric commanded. Vahldan had all but forgotten his friend. It was his fault Arnegern was involved in this. Arnegern complied, sheathing his sword and raising his hands out at his sides, moving to the shore.

"No trouble now, son," Jhannas said to Vahldan. The big man's tone was the warning growl of an alpha. Vahldan glanced to Teavar.

The big man shook his head. It was over. For now. Jhannas held out his hand. "Blade." Vahldan drew his sword and laid the hilt in Jhannas's palm. The forge began to cool.

Vengeance would have to wait.

THE SKOLANI HAD all left the scene, and yet Icannes lingered in the shadows, watching the accused being hauled away. She tried to shake her regret. Things had gone even worse than she'd imagined. Icannes was surprised by how badly she felt for him. She should've been relieved. Even at his best Vahldan was a distraction to this campaign.

Plus, she had to admit, she still worried about his hold over Elan.

Of course he'd find a way to regain his footing. Icannes had uncovered a natural in their training sessions—deft and nimble. Indeed, he'd inherited the instincts of a lauded bloodline. This was what Vahldan did—he blundered, then regained his footing. He was stubborn that way.

Icannes noticed another lurker at the scene. Seeing that Urias had also stayed back made her curious. They'd been friends as long as she could remember, although their interactions were few these days. It seemed adulthood, and the responsibility that came with it, had conspired against their friendship.

Urias's loyalty to his adoptive family was beyond question. Which made her wonder if he'd stayed at the behest of the Wolf Lord. And if so—if the man cared enough to have his captain stay behind—why had Thadmeir abandoned Vahldan to the whim of Desdrusan?

The flames of the burning cypress trees began to sputter and hiss. The Gottari column was nearly complete again as those escorting the prisoner marched uphill. Urias drew his mount up next to the Lion Lord, waiting to take up the rear. Icannes gently urged

Starfire a few steps closer. Urias said, "So you'll send Vahldan to the slave markets, my lord?"

Desdrusan glowered. "I'll do as I see fit, without meddling from the likes of you."

"I don't doubt it. I just wonder for the timing."

"It was the killer who chose tonight to reveal his true self, not I."

"Also true, my lord. But if you send him away just now, along with—what?—at least two guards to see him to Thrakius, I'm sure no few will question your sending off three able swordsmen on the brink of battle."

Desdrusan smirked. "Then perhaps I'll just have him executed."

"In seriousness, it's a thorny situation, isn't it?"

"Not at all, Captain. It's as simple as it could be. At long last."

"Are you sure? Certainly you've noticed how many young Amalus warriors have come to admire him. No few all but revere him. I doubt his killing a Carpan will tarnish their ardor."

"Hmph. They'll soon forget him. Particularly once the Spali arrows fly."

"Speaking of Spali arrows, what about sentencing him to the Penance Line?" Desdrusan glared uphill after his prize, but didn't speak. "Think of his humiliation in the eyes of his admirers, being chained to a line of degenerates and thieves."

"And fellow murderers," Desdrusan added musingly.

Icannes saw that Urias had him. Urias knew it, too. "Yes, I believe there is a murderer on the Penance Line. The vital thing is, Vahldan would see it as a chance to die with honor. Which would encourage his supporters to see it as such. Who could argue that his fate was rightfully in the hands of the gods? And those in the Line rarely survive past the opening moments of battle."

"I said I'll do as I see fit, Captain. And I'll thank you to stay out of it." Desdrusan heeled his mount and fell in behind the column.

Urias allowed himself a secret smile before he reined to follow. She was impressed. The clever manipulation reminded Icannes of someone. Which made her wonder.

Icannes urged Starfire into a trot and fell in alongside him. Urias startled. "Oh, it's you. Good evening, Princess."

Rather than offering a greeting, Icannes said, "Why concern yourself?"

"With what?"

"Him, of course." She nodded toward the prisoner at the front of the column.

"I've been meaning to ask you the same question. For some time now, actually."

"Fair enough," she said, "but I asked first. Your brother...?"

"Oh, gods no. Thadmeir wouldn't approve."

"Why, then?"

Urias slowed their pace as the front of the column crested the hill above them. He turned in the saddle. "Honestly, it just bothers me. It's all been so convenient."

"Convenient?"

"Yes. Convenient that it was Desdrusan who woke my brother tonight, and insisted he come out to see the Skolani victory in the works. Convenient that Desdrusan was the one who managed to broker a deal with the Carpan priest to betray the Paralatoe. Convenient that Angavar's death came at the hands of this same Spali clan and their Carpan guides." He glanced uphill and lowered his voice. "Vahldan made a good point, on the night he petitioned the council. I've long considered it damn convenient that Desdrusan and his supporters were the only witnesses to Aomeir's death."

"You believe the Outcast was unjustly banished?"

Urias reined to a halt. Icannes drew up beside him. His voice was pensive. "I have no proof of much that feels to my heart like truth. For instance, I have no proof of Amaseila's claim of having foreseen Vahldan's place in the Urrinan. I also have no proof that Vahldan could one day play a role in restoring balance to the futhark." His smile shone in the dim light. "But then, it's lack of proof that provides the need for hope. And it's hope that keeps us striving."

Icannes smiled back. That, too, reminded her of someone. Several someones, in fact. It made her regret over Vahldan a bit keener. People actually believed. People she cared for. She thought she'd better change the subject. "You handled him beautifully." She nodded at the column, growing ever more distant.

"Oh, Desdrusan? He's not so difficult."

"Still, cleverly done. Your performance reminded me of my mother, actually."

"I'll take that as a compliment." He set his horse to a walk again.

"If you don't mind my asking, when did the queen last have the pleasure of your company, Urias?"

He looked again, reading her, considering his reply. "The queen summoned me the night after the first day of battle, at the ford. Why?"

"Oh, I just find it interesting. Keisella is quite a judge of character, don't you think?"

"I do," he said.

"It's part of what makes her so perceptive."

Urias raised an eyebrow. "Makes her damn near prophetic, I'd say." Icannes laughed, and he joined her. "So, now it's your turn," he said. "Why concern yourself?" She paused as he had, mulling over how much she should say. "No need to filter it," he prodded. "Haven't we always kept one another's secrets?"

"Aye, we have," Icannes conceded. "How far back would you have me go?"

"Oh, all the way. From the beginning. I've often wondered how you came to be the one to bring Vahldan into our lives."

"That far, eh?" She paused again, lips pursed.

"If you'd rather not say," he offered.

"It's not that. It's more that I haven't completely figured it out for myself." She huffed a laugh. "At first it was just wanting whatever Keisella wanted. If she was going to have a hand in the stirrings of Urrinan, in posing the players in their roles, so was I. Not to mention Elan."

"Well, I didn't mention Elan. But since you did..."

"Elan has a way of bringing out both the best and the worse in me. Seems she does the same to Vahldan. Anyway, difficult as it is to admit, since she met him I've worried about her. Oh, at first I thought it would be fun, of course, teaching him and needling her."

"And his trial performance certainly didn't hurt your reputation."

"That too. But as a bonus, Vahldan presented an opportunity to measure Elan's devotion."

"You wanted to make her jealous?"

"Well that sounds uglier. But it's true enough, I suppose."

Urias paused. "Setting aside their little incident in the Spali camp, I've seen the way they look at each other. Makes me wonder if the prize you snared turned to snap at you?"

That stung. But again, true enough. "I've got the bite marks to show for it. Tonight might go some way toward healing them, though."

They crested the hill. The torchlight of camp illuminated Urias's face as he drew to a halt. "You said *at first* you sought a part in your mother's workings. What about now?"

Another tough question. And at its heart, the source of her regret. Icannes scanned the camp, alive with activity in the middle of the night. A group of Desdrusan's minions busied themselves placing their brooding prisoner into shackles, while others gathered around to jeer him and gossip over what had happened. Gods, Vahldan hadn't just stumbled but tumbled. Her regret made her feel off kilter —perhaps even self-doubting. How had it come to this? Did Keisella ever feel this way? Icannes wondered if a good night's sleep would help. It seemed an age since she'd gotten one.

A pair of Blade-Wielders trotted toward the Skolani side of the camp. Elan wasn't one of them. Icannes wondered when Elan would return to her bed. She supposed she could just command it, but resorting to that would steal the thunder from tonight's storm. Elan might resent Icannes at the moment, but at least her dearest had finally been thrown clear of this wild ride.

Icannes turned to Urias. "Now? I think I'm done with it, actually.

Whatever comes will do so without my meddling. Even if he survives this, I'm not convinced Vahldan will restore balance to the futhark. In fact, I think he's likely to continue to cause turmoil." She paused. "But come to think of it, isn't that what the seers tell of Urrinan, that it's to be born of strife?"

Urias scratched his chin. "I suppose so, now that you mention it."

"There is one thing I've come to agree with Mother on."

"What's that?"

"That the Skolani can no longer keep the outside world at bay. I suppose rather than simply hoping we can remain untouched by what comes, I'd like to be on the front lines, facing it with sword in hand. So to speak, of course." She winked.

"I can't imagine you anywhere else, Princess Icannes." Urias smiled. He'd been a beautiful boy, and he'd become a handsome man. When had that happened?

Icannes wondered how much he'd gleaned of what she'd left out. She'd nearly forgotten how perceptive he was. "So, Captain. Can we still keep one another's secrets?"

Urias nodded. "As always, old friend."

CHAPTER 25—FETTERED
TO FATE

"It was not Angavar alone who suffered Desdrusan's treachery and wrath. For years after Angavar's banishment, those who had remained loyal to him were singled out for abuse. A case in point was the Rekkr Keffric, who had ridden in Angavar's host. Many named him the realm's finest tracker. But after Desdrusan seized power, Keffric was accused of livestock theft and stripped of his land and status. Some whispered of his subsequent aid to Angavar. A few have even claimed it was Keffric who led Angavar to his capture of the Carpan priest Túkash.

The rumors seem supported by what next happened between Keffric and the Rekkr who'd accused him of theft—a man loyal to Desdrusan named Erwig. Several years after the supposed theft, and just after the time of Túkash's escape from Angavar, Keffric's teenage daughter was taken from his home. Keffric tracked the kidnapper to find that the guilty party was Erwig's son. The girl was held at Erwig's homestead, the father claiming she'd come willingly and sought to bond with the son. Keffric rode to Danihem to request his right to challenge the boy to trial, which was refused. Keffric then stole his daughter back in the night, and took her home. Oddly, no complaint was raised, and Keffric and his daughter were *left in peace. In time it became clear to neighbors that the girl was with child.*

No one knows what confessions were shared between father and daughter. Just as no one can know the truth of what happened the night Keffric rode to Erwig's for a second time, save Keffric himself. All that is certain is that Erwig's and his son's corpses, as well as those of two men-at-arms, were all found fully dressed and armed. Few who knew Keffric believe he had crept in stealth to murder all four as they slept, as he was accused and for which the Lion Lord sentenced him to the Penance Line." –
Brin Bright Eyes, Saga of Dania

THE BOYS WERE MOSTLY APPRENTICES to the smiths and servants to the cooks. Vahldan wasn't surprised that they enjoyed taunting the chained men of the Penance Line. But the lack of surprise didn't lessen his annoyance. The other prisoners seemed to have become inured. The chained men utterly ignored their tormentors, even when they were hit with rotten food or slung mud. The first evening Vahldan had stood and roared, putting them to flight, he'd been scolded by the grizzled curmudgeon chained beside him. "Don't make a game of it," he'd growled.

"I'm not playing," Vahldan retorted. The grump then ignored him.

"Just prolongs it," a young man on the other side of Vahldan explained. "They get bored faster if you don't give them the satisfaction."

Vahldan had done his best since then. It wasn't that being a prisoner had gotten easier on this, his fourth night chained to the Penance Line. In fact, the pain from his lingering wounds and the chafed skin on his ankle had only gotten worse. It was more that he'd gained a sense of resignation—something he shared with his chainmates. There was nothing to do but endure. Thus, he didn't react when something wet hit the hair on the back of his neck, or even bother trying to identify it. Once you were this dirty, you really did start to lose interest in hygiene.

Thankfully, the arrival of the skirmishers to the camp sent the nasty boys scurrying to welcome the returning Rekkrs. Vahldan wondered if Arnegern and Teavar had been allowed to ride with them. He stood and stretched to see, causing his legging to pull from the oozing tissue of his thigh wound. He hissed. It was beyond sore. Pain radiated up and down his leg from the spot. It needed to be washed and newly bandaged, but that wasn't going to happen. He still couldn't see the arriving Rekkrs. He took a step, drawing the chain taut.

"Ease off, cub. You'll get your chance soon enough." It was the curmudgeon, stretched back with his arms crossed over his chest and his hood pulled over his eyes.

"Chance for what?"

"To clutch the hilt of that blade that you love so much."

"They'll give us our blades?"

The curmudgeon peeked from under his hood. "Oh yes—your shield too. You'll be naught but Spali arrow fodder. But at least we'll all die with a sword in our hand." The man laid back and covered his eyes again. "It's all that's left to us."

Vahldan bristled. What did he know? "My friend told me the scouts sense that the Spali may continue to flee, that the queen may soon call off the chase." Which would actually only serve to put Vahldan right back to facing judgement, this time in chains.

"Ha," the grump barked. "Your friend ought to know better. The Spali are guiding us better than a pack of prize hounds herds a flock. And the rising rate of their little strikes tells me we're nearing the pen they want us in."

Vahldan didn't want to argue. Partly because he sensed the grump may be right. He sat heavily, his back to the others.

With everyone focused on the returning warriors, Vahldan sensed it was safe enough. He pulled the small knife Arnegern had slipped to him from one boot and the smooth length of heart oak from the other. He slid the knife down one tapering end, curling off a thin shaving.

He sighed. Gods, it wasn't just that carving soothed him. He used to think carving kept the ugliness at bay, but it was more like an antidote. Like eating bread to soak up stomach acid.

Vahldan cupped the cut wood, lifted it to his nose and sniffed. The smell took him back. He cut another slice. The color was reddish but bright, the grain fine. He could almost hear the hum of his mother's approval.

Vahldan couldn't help but wonder. If he'd stuck to carving, even after the Spali attack, would he have become a killer? Icannes and Elan had taught him the path to better control, to accepting Thunar's Blessing. But had his training—the focus, the dedication—really made him a better person? Or just a better killer?

The wood was hard and well-cured, perfect for what he planned. The work called for patience—something that was tough to come by at the moment. And, damn, he wished he could work in better light. It had to be done in the dark, of course.

It seemed an almost impossible task. But trying felt necessary. Like it might just save him, even if he failed. Or perhaps it would save whom he'd always hoped he would become. The person his mother had been so sure was inside him. If dying was certain, he'd rather die as that person.

The grump sat up, craning to see over Vahldan's shoulder. "You planning on more killing, cub?"

He slid the items back in his boots. Apparently the grump presumed he was making a weapon. It was close enough. Vahldan did have one more kill to make, and he needed to finish this beforehand. "We may be in chains, but it's still a war."

"That's not what I mean and you know it. Easy enough to see how your mane gets up and your eyes glow when the fat one and his ilk come 'round. Best let it go, cub. The only one certain to end up dead is you. Whether you succeed or not."

Just like that, the ugliness was back. His father's voice came with it. *'I know what's inside you, because it's inside me too.'*

"Certain is certain," he muttered. "And dead is dead. Might as well mean something."

"Don't bother, Keffric." It was the beefy youth on the far end of the chain whom everyone called Lummox. "Thinks he's above the likes of us. Be better he gets hisself killed afore, rather than getting the rest of us killed come battle day."

The man on Vahldan's other side—a jittery, pock-faced rapist they called Coil—agreed. "Yeah. The last thing we need at battle time is to be tripped up by his highness."

Vahldan's lip curled. "Don't worry. The last thing I want is to spoil anyone's glorious death." Under his breath, he added, "Including mine."

'I won't let them get away with it!'

Ah, what was the use? Carving might soothe him, but it also reminded him of whom he'd failed to become when it mattered. Besides, if everything went as planned, he'd be remembered as a killer no matter who he thought he was.

ELAN HURRIED THROUGH THE BUSTLE. Everyone around her was excited and energetic. It only made her feel more anxious. The sun hadn't quite risen and already horses were being saddled, armor donned, and weapons readied. After the slow trudge through Afletam, today they would march out of the forest's gloom and onto the Oium plains.

Rumor had it that they would finally face their foe in the field. The thought only seemed to tighten the knot of anxiety within her.

As long as she'd waited for the chance to fight, Elan felt only gnawing dread. Battle was easier to face when one was fighting for something they believed in. Or at least *with* someone they believed in. Those things had been taken from her.

Everyone was busy. Elan wished she were, too. She wished she were at the corrals, saddling Hrithvarra herself rather than trusting a protégé to do it. She'd rather do anything but go where she was headed. She was still too angry to face her, but this time she'd been summoned.

Elan hadn't seen Icannes since the night of the failed ambush. Since she'd fully absorbed what had happened. By day, Elan had taken to riding among strangers, alongside the supply wagons at the rear. By night she slept outside, usually near the corrals, head propped from the cold ground on her saddle. In truth she spent as much time trying to refrain from furtively checking on the Penance Line as she did sleeping.

She arrived at Icannes's pavilion and Kukida waved her in without a word. Elan parted the flap, stopped and stiffened. It was worse than she'd imagined. Anallya was on her knees, lacing Icannes's shin guards. Perfect spot for her, actually. Sochana was also there, lacing one of Icannes's arm guards while the youngest of the Blade-Wielders, Kunna, laced the other. Sochana saw her first and smiled. "Elan. Where have you been hiding?"

"That's just what I've been wondering." Icannes didn't bother turning to her. She was painted with her typical bright red swath across the eyes, with sloping slashes on her brow and down the hollows of her cheeks, all to enhance her scowl. Her fair hair was tied into a dozen thumb-thick braids, gathered behind her head to hang down between her broad shoulders. The hoof scales of her breastplate were polished, as were the torcs on her bare biceps. Under the breastplate she wore her crimson doeskin tunic over sand-scrubbed leather leggings.

Damn. She was magnificent.

Elan bowed her head, trying to summon her anger back. "I came as soon as I heard you sought me, my princess."

"I would've given you more time to sulk, but our time's up, I'm afraid. You're here to ride with me, as one of the queen's guardians. Full regalia. I know you don't care for it, but wear an axe on your back and your sword at your hip. And have someone with some skill apply your face paint." Icannes finally looked at her. "Oh gods, and your hair! When was it last rebraided, Elan? When I did it after the crossing at the ford?"

"No." She felt a flush crawling up her neck. "Well, maybe. So?"

"So, you look like a protégé after a scrum. It needs to be redone. We seek to honor our queen, not shame her."

Elan glanced to find Anallya smirking. She hardened her glare. "Yes, my princess." How could she mention a protégé scrum in front of Anallya?

"Sochana can do your hair, and you and Kunna can do each other's faces. But let's make it quick, people. We won't be striking camp. We muster right after morning meal." Kunna gave Elan a shy smile. The girl was a quiet one, with dusky skin, brown eyes, and almost black hair. She'd just earned her blade the prior summer. Elan thought her stunningly beautiful, but she knew Kunna's dark complexion incited speculation about her father. Over the generations, no few Skolani had raised daughters born of encounters with foreigners, but it was rare enough that those with non-Gottari fathers tended to stand out. And those among them who trained to become warriors were often subjected to extra bullying because of their appearance. Which might explain why Icannes had begun keeping this girl close. But that sort of altruism did nothing to explain Anallya's presence here.

"So it's true?" Elan ventured. "The Spali are forming up to fight?"

"Yes, they've picked a ridge on the plain. We can reach the site before the high sun. Seems it's the best they can manage for higher ground."

"And the scouts have all made it back?" Elan had heard that the scouts were having a difficult time in Oium. The sort of stealth and horsemanship they relied on was all but useless on the open plain.

"Four that were due back are still missing," Sochana said, sounding worried.

Icannes brushed it aside. "Enough have returned for us to gauge the lay of the land."

"Seems strange the Spali would choose such exposure," Elan said. "There were so many places they could've ambushed us on the way through Afletam. And they never committed."

"Proving them craven once again," Sochana said.

"Nothing new there," Icannes added.

Still, it didn't make sense. "Then why make a stand here?"

"They don't have a choice. Their army can't retreat much farther before overrunning their own women, children, and herds."

"I just wonder about pressing them. Maybe if they're given the chance they'll continue to flee. All of them. Maybe the Wolf Lord is right to call for laying back for a time."

Anallya smirked up from her lacing. "Speaking of being proven craven. How perfectly like you to seek to avoid a fight."

"How perfectly like you to always be a blood-bitch," Elan said. "What's wrong, Anallya? Haven't bloodied your fangs in a few days?"

"That's easily fixed!" Anallya leapt up and lunged, the butts of her palms jarring Elan's chest so hard it stole her breath and nearly knocked her over.

Elan caught her balance and flung herself back. They collided and Elan's shove was completely absorbed by Anallya's counter push. Someone grabbed her from behind—she realized it was Sochana. Who's side was she on?

Icannes grabbed Anallya and threw her back like a child. Anallya didn't take the hint, and came at Elan again. "Where's your stud now, you rutting filly?"

"Enough!" Icannes stepped in front of the blood-bitch, nose to nose, her scowling face paint made all the more vivid by the real expression beneath it. "Save it for the Spali," Icannes growled. "Both of you," Icannes added over her shoulder. "Horsella help me, if either of you embarrasses me today you'll have worse to worry about than Spali. Understood?" Still glaring, Anallya gave a half nod. Elan only followed suit when Icannes faced her and narrowed her eyes.

"You." Icannes thumped Anallya in the chest. "Out! See to our horses." The blood-bitch left slowly, never taking her eyes off of Elan.

"And you." Icannes grabbed Elan's arm. "Sit." Icannes pulled Elan to the bench by the brazier. "You." She pointed at Sochana. "Get busy on that squirrel's nest on her head. And you, get the face paint together," she added, sending Kunna scurrying.

Elan sat heavily and Sochana started untying her braids. Icannes fiddled with the stays on her arm guard. "Gods afire, Elan. You really had to twist her nipple *today*?"

Elan couldn't properly catch her breath. "You think *I* started that?"

"It doesn't matter who started it!"

"She called me craven. What did you expect?"

Icannes spun, boots thumping to loom over her. "I *expect* you to know you're better than her. I expect you to not need to lash out to prove yourself." Icannes paused, composing herself. "I expect you to put your emotions aside and attend to your duty, Elan."

Her duty? They'd made a mockery of it. Elan sought for a retort, but she swallowed it. It would only make things worse. She made herself say, "Yes, my princess."

Icannes stared a moment longer. "Good." She went back to her arm guard.

Sochana tried to comb Elan's hair. The snags and snarls, yanking and tearing, matched up well with her thoughts. Icannes had the gall to mention her emotions? After manipulating them all the way across Dania and back? She dared mention duty? After all that had happened, and Icannes's role in it? What, in the nine realms, was Elan's duty now?

To Icannes and Keisella, duty was just a hilt by which to wield her. Her duty to Vahldan had been a joke to them.

Kunna came with the face paints and sat before her. "Are you ready?" Elan nodded, lifted her chin and closed her eyes.

"I have to report to the queen," Icannes announced. "I'll leave you two to it. Make her look the part."

"Yes, my princess," Kunna and Sochana droned in unison.

Eyes still closed, Elan heard Icannes leave. She had to be sure.

"Sochana," she started in a sunny tone. "When Princess Icannes sent you to fetch me on the night of the ambush, you thought Vahldan already knew about the plan, didn't you?"

The silence stretched. Finally: "I've been feeling awful about that, considering what happened."

Elan drew an even breath, kept her eyes closed for Kunna and feigned a smile. "It's not really your fault, though, right? After all, Princess Icannes must have believed Vahldan knew. She did mention it, didn't she?"

"Well, yes, she did. I wouldn't have said anything in front of him otherwise."

"See? Not your fault, then." Both women resumed their work in silence.

How perfect. They'd made both she and Vahldan players in a mummery. First the queen, then her daughter. Let alone Badagis and Amaseila and the rest. They all used the bedamned prophecy like a lever. Or maybe like a cudgel. They prodded Vahldan until he tripped, and they threw him away—and her with him. Now what was Elan supposed to be? A painted and preened guardian to the queen who had used her? Another part to play? For which one? The mother or the daughter? Both? Worst of all, she was supposed to play her role alongside the blood-bitch.

At least now she knew. She owed them nothing. Her duty had been a joke. Her whole life had. By using Elan in her little games, Icannes had thrown away everything they once shared.

Elan remembered a time when she'd longed for the chance to win glory—to take trophies and prove herself as a warrior. Seemed like ages ago. Now she just wanted to get through this bedamned war. Then she'd figure out where she belonged. The gods knew it wasn't riding in the queen's retinue, or sitting at her daughter's heel like a prize hound.

The whole thing made her wonder if her dream had been

nothing more than an ordinary dream—the fading fantasy of a girl who'd been shaken awake by adulthood.

VAHLDAN COULDN'T SEE MUCH. Just grass and sky. The grass was wet and matted, and the sky was a vast rumple of low, gray clouds extending to every identical horizon. After so many days spent under Afletam Forest's dense canopy, Oium felt like another world. The brisk northerly wind chapped Vahldan's cheeks. His tunic clung to him, damp with cold sweat. His leggings were so stuck to his thigh wound they were beyond being pulled free. It wasn't just his raw ankle anymore—everything about the situation chaffed. His only consolation was its impending end.

Vahldan leaned to one side, trying once again to see beyond the Penance Line's mounted guards. He knew the Skolani were out ahead, leading the Danian army onto the field, but he couldn't catch a glimpse. He hated that it had come to this. He'd failed to live up to his father's aspirations even more swiftly and completely than Angavar had feared. Only one thing was left to him. It would be his last act, but he would fulfill one oath, at least. Afterward, he would have no last words. He would be swiftly executed, his body left for the carrion-eaters.

Some legacy.

But there was one thing he hoped to be sure of before any of that.

His leaning to look made him stumble, and Coil cursed. The entire line's step was yanked short again. Lummox nearly fell, further impeding the line's progress. The large young man could barely keep up, let alone maintain a cadence. The chain reaction reached the only man ahead of Vahldan. The grouch stumbled and cursed. Keffric looked back. "Step lively, Haimlan." Apparently Haimlan was Lummox's real name. Odd to be learning it now. "All of you," the grouch added. "Let's try for one last bit of grace, shall we?"

Lummox grunted ambiguously and belched into blown cheeks,

and Coil replied to Keffric's turned back with an obscene gesture. Such grace. Vahldan hated that his chances for the success of his final goal could be hindered or even ruined by these misfits. His shitty legacy was utterly dependent on the dregs of Gottari society.

At least the ugliness was starting to fill his belly. It wasn't the clarifying energy of Thunar's Blessing, but no matter. Bitterness, frustration, and fear might just carry him through.

Oddly, for the first time since Vahldan had been on the chain, the grouch seemed to have lost his bitterness. Today it was as if he'd transformed into their concerned captain. It wasn't just age that made Keffric the leader of the Penance Line, although he was clearly the eldest—his graying hair and beard and creased face attested to it. There was more to it. The man had a way of making others take heed, without raising his voice. In another circumstance, Vahldan might have named it a noble bearing. Or perhaps it was spiritual.

This dignified air stood in contrast to the fact that Keffric was the only other prisoner accused of murder. One of the few things Vahldan had learned of proud, solemn Keffric's past was that when he'd faced his judgement for his crimes, he'd actually requested the Penance Line.

The man sought honor in death. That hit close to home.

Angavar had sought honor in death, but what good had it done? His father's enemies had not only outlived him, they had thrived. Hel's bridge, they even had Angavar's son in captivity. The victory of those who'd conspired to consolidate their power was all but foregone. And they'd done it all in the name of ongoing privilege. Honor, sacrifice, and duty meant nothing to men like these. To the guildsmen and the landowners, even this war was about ensuring their status and protecting their profits. Few of them would die to keep their lands free of Spali incursion. Their tenants, however, would bleed for the opportunity to continue to be exploited.

Vahldan might not die an honorable death, but he wouldn't let the bastards get away with what they'd done. At least the villain at the center of it all would pay.

The cloud cover made it difficult to tell, but he gauged they'd shuffled across rolling grasslands for over half of the morning before the warhorns sounded. Commands rang from the front of the procession. The Amalus column was turning left off the muddy trail, marching across matted brown grass. The Skolani were spreading out straight ahead, at the top of an upcoming ridge. The trailing Wulthus Rekkrs and their footmen would be aligned to the queen's right. The battle site had been reached. The lines were being drawn. Time was running out.

Vahldan's belly churned, but it wasn't with the rage he needed. This was anxiety. He thought by now he'd have come to terms with his plan. Nothing felt true or right about this day.

As the Penance Line moved parallel to the Skolani line, he spotted her auburn braids. She was among the queen's retinue, facing away. "Elan!" he called, earning the glare of his guards but not the slightest reaction from a single Skolani. Anxiety turned to panic. He considered breaking the chain early. His heart told him this was even more important than his final goal.

But if he failed, he could lose his chance to accomplish both of his goals. They moved on as he vacillated, beyond Elan. He kept moving farther away. Gods, he was torn.

Galloping hooves. Vahldan leaned to look and relief suffused him. He knew both the rider and the horse that galloped back against the column toward him. Arnegern. His friend hadn't forsaken him. And he rode Ardua. Arnegern reined the sleek gray mare to a walk beside Vahldan's progress. He held up a finger to the scolding guard. "Please, spare me but a moment with a friend, before he faces what comes."

"Just keep him moving," the cross guard conceded.

Arnegern leaned to Vahldan. "I gather you have something you'd like delivered before the battle?"

～

THE QUEEN'S retinue crested the last ridge and Elan sat tall in the saddle, straining to see ahead. The foe came into view atop the next ridge, beyond a deep, grassy swale. The Spali were a blur of activity. Mostly ahorse, the colorfully dressed, tattooed warriors rode back and forth as if they were in a swagger competition. They hooted, jeered, and waved their weapons overhead on prancing, rearing ponies. But for all of that, their numbers didn't suggest the vast horde that the Danians were led to believe they'd face.

Elan leaned to look down the line as the Amalus marched into place to the Skolani left. She couldn't see him. Her wound ached, spreading from her shield arm to her chest. It was healing so damn slowly. The wind was bitter, yet her under-tunic was soaked. Soon, the Penance Line would be marched out into the swale to goad the Spali archers—fodder offered up to gauge the range of their poisonous arrows. How could she face a battle without making things right? Elan considered riding off to find him. Damn the consequence. This was it—likely her last chance to see or speak to him. She vacillated. He'd been so furious with her. But if she survived him, could she live with knowing she'd left things as they currently stood?

"I need only a quick word with Blade-Wielder Elan." Elan turned to the familiar voice. Arnegern had dismounted and was being waved through to her by Sochana. Anallya eyed his passage, looking peeved. Elan reined to gain a few steps clearance from the blood-bitch.

Arnegern came to her stirrup wearing a sad little smile. He bowed. "Blade-Wielder."

"Rekkr," she replied.

"I bring you a boon. Both a charm and a message—well wishes from a friend." He proffered a small wad of cloth. She took it. There was something wrapped inside. She carefully extracted a polished carving of wood, wrapped in a leather cord. She unwound it with trembling fingers, and dangled the carving by the attached cord.

Though it fit in her palm, the kestrel's details were intricate. Her outstretched wings and fanned tail were thin but strong, poised to hover and hunt. The hard eyes, the hooked beak, even the curled talons, were all to scale and lifelike. She hung in perfect flight from the cord.

Elan drew a shaky breath. Her eyes stung. Arnegern smiled up at her. "You are pleased?" She nodded, lips pressed tight.

He waited. "And the message?" she finally managed.

"Our friend bid me to tell you he regrets much, but nothing more than his behavior when he last saw you. He realizes that a bird such as this can never be tethered or caged. He wants you to know this bird was fashioned with his heart as well as his hands. And it now belongs to you. He bids you to soar and hunt, keeping the hope of your dreams in your heart. Come what will."

Elan kept her face and her gift turned from Anallya, firming herself, staving off tears. Her breath came haltingly. "Please thank him if you see him."

"I will." Arnegern tipped his head and started to leave.

"Arnegern." He turned back. "If there's any way, any chance, for you and the others to... to watch over him, to help him..."

Arnegern's sad smile reappeared. "If the chance arises, we will do all we can. That much I can promise." He bowed his head, mounted Ardua, and rode off down the Amalus line.

THE GUARDS PRODDED the Penance Line out to the front of the Amalus formation, and the foe came to view, lining the next ridge. Vahldan had never seen so many Spali. They were so colorful, so animated, it was almost laughable. Until he recalled the potency of their poison.

None of it mattered. Vahldan would soon have a sword in his hand again. The time to act had nearly arrived. He sought for his anger. Damn, he felt nothing but cold fear. Even the ugliness eluded him. Such a betrayal. Predictable, he supposed, that his lifelong curse would abandon him when he finally needed it.

Vahldan still believed in his goal. He considered the source of his inner conflict. He craned to scan the center of the Skolani battle-line. He spotted Keisella at the fore, her golden braids stiffened into two great horns behind either ear and her face painted in red, white, and black, giving her the look of a mythological being. But he couldn't see the one he sought. He would simply have to trust Arnegern had gotten to her.

Vahldan realized that it didn't matter what anyone else thought. He simply couldn't face what came next without knowing he'd given his all to gain Elan's forgiveness—to have her remember him well.

The Penance Line was marched out directly in front of the Amalus vanguard. As he took his spot, Vahldan glanced to find Desdrusan, sitting ahorse behind a row of his loyal Rekkrs. Those loyal to the false-lord sat behind another row of young bannermen. The usurper was well-insulated, of course. Added to that, Desdrusan's mount stood between those of his formidable guardians, Jhannas and Ermanaric.

A guard pulling the prisoners' weapons and shields on a litter rode out before the Penance Line. The horse stopped and another guard hacked the ropes that bound their gear.

This was it. Vahldan had to move fast once he got the sword. He sought for the flames he was about to need, but the forge in his belly was still cold.

After he'd finished the kestrel he'd worked diligently on the connecting link of his ankle shackle with Arnegern's knife. He'd ruined the knife's blade, but made significant progress in weakening the link. It should only take a strike or two with the sword to free himself. He needed to be accurate and swift. Surprise was vital.

The guards began at the far end, returning each man's weapon and shield. Vahldan gauged the scope of the various threats. Jhannas was the most likely to kill him. He simply had to get to his target before that happened. He would attack from Ermanaric's side.

"It's the wrong kill."

He turned to the voice. Keffric squinted out at the field. Vahldan wanted to ignore the grouch, but his annoyance wouldn't allow it. "You don't know what you're talking about."

The older man turned to him, eyes hard. "Oh, I do." Keffric glanced back, toward the vanguard and the usurper. "And I'm telling you, it's the wrong kill."

The ugliness finally flickered to life. He kept facing forward. "What would you know?"

"Plenty. It's why I'm here."

So *now* the grouch wanted to talk? "I don't know why you're here, and I don't care." The guards were taking forever, sorting out each man's weaponry. Vahldan sought for focus.

But Keffric kept on talking. "I'm here because I made the same mistake you're about to make. It's all wrong. He's going to hate that you threw yourself away."

The ugliness flared, spreading up, nearly choking him. "Doesn't matter what you think. I made a vow. I'm going to make things right."

"Sorry. The kill you're planning won't honor the vow you made. It's not what he wants."

Vahldan's head snapped to face the man. "How would you know?"

Keffric huffed in laughter. "I knew him longer than you."

It hit Vahldan like a slap. "You knew my father?"

"Freya's grace, I was with him on the day you were born, Vahldan." It was the first time the grouch had called him by name. "Angavar was my chieftain, my commander. But he was also my friend. I loved him like a brother."

Vahldan's thoughts whirled. The guards were drawing closer. "Why is this happening?"

"I told you—it's what I'm here for. I know it now. I was sent to help you see."

"See what?"

Keffric faced forward but closed his eyes. "Angavar is of the gods now. They guided me here—I can feel it. They guided me to this moment, over long months. Starting before I could ever know why. But I know now. Your father wants you to let him be a part of you. You always held him apart. He wants you to dig deeper, to find and embrace it."

Angavar had always said as much. Vahldan still didn't understand. "Embrace what?"

Keffric's eyes sprang open. "Him! He spent all the years of your life striving toward what he believed you might become. He wants you to embrace his belief in you. He wants you to be bold, to go all the way. Just as he knows you can."

They were so near to his father's dying words. "How... how can you know this...?"

Keffric stared skyward, eyes unfocused. "The gods, They revere his valiance. They accept his choice of you. It's why he chose his death." His father's friend turned to Vahldan, a sad kindness written upon him. "He gave his all for you. He knew you'd be better."

Tears filled Vahldan's eyes. "No. He didn't. Or if he ever did, I changed his mind. Everything that happened was my fault. I killed him."

"Just as he will be the death of you. But not before you take it back. For all of us."

"What did you say?" he whispered. It was as if Keffric had been there on the day Vahldan ended his father's life. It had to be a trick.

Keffric tilted his head back, as if to receive divine communion. "Glory is the way. You must take it back. He asked you to stay true to him. He knows you're the one." Keffric opened his eyes and faced him. "He can only be right if you try. Only you can honor him."

Vahldan stood stunned as the guards came before them and handed them the final two swords and shields. "Gods grant you a worthy death," one of them muttered by rote. He and Keffric bowed their heads in turn.

Still feeling stunned, Vahldan buckled on his sword belt and slipped his arm through the shield straps. His hand tightened on the hilt. It had been a long while. He realized it felt like getting back a part of himself. One that he'd been missing. He felt Keffric's eyes upon him, waiting. "I...I don't know how."

"Let him in, son," Keffric said.

"I can't. I'm not like him. I'm a killer."

Keffric nodded, as if Vahldan had told him winter was coming. "Killing isn't the problem. It's who you kill and why. That's what I've been trying to tell you."

"You don't understand. There's an ugliness. Inside me. I lose myself."

"Listen. Hear me?" It sounded like Elan. Vahldan turned to Keffric, met his fervent gaze. "You won't be lost if you let him in. That's what staying true means. Feel him inside you. Let his blood mingle with yours. You've fought it for so long. Forget about the fat man and his ilk. Just let it go." Vahldan took a deep breath and released it. "You feel him, don't you?"

"Yes. But I'm... I'm not like him," he repeated.

"You're afraid. I get it. But you've got to trust me. Look, if you insist on focusing on the ugliness—on the bad that comes of what's inside—you've at least got to acknowledge that good can come of the bad. You need it today. Your people need it. They need you. All of you."

Vahldan squeezed his eyes shut. The ugliness pulsed at his temples, churned in his belly. "I still don't know how."

"You do. He's there. You share the blood of the Amalus kings. Let it flow through you."

He kept his eyes closed. His father's face came to him—the sad smile. *'Trust me, I know what's inside you. Because it's inside me, too.'* The ugliness morphed. Indeed, he felt his blood warming. He recognized it, flowing to his limbs. He'd felt it before. This was the clean version of Thunar's Blessing he'd channeled during his trial.

"Now, you see? Killing the usurper would be a stain," Keffric said. "A waste."

He squeezed his hilt, tucked his chin and tapped his helm on the top rim of his shield. He felt it, but he still felt lost. "What then? What do I do instead?"

"Look." Vahldan looked at the man. He was gazing out across the field. "Look at them, Vahldan." Keffric nodded toward the Spali. "There is the real foe. They want to kill your people, to take everything from us. If you accept Thunar's Blessing—if you accept the blood of your father—you accept that you are a killer."

Vahldan started, his chest tightened. The ugliness flopped in his belly, cooling his blood.

"Yes, the gift comes at a dear price. But right now it's a boon for our people. Out there." Keffric pointed with his sword. "There you shall wreak death that honors the gods. Death that bestows glory. You shall be Their instrument. Yes, the people will see the killer in you. After today, all will see and know what's in you. And they will praise and thank you for it."

Vahldan closed his eyes, still unsure.

"Breathe," Keffric said. "Breathe and let it flow."

He did. And he felt the heat in his blood once again. It pushed away the ugliness. "Why?"

He didn't need to elaborate. Keffric laughed. "Because of what you'll bring."

His eyes snapped open. "What, you think I'm the Bringer?"

"Of course! And I'm ready to put my belief to the test. The question is: are you ready to accept your true calling—to seize your destiny?"

Vahldan gazed out at the Spali. From the center of the raucous commotion, a white horse emerged, leading a cluster of riders. The leader halted at the lip of the ridge, directly across from the Skolani vanguard. Death's Grin. The warriors around him were heavily tattooed, their hair tufted. Auchote would lead the Paralatoe against Dania's leaders.

Vahldan felt the familiar longing, but it wasn't to kill Auchote. Something stronger pulled at him, made him look over his shoulder to the queen's scowling retinue. He spotted Icannes first. Then there, at Icannes's side, she appeared. Finally. Hrithvarra was in the front line. Elan's gaze was already locked on him. She'd drawn him to look.

Strength and conviction flowed from Elan, to and through him. She nodded, and placed a hand on her breastplate, over her heart. She'd gotten it. She wore it!

Elan pointed to the sky and he followed her gaze. The sight stole his breath. There, soaring over the grasslands between the two poised armies, were two kestrels—one hovering above the other, both ready to swoop, one to guard the other during the dive on their prey.

Vahldan looked back to her. Elan started to laugh. Happy tears sprang to his eyes.

Yes, their connection was still there. The gods had seen to it. It didn't matter whether or not he was the Bringer, or whether or not the Urrinan was nigh. She was still his anchor.

Yes, there was still something to live for—to strive for. The flame within burned clean and bright, heating the blood of his father, of his ancestors.

Yes, he would kill again. But he could also seek honor. And take back his clan's glory.

Vahldan nodded in reply, kept his gaze locked with hers, and said to Keffric, "I am."

CHAPTER 26—THE BATTLE OF THE OIUM PLAINS

"The terrain of the Spali's homeland on the steppe engendered their horsemanship. The flocks their various tribes depended upon, for clothing and for sustenance, were vast, and best driven and herded from horseback. Spali warriors are trained to fight from horseback from an early age. And yet only the elite clans owned the famous Spali ponies. It's said that through keeping their pony strings closely held and selectively bred, the noble and royal clans of the Spali kept the common herdsmen among them from rising above his station."—Brin Bright Eyes, Saga of Dania*

THE THRILL of it set Elan's skin to gooseflesh. It had happened again. The kestrels had appeared just as Vahldan received his sword and shield. And then she was able to reach him again. She sought for him and he looked. And the change in him was clear.

Vahldan believed again.

Since his murder verdict, Elan had watched him from a distance, more than she cared to admit. It had become clear that he was lost.

What he'd become was different from when he lost himself in his rage. It was even more alarming, as it didn't seem temporary. She'd feared Desdrusan had actually broken him. It terrified her. She felt responsible, as if her loss of faith in her dream had incited his giving up. But he was back!

She'd been conflicted, wanting to see him one last time before he marched, but afraid, too. Afraid of what would happen if she was caught, yes. But there was more to it. A part of her longed to confess her wrongs, to beg for his forgiveness, and what she feared most was that he would refuse to give it. But seeing and feeling his change made her believe again.

There was still hope.

The queen gave a signal. At the command from the Amalus vanguard, the guards directed the Penance Line to march to a cadenced call. Vahldan gave her one last nod of reassurance, then one last look at the sky, before he hoisted his shield to march into the swale.

Arrows began to fall, picketing the turf short of the Penance Line's progress. The chained men tightened and formed their shield-wall, some dropping behind and raising above the others to create the ceiling. Hrithvarra stirred under her, sensing her tension. It took everything she had to keep from riding out to him. She reminded herself how ridiculous the idea was. He was between the foe and those who'd condemned him. Not to mention being chained to ten men.

Elan had to hold to the hope she'd just found. And to focus on her own duty—whatever that was. No, she knew. She was Skolani. She'd been assigned as a guardian to the queen. Focus! Arrows began to thunk into the shields of the Penance Line.

Elan glanced at the kestrels, then looked around at her sisters' stern, proud faces. They all buried away their fear, chins high, ready to swoop. She looked across at the boiling mass of the foe—those who sought to kill her people and invade her homeland. Those who hadn't hesitated to kill a healer. The tingle of Thunar's Blessing flowed from Biter's hilt, swept across her bare arm and up the back of her neck.

"Death's Grin!" Icannes pointed across the field. Auchote stood in his stirrups, raised a javelin, and bellowed in command. Rather than charge, the Paralatoe parted the line. Up onto the crest from behind them came two horses pulling a staggering, tethered and naked human. Elan first perceived the braided hair. Then the captive's shape. The shape of a woman.

"It's Meika!" Sochana cried.

"Gods be damned," Elan hissed. The missing Skolani scout's arms were bound behind her. Elan squinted and made out the purple bruises and gashes that covered her body.

At a command from the tattooed chieftain, one man dismounted. The other turned his horse to face the way he'd come. The lines that bound her went slack, and Meika's knees buckled. One tethering line wrapped her at the hips, the other up under her ribcage. A wave of dread washed through Elan. "We've got to do something," Sochana said.

"It's too late," Anallya spat. "But they'll pay for this."

The chieftain thrust his javelin into the air. The man who'd dismounted swatted the riderless horse, launching the beast into a gallop toward the Gottari lines while the other man kicked his mount to gallop in the opposite direction.

Elan not only heard Meika's brief, piercing cry of agony, she felt it in her teeth. The Spali lines erupted in raucous cheering. The horse galloped in terror, dragging the ragged and bloody mass that had been the upper half of the Skolani victim directly toward the queen's vanguard.

Icannes's battle-cry was equal parts anguish and fury. Others took it up, and Elan realized she was screaming too. Elan glanced up. Just then, the female kestrel folded her wings back and dove. The male followed, and both raptors disappeared in the greenery of the basin before them.

The roar of the Skolani would not abate. Keisella must have realized there could be no holding back. The warrior queen raised her broadsword, pointed at the foe, and galloped downhill, leading the Skolani host into an all-out charge.

"I THINK THEY'RE CHARGING," Lummox called. Vahldan knew something was happening, but he wasn't sure what. It was difficult to see much through the cracks between their shields.

Coil peered out. "No, they're only cheering."

"Keep moving," Keffric growled.

It was slow going, dragging their chains over clumps of brown grass without tripping, all while holding their shieldwall intact. But once the cheering began, the foe's arrows seemed to falter. It made Vahldan anxious. He looked up just as the kestrels dove and disappeared, and he knew. It had begun.

Then he heard it. A chill ran though him, and the line stutter-stepped to a halt. "What is it?" Coil asked.

"Skolani," Vahldan cried. He'd heard it before, but never like this. "Cluster and squat! Make it easy to get around us." The distant rumble became a rolling thunder as the men of the Penance Line stumbled into a tightening circle, trying to keep their shields side by side.

Keffric peered out. "They're charging already?"

It surprised Vahldan, too. They'd assumed the allies would move to just beyond the Spali's bow-range and reassemble before charging. Vahldan gapped his shield to look, too. He was relieved to see the Skolani would mostly pass to their right. He scanned till he spotted the rider with auburn braids, same color as the horse that bore her. The fires were stoked again. An energy surged, the hot blood rushing through him.

Horns floated over the rumble of hoofbeats. Now both wings of the Gottari army were on the move, fanning out like a trailing wake behind the surging Skolani.

"Double-time, men!" Vahldan called. There would be no getting clear of this. "Stay ahead of them."

They reformed their wall and hurried on as Keffric called a faster cadence. "Step and pull and step and pull..."

"Come on, men!" Vahldan coaxed. "We can either fight with them, or be trampled by them." The chained men all huffed and pushed on. Even Haimlan managed to keep up.

The queen's charge was past, and the Gottari came on from behind as the Line reached the foot of the slope below the Spali position. As they started to climb, Vahldan expected the foe to attack. He found himself longing for it—hungry to fight. The heat of his father's blood had cleansed him of fear.

Vahldan peered through the cracks between shields on both sides. The Spali were standing their ground, spearmen interspersed by riders sitting their mounts. They scarcely looked like an army about to counterattack. Something was off. "The bastards are going to run."

"What're they waiting for?" Coil asked.

"To draw us in," Vahldan said. "It's a ruse! It's got to be."

Keffric looked over the top of his shield. "Well, the buggers straight ahead of us aren't running. Get ready to hit 'em, lads! Stay with my count. Go, step; go, step; go, step..."

They all churned their feet to the cadence, no longer bothering over the tightness of the shieldwall. In less than a dozen steps the javelins of the Spali stabbed down, thumping the shields and popping through the cracks and into the armor of his fellows. Both sides roared, and their wooden shieldwall slammed into the scattered wicker shields of the Spali spearmen. The foe's line almost instantly gave way, and the Penance Line rushed forward.

Feeling almost giddy, Vahldan put his shoulder to his shield and rammed a horse. He thrust his sword through the gap and found flesh. The horse screamed and reared. The Spali rider loomed over him, jabbing down as he fell from the wounded horse. The man's spear-tip glanced off Vahldan's mail. The forge flared, and his sword flashed, hacking the Spali's bare back as he crashed down. Vahldan savagely kicked, snapping the fallen rider's helmless head. He'd either knocked the man out or killed him. The carnage fueled Vahldan. He stepped on the flopping body as he pushed toward another victim, feeling invincible.

Metal clanging, shields thumping, boots squelching, hoarse voices shouting curses, the Penance Line pressed forth, grinding their way onto level ground.

A call went up in a foreign tongue, and in a heartbeat, the resistance was gone. Vahldan peered out to find the Spali in full retreat, running or galloping downhill on the backside of the crest their formation had been lining. He roared after them.

"We made it!" Coil cried. Vahldan gathered himself. Indeed, the Penance Line was alongside their fellow Gottari. A few of Vahldan's chain-mates were bloodied, but they were all still standing. Behind them lay a half-dozen fallen Spali and two downed horses. Their feat had required teamwork that he'd have never imagined possible. The dregs of Gottari society had become brothers—a bond forged in blood.

A cheer went up. Lummox doubled over and retched. The fleeing foe made way across a marshy flat below them, headed for another ridge a little more than a bowshot away.

"The bastards are getting away," Vahldan grumbled.

"Not much we can do about it," Keffric said.

"What now, then?" Coil asked. It was a valid question.

"Looks like a riverbed," Keffric said, gazing at the terrain ahead. Vahldan was pleased with his clarity of thought and vision as he studied the lay of the ground ahead. There was a small stream at the near side, but the breadth of the bottom had recently been underwater.

"It's a lure. That's where they want us," Vahldan said.

"Good reason to stay up here," Haimlan offered.

THE SEVERING SON

Keffric squinted. "If I were a chieftain, I'd send the Penance Line down there first. It may not be over for us yet, lads."

Oddly, no one along the Gottari line was paying the Penance Line any heed. Not even the members of the Amalus vanguard, off to their right. Vahldan scanned the foe and spotted Auchote, already prancing across the top of the next ridge. Two more Paralatoe warriors rode up to their chieftain with a pale form tied to their mounts. The newcomers came to better view. The Spali were pulling along a naked woman. She was on foot, her arms bound behind her, running to keep up with her captor's progress.

"What wickedness is this?" Keffric asked.

Auchote rode over to the bound woman, raised his javelin and jabbed down. The captive shrieked as her knee was stabbed. She fell face first, no arms to soften the impact. At the same instant, a cheer rose from the Spali and a roar of outrage went up from the allied lines. Vahldan felt it, same as his cohorts—very near to the flare of the ugliness. The sight was a potent lure to bloodlust. He was grateful to recognize it. Thunar's Blessing still burned cleanly as it flared.

Auchote's mount reared as he raised his javelin overhead. The trio of Paralatoe turned and fled, yanking their captive around and dragging her by her bound wrists through the mud and tall grass. The rest of Auchote's men reined to follow, all of them vanishing over the next ridge.

An instant later, Icannes's chestnut mare shot into view, charging down into the swale, hooves throwing mud as her mare stomped across the riverbed. A score of Blade-Wielders galloped not far behind her. Sure enough, there was Elan, trailing the leaders but still prominent among the vanguard.

If Auchote had intended to entice a chase, he'd succeeded.

Calls to form up echoed along the Gottari lines. Keffric said, "Doesn't look like we'll be the first to make it across."

Regardless of whether it was a trap, or whether or not the Penance Line's role was over, Vahldan and his companions were honor-bound to seek to fight for their people. "That's no reason to stay here," Vahldan said, his blood running hot again.

IT WAS TOO much to bear. The second captured Skolani was Nahlay, Meika's scouting partner. The spectacle of Auchote's mocking, and then Nahlay being dragged away, refired the rage of the Skolani. And yet, a warning stirred inside Elan. Such blatant enticement.

Elan reined closer to Keisella. The queen silently observed the scene, her simmering fury evident. "My queen, surely they lead us to some trap or trick."

Down the line, Icannes bellowed and plunged downhill at a gallop. The Blade-Wielders nearest to the princess cried out and followed.

"He leads us to war," Keisella said, reining her mount to ride after her daughter. "Which is where we were destined to go." The queen galloped off with a resonant battle-cry.

"But it could've been on our terms." Elan muttered, and urged Hrithvarra to follow.

The far ridge was lined with Spali spearmen, mostly on foot. Only the Paralatoe near Auchote were mounted, forming a cluster at the center of the enemy host. Only the mounted Paralatoe followed Auchote and the pair dragging Nahlay. The band swiftly disappeared from view, leaving a gap in the Spali line.

The Skolani leapt the trickling stream at the base of the hill with ease, but their mares' hooves started to throw mud. Their pace slackened as they advanced. Hrithvarra was soon blowing with effort. Elan heard the throaty cheers of the Gottari behind them. They were charging as well. The arrayed Spali began to fire, but their arrows landed sporadically. The Skolani charge ground on, many of Elan's sisters readying their weapons for another chance at the foe. Icannes led the vanguard straight for the gap left by the retreating Paralatoe.

As the lead riders headed uphill, Elan's dread gnawed at her.

Icannes would crest the ridge first, leading from well ahead of her followers. Elan glanced back. The Gottari were making their way across the basin. At least the Skolani still had an army at their backs.

Icannes reached the hilltop. Starfire reared and Icannes called and beckoned. Then both horse and rider disappeared from Elan's view. Something was amiss. Skolani battle-cries erupted around Elan as her companions spurred their mounts to answer their princess's call.

Elan gasped as she crested the ridge. The Spali standing along the ridge were not alone. To either side of the gap left by Auchote stood a mass of humanity. She'd never beheld an army so large. Those at the front bore bows or shields, and behind them stood row upon row, spears bristling from their waiting ranks.. Auchote and his Paralatoe rode on through the broad gap, left all the way through the massive formation. Icannes rode into the gap in pursuit.

The queen reined aside and raised her sword. "Hold and retreat!" Keisella bellowed. "To me, Blade-Wielders!"

Kukida and Anallya reined tightly to create a block between their queen and the foe. All along the attacking host, Skolani horses reared and stomped to turn, sliding and colliding on the hillside. Elan stared after Icannes, fear for her near-sister thrumming through her. Sochana and Kunna had already ridden on after Icannes. Elan hesitated. She was alone between her queen, who'd ordered a retreat, and her near-sister, who'd either not heard or was disobeying. A javelin whizzed by Elan's head. When she looked again, Keisella and the Skolani host were in retreat, the queen roaring for all to follow.

Elan had been assigned as a queen's guardian. She should obey.

But she simply could not leave her dearest friend—even as Icannes plunged into an impossibly dangerous situation. The grip of Thunar's Blessing tightened, urging Elan to follow. She glanced back a final time, only to find Anallya, the last Skolani to vacate the hilltop.

"Elan, do your duty!" the blood-bitch bawled. The outrageous command provided the final nudge, her oldest hatred sparking her unshakable loyalty to her savior. She accepted that she would die for Icannes, just as she knew Icannes would for her—just as her hero risked everything for Nahlay now. Elan bent her head to Hrithvarra's neck and galloped into the opening in the Spali ranks, following her near-sister into what seemed certain death.

Squealing horns blew around her as she sped through, and Spali calls rang out along the length of the sprawling formation. She was certain they would turn on her, but instead, and in amazing unison, the Spali horde started marching forward at her either side, heading for the top of the ridge. Even as Elan realized she might make it past the advancing Spali army, she thought of the outnumbered allied army, floundering in the hoof-sucking muck of the riverbed below.

The trap Elan had sensed and feared was being sprung.

"Let's go!" The Skolani host had reached the far hill. The fight was about to begin. Vahldan beckoned his mates and started to follow. The chain that held their shackles together snapped, stopping him short.

"Hold on. Let's consider our options," Keffric said.

The allied Gottari were in the basin, following the Skolani. The Penance Line were already the last to leave the ridge.

"Why should we go?" Haimlan asked. "Who's to make us?" He had vomit in his beard.

"Yeah. Besides, we're still in chains," Coil added in support.

As the Line bickered, Vahldan spotted her, his gaze locked on Elan's red braids, riding behind Icannes, disappearing over the next ridge. The forge flared. He pulled his foot, popping the chain. "Enough!" he shouted, rounding on them. "We must go. Have you no honor?" They all stared, eyes wide.

"Vahldan's right," Keffric said. "We're honor-bound to fight. We must go."

Vahldan looked again, then did a double-take. What he saw he would never have imagined possible. The mighty Skolani were splitting in two, the bulk of their force turning back from the Spali at the top of the ridge. He was fairly sure Elan was not among those retreating.

Newfound urgency shot through him. He turned to Keffric. "Time to go! Form them up."

"Not me." The older man turned to the others. "It's clear to me that this man is the blood of our rightful chieftain. And chieftains lead. Anyone else see it as I do?" Coil frowned and Haimlan rubbed his nose, but several others nodded and a few even murmured in consensus.

"Looks like you're our leader." Vahldan was about to object, but Keffric went on. "If I might make a final suggestion, it would be to rid your followers of this chain. We're sure to fight much better that way. My lord." Keffric winked.

"Over here." Coil pointed to a protruding rock at the crest of the ridge.

"Good idea. Quickly now." Vahldan rushed to lead them shuffling to the rock. The sooner he could be on his own, the better.

"Can I try?" Haimlan asked.

"Yes, go," Vahldan said. He considered just hacking his own weakened shackle link, but that would take just as long, and posed a risk to his sword.

Keffric leaned back and Vahldan held the link connecting the chain's end to Keffric's shackle tightly against the rock. Haimlan raised his blade and lunged with a grunt. A spark flew as metal gashed metal. He'd bent his blade's edge, but he'd also cut one side of a filthy link open. Vahldan and Keffric pulled it wide enough to release the next whole link.

"I did it!" Haimlan beamed.

"We're free," Coil exclaimed as they pulled the chain through.

"But we're all still honor-bound," Keffric added.

"Let's go," Vahldan called, starting off.

Haimlan, being last on the chain, ended up with the entire length. "What am I supposed to do with this?" the big man cried.

"Either cut it or carry it," Vahldan called back as he loped downhill. He didn't care whether the others followed or not. He had to try to get to Elan.

It was exhilarating to take full strides again. Thunar's Blessing burned brightly, fueling him, boosting his speed. His head and vision were clear. The wind and his father's words sang in his ears. *'Remember, where I end, you begin. You will live up to me.'*

He sensed someone running just behind. It was Keffric. And the others ran behind him. Even Haimlan, a great wad of chain in his hands as he struggled along at the rear. Gods alive, even after all that had happened, Vahldan was leading men to battle. The Danian army was charging, and he was a part of it. He'd survived the Penance Line. He was truly free. Free to fight, to strive—for worthiness and for honor. For his dearest friend—if he could only catch up to her. He couldn't worry about that. He could only try. He squeezed his hilt, realizing that Keffric was right: he would wreak death this day, and the gods would approve it.

Vahldan jumped the muddy stream at the base of the hill and set out across the soggy bottomland. Even with mud sucking at his boots, he felt like he could run forever.

He moved into the center of the swale, each step sinking a little deeper. Desdrusan's vanguard continued to fall further behind the Amalus advance. Vahldan and his companions would likely overtake the laggards before reaching the base of the far slope. Some vanguard. He pushed the possibility of revenge from his thoughts and focused on Elan, and on the true foe.

The shrill squeal of the Spali horns rang through the valley, pulling his attention back to the top of the ridge. When the discordant Spali horns screech finally ended, it was answered by an otherworldly guttural call. He and Keffric beat to a halt as the others caught up. "Gods, that sounds like..." The fear from which he thought he'd been unshackled instantly reappeared.

"More Spali than we've seen so far?" Keffric said, validating his thought as the men of the Penance Line gathered, huffing.

"Or more humans than we've seen, ever," Coil added.

Haimlan arrived last and threw the chain in the mud. "That didn't sound good, lads" he said breathlessly. "I think I better get rid of this chain." The big man had a talent for stating the obvious.

CHAPTER 27—AGAINST A TURNING TIDE

"*Not without cause is the claim made that Blade-Wielders value their friends above all other relationships—sisters and even their mothers. Fillies of the finest lineage are customarily paired with young girls of promise. Even before they begin their warrior training, the bonds between girl and horse are deeply embedded. The pairs come to rely on one another.*

A Blade-Wielder may have other horses in her string, but her friend is the one being with whom she spends the most time in this life. Amazing tales of trust and loyalty and devotion are commonplace. And true! I can personally attest, for my dearest friend Foyra and I lived no small number of such tales."—*Brin Bright Eyes, Saga of Dania*

ELAN WAS AMAZED. No arrow or spear struck her or her friend. Not one of the foe had sought to rush them, or even to impede their passage. The main body of the Spali seemed utterly focused on moving off in the other direction. Elan was the last of the Skolani to come clear behind the foe's lines. All four of them had made it. Icannes had led them though unscathed. She had to wonder if it was yet another trick. Or was it the workings of the fickle gods—feeding their hopes only to better squash them?

Elan looked back across the sea of Spali warriors, now arrayed between her and the rest of her people. Between her and Vahldan. She felt the kestrel necklace beneath her breastplate, pressing on her heart.

Instant remorse bordered on panic. How had she allowed this to happen? What in the nine realms could four Skolani accomplish now? What if she never saw Vahldan again?

No. They had both seen the kestrels. Elan had to hold to hope. She'd tried to deny and resist her connection to Vahldan, but it was futile. Just as ridiculous as denying her devotion to Icannes would have been. Elan was following the only path available to her. And she knew Vahldan would do the same.

Whether they lived or died didn't matter. They would both do what was rightful. No sister or daughter deserved the torment and desecration Nahlay suffered. The poor captured scout deserved mercy, no matter the cost. Elan sensed her mother's spirit within, speaking to her, guiding her. Yes, she was doing what Ellasan would've done.

A series of commands echoed from the Spali lines. She turned in the saddle just as the largest volley of arrows she'd ever seen arced out over the ravine. The tips likely carried lethal poison. Death was about to rain down upon the Danians below. Many of her people would die.

Was Vahldan among those in harm's way? Had he survived the initial charge? Gods, he was in chains. Had the premature attack of the Skolani spared him?

No—she wouldn't allow herself to fret. She had to fight the battle before her. She focused on being one with Hrithvarra, focused on their pursuit.

A series of squealing Spali horns blew, and as one, the vast horde called out in refrain, and headed into the swale. Auchote curved left, leading his host north, crossing along the backside of the departing Spali lines.

Icannes closed on the dragging form of Nahlay. The primary mission was to end her suffering, of course. But Icannes would also seek to retrieve her body. Icannes was trying to cut her free. Only then could the objective become killing Spali.

Auchote turned in the saddle, always grinning. The chieftain signaled and a half-dozen of his warriors peeled off, three in each direction. The pair dragging Nahlay was among those he directed to separate, one in each direction. Nahlay was savagely yanked. One of her arms was pulled off, leaving her a bloody heap in the grass. It seemed nigh impossible for her to yet live. The six Spali fanned out and turned to face their pursuers. Auchote led the bulk of his host on in flight. Icannes raised her sword and shield and headed for those on the right. Kunna stayed at her princess's shoulder.

Witnessing the horror of Spali viciousness brought Elan's rage roaring back. Thunar's Blessing offered her focus and fuel. She raised Biter and aligned Hrithvarra to trail to the left of Sochana's honey-colored friend, Litlauss. The trio of Spali separated, which was unwise. Sochana tilted her head left as they neared impact, signaling the direction she would rein. The lead Spali of the trio raised his curved sword and hunched behind a woven shield. His comrades brandished javelins.

A heartbeat before meeting, Sochana yanked the reins left. Her agile warhorse veered sharply toward the second rider. The stunned Spali leader had already started his swing, and Elan easily avoided it and scored a solid blade strike, slicing flesh on his upper arm and bare chest, knocking him from the saddle. She was certain her victim was badly wounded or as good as dead. Sochana's maneuver had surprised the second rider into an early throw of his javelin, which glanced harmlessly from her raised shield. The thrower peeled off in flight. It appeared Sochana would easily ride that one down.

Elan refocused on the third. The Spali seemed to dislike his odds. He turned and shot off across the open field in flight. Elan trailed him long enough to see he'd gained too large a lead to be caught. Not without another lengthy chase. Her friend had done too much already. She slowed to a trot to give Hrithvarra an overdue rest.

Elan stroked her blowing friend's neck and surveyed the field. Icannes and Kunna had gained command of their circumstance. One Spali was down, one in flight from Kunna, and the third was engaged with Icannes, and therefore about to lose. All was well in hand.

Sochana had dismounted. She had already ensured Elan's first victim's demise, and was running to Nahlay's body. Elan shaded her eyes and looked back west. The remainder of Auchote's host was lined along the top of the now empty ridge, overlooking the battle below.

Auchote pointed, shouting to his fellows, and then pumping his javelin, jubilant. Elan halted Hrithvarra, listening. Auchote's words drifted to her. "*Laieenz puca!*"

She'd heard the words before, during the attack on Angavar's compound. Elan had been beside Old Gahtala, who knew the Spali tongue. "Lion's son," he'd shouted, then and today.

Death's Grin had spotted Vahldan. He was still alive!

Elan's adrenaline surged, but then quickly morphed into fear. He was alive, but Auchote still hunted her subject. Vahldan was the target of all of Auchote's Paralatoe.

Elan suddenly recognized her truth—*this* was her duty. In spite of all she'd done wrong, all that had gone awry between them, the gods had delivered her to this reckoning. Their destinies were entwined. Responding to destiny's call was all that mattered.

The Paralatoe cheered. Auchote pointed his javelin and whooped before kicking his mount and disappearing over the ridge. His host spurred to follow.

Elan glanced back at her companions. Icannes fought on, and Kunna was still in pursuit. Sochana was kneeling over Nahlay's body. They were all too far away and distracted to be signaled. She could not dally, could not lose track of her quarry.

Elan had already asked so much of her friend. She leaned to

her neck, stroking her mane. "Once more, dear one," she said. "Once more, let us show them your strength, your speed, my glorious girl. Let us show them the price of our wrath. Fluga fram, Hrithvarra!"

Without hesitation, the mare set out again. Together, Elan and her valiant friend charged toward the ridge, angling for the spot where the Paralatoe had descended.

A DARK SHADOW moving above caught Vahldan's attention. "Gods afire," he muttered.

"Now what?" Haimlan said.

There wasn't time to explain, or even to point. "Shields up!" Vahldan called.

They were near enough to the vanguard that others heard and took up the call. The members of the Penance Line clustered once again, squatting with their shields overhead just as the pouring rain of Spali arrows thumped on wood and picketed the field around them. The screams of wounded horses and men surrounded them. For the first time that day, it seemed more fortunate to be on foot than mounted.

The arrows finally stopped falling. "Stay put and keep 'em up!" Keffric shouted.

Vahldan gaped at the picketed ground. "Gods, that's a lot of arrows."

"Worst part is, there's sure to be as many Spali," Keffric replied.

"Or more," Haimlan added unhelpfully.

A rumble became a roar and grew, as if the sea were rolling across the plain on the hilltop above. Vahldan and his followers lowered their shields and stood.

They appeared at once, thousands of them, all across the ridge. Spali on foot cascaded over the crest and rolled downhill like a tide rushing to the low ground. And they just kept coming, row upon row with no end in sight. The breadth of their ranks exceeded the allies' line in either direction.

The massive Spali horde the scouts had long warned of was finally revealed.

Vahldan felt a moment of overwhelm—the ugliness seizing him as the purest sort of hopelessness. It seemed he had gone through so much: had reconnected with Elan, had accepted the blessing and curse of his blood, had survived being chained and sent out at the fore of an army, only to now face the extinction of his people.

Vahldan's ancestral spirit rebelled, relighting a spark within. "No," he said aloud. "Not yet." The forge flared hot once again. Thunar's Blessing still imbued him, snuffing the ugliness. Killing these who came against him was not only honorable, but vital to existence. Even in facing likely eventual death, killing their attackers was righteous. He may be doomed, but he would never relent.

His instincts had him searching his surroundings. The Gottari needed to pull together and fight, and it needed to happen fast. They needed leadership to survive. Vahldan was born for this.

The nearest cluster of comrades was the Amalus vanguard. Desdrusan had been unhorsed, but Ermanaric had dismounted and was helping his obese chieftain onto his own mount. Jhannas, Hjalmar, and several others were forming up to protect their false lord. Dozens along the ally lines attended the wounded or flailed over the fallen. Still others were in flight. But there was no fleeing this. Some Rekkrs called to their bannermen to form up, but the result was clusters rather than cohesion.

If an Amalus host didn't come together now, they'd be overrun.

"Lions of the Amalus!" Vahldan bellowed. "To me, to me! Form up!" He ran to the fore, out ahead of the disjointed Amalus, and turned back. "Shield to shield! Form up! As one!"

Amazingly, several of the clusters moved together and beckoned to those beyond them. A group of riders to his left galloped his way. "Over here! Join us!" he called, waving his sword.

The lead rider pointed at Vahldan, shouting over his shoulder.

"Rally, brothers! Rally to our rightful lord!" Vahldan knew the voice, knew the horse. Even now, on the precipice of doom, the sight filled him with joy.

Arnegern rode Ardua toward Vahldan and the Penance Line members. Teavar and Badagis rode at Arnegern's shoulders, and his kinsmen rallied behind.

Badagis grinned, his fur cloak flapping behind him. "Did I not say? The Lion Lord lives!" Belgar carried a pike with Vahldan's father's red snarling lion banner snapping in the wind over his head. The entire Amalus flank followed behind, marching at double-time, rallying to their legacy banner.

The host his father had gathered for him led the way, and reined around him. "Back from lunch?" Vahldan asked. Ardua came right to him, blowing but clearly happy to see him.

"A brief shower delayed us, Lord Vahldan." Belgar bowed from the saddle.

"Glad to see you all stayed dry." Vahldan scanned those who remained loyal in spite of his failures. "Thank you for finding me, my brothers. I would die for you."

Most bowed their heads in reply. "Works out well," Teavar said, looking beyond him. "We feel the same, and it looks likely."

Gottari horns blew. The front edge of the still-reforming line of the allies was meeting the leaders of the Spali horde at the base of the hillside.

"Here Vahldan, take your horse." Arnegern started to dismount.

"No, stay. There's no time. All of you! Riders and footmen. We meet them together. "

Arnegern called, "Form up around Vahldan. Protect our rightful lord!"

His newly reinforced host came together just as the spears of the foe struck their shields. Within moments, the nascent Amalus line was slammed by a mass of shrieking, jabbing Spali. Most of these Spali were bearded and not tattooed. Few had shields and almost none had armor of any sort. For all their numbers, they were clearly not warriors. As many of them fell as advanced, and still they came, wave after wave, pushing their comrades and trampling their own fallen, wild-eyed with terror and rage.

From the onset, Arnegern and Teavar rode at Vahldan's sides, with Badagis at the fore, slashing a path into the thick of battle. Keffric's and Haimlan's larger shields were pressed close to Vahldan's once again. As a team, the men of the Penance Line pushed and stabbed and chopped at the Spali who made it past his mounted host. With churning feet, they drove into the Spali press. Coil shrieked and fell, blood pouring from an eye. The Penance Line's Spali victims piled up around them. Vahldan's world had been reduced to this encroaching circle. It was mud and straining muscle, grunts and curses, cries of pain and rage, the stench of piss and sweat, all splattered with blood.

Again and again, his sword found Spali flesh to stab and slice. Thunar's Blessing, indeed. The killing of these non-warriors, these lesser men, was brutal and bloody, but relatively easy. He found himself believing that glory could yet be won.

He lowered his shield for an overhead chop, felling a Spali. It gave him a brief view beyond. They'd cleaved the ranks of Spali formation and were beyond the press of the attack. The Spali still coming downhill were stragglers, and these gave broad berth to avoid the blades of the roaring lions fighting under the red banners.

Desdrusan's vanguard was to their right, and Vahldan's mounted followers now intermingled with those flanking the usurper's loyal Rekkrs. It was only a portion of the broad battle, but it was a portion in which the mighty Amalus were holding sway.

The screech of Spali horns and the sound of galloping hooves drew his attention back to the ridge. A host of mounted Spali came in a downhill charge. The lead rider's dark eye sockets stared Vahldan's way from a pasty white face above a jawline of grinning teeth.

"Auchote," he said aloud. No one heard. The battle's outcome was far from certain, but the gods were delivering his father's murderer to him. Auchote bore down among a raging Paralatoe host, coming right for him. The forge flared, his blood pumping hotter than ever.

"Paralatoe!" Vahldan shouted. "Reform the line!"

Arnegern and Teavar reined and called to the others. His host gathered to face the newcomers. Vahldan glanced to find Desdrusan prancing behind the increasingly cohesive Amalus lines. The usurper was looking right at Vahldan, a traitorous grin on his ruddy face.

Keffric and Haimlan were still at Vahldan's either side. "Shields up, my lord," Keffric huffed with feigned cheer. Vahldan nodded and raised his shield. His Penance Line comrades clustered in the crescent of his mounted Rekkrs. In what seemed only a few drawn breaths, the Paralatoe hit the Amalus shieldwall. Vahldan was surrounded by stomping, neighing horses. Teavar bellowed, "Protect Vahldan! They target our lord."

Vahldan lunged, sliding between his shield-mates to slash down an attacker. In doing so, he'd exposed himself. A Spali pony appeared, rearing over him. The rider grinned down, brandishing a battleax. Vahldan recognized the scarred face. He and Elan had faced the man in Auchote's camp. The Spali's gaze held a murderous glee as he swung. Vahldan contorted to parry, off balance. The ax glanced off the top rim of another shield that appeared over him, deflecting it with a clang. Haimlan's big body dropped, blood pouring from the top of his head.

Keffric sprang in with a guttural cry, skewering the Spali mount's neck. The beast screamed and twisted to the ground. Vahldan vaulted, thinking to land on the fallen rider. His attacker was sure to be trapped by a ton of horseflesh. But once again the giant Spali defied him with agility and speed. The man hopped clear of his falling mount and stayed on his feet, ax raised and shield up. Vahldan had to twist to face him, putting him off balance again. Still, he found the strength to hurl his entire body at the giant, sword tip leading the way.

His sword slid a hand's length into the weave of the giant's shield, and the stubborn mesh held it fast. Vahldan struggled to yank the blade free, but his larger opponent pulled him off balance instead. He fell forward, exposed again. Even as he fell he knew an ax-blow would land on his back as soon as he hit the turf.

Instead, he felt the weight of a body, pushing him to the ground. Keffric's voice was in his ear, "For Dania!" They hit the ground together with his father's friend on top. Vahldan heard and felt the crunching thud of the ax-blow Keffric had taken for him.

"Keffric?" he called.

"It's my honor," Keffric wheezed. The next blow made a ghastly cracking sound on the head beside his own.

The fire of rage flared. Vahldan pushed Keffric's weight to his left then rolled to his right. His blade came free, but his shield was still trapped. He'd been forced to his back, and could only bring up his blade to parry as the giant raised his gory axe to strike again.

His nemesis grinned, making his scars rise to his ears like a mocking puppet.

CHAPTER 28—
VENDETTAS WITHIN

"An old saying among the Amalus loyal goes, 'When a battle falls to close combat, a lion seeking his chieftain has but to look to the heart of the fight. For if he is not there, the Amalus of the blood that is there in his place is most likely your new Lion Lord.'"—Brin Bright Eyes, Saga of Dania

ARNEGERN QUAILED. Not for his own safety, but for something even more important: the possible loss of all he'd fought for since he first laid eyes on Angavar's son.

The Paralatoe attack delivered the most ferocious fighting he'd witnessed. Not just this day or in this war, but ever. The formation around Vahldan was crumbling. Teavar was engaging a half-dozen foes, and his horse drifted. Arnegern could only steer Ardua with his knees as he slashed and blocked. The gray mare was remarkably responsive as well as unflappable, her hooves doing their own share of damage. And yet the Spali relentlessly pried the Amalus formation apart. There were just so many, all targeting this one spot—this one man.

Then the worst happened. Vahldan fell to the ground, helpless before the onslaught of the biggest Paralatoe Arnegern had ever seen. Arnegern couldn't get through. He was too far, and he was losing ground. Teavar bellowed in rage, but the giant couldn't reach their young lord either.

In the depths of his despair, something flashed in the periphery of his eyesight.

The sorrel warhorse galloped into the melee at full speed.

Arnegern's breath caught. Elan! Where had she come from? Had she come to save Vahldan? Would she be too late? Vahldan was surrounded, unreachable.

Elan arrived squatting on her feet atop the saddle, rolling with the galloping gait. The mare slid to a halt in the churned mud to collide with a Spali pony at the edge of the fight, launching Elan into flight over her mount's head. The Blade-Wielder landed a foot on the rump of another Spali pony and instantly sprang again—arms raised, buckler and broadsword spread like a soaring raptor's wings. With a Skolani battle cry, she brought the broadsword arcing down as she plunged into the axe-wielding Spali straddling Vahldan. Her victim only gleaned her presence in time to turn and watch her blade slice into his forehead—undoubtedly a terrifying final sight.

Arnegern's opponent had also been distracted by the Skolani spectacle. But Arnegern recovered his focus first, and the next swing of his sword opened a red slash across the tattooed pectoral of his opponent, knocking him off balance and tumbling from the saddle.

"Skolani!" Arnegern cried, releasing a spontaneous surge of joy.

It was like a trick of the gods. In a blurring flash, the scar-faced Spali was gone and Elan was standing over Vahldan in his place.

Vahldan lay stunned. She'd saved him. Again.

Elan dropped to her knees beside him. "Vahldan? Can you speak?"

"Where did you come from?"

Her apparent concern morphed to relief. "Gods, I thought... "

"It's as if you were soaring above, waiting for the moment I needed you to strike."

She smiled slyly. "Maybe I was." Elan put her hand over the spot where the kestrel hung.

In spite of everything, he couldn't keep from grinning. "I don't doubt it."

"Are you wounded? You're wearing so much blood."

"I don't think too awfully much of it is mine. And yours?"

She looked down at herself. "Same here. Hope not, anyway." Elan's smile faded. The clamor seemed suddenly nearer. "We'll have to figure it out later. This fight's far from done. Can you stand?" He nodded. She rolled Keffric's body aside and helped him up.

They stood back to back, shields and swords up, surveying the field.

Their readiness came just in time. A Paralatoe horseman was nearly upon them, curved blade ready to swing. "Inbound!" Vahldan shield-blocked the rider's stoke and Elan lunged over his shoulder to gash the man's sword arm. The Spali's blade dropped nearby and the foe rode on.

Just like that, he and his guardian were as one again.

Vahldan's host had thwarted the progress of the Paralatoe attack, creating a perimeter. On his host's right flank his men had been joined by members of Desdrusan's vanguard. Those who'd joined with his host on the left had been pushed toward the center, and were now flanked by the foe, but together they fought on. The Amalus were virtually surrounded, but the Spali weren't rushing to engage them. Just beyond their formation, Vahldan spotted the lurking skull-faced rider. The forge flared anew, its heat instant and energizing.

"There you are," he said. "Auchote, he's still here!" he called to Elan.

"Knowing him, he won't linger," Elan replied.

"Stay with the others," Vahldan said, gesturing to his host. He started to run, straight at his father's killer. Taking Auchote out of the fight would make a good start on righting his many wrongs. He couldn't imagine a more honorable kill. Which only made the longing grow.

"He sees us. He's still targeting you." Elan was running just behind him.

"Works out. I'm targeting him, too. Go get Hrithvarra. Bring the others." He sped up.

"I won't leave you again," she said, surging to stay apace.

It wasn't the time to argue. Honestly, he was relieved. "As one, then."

Auchote cantered around the right flank of the Amalus and Desdrusan drifted along the nearest backside edge, both of them keeping their distance from the fighting. Vahldan didn't think the usurper saw either him or Auchote approaching, but Desdrusan seemed to have sensed the momentum was shifting. The false lord looked to the rear to find a clear gap behind the Amalus lines. Desdrusan kicked his mount into a galloping retreat, heading across the muddy river bottom toward the far hill. Jhannas noticed, and the big man broke away from the fight to ride after his lord. By then Auchote and four of his henchmen were already on the move, circumventing the perimeter at a gallop, clearly in pursuit of the retreating Lion Lord. Two of Auchote's men split off, galloping at angles to limit Desdrusan's avenues of escape.

Vahldan remained fixed on his target. He and Elan ran right past several of the encircling Paralatoe riders as if they weren't there. Not a single one pursued them, confirming that the gods favored their boldness. As he and Elan neared, Auchote seemed to have lost track of their approach. The Spali chieftain sent his two remaining henchmen into a charge on Desdrusan. Jhannas turned to face the henchmen.

Which left only open ground between Auchote and Desdrusan. It also left a clear approach for Vahldan to get to his two worst enemies. He kept running directly at Auchote.

Desdrusan saw he was all but caught, and reined to face his former ally. He too seemed to have lost track of Vahldan. The usurper had drawn Bairtah-Urrin, the Amalus futhark blade, but he had no shield. Desdrusan's false smile belied his evident terror. His blathering drifted to Vahldan's ears. "Remember, your task remains unfinished. But I am still willing to pay."

Auchote grinned and kept coming. "Yes," he called in accented Gottari. "You will pay." Death's Grin readied his scythe-like sword and kicked his mount into a gallop. Desdrusan brandished the futhark sword awkwardly, looking like he was pissing himself. The heinous pair would meet before Vahldan arrived, but not by much.

The Spali chieftain's blade whirled and Desdrusan barely brought his up to parry. The clang was resonate, and sent Bairtah-Urrin flying from Desdrusan's grip. In a single stroke, the fumbling usurper had lost the Amalus clan's most sacred relic.

Auchote wheeled to charge again. Vahldan was almost in striking distance when he noticed one of the chieftain's minions who'd been engaged with Jhannas now galloped on a path to intercept him. "I've got this one," Elan called. "Go!"

Vahldan ignored the threat, confident in his kestrel guardian. Auchote was focused on Desdrusan when Vahldan leapt and swung. Auchote caught sight of him just in time to jerk the reins. Auchote's mount was well-trained, instantly pivoting to face the threat and rear up. In mid-flight Vahldan suddenly faced flailing hooves. He raised his shield, absorbing a pair of thumps. He was unsure what the wild arc of his sword struck, but he hit something. He landed and rolled, fully aware that a ton of horse would be coming down, too.

After two rolls, he got his feet under him. He oriented himself and regained his stance just as Auchote bore down on him. He'd unhorsed the chieftain, but Auchote still had the advantage. Vahldan stutter-stepped, defending in retreat as Death's Grin came on swinging both the crescent sword and a long dagger. It took everything Vahldan had to block and parry the cascade of slashing blades.

Each of Auchote's blows struck with force. The chieftain was fast and strong, his attack relentless.

Vahldan's rage surged, but his head remained clear. He began to see the attack as if it came in slow motion. He blocked, parried, repelled, and found his footing. Then, at last, he spotted his moment. Auchote placed a foot awkwardly, and Vahldan lunged to shove with his shield. He finally gained the space to counter. Auchote managed to cross-block backhanded, but Vahldan had seized the momentum. Now Auchote was retreating.

He stepped into the attack, Thunar's Blessing pulsing at his temples and in his chest. His sword strokes were fast, accurate, and forceful. Auchote's smug smile faded, his movements jerky, almost panicky. Vahldan's training with Icannes shone through; he set his opponent into a lull with repetitive strokes, and then feigned and switched from delivering overhand, dropping his shoulder and slashing from the side. Auchote only managed to save himself by parrying with the dagger. Vahldan's sword slid down the smaller blade to slice into Auchote's left hand, sending the dagger from his grasp.

Death's Grin was his to beat, and they both knew it.

Auchote's distressed expression morphed into a grin just as Vahldan processed the sound of galloping hooves, coming from behind. He spun just in time to shield-block the first rider's javelin thrust. He could only fling himself, tumbling aside to avoid a second Spali horseman. The two Auchote had sent to block Desdrusan's flight had ridden to the rescue of their chieftain.

By the time Vahldan regained his feet, the first rider had pulled Auchote up to ride pillion. He'd lost his chance to finish Death's Grin man to man, but he would not face this trio alone. Jhannas and Elan had both dispatched their opponents and rushed to Vahldan's side. The Spali were mounted but remained cautious as the two trios faced off. Desdrusan was nowhere in sight.

One of Auchote's men pointed to the north, and everyone looked. Badagis and Arnegern rode toward them, leading the rest of Vahldan's host. And they weren't alone. Scores of Amalus Rekkrs and their bannermen rode behind his cousins and supporters. Even those of the vanguard.

Vahldan actually laughed. The lions had reunited, and damn, they were a glorious sight.

Auchote barked a command and one of his men raised a horn and blew a series of squealing notes. Every nearby Paralatoe warrior broke off their fighting and rode to their chieftain, forming up between him and the gathering Amalus host.

From the center of his men, Auchote raised a fist with his wounded left, emitting a screech of rage as blood oozed between his fingers and dripped down his arm. Death's Grin held up the bloody fist and pointed his curved blade at Vahldan as he ranted in his own tongue.

"He's trying to stall us," Elan called. "Just the yowling of a cornered cat."

Badagis turned and shouted, "Attasar! What's this savage blustering about?"

The young scholar reined his horse in closer. "He says, 'Whore-spawn bastard son, gaze upon your destiny. I shall cleave from you both nose and nuts before slicing you open to choke you with your own maggot-ridden guts.'"

Vahldan laughed. "Come and try!"

Auchote snarled. "No more luck, little rabbit," he called in broken Gottari. "Know I cause you much to suffer before you die."

Elan was right—Auchote was biding time. "Form up!" he called to those still arriving.

Teavar's mount stomped to a halt. "Vahldan, heed the flank!" The giant pointed. A newly reformed mass of Spali footmen were mounting a charge. The squealing horn must have signaled them. Once again, the Amalus were in danger of being overrun by the masses of Spali infantry.

Even as his host gathered to face the Paralatoe, the Spali horn squawked again. As one, the Paralatoe reined and fled, their chieftain in the lead, riding directly to and through the ranks of their Spali foot-soldiers, who parted to let them pass before reforming a shield-wall behind their departure. The protective Spali line bristled with spears.

Auchote and the Paralatoe were escaping. Again.

The ugliness boiled. Vahldan roared till his voice gave out. He stood watching the bastards getting away, his head swimming.

"My lord?" Arnegern had dismounted next to him. "Vahldan?" He finally turned to his friend. "The way is clear." Arnegern gestured to the back of the Danian's lines. "I'd suggest we take the opportunity to retreat and regroup."

Vahldan looked back at the advancing Spali herdsmen, coming on slowly now, warily. He realized that all of his men—and even many of the Amalus Rekkrs who'd remained loyal to Desdrusan—stood staring, waiting. For him.

Arnegern was right. It was time to regroup. Vahldan nodded. "Yes, let's go," he said softly. The call went up.

As his heart slowed, his blood cooled. His head finally began to clear. His host had not only survived, but held their own. The battle was far from won, but the Amalus were a fighting force to be reckoned with once more. *"Lead them back to glory."*

Somehow Vahldan had found his way to a part of his father's bidding. Vahldan suddenly realized that there was still another part of his oath to his father he might yet fulfill this day. To pursue it would be a risk. But it was a risk he knew he must face alone.

CHAPTER 29—THE SIGNIFICANCE OF RELICS

Although many puzzled over it, few could discount the loyalty shown by the Amalus Rekkr Jhannas to Lord Desdrusan. His size and skill as a warrior were never in doubt, and perhaps only Mighty Teavar was his equal. But few knew the extent of his indebtedness to his clan's lord.

It's said that even before Angavar's downfall, Desdrusan had pursued the allegiance of some of the finest young Amalus warriors by any means available. Few outside of Jhannas's circle knew of his father's compulsive lure to games of chance, how the elder had wagered his herd and then his homestead and lost; how Desdrusan had paid off the father's debts in exchange for the indentured service of his son.

Fewer still knew that Jhannas's qeins Glismoda, along with their two small children, lived in Desdrusan's country homestead in relative luxury. But among those few was rumor passed of Desdrusan's fondness for his guardian's young qeins, whom he kept as his personal handmaid. Among those who heard such rumors, rarely was it spoken beyond a whisper that the decadent lord's fondness was almost surely rooted in lust."—Brin Bright Eyes, Saga of Dania

. . .

ELAN FELT like she could finally take a breath. Vahldan had called for a retreat, which allowed them all a moment of relief. They'd turned the tide of the Paralatoe attack, and although Auchote had escaped, surviving the deadly onslaught felt like a small success, perhaps a step toward victory.

But no more than that.

Elan appraised the Spali spearmen forming a growing shieldwall, and her anxiety flared again. She franticly scanned the battlefield, feeling a gnawing fear for her friend's wellbeing. Elan hadn't seen Hrithvarra since she leapt from her back.

She finally spotting what she sought. Herodes rode toward them holding the leads of two horses. One was Hrithvarra. Relief suffusing her, she ran to greet her friend. Hrithvarra seemed as relieved as Elan felt, likely due in part to no longer being led by the nose.

"Thank you," Elan said.

Herodes bowed from the saddle. "I brought Arnegern a horse as well, so that Ardua can return to her rightful rider."

"Good work, cousin!" Arnegern dismounted and handed the reins to Vahldan.

Badagis looked beyond their gathering. "Now about that retreat." The foe's shieldwall continued to approach, albeit cautiously.

"Yes, before any of them finds a bit of bravery," Belgar said.

Vahldan nodded. His frustration and exhaustion were apparent as he pulled himself into Ardua's saddle. He said nothing before setting out, leading them west. Elan felt it, too. She had no idea what time of day it was. Life was war, the day unending. There was no horizon. Nothing existed but brutal battle in the mud-churned swale under a ceiling of gray clouds. It was as if the gods had thrown them together like dogs in a fighting pit, seeking to amuse Themselves.

The worst part was, no one—at least no mortal—knew when, or how, it would end.

After they cantered through the heaviest mud at the base of the swale, Vahldan reined in and called for them to gather round. "I want you all to ride to the stream at the foot of the slope. Regroup and water your mounts, then ride south and rally to the queen." He pointed with his sword. "Guard her left flank as she drives the foe back uphill."

Elan saw the wisdom in the plan. The Danians had driven a deep bulge into the foe's lines, and the queen's force was in danger of being outflanked as it advanced on the precarious slope. The puzzling part was that he'd notably excluded himself.

Everyone sat waiting. "Did you all hear my orders?" Several of them nodded and murmured that they'd heard. "Well, go. Ride now," Vahldan shouted hoarsely.

Arnegern said, "We'll be right behind you. Leading is what leaders do."

Vahldan shook his head. "No. This time I'll be behind you." No one stirred. The calls of the foe echoed to them. Some of the Spali footmen had ceased to press their initial retreat, but their leaders seemed to have noted the Amalus host's withdrawal and were calling them back into formation. Vahldan went on. "If you really consider me worthy of becoming your lord, you must heed me now. Badagis, I am putting you in command. Lead them." The older man frowned. "Please," he added. He'd abandoned the commanding tone. It was a plea.

"Where will you go?" Arnegern asked.

"There's something I must do. Alone," Vahldan added more forcefully.

"Come on then," Badagis said. "Apparently he's as secretive and stubborn as his father was." The big man beckoned the others and started out, back toward the base of the far slope. The others reluctantly followed, no few looking back with puzzled or concerned expressions.

"You too." Vahldan was staring at Elan now. She noted that his eyes were clear. He wasn't acting in the fog of what he called his ugliness.

She shook her head. "I've already told you. You're stuck with me."

He frowned but didn't argue. He kicked Ardua and rode back, angling across the open ground in front of the Spali line. She set out after him. "May I ask what we're up to?"

"Going back to where we first fought the Paralatoe. There's something there I need."

She suspected she knew what. "We can't look for it later?"

"Later might be too late."

Vahldan looked back, waiting for her retort. Elan simply nodded.

The reformed Spali had settled in place, leaning on their spears. No few of them had actually sat down in the mud. They seemed relieved that their opposition had fled, although several were watching Vahldan and her—no doubt wondering what they were about.

Vahldan ventured into bow range and a few arrows fell nearby. He slowed, ignoring the lobbed arrows and the increasing stir among the Spali footmen. He leaned from the saddle, scanning the matted grass below.

A Spali commander had roused a squad to march out against them, wicker shields at the fore. "Might be nice to actually have a later, though," she suggested.

He kept searching. "True, but I consider this worth the risk."

The approaching squad came on with supreme caution. They seemed reluctant to revive the fight, but if they got close enough, a lucky spear throw would still be deadly. "I suppose I'd better try to buy us some time, then."

Elan heeled Hrithvarra, raised her shield and blade, and charged the squad. Her throat was raw, but she offered up her best Skolani battle cry and waved Biter overhead for show. As expected, the Spali halted and tightened their formation.

Elan arced back in retreat. She knew she'd only be able to cow them once. She rejoined Vahldan just as he leapt from Ardua's back and swatted the mare's rump, sending her trotting away from the Spali squad. Vahldan sheathed his sword, bent and thrust his hands into the mud.

He came up with another blade.

He swiped the mud from the hilt on his leggings. She recognized his find. It confirmed her suspicion as to why he'd come.

Elan glanced back. The Spali squad had split up, one segment seeking to cut off their angle of retreat. Both segments were moving at double-time, the main group on the verge of a full-out charge. "Time to go!" she cried.

Vahldan whistled and ran toward Ardua. The gray came trotting to his call. Elan marveled at how quickly they'd bonded. Vahldan landed in the saddle just as the Spali line roared and charged. "They're too close," Elan cried. "If we run they'll all throw."

"Only one choice, then," Vahldan said, reining to face the larger Spali division. With a shared nod, they charged. The Spali halted and formed up again, shields tight and spears braced. They reined left to make a pass, swinging to break a few spears. The flanking squad rushed to return to their mates.

Their feint had created the needed space. "Good enough," she said. "Let's get clear."

They both bowed over their mares' necks and galloped. The foe had foolishly sent only spearmen to meet them, thank the gods. A few spears hit the turf as they fled, but with no archers to attempt a longer shot, the threat was swiftly diminished. Elan's heart filled with love for her friend, who had galloped more this day than Elan had a right to ask.

Elan and her subject had survived again. It reaffirmed her belief that their destinies were indeed entwined. Even after all that had happened—all of the forces that seemed intent upon prying them apart.

Vahldan led her to the stream at the base of the far slope. The Amalus host had already moved on. "Whoa!" she called. "These two need to drink. And rest." The mares bent to the flow.

Vahldan stared out across the battlefield, scattered with bodies. "So many have fallen."

"It's difficult to tell how many are theirs and how many ours."

"Whether we succeed or not, the cost is high." He was looking at his bloody hand, gripping the futhark blade's hilt. She wasn't sure if he was talking about the war or his retrieval of the sword, but he'd definitely been released from Thunar's Blessing.

Elan thought about the choices made; about the risks she and Vahldan had taken; about how they'd been ripped apart and had ended up together again. "Would the cost have been higher had we done nothing?" His gaze rose to hers, pensive. "Had we waited to pay it in Dania—had we not chosen to seize destiny—would more innocents have died? Would we have been forced to kill even more Spali to repel them?"

"Likely so," he said softly, looking back to the sword. "A wise friend told me that sometimes there's honor to be found in killing." He looked up at her. "Seems it comes naturally to me. Might end up working out this time, but..."

"But what?"

"The friend didn't make it today."

"Part of the cost," she suggested.

"I suppose," Vahldan said. He shook his head. "Killing and death seem to follow me around. Guess it's the burden of my legacy. One I'll bear for all my days."

Elan knew better. All Blade-Wielders did. "Seems like you're the one making it a burden. It doesn't need to be." He cocked his head. "No offense, but either your friend wasn't quite as wise as you think or you didn't quite take him right. The honor isn't in the killing. It's in the justice. Sometimes death is the cost of it. The wisdom comes in knowing when it's truly necessary. And in preventing it when it's not."

Vahldan gazed out across the field again, deep in thought. Elan sheathed Biter and pulled a skin from her saddlebag. She drank and held it out to him. He had no free hands. He seemed reluctant to even lay the famous blade across his lap. She beckoned. "I'll hold it." He hesitated. "Promise to give it right back."

He smiled. "There are few I'd trust with it, but you're one." They traded sword for skin.

Elan wiped mud from the bright blade with the hem of her cloak. Then she swung it as he drank, testing its weight. For its age, Bair-tah-Urrin was remarkably light and balanced. Vahldan drew his old sword from its sheath and stowed it with the blanket roll behind Ardua's saddle. "Nice sword," she offered as they exchanged again.

"Thanks. It's an heirloom."

"Part of that burdensome legacy, eh?" She winked and he laughed. "I suppose I almost get risking our lives for it." She shot him a wry smile. "Almost."

"It'll be worth it," he said with a resolute nod. "You'll see. And they will, too."

"I get the feeling you're referring to someone other than the Spali."

"All I seek is justice. I'm thinking this will help." He sheathed it with a nod.

"See? You're already getting wiser."

Vahldan laughed, but she meant it. Elan recognized that it was more than a sword. Bearing it, he already seemed more solemn, more assured. Relics had power. Possession of this ancient symbol, this family heirloom, would likely change much. Including him.

"Come," she said. "Let's join the others, and see this awful thing through."

ARNEGERN REINED in with his Amalus brethren, surveying the field. Most of the fighting was now on the hillside, as the Spali continued to fall back. The ferocity had gone out of the Spali counterattack. They were fighting for survival now, but Arnegern sensed that the foe's resolve was beginning to falter—particularly among the herdsmen who made up the bulk of their numbers. Even the volleys of the archers behind their shieldwall had dwindled in frequency. Perhaps the Spali were finally running out of arrows. At the battle's center, the queen's Blade-Wielders continued to push the crumbling Spali line back up the slope. He sensed that if the foe hadn't perpetually been on higher ground, their retreat would've become full flight by now.

Beyond the Skolani, on the queen's right flank, the Wolf Lord's Rekkrs had stemmed the tide, and were now driving slowly to the base of the slope. Everything was slathered or splattered in blood and mud. Vahldan had been wise to send his host to protect the queen's left flank. The lacking Amalus presence had created a gap that the Spali had sought to exploit. The lions had arrived just in time, and Badagis had led the first Amalus charge that sent the Spali's flanking attack back to rejoin their brethren on the hillside.

Arnegern spotted a few mounted Paralatoe at the hill's crest. At the tattooed warriors' direction, the spearmen were regrouping for another flanking surge. Near the hill's base, Badagis held up his sword to reform the Amalus lines. Arnegern rode to his side. "They're desperate to hold the top, to keep us on the slope."

Badagis nodded. "The gods know they fear what the Blade-Wielders will do once they're level with them." Arnegern sensed the Spali's desperation to stay out of reach of the Blade-Wielders, who showed no mercy for those they caught in close combat. The hillside below the queen's center was littered with Spali, many of them mauled—some missing limbs or disemboweled. Enraged Skolani were even taking scalps in the midst of the raging battle.

Arnegern surveyed the wary Spali reforming above the Amalus, peering over their shields. "I sense these herdsmen are about to break. One more hard punch might do it."

"Theirs may be near to breaking," Badagis said, "but ours are near to exhaustion." He nodded toward the mud-slathered Amalus host. "Particularly the horses."

"To me, Amalus Rekkrs! To me! Rally to Bairtah-Urrin, my brothers."

The clarion call came from behind. Everyone turned. On came Vahldan and Elan.

Vahldan held a sword raised before him. The way he held it, the way it shimmered—there could be no doubt. Vahldan indeed held the futhark blade of the Amalus clan.

Galloping toward them on the fine gray mare, without his helm, his golden hair flying, Vahldan looked like more than just their rightful lord. He'd transformed into one of his ancestor kings, galloping forth from another age.

Arnegern knew the coming of the Bringer of Urrinan was as much political theater as it was widely held belief. But he'd always suspected that most Amalus clansmen held a secret hope that there was truth to it. As did he. Hope had been hard to find since Vahldan's arrest. But in the moment, witnessing the arrival of their rightful heir, with Bairtah-Urrin held high, Arnegern's hope was rekindled. He could believe again.

Theirs would be glorious times.

"Forth comes the Bringer!" Arnegern shouted, his eyes suddenly blurred by tears.

All of them cheered, even those who had yet to renounce Desdrusan. The Amalus host parted to allow their dashing leader and his fierce guardian through to the fore.

Vahldan reined Ardua before them, their clan's most famous blade held like a rallying standard. "Lions of the Amalus! Let us banish this awful foe from our lives. Forever!" He turned in the saddle, pointing at the Spali above. "Once more for Dania, my brothers. Ride! To glory!"

Arnegern's heart filled, and all weariness seemed vanquished. With a fitting roar, the lions rode into battle as they had not done in long years: together and behind a leader.

Better still, behind an heir to the blood of the Amalus kings.

ICANNES RODE toward the advancing Danian army through the hordes of the fleeing foe, leading back the remains of her errant band. Rather than posing a threat, the retreating Spali gave their passage wide berth. She continued to scan the surrounding grasslands, but to no avail. Regardless of her growing concern over having yet to find a trace of Elan, nor even of Hrithvarra, Icannes still had vital news to deliver to the queen.

The Skolani line spread out ahead, holding at the top of the ridge. The queen had managed to halt them to allow the foe's flight. Icannes sensed the Skolani warriors' seething. If they hadn't been restrained, it would've been a slaughter. No matter the circumstance, her mother always maintained her composure, weighing the costs and advantages of her actions. If Icannes had been in her mother's position, she doubted she would've remained so poised.

Keisella stood at the Skolani's center, her blade Douthrond blood-smeared and resting on her shoulder. The queen looked smugly satisfied. Icannes sped to a canter.

Keisella walked her mount out to meet her. Icannes dismounted and bowed, as did her companion. The queen remained ahorse. "So, you managed to survive."

Why had she imagined her mother would be relieved to see her safe? "I did, my queen."

"And also to retrieve Nahlay's body?"

"Yes, my queen." Icannes tried to change the subject. "Congratulations, Mother, on your victory. You've won not just a battle, but the war."

Keisella raised her chin. "You could've been a part of it. Perhaps you'll heed me next time." Funny, but Icannes thought she had been a part of it. Though she couldn't deny there were indeed lessons to be heeded.

The queen looked beyond her. "So you brought back a dead scout. But what has it cost you, Daughter? Where is Elan?"

She fought to rein in her emotions. "I... I don't know, my queen. Not yet."

A dark look crossed Keisella's face. "We'll speak of this later," she hissed.

"My queen, in our pursuit, we came upon the Spali's tent city. It's as the scouts reported, lying across a large vale, beyond this high plain. As we surveyed it, I was beckoned by a Spali holy man. He managed to convey that he and his fellow priests wish to surrender. They wish to offer terms, that their women and children might pass from here unharmed. They claim to have renounced the Paralatoe, whom they blame for leading them to folly and darkness."

"This priest relayed this to *you*?"

"He did." Was she really going to be fickle about to whom they surrendered?

"Huh. A Spali priest, deferring to a woman?" Her mother gave her an up-and-down look. "Or perhaps he mistook you for a man. I suppose we soon shall see."

Off to the queen's right came the Wulthus vanguard, cresting the hill. The Wolf Lord gave the queen a solemn nod. Keisella returned it. She pitched her voice for Icannes's ears. "If you can believe, the wolves actually stayed at our side. As best they could, anyway. Better than can be said for that puffed up lion and his ilk."

Icannes looked to the other empty flank, but said nothing. Now was not the time to ask about Vahldan. She had more pressing concerns, and didn't want to be questioned herself.

Keisella started riding past her. "Well, Daughter. Lead me to these Spali priests. Let's see if they really have been brought low enough to submit to a woman."

Vahldan rolled Keffric onto his back, and placed his helm back on his head. The grouch looked so peaceful now. He laid his father's second sword on Keffric's chest. "Thank you. For coming when I needed you. And for saying what I needed to hear. The honor was all mine."

Vahldan shook out the Amalus banner he'd asked for on the way, and laid it over Keffric. "I know you're already at the banquet, but this will keep the crows away until we can come and collect you, to give you a proper sendoff." He laid Keffric's shield over the banner.

Elan came up, tucking the trophy she'd taken from the Spali giant into her belt. "If not for him, I wouldn't have made it in time. Thank the gods he was here for you."

Vahldan raised a brow. "Really? You, thanking the gods?"

"Good point. We can only rely on ourselves."

"And sometimes on each other."

Elan nodded. "Aye, and on each other."

"I suppose our thanks should go to Keffric. And to my father, who knew his worth."

Arnegern and Teavar galloped up and reined in. Arnegern called, "We've seen the Spali camp. It's vast. Everyone's gathering above it. The queen says she'll accept their surrender. Their holy men are about to come forth to formally submit."

Vahldan strode to Ardua. "Any sign of Desdrusan?" He and Elan both mounted.

Arnegern turned his head and spat. "Believe it or not, he's actually crawled out from whatever rock he's been hiding under. He's put himself right there next to the queen. As if he played a part in the victory."

The ugliness burst to life, filling him like a smudge pot in a tent. "No," he whispered.

Teavar shook his head. "Hard to believe he's got the guts to show his face."

Arnegern said, "All the more reason for you to be there—to show everyone who the real Lion Lord is now."

Vahldan hardly heard them—could hardly see or hear anything past the thrum. "I won't let him get away with this." His words came as a growl.

"He won't," Teavar said. "Too many saw the truth."

Realization came through the fog of the ugliness. He may have been the only one who heard the usurper's interaction with Death's Grin. Other than…"Did you see Ermanaric?"

"At his side," Arnegern said. "Jhannas, too. As if nothing shifty has happened."

Vahldan shook his head. He had to maintain a grip. If he lost himself, he could doom the rest of the victory that was rightfully his.

This was far from over. Besides Desdrusan, there was still another murderous rival yet to vanquish, as well. "What about Auchote? Any sign of the Paralatoe?" Teavar and Arnegern shared a look. "Well?" Vahldan pressed, feeling the heat suffuse him.

"No sign of Auchote, but we spotted a pair of Paralatoe," Teavar said. "They're watching from the hills on the far side of the Spali camp."

Elan's lip curled. "Those dogs. They're abandoning their people. They mean to flee."

The rage hit him like a thunderclap. "No!" Vahldan kicked the mare into an uphill gallop. "I won't let them get away with this."

He sensed his supporters following. "Which ones?" Arnegern called from behind.

"None of them!"

～

ICANNES LED THEM FORTH, as her mother's second. Seemed Keisella considered interaction with lowly savages beneath her, even to accept their submission. Icannes had already sent Kunna back to the Danian camp. She would deal with the fallout of what had happened afterward. Starting with organizing a search party.

The queen had the lords of Dania at her either side, though Desdrusan seemed to be lurking behind his guardians, and Keisella hardly gave him a second glance. Dozens of prominent Blade-Wielders and Rekkrs kept a respectful distance behind, and scores of warriors from the Danian army meandered behind them. Few were willing to miss out.

The allied leaders reined in and formed a line along the crest of the vale. Icannes still found the sheer scale of the tent city startling. Dun-colored hide roofs filled the basin, lining a stream that ran through it. On the hillsides beyond were makeshift corrals filled with large flocks of goats and sheep. Many of the tent-like structures were built out from rickety wooden wagons. Drying garments flapped in the cold breeze from lines strung between them.

The Spali who'd fled the battlefield arrayed themselves before their makeshift homes, looking beaten but grim. Icannes respected that—seemed if necessary, these herdsmen would still give their lives to protect what was left of their shattered world. Many clutched spears planted like staffs, and others wore bows on their backs. Behind the Spali men, at the edge of the camp, furtive women stood watching, many with ragged children peeking from behind their skirts. Icannes had heard how the Spali treated their women. Seeing them, she could believe that theirs was a wretched existence. She feared it was about to get worse.

The priest Icannes had met earlier emerged from the largest structure, leading a dozen more with similar ankle-length robes. She dismounted and moved to meet them. The priests were all beardless, like the Paralatoe, but they wore their shoulder-length hair tied behind their heads. Near the end of the procession, two younger priests hauled a naked woman between them, and another held a naked infant under his arm like a bedroll. The infant was oddly limp and silent. The woman's arms were tied behind her. She hung her head, her dark hair curtaining her face.

Two span away from her, the Spali procession halted and lined up behind the priest who'd spoken to her earlier. He carried an odd knife on the palms of both hands. He bowed his head, but the others did not. As she and the priest had the first time, they found words in common from both languages. The priest said, "Is to yield we are here. Yield for all." He nodded over his shoulder, indicating his gathered folk. Then the priest scanned the Danians beyond her. "Is wish to yield to king of Gottara."

"The Gottari have no king. This army is led by the Skolani queen." Icannes pointed to her mother.

The priest frowned. He turned to blather to the others. Several shook their heads. The priest shook his head to Icannes in turn. "No. Laieenz puca is defeating Auchote. Ah xsaya—a king, he rises, no?"

As if in answer, hooves rumbled and a chorus of Gottari horns blew. Icannes looked up as the Danians lining the hillcrest parted to make way for some sort of arrival. It shouldn't have surprised her, but it did when the first rider to emerge was none other than Vahldan, son of Angavar. In spite of herself, Icannes let out a gasp, her heart trilling at the sight of the auburn braids of the rider beside him. She shook her head and silently cursed. She wanted to be royally peeved, but her skin had gone to gooseflesh. Surely she was cursed by the gods to love that beautiful, infuriating woman as much as she did.

When their eyes met, Icannes easily read Elan's worry and regret. Elan mouthed, "I'm sorry." Icannes clenched her jaw and offered the slightest of nods. More than an apology would be needed to mend what Elan had wrought.

Vahldan leapt from the saddle and stormed out in front of the Danian leaders. "Where is he? Where's Desdrusan?"

Icannes turned to find that, indeed, the Lion Lord had slipped away.

Keisella scowled. "This is not the time, Young Lion."

"It is he," the lead Spali priest cried. "Laieenz xsaya!"

Vahldan spun to face them, panting like a lathered stallion. All of the priests except those holding the woman and babe fell to their knees and bowed their heads. The lead priest proffered the knife he carried, but Vahldan strode past him. "I see you, Auchote!" Vahldan bellowed, pointing over the tents. "I see you!" His voice echoed through the vale. "You won't get away!" His eyes were dazed, beastly. Icannes had seen him like this before. Vahldan was lost to his rage.

A group of Paralatoe horsemen sat on the far hill. And, indeed, there among them was Auchote's skull-painted face. Vahldan ranted on, "I will hunt you down! All of you! You hear me? I will sever the fanged head from the snake!"

Auchote and most of his followers reined and disappeared behind the hill, leaving only two behind. Vahldan tilted his head back and roared. Only then did he seem to notice the surrendering Spali procession. He drew and pointed his bloody blade at the gathered Spali below. "Fear me! For I am your ruin. I am the Severing Son —the Bringer of Urrinan! You, your children, all of you. From today forward you will mourn that you dared awaken my wrath!"

Vahldan stood huffing and growling. Icannes glanced up at her mother and the Wolf Lord. Both were clearly appalled by the spectacle. The lead Spali priest stood, resolutely offering the knife to Vahldan and speaking rapidly in his own tongue.

Vahldan shouted over his shoulder, "Attasar!"

One of Badagis's young warriors dismounted and hurried to Vahldan's shoulder. The young man said, "He is offering you the dagger their gods bestowed upon the Paralatoe's ancestors, for they are renounced. Auchote and his followers are exiled. The Spali nation places themselves at the mercy of the lion's son—now a king risen. For it is foretold that should the son of a Paralatoe foe vanquish their chieftain, he would then ascend and blaze, to devour the grazing grass of all the lands, unto the seashore. It's said that only through the surrender of this great gift will this risen king show mercy upon them."

Vahldan wouldn't touch the dagger. His face glowed red, but his eyes seemed to be clearing. He moved several steps downhill of the priests, still glowered at the remaining Paralatoe on the far hill. The lead priest beckoned, and the priests holding the woman and the infant brought their captives forward. Young Attasar continued to translate: "These are Auchote's favored woman and his newest son. They are yours to take and to do with as you see fit." The captive woman looked up. She was beautiful but for a black eye and swollen lip. Icannes now saw that she had lash marks and bruises all over her shapely form.

Vahldan wrinkled his nose. "They're what? No, I don't want his woman, or his babe."

Attasar said something to the lead priest, and the man nodded and replied. "He asks if you would have them dealt with as the Spali people would then deem fitting."

Vahldan was watching the Paralatoe again. "Whatever. I don't want them."

Attasar spoke to the priest, who nodded and, swift as a snake striking, snatched the woman by the hair with one hand and sliced her throat with the other. A roar of approval erupted from the gathered Spali. Before Icannes could move to interpose, the man had plunged the knife into the chest of the babe, as well. Their cheering swelled.

Vahldan abruptly spun away and started uphill. Icannes glanced to see the last two Paralatoe disappearing over the hill.

The priest casually wiped the relic's blade and hurried to get in front of Vahldan, bowing his head and proffering the knife again. It had some sort of bone handle. Its blade was dark with age. Vahldan took it, placed it under his boot and pulled, breaking the blade. He glared at the priest as he tossed the remnant hilt on the ground between them. The assembled Spali gasped. The alarmed priest bent to retrieve it, but Vahldan's sword tip was instantly at his throat. Vahldan twisted his boot, pushing the broken relic's blade into the mud.

Vahldan withdrew his sword from the priest's neck, spat on the ground, and turned to stride back up to his mount. The young translator started after him. Icannes grabbed the young man's shoulder. "You. Stay. We'll need help to talk our way out of this mess." The battle was won, and by rights this war should end the enmity between Dania and the Spali. Icannes knew they couldn't allow a young hothead, lost to rage, to ruin their chances for a lasting peace.

Attasar called after Vahldan. "My lord?" Without looking, Vahldan threw up a hand of either assent or dismissal and stormed on. As Vahldan mounted, his followers started to cheer. The throaty cheering was taken up by the Amalus ranks as they parted to allow him passage from the site. Surprisingly, the ovation continued to rise, spreading to all of the lesser soldiers, wolves and lions alike. Even a few Skolani cheered.

Against all odds, Vahldan had managed to win the acclaim that had eluded Icannes. He'd been rude, callous, petulant, and the Gottari seemed to admire him all the more for it. In spite of his outrageous insult, even the bedamned Spali seemed awestruck by him, most of those gathered below bowing and murmuring as he departed.

Icannes supposed Vahldan would still have to face his judgement. She doubted that the wolves and the guild would allow him to ascend unchecked. But it seemed he'd truly seized a new level of stature.

Too bad he clearly still hadn't learned how to utilize it.

CHAPTER 30—OF INTENTION AND CONSEQUENCE

"Though the Skolani oath to Horsella, offered upon each girl's first moon-blood, forbids recurrent celebration of the fertility rites with the same male, it is hardly a well-concealed fact that most queens—as well as many powerful elders and Blade-Wielders— have enjoyed ongoing engagement with their favorites. As it was with Keisella and her favorite, Badagis of the Amalus.

Despite such leniency, some laws and customs could never be over-looked, even by a queen. As fond as Keisella was, as close as she and Badagis became, as often as he was invited to the Fagna-Allramani and other celebrations, after each such occasion Badagis rode home alone."— Brin Bright Eyes, Saga of Dania

THE CAMP WAS JUBILANT. It couldn't be denied, the Danian allies had won a great victory. But Elan felt anything but jubilant. She sat alone at Badagis's pavilion fire, watching young men swarm to fawn over her subject. She'd forgotten how much she hated this before. Now it was worse. Much worse.

In the beginning it had been cousins, rounded up by Badagis to pretend at the certainty of Vahldan's ascent. Tonight the ranks of Vahldan's devotees had swelled, and no one seemed to be pretending anymore. Whatever happened with Desdrusan now, it couldn't be denied that circumstances had changed. And once again, Elan was pushed to the margins.

Elan gazed up at the sparse brown oak leaves still hanging overhead, dancing in the rising heatwaves from the fire. It was some comfort, being back in the forest. She'd felt so exposed out on the plain. There was no hiding out there. She'd never realized it more fully than when Icannes had fixed that scowl on her after the battle.

A hand holding a cup appeared at her shoulder. She looked up to find Badagis standing over her. "Take it." She did. Even the smell was potent. "No one deserves a drink more than you." He raised his own cup in salute and drank. She sipped hers. It burned all the way down. The warmth was welcome, at least. Badagis indicated the bench next to her. "May I?"

"Your bench, your fire." The aging warrior sat with an exaggerated groan.

Two young warriors Elan didn't recognize passed by, heading for the fawning swarm. "...I hear he crossed blades with Death's Grin himself," one said. "And lived to tell," the other added. "Near single-handedly chased the tattooed savages off..."

Badagis softly laughed as the pair joined the throng. "Every so often, a person appears and seems to incite legend in the telling of them. I used to doubt I'd live to see another like his father. Suppose it'll be fitting if it's the eldest son who surpasses him, though."

She sipped again. It made her eyes water. "If it happens, it'll be in no small way due to his father's foresight. And to you, Rekkr."

"Ah, I'm no Rekkr. Not anymore. I walked away from that years ago."

Elan studied him, curious. "Does it ever bother you?" His sideglance was puzzled. "To have lost your status," she explained. "After all you've done for the realm."

Badagis gave a dismissive wave. "Nah. It was my choice. I know in my heart I did it for the right reasons." He laughed softly and nodded toward the gaggle. "That used to bother me, though. Back when we were much younger, and I was much more foolish."

"What's that?"

"How he always got all the credit. I was the better warrior, but somehow Angavar was always the one lauded for winning the battle." He cocked a brow at her. "Like today. Vahldan wouldn't have even survived to face Auchote if you hadn't bested at least two of his thugs."

Elan shrugged. "I did my duty."

"As did I. For years. You do know why, don't you?"

"Why we do our duty?"

"No. I mean why we serve them. How we make it our duty."

She furrowed her brow. "I was assigned to it." It came out snappish.

"Oh, but surely you see it goes beyond that. Surely you did much more than your assignment this day, Blade-Wielder. Let me ask you this: what you went through today—how did you endure it? How did you make it from behind enemy lines, just in time to save him, and then battle on through most of an entire day without rest or food?"

"I don't know. I just... did."

"But what did you hope to achieve?"

Elan stared into the fire. "I wanted to save people. Like my mother before me."

Badagis grinned. "Ah, but your mother was a healer, Elan. You and I are warriors. And this"—he nodded toward the throng surrounding Vahldan—"is about more than being a warrior. This is about inspiring others. You see how they're drawn to him? You see the light in their eyes? Men like Desdrusan can only thrive by making other men believe they're small, weak. Afraid. Men like Vahldan make other men believe that they're bigger, stronger, fearless. Fit for something more. Like Angavar before him, your subject manages to make men believe they can achieve more than they'd dared to dream. They long to see something of themselves in him."

Badagis pointed at himself and then her. "Warriors like you and I do well to make it our duty to serve leaders like him. We're drawn to him, too, but in a different way. Even at our very best, we warrior elites can only more deftly kill. We destroy, we know it. But we long for more. By serving a presence like Vahldan's we can help to make magic happen. It's how we create rather than destroy. And so we have. What we've helped to create is right here before our eyes." He grinned at Vahldan with fond satisfaction.

"So it is," she said, pushing aside her annoyance, and seeing the man in a new light. Badagis really had willingly taken a supporting role. Twice now, actually. She glanced at the trophy she'd taken from the scar-cheeked Spali, stuck in her belt. Badagis had foregone the credit he'd earned, and yet he was satisfied. Likely moreso than if he had sought credit and received anything less than what was due. As was usually the case.

Badagis raised his cup. "To us." She raised hers and they drank. Gods, the stuff went straight to her head. Badagis sighed. "I imagine you're relieved to be done with it, though."

"Done?"

"Your assignment. After today, clearly the man will have no shortage of guardians."

Elan instantly bristled again. "None like me."

Badagis eyed her. "Undeniably so." He drank deeply and hissed. "May I tell you something, Blade-Wielder?" She gave him a reluctant nod. "I share this only because you and I are two of the few who can fully grasp it. Look at him and tell me you can't see that he belongs to them now."

She gazed at Vahldan. Her subject stood at the center of dozens, all facing him, all beaming—as was he. She couldn't deny it seemed a joyous communion. She knew it should be satisfying. She looked back to the fire and swallowed the biggest slug from her cup yet. Was it this gods-awful drink that made her chest hurt?

Badagis leaned in, softening his voice. "Freya knows I understand how hard it is to love someone who belongs to their people. But I assure you, it's worth it. And yet, one warrior to another, I advise you to keep your armor on. Keep your shield up. No matter how tough we are, our hearts still beat the same as a babe's."

Elan's hand drifted to her chest, resting on the talisman hanging under her breastplate.

Badagis squinted out into the darkness beyond. "I'm guessing that one's here for you."

Elan followed his line of sight. Kunna stood between two tents, just out of the firelight. The young Blade-Wielder waved for Elan to follow, and disappeared into the night. "Seems the real world beckons," Badagis said knowingly.

Gods, going back would be even worse than watching the fawning gaggle. It seemed like ages since Elan had crawled into this nettle patch. Now every move she made offered a new prick, every direction she turned, a new series of stings.

"So it does," she said. She could no longer avoid facing the barbs of her changing life.

VAHLDAN STOOD IN SILENCE, hardly paying attention as Arnegern retold the tale of his face-off with Auchote for the tenth time. He was even too worn out to insist on the inclusion of Elan's vital role. Arnegern raved on and Vahldan checked on her again. Elan stood and handed her cup to Badagis. Would she finally join him? Or better still, pull him away from this torture?

He'd finally come free of the ugliness to find himself in this dizzying vortex. Even a bottomless cup of mead and unending praise eventually became tiresome. He'd long since had his fill of both. Vahldan felt the need to gather himself, to see where he stood, to consider what came next. He'd splashed his face and rinsed his arms, but he'd yet to manage a thorough washing of himself.

Oh gods, Elan was leaving. He hadn't even properly thanked her for saving his life. Let alone for her role in his having found himself again. After he'd retrieved the sword, she'd provided him with such clarity about whom he needed to become, and why. As no one else could have. Then he'd gone and lost himself again right afterward. Surely she must be as disappointed in him as he was in himself.

No one here seemed to care that he'd raged like a savage at the surrender. They all seemed to have forgotten how recently he was in chains, dodging thrown rotten food and absorbing curses and mocking laughter. But he hadn't.

Vahldan knew he wouldn't have seen his way through to this reversal of fortune without Elan. She'd even inspired him to carve again. Vahldan set out after her, pushing through those surrounding him. How could he have let this happen?

Badagis stepped to block him. "Let her go, son."

"I can't. There's too much I didn't say." He tried to move past the bigger man.

Badagis wrapped an arm around him. "It can wait. Besides, she already knows."

"But I didn't even—"

"Vahldan, don't. She has her own responsibilities, her own people. Just as you have yours. Now more than ever." Badagis nodded to his followers, most now silent and gaping.

Vahldan made a fist, waking the ache in his hand. He deserved it. He needed it. He'd been an ass that night, too. But she came back. Right when he needed her. He didn't deserve her help, let alone her loyalty. But she gave it. Without question or condition.

The ache would remind him that he needed to start being the friend she deserved.

Vahldan turned back to his mulling admirers. A trio of young wolves who'd come to congratulate him had started back toward their side of the camp. They were stopped by a group of four men in the shadows beyond the firelight. Vahldan squinted. One of the four was Ulfhamr, the captain of the Wulthus infantry. His companions were wool guildsmen. It was clear the wolves who'd come to congratulate him were being scolded for doing so. The young men bowed penitently before hurrying on to their own pavilion fires.

"Seems not everyone is an admirer." Badagis had followed his gaze.

"No matter what I do, it'll never be enough, will it?" he said. "They'll do whatever they have to. They'll find a way to keep us down."

"Aye. The wolves think the only way to keep their place is to stand atop of us."

Vahldan shook his head. "It's not just the wolves. You know as well as I do that somewhere out there, Desdrusan is plotting, brewing up the perfect lies, twisting what happened. And too many will happily gulp it down. No matter what good I do, to them I'm a threat."

Badagis sighed. "Sometimes I wish we could just take back our glory. We used to bathe in it. We lions were the warriors, and everyone knew the nation needed us. Those were simpler days. Even most wolves respected us, then."

Vahldan stiffened. His head swam. "Take it back?" His father's voice whispered in his head. *'Lead our clan to glory. Take it back.'*

"There was a time before those greedy bastards had such a hold over the herdsmen," Badagis said. "A time when defending our people and our homeland meant more than the earnings one man could squeeze from another man's needs. Back then glory was worth more than coin."

"Take it back," Vahldan repeated wistfully.

Badagis tilted his head. "You still here, son?"

"Yes, I'm here. *'I trust you'll see it soon enough. Besides, you've already promised to stay true to me. Remember, Badagis will show you the way.'* Vahldan grinned at the big man. "And oddly, somehow he knew that you'd be here with me."

Badagis returned the grin. "So, you're speaking in riddles now? You sound like the priestess."

"Sorry. It's just that you've reminded me of something my father knew you'd do."

"He knew I'd what?"

"Show me the way."

"So it's just riddling from now on?" Badagis asked, sounding amused.

"No. Well, maybe. I'm guess I'm just glad you're here. You've shown me what I must do." Vahldan gazed at the lurking guildsmen, and a very recognizable pair of figures appeared, coming from the Wulthus side of the camp—one squat and the other towering over him. The pair was trailed by a half-dozen members of the Amalus old guard. "Speaking of which." He pointed.

Badagis harrumphed. "I was wondering when Lord Lard-Barrel would show his face." His father's friend nodded at the hilt of Vahldan's new sword. "He'll be coming for that, I'll warrant. Say the word and we can make a stand here and now. I'm with you, all the way. Others will be, too."

Vahldan gripped Bairtah-Urrin's hilt and shook his head. "Not yet. What I have in mind requires the right time and place. I'm not sure what might come of it if he pushes tonight."

"Get yourself inside my pavilion. Your cousins and I can see that Desdrusan and his thugs leave you be. At least for the night."

"No. I don't want any lions facing one another in anger over this. Especially not tonight."

"Sorry to be the one to tell you, but this is bound to come to a fight, son."

"I know. But it has to play out just right. And not on the night of a victory. There are already hard feelings among good men. Men I hope to lead one day." Badagis's gaze narrowed. "What? You disagree?"

The older man shook his head. "I don't. It's just... You're certainly not your father."

'Angavar was a gifted warrior, perhaps the finest in the realm. You may never live up to that.'

The remnants of the ugliness fluttered in Vahldan's chest. "Meaning what?"

Badagis laughed. "Meaning you are wise beyond your years. Certainly wiser than he was at your age. Perhaps wiser than he ever became. Makes me think you really are the Bringer, after all." The big man winked. Vahldan looked down and shivered as he shed the ugliness. Badagis stepped around him to block the oncoming usurper's view. "Whatever you're up to, you'd be wiser still to be gone from here. And quick."

Vahldan had to agree. "I'll send word when I figure this out. Thanks again. For everything." He set out into the darkness of the forest at the far edge of the Amalus camp.

KUNNA STAYED AHEAD OF ELAN, never glancing back. The Skolani camp was quiet. They encountered only protégés, scurrying with pots of cleansing paste and armor to be polished. They all avoided eye contact with Elan, same as Kunna.

Kunna led her to Icannes's pavilion. Elan didn't know whether to be relieved or more anxious. It wasn't the queen she'd face, but she almost dreaded Icannes's judgement more.

Kunna held the flap open. Elan hesitated. The soft glow and the scent of the warm cleansing paste beckoned. She firmed herself and strode in. The flap fell shut behind her.

Elan came face to face with Ursellya. She sighed. "Oh, it's just you."

"Yes, just me." Ursellya stiffened then looked away. "Princess Icannes bid me to make ready for your cleansing."

A cleansing. Maybe this wouldn't be so bad, after all. "I presume she's with her mother?" Ursellya nodded and bent to stir the pot on the brazier. Something felt awkward. Maybe she was imagining it. It'd been a long day for everyone. "What can I do?"

Ursellya all but harrumphed and stood to face her. "Turn." Elan spun away from her and Ursellya unbuckled the stays for her holster and lifted it over her head, mussing her braids.

Ursellya seemed put out, her movements jerky. "Tired?" she asked.

"I suppose."

Not much of a conversation. Elan fumbled for something else to say. "I rode with your sister today. She fought well."

Ursellya's fingers paused. "So I understand. Or at least that you started off together." Ursellya began again on the straps to her breastplate, her actions growing rougher.

"Yeah, it was a long day."

Once her breastplate was off, the healer came around to face her. Ursellya's body was rigid, her eyes hard. "Actually, what I heard was that you rode with her, and then left her." Ursellya's lip quivered.

"Well, yes, we were eventually separated. As I said, it was a long day."

"So it's true? That you left Sochana, in the heat of a fight? Left her to ride off to your young man?"

Elan's scalp tingled. Her face and all the rest of her exposed skin pricked hot. Like the wrongness of the conversation was burning the pavilion around them. "Oh, gods. What's happened? Where is Sochana?"

Ursellya stiffened, rising into brave shoulders. "She's dead, Elan."

"No! How?" Elan felt slapped. It sent her from prickling to stinging.

"That's what I hoped to learn from you."

She told herself to stay standing, to somehow face her friend's accusing eyes. *Was* she at fault? She ran though the day's events in her head. "Sochana was fine, when I..."

"When you left her?"

"Yes. I mean, when we parted she'd downed her quarry. She dismounted and was heading over to check Nahlay's body."

"So it's all true? You ended up paired with my sister. You were behind the Spali lines, outnumbered. Sochana was off her horse, exposed, checking on a fallen comrade. And you chose that moment to gallop off."

"No! I mean, Sochana seemed safe. Yes, we'd fallen into pairs. We were pursuing Paralatoe. And I continued to pursue them."

"Because of him!" Ursellya's shining eyes flared. "Admit it, Elan. My sister was struck down while she prayed to Hel for her friend, thinking her partner had her back. And in return for this act of grace, she was abandoned—left to have her skull caved in. And not just by some random Spali. By the one you let go. You gave up the chase. But you hadn't just given up, had you? You left her for someone more important. You left to go running to your lover."

Elan shook her head. "No, no, no. It wasn't like that. I... I didn't realize... I—"

"Of course you didn't realize. You left!" Ursellya hugged herself and walked to the brazier. "I just don't know anymore, Elan. Maybe they're right about you. Maybe Anallya is right, that you don't deserve your blade."

"Anallya has always hated me. Everyone knows it. No one listens to her."

"They're listening now! Even the queen. Everyone saw you gallop off when Keisella called for a retreat. Everyone knows you heard and disobeyed. If I were you, I'd get ready to defend that blade. I'm betting you'll soon be summoned to do just that. And when you are, will you really be able to deny it, Elan?"

"Deny what? That in the heat of the fight I continued to pursue the foe?"

"No. Can you still deny that you're gone to Freya's Curse?"

"I'm not... He's—"

"Everyone knows what he is. How could we not? It's obviously true that you fucked him. And not just outside of the rites, but during the *heat* of the last fight. Seems like the heat tends to get to you, doesn't it?" Ursellya glared.

Elan gulped for air. "I can't believe you're saying this."

"Believe it. And believe I'm not the only one. I'd suggest you practice denying it. Or at least come up with an excuse you can memorize."

"An excuse? I didn't mean for any of this to happen."

Ursellya folded her arms. "You didn't mean it. Huh. Nah, that's lame. Better work on it. And while you're at it, ask yourself how long you can continue to avoid making a choice."

"What choice?"

"Between him and us. You can't live in both worlds, Elan."

"I never wanted..."

"Clearly what you want is to have it both ways. But you can't. It's part of the Skolani oath for a reason. Or have you forgotten?"

"I know the oath."

"Do you? If so, you're excellent at ignoring it. You're being selfish, Elan. And people are suffering for it." Elan shook her head, trying to process. "Oh, you don't think so? Need proof? My sister is dead. I'm suffering. Isn't that enough for you? Do you even care?"

Elan opened her mouth, but all that came was the threat of a sob. Now she felt both prickly hot and shivery cold. And nauseous. And so weary. She knew an apology would ring hollow, but she had to try. "Listen, I am so sorry about Sochana. I'm sorry that I left her."

Ursellya raised her chin. "I'm sorry, too. Sorry that I can't obey my princess just now. She asked me to untie your braids, but the thought of touching you suddenly makes me feel ill." Ursellya spun around and headed out. She stopped at the exit. "But that shouldn't bother you. You're used to ignoring commands." The flap fell shut behind her.

ELAN DIDN'T KNOW how long she'd been on the ground in Icannes's pavilion. She was curled in a ball on her side, her face wet with tears and snot.

Elan opened her hands and focused on the kestrel carving she'd been clutching. It had darkened with oils from her rubbing fingers.

She realized she was mourning. She mourned not just for Sochana, but for all that was lost. From her mother to Vahldan. From her dream to the looming loss of her blade.

Icannes greeted Kunna outside. Elan slipped the kestrel into the pouch on her belt. She clumsily straightened and pushed herself upright, wiping her face on her sleeve. She needed to face her for this.

Icannes ducked in and straightened. She wore a loose frock and sandals. Her skin glowed in the lamplight, her cheeks pink from scrubbing. Her braids were freshly retied. Gods, she hated that Icannes looked this good and she was a complete mess. Seemed to be happening a lot lately.

Elan firmed herself. "You did that on purpose." The fury in her voice surprised her.

But not Icannes. "You two needed to cleanse a shared wound, before it became infected." Icannes strode past her and dropped her saddle bag.

"Cleanse it? You left her here to scrape me raw, and you knew it."

"You think it'd have been better to let it fester? Because that's been working so well for you, hasn't it, Elan?"

Her face and eyes stung again. Just a short time before she'd had the audacity to hope that she could find her way back to some sort of satisfaction. That she could live as Badagis seemed to. How would that work for her, exactly? Had she imagined she'd find her way to some sort of new normal with Vahldan? Or with her Skolani sisters? Now she couldn't imagine either.

After all she'd endured, the gods were fickler than ever.

Her hopes hadn't even lasted the night. "I can't do this anymore."

"You don't have to. That's why you're here. It's over, my love." Icannes opened her arms, beckoning.

Somehow, Elan's longing to be held won out. She fell into Icannes's embrace, hoping her oldest friend could somehow regather her shattered pieces. "Everyone thinks I'm awful. The Gottari ignore me. My own sisters won't even look at me."

"They'll all get over it. And you will, too."

"They all think I betrayed Sochana, betrayed my people."

Icannes hummed, deep in her chest. "I don't think that. And no one else matters."

"The queen is going to take my blade."

"I doubt it. If she tries, I'll remind her that she's as much to blame as anyone."

Icannes stroked her back and fussed with her braids. Elan's body betrayed her. She wanted to stay mad, wanted to sulk, to run away, to never face anyone again. But she felt gathered up if not healed. Warmth spread through her, into her core.

Icannes knew holding her like this would ruin her tantrum. Damn her.

With Elan's ear pressed to her chest, Icannes's voice was like a big cat's purring—deep and soothing. "Even if you do lose your blade, you're home, dear heart. It's over now. As long as we have each other, we'll find the way back to who we used to be."

CHAPTER 31—AN AMALUS AFFAIR

"Although Vahldan grew up in isolation, he was raised by two parents who impressed the import of legacy upon him, even if each parent held their own view of how he might honor that legacy. Being a curious and clever child, he sought to learn from each of them. But so too did he discover that he could utilize his parents' differing perspectives to gain insight. He not only constantly questioned whichever parent he was alone with, he also plied one with the positions of the other.

It's true, he went through a rebellious period, and was repelled by the notion of being at the center of the political divisions of the Gottari nation. But through examining issues from opposing viewpoints, Vahldan gained both a broad outlook and a keen mind for debate and persuasion." –Brin Bright Eyes, Saga of Dania

DESDRUSAN HAD FINALLY REGAINED his composure. He was reconsolidating his grip on the reins of power. Events had spiraled from his control during the battle and briefly afterward. But the battle was won, the surrender accepted, and he was still the Lion

Lord. He might have mishandled the futhark sword, but he still held the political advantage, gods be praised.

Soon, all would be made right again. There could be no debate. The Amalus blade was his property. Desdrusan still had the authority to see to its just return.

Once he'd managed to speak with most of the prominent landowning Rekkrs among the Amalus, it had only taken a moment each to remind them how dangerous Angavar had been to their interests—how recklessly he'd stirred the resentments of their tenant herdsmen.

From there, he had only to point out that the son was proving himself even more volatile.

Admittedly, Desdrusan had been rattled during the battle. It was as his mother had always said: he simply wasn't born a warrior. Instead, he'd been born clever. Which was a far better gift. Most people with an ounce of sense realized that men weren't natural warriors, even if they made a show of it. When it came to arrows flying and blades swinging, the wise sought shelter, and let those with witless passion do the shooting and stabbing. And the bleeding.

Once Desdrusan had sought and reconfirmed the backing of his oldest allies, he had cleverly gathered them to petition Thadmeir on the Wulthus side of the camp. He even saw to it that a dozen prominent Wulthus guildsmen were in attendance. With his supporters around him, Desdrusan had made the issue of his stolen futhark sword paramount. The pariah's possession of such a cherished relic was intolerable. If they wished to maintain any semblance of the futhark uniting them, they had to admit this was so. Desdrusan made the stickler and those who kept him in power admit that such an outrageous scenario could not be tolerated.

He pulled this off in spite of the ongoing victory celebration. All the while, drink had dulled the wits of the celebrants—particularly those of his clan. That worked to his advantage, too. Not only were those who might refute him addled and distracted, everyone who mattered recognized that left unchecked, the drunken celebration could carry on for days. They all saw how vital it was for Desdrusan to regain control over the unrulier of the two ruling clans.

Stickler that he was, Thadmeir, more than any of them, recognized the need to reestablish order, and that possession of the Amalus futhark blade was a logical, and vital, step to it.

With the battle behind them, it was a short leap to convincing Thadmeir that a ruling in the field on the status of the murderer in their midst was not only warranted but urgent. Of course the Wolf Lord saw the potential for the pariah to leverage the passions of victory to his advantage. As well as how dangerous such levering could be. The young hothead's outrageous showing at the Spali's surrender certainly didn't hurt Desdrusan's case. The shock of such behavior had even erased the potential stain of Desdrusan's disappearances—both during the fighting and at the surrender. None of them had even asked him where he went.

With things back in his control, Desdrusan led a few of his followers and his loyal guardian to the Amalus side of the camp. Although Desdrusan seemed to have lost Ermanaric to drunkenness, it was only a temporary setback. Jhannas, of course, remained steadfast.

The time for a confrontation had come. The raucous group of the pariah's young fans stood guzzling and gabbling as Desdrusan approached. He spotted their decadent role model, Badagis himself, standing at the edge of the gathering, oddly alone. Desdrusan made for the bushy-bearded oaf, scanning the crowd for his target. "Well, Badagis, what have you done with him? Already drank him under?"

The oaf raised his cup, grinning. "Ah, you know me well, my lord. When it comes to drinking, I'm always happy to oblige. Though I'm not sure to which of my victims you refer."

With Jhannas and his old guard supporters fanning out behind him, Desdrusan stood before the drunken throng. The louts gradually fell to silence, most fixing him with boyish scowls. They'd learned well from their insolent hero, and they looked just as ridiculous.

"I'm looking for our clan's convicted murderer. He's supposed to be in my custody."

Badagis laughed. "That's funny."

Desdrusan rounded on the grinning oaf. "What's funny about it?"

"If you refer to Vahldan, it's funny because he's been wondering where you were."

"I can't imagine when this was. Lord Thadmeir and I have been conferring with senior Rekkrs all evening, as one would expect of the lords of Dania."

Badagis stroked his beard and looked skyward. "When was it? Oh yes. He was looking for you just after he saved your fat ass from Death's Grin. Who seems to have turned on you just before Vahldan's attack intervened." The drunk's gleeful façade morphed to a glower. "He looked for you then. But you were nowhere to be found. My lord."

Desdrusan was not about to be intimidated. Or dragged into a debate with a drunkard. He turned to face the malevolent boy brigade and raised his voice, "Hear this, all of you. It matters not what you think of me, nor of him. This is a matter of Gottari law. I am still the chieftain of this clan. Vahldan is still a convict. His absence puts him in violation of his oath. Besides that, he has something that does not belong to him. These transgressions will not be tolerated."

"Vahldan survived the Penance Line." Unsurprisingly, this outburst was from Arnegern, son of Vildigern. "By the will of the gods, he is proven righteous."

"His survival reveals nothing of the sort. By Gottari law, his survival wins him only that—his life. It does nothing to absolve him of his original crime. He is an exile. He illegally reentered Dania. And I shall see the issue settled. Lord Thadmeir feels the same. Our nation's two chieftains stand together in decreeing that Vahldan's status must be resolved. By the Lag of the Arrivals, I shall convene a field council. At sunset tomorrow. Vahldan's fate will be settled by a tribunal of the Rekkrs present. The law must and will be upheld."

"Vahldan won't stand for this."

Desdrusan wheeled to face his sullen nephew Belgar. "He will, or his absence will be his confession of guilt. He will return our clan's sacred relic, and he will comply with the law by never setting foot in Dania again. Trust me when I say that the council shall see to it."

Satisfied with the looks of uncertainty and even distress that he'd inflicted, Desdrusan turned and pointedly avoided Badagis as he strode back toward his pavilion, signaling for Jhannas and his own supporters to follow.

VAHLDAN HEARD footsteps just before the flap to the pavilion stirred. He sat up straight and drew a deep breath, hoping he hadn't miscalculated. A bent head came through. The pavilion's resident raised his face and stopped short, startled. "Oh. Vahldan. You're here."

"I am. Sorry for the intrusion. I'll leave, if you prefer."

Urias's smile seemed genuine. "No, it's just that they've been looking for you. And here you are."

"In one of the last places they'd look."

"Why yes. I suppose so. Well done, if that was your intent."

Vahldan shrugged. "Suppose I'd prefer not to be found. Not tonight, anyway."

Urias moved to a small table and pulled the stopper on a jug. "Drink?"

"No thanks. I had my fill earlier. This sneaking around has given me a bit of a headache."

The Wulthus Captain poured himself a cup and sat across from him. "So, besides not wanting to be found, is there another reason you chose me? I mean, is there something I can do for you besides hide you?"

"Perhaps."

"Such as?"

"I was just wondering where things stand. With your brother, I mean."

Urias leaned back. "I see. Well, for starters, Lord Thadmeir was pleased by your role in the battle. He applauds your host's holding of the left flank at the crucial moment. He's admitted aloud that you were vital to our victory. Several times, in fact."

"But...?"

Urias laughed. "But he was far less pleased by your performance with the Spali priests." One of Urias's eyebrows rose. "It rattled him a bit, I think—when the Spali named you as an ascending king. Rang too close to the prophecy for his taste, I suppose."

Vahldan was impressed by his candor. "I suppose it would." He tapped the hilt jutting from his waist. "I'm guessing Lord Thadmeir is less than pleased with my having this, as well?"

"Oh, he's not half as displeased as Desdrusan. It's mostly due to your having it that the Amalus Lord and several prominent Rekkrs have convinced my brother that a field council is in order. They're demanding that you appear to surrender it, tomorrow at sunset. Desdrusan is citing the Lag of the Arrivals."

Vahldan fingered the rune ring dangling from the roaring lion's head pommel. "Reclaiming this sword was part of my final vow to my father."

"I understand how difficult all of this must be. But be patient. Keep fighting. You won a lot of folks over today. It's a big step forward."

Vahldan softly chucked. "Being patient was part of my final vow to my mother."

"It's good advice. Things will grow clearer in time."

"You sound just like her. And yet." He gripped the hilt. "She also said I should stay true to my heart. She warned that some people would try to rein me, to use me to advance their ends. It's what your brother and Desdrusan and these, as you say, *prominent* Rekkrs are doing. They all seek to rein me, even as I *step forward*, as you put it. They want to keep things as they are."

Urias drank, watching him over the cup's rim. "They seek stability."

"They're afraid of change."

"A man who's cautious of change is a wise man," Urias said. "Many tell themselves their caution is in the service of protecting the futhark."

"Ha. The futhark is already broken."

"Maybe so," Urias admitted. "But many also claim it was your father who broke it."

A surge flowed through Vahldan. He released the hilt and bowed his head, seeking to regain control. "May I ask you, Captain, if you would say the futhark is intact?"

Urias squinted, weighing his words. "I suppose I'd say it's far from healthy and sound."

"Would you agree that the futhark cannot be made sound again without balance between our two clans?"

"I suppose I'd say that balance is the vital ingredient to the futhark's soundness."

Vahldan leaned in. "And do you really believe balance can be achieved if the Amalus clansmen do not control their own destiny? Do you really suppose that returning things to how they were before the war will steer us toward any semblance of unity, with the guildsmen and their lion puppet holding sway?"

Urias gazed in seemingly deep thought for a long moment. "I suppose I see your point." The Wulthus Captain stood and set his cup on the table. "I have a feeling, so I'm going to ask again. Is there something you wish of me?"

Vahldan stood to face him. "I wish only for you to understand me —which I sense you do. Maybe even more than you'd care to reveal. Because of the understanding I sense, I would wish only for you to remember two things: First, that I believe in the futhark and will strive to restore it. Through balance."

"And the second?"

"I am keeping this sword. And I hope that you, and your brother, will understand that I do so not out of spite. Rather, I do so out of a desire to seek honor. Not just for me, but for those who fought so valiantly—whose effort and bloodshed helped to lift my clan up, so much closer to a position from which balance can be achieved. Please remember that this is an Amalus relic, and the choice of its bearer is an Amalus affair." He bowed his head. "No need to reply. I thank you for your hospitality, for listening, and for your service to the realm." He strode to the exit.

"Vahldan," Urias called. He stopped. "Will you come to the field council?"

"I'll be there."

"Promise me it won't come to bloodshed. There's been too much already."

"I wish I could. Honestly, it's not entirely in my hands." Urias raised his brows. "But perhaps there are ways to help see to it," he added.

"Such as?"

Vahldan smiled. "As I said—it's an Amalus affair. And being left to decide our fate for ourselves might go far toward a satisfying— and peaceful—resolution. As far as I'm concerned, Wulthus Rekkrs need not trouble themselves over it."

"I doubt our lords will feel that way."

"Perhaps *our lords* need not be troubled over a decision best left to each Rekkr."

Urias frowned. "Hmmm. Perhaps."

"Cheer up, Captain. I've already promised to be patient." He slipped out into the cold night, and moved silently into the shadows between the Wulthus pavilions.

CHAPTER 32—UNBOUND BY TRADITION

" *It must be remembered that the seeds of Gottari clan division were sown by a young man's lovesick obsession. None of Angavar's friends have ever denied that he coveted the Wulthus heir's betrothed. Long before Angavar's ascent or Frisanna being promised to another, the two preened and posed for one another's attentions.*

No few recall how forlorn Angavar was at the announcement of Frisanna's betrothal to his rival, how pale he became in watching his beloved dance for Aomeir. But so too do many recall seeing how Angavar's smirking cousin Desdrusan whispered in his ear during that performance. With what ideas the glutton filled the mind of the forlorn young man, only the gods now know. Regardless, it is no secret that the passions of the players led not just to a tragic incident, but to generations of strife." *–Brin Bright Eyes, Saga of Dania*

MORNING DREW NEAR. Vahldan couldn't show himself in the camp until after the field council began. He had to trust his campaigning to others. Before dawn, he snuck into Arnegern's tent and conveyed his wishes to his most trusted friend among the Gottari.

He was still dressed in his filthy battle gear when he arrived at the corral in the predawn twilight. He sent the boy attending the horses to gather a sling of the driest firewood he could find. The boy returned just as he finished saddling Ardua. Vahldan tossed him one of the apples he'd packed for the mare, stowed the sling behind the saddle, and mounted.

He longed to see Elan, but he knew Badagis was right. She had her own responsibilities, as he had his. Instead he would take a lesson from her. Vahldan loved the Skolani idea of a post-battle cleansing ceremony. If he'd ever needed cleansing, it was now.

He rode by the clearing where the fallen were laid out. During the night he'd made sure Keffric was there among them. Vahldan had never been much for praying, but he'd done his best to plead Keffric's honor to Hel. Even now, the thought put a lump in his throat. Once they were out of the forest, he urged Ardua to a trot, heading out across the plains through a light snow, the frozen coating on the brown grass crunching under the gray mare's hooves. He avoided the battlefield by riding north. As he surmised, at the base of the third swale he found the clear stream that ran down to the Spali camp, far enough away to keep him out of their view. He doubted their scouts would bother him.

Vahldan found a firm grassy patch along the bank and dismounted. He stripped off not only his hauberk and leathers, but his clothing, too. He soaked and wrung each piece, and scrubbed both his armor and body with the fine sand from the stream's bottom. He carefully washed the leg wound. It had regained its scab, thankfully. His arm wound, given to him by the first man he killed, had healed but left an ugly scar. His torso, arms and legs were scattered with lesser cuts and scrapes, and bruises and welts of various colors and shades.

He managed to rid himself of the blood and mud, even from under his fingernails. The bodily marks of battle would eventually fade, but he knew the war would remain with him long afterward.

He caught sight of his reflection in the water. It startled him. His beard had filled in and darkened. He thought of himself as a man's son. But the face that looked back at him was simply a man's. He looked like Angavar. *'This is where I end and you begin.'* He supposed it boded well for the night's purposes.

Or perhaps not. *'Angavar was a gifted warrior. You may never live up to that.'*

The cold rinse braced him, made his skin glow pink. Shivering, he wrapped himself in his cloak and walked Ardua back to the top of the ridge. With Afletam in sight on the western horizon, he started a fire with the wood he'd brought.

Vahldan propped his clothes around the fire as best he could to dry. He ate the hard cheese and brown bread Arnegern had provided before splitting the last apple with Ardua. He sat polishing and sharpening the futhark blade while the mare grazed.

He spent the afternoon sorting his thoughts, weighing all he'd come to know, and scanning his memory for lessons long forgotten. He wished he'd paid closer attention to those on the old lag—the customs and laws that bound Gottari warriors in the field—but he thought he remembered enough. Hopefully enough to at least fake an expertise.

Vahldan thought of his brother and sisters, beholden for food and shelter to Arnegern's parents. Little Kemella was so tiny, so fragile, with only Mara to offer the motherly touch that had nurtured the rest of them. Their well-being and safety was far from set. The only way to ensure their welfare was to succeed tonight.

Vahldan wondered what the coming night would require of him, if more blood might be spilled. Urias was right—there'd already been too much. He felt a stirring deep down, at the pit of his belly. Surprisingly, there was no sign of the ugliness. Not anymore. Today he would act with honor, with justice. The confidence he felt in that seemed to have banished it. He gripped the futhark blade. It was lighter, keener than the sword with which he'd first killed. If anything, it felt more natural—more a part of him. More lethal.

This deadly instrument was the age-old symbol of Gottari law and prosperity, long borne by his ancestors. Keffric's voice sang in the wind, rustling through the grasses: *'You shall be an instrument of death. You shall wreak death that honors the gods—death that bestows glory.'*

Then his father's: *'Take back our clan's glory. Glory is the way.'*

The snow tapered off, and the low clouds darkened with evenfall. He dressed himself and mounted. His leathers were stiff as new and his hauberk gleamed in the day's last light. His hair was finally dry, but he didn't tie it back. It'd grown long. He left it unbound on his shoulders.

Vahldan arrived at the camp corral at dusk. Torchlight drew him to the clearing beyond the royal pavilions, where the dead were laid out. He stopped short, bristling in outrage. There, offering ceremonial prayer, was not just the Wolf Lord but also Angavar's craven murderer. They stood over Keffric and the others. The usurper was an insult to those who'd faced their deaths with honor and valor.

He pressed down the stirring in his belly. He would not allow the ugliness to reappear.

Jhannas and Urias walked behind the pair. Lord and usurper finished their ceremony and strode toward the gathering at the far end of the clearing. Vahldan looped around the outside of the camp, keeping to the trees beyond the field council.

Lamps hung from the low branches of the oaks surrounding the clearing. His mission with Urias had succeeded. He saw no one he knew to be of the Wulthus, and very few guildsmen. It seemed every man present was an Amalus Rekkr or bannerman, mostly herdsmen of the eastern marches. Most had their shields slung behind their shoulders. Several wore armor and battle gear. They all wore grim expressions, with the steam of their breath rising over them.

Vahldan hovered on the outskirts. The Wolf Lord studied the gathering, looking concerned. Desdrusan lurked behind Thadmeir, unable to hide but doing his best. Thadmeir raised his hand as if to ask for a silence that already existed. "Where is young Vahldan? Does he avoid justice?"

"No, justice is precisely what I seek. I am here, Lord Thadmeir."

Vahldan stepped into the torchlight. Desdrusan sneered but stayed behind his counterpart. Thadmeir's gaze settled on the hilt of Bairtah-Urrin. "Well, what have you to say of yourself?"

"Of myself? In regard to what?"

Thadmeir frowned. "In regard to your judgement, of course."

"As you can see, I survived the Penance Line." Several Rekkrs chuckled. "Though it's rare, as I recall the Lag of the Arrivals, those who are sentenced and survive are judged worthy by the gods. Several of us survived, my lord. Is the judgement of the others in question, as well?"

Thadmeir turned to Urias, who whispered briefly in his ear. Desdrusan continued to cower. Thadmeir faced Vahldan again. "You have a point. And too few have come tonight to render a lasting decision on the issue." The Wolf Lord nodded toward the sword. "It's well that you brought the blade. You might have brought it back sooner, but we can still put this mess behind us for now. Just return it to its proper owner, and let's be done for the night, shall we?"

Vahldan drew the futhark sword. "You mean this blade? The Amalus clan's most sacred relic? The blade that was knocked from the grasp of the man hiding behind you, on its first battle contact since he's wrongfully borne it? The blade that, in his haste to flee, he so willingly deserted to fate?"

"Yes, yes—you've made your point, Vahldan. We all understand your grievances. They can be discussed once we're back in Danihem. But for now—"

"No, my lord," Vahldan interjected. "I don't think you do understand. I have no complaint for your consideration. So, if my possession of this"—he raised the sword—"is the only matter you wish to address tonight, rest assured it's about to be indisputably resolved. In fact, if you're weary, I'm sure no one will mind your departure. As I see it, the rest of what must be settled here is strictly an Amalus affair."

The usurper's eyes widened and the Wolf Lord's scowl deepened.

"By Thunar's balls, boy—who do you think you..." Urias touched his brother's arm as the grumbling and fidgeting of the encircling Amalus Rekkrs rose.

Urias smiled and stepped between them. "Vahldan, no one disputes that your survival of the Penance Line releases you from your sentence for the murder of the Carpan. What Lord Thadmeir is trying to say is that judgement still awaits you in the longhouse. As was agreed before we marched."

"Thank you for explaining, Captain. What I'm saying is that my judgement in Danihem is about to become unnecessary. As you recall, the judgement in question was whether or not I was worthy of a new trial after Rekkr Teavar and I fought to a draw. The point will soon be moot. For the trial I sought then is about to happen. This very night."

"This is an outrage!" The quaver of Desdrusan's first spoken words revealed his terror.

Vahldan laughed, and Thunar's Blessing thrummed through him, heating his blood. "You're outraged? After your pathetic showing yester-day? I'm surprised you aren't still running, all the way back to Danihem. Too bad for you that your instincts to flee didn't keep you going. But I, for one, am glad you're still here. Makes things simple." He signaled to the Rekkrs. "Since we have no tarp, I'll need Amalus Rekkrs willing to make a vow to fairness to form the trial's shield-circle. Are any of you willing?"

Dozens of lions slung their shields around and onto their arms and moved to form a tightening circle around Vahldan and those he debated.

Desdrusan turned to Thadmeir. "My lord, you mustn't allow this, this... lawlessness."

Vahldan shook his head. "Actually, it's the opposite of lawless. And it has nothing to do with Lord Thadmeir. This has only to do with the Amalus clan, and the ancient laws that bind us all." The Rekkrs shields were edge to edge. The remaining onlookers had gathered two to three deep surrounding them.

Thadmeir looked distressed. "How do you presume such actions?"

Vahldan pointed the futhark blade at Desdrusan. "This man, our supposed chieftain, has disgraced us in the face of the foe. It's a matter of clan honor. By the Lag of the Arrivals, it's within my rights as a witness to demand satisfaction. And since we are beyond a day's ride from the longhouse, the old laws dictate the proper form for such satisfaction. And that form, should the claimant so choose, is by field trial. Which is fitting, since a trial is what you all had secretly planned for me. A trial between the two of us will resolve so much, don't you think?"

Thadmeir's eyes narrowed. "Is this some sort of threat, Vahldan?"

"Oh no, my lord," Vahldan said. "It's not a threat. It's more like a promise. A promise that our clan will resolve its inner strife, and be made sound again. As the futhark demands of us. In fact, I'm going to have to ask you and your brother to step out of the circle. You're free to stay and watch, of course. But since neither of you is of the Amalus, I'm afraid you're forbidden from holding a shield. Or even from voicing opinion once we're underway."

Thadmeir turned to his brother, who again whispered in his ear. Desdrusan's cheeks glowed as if sunburnt. Jhannas glowered, but remained the unreadable rogue element.

The brothers continued to whisper. Vahldan sought to help them along. "Trust me, my lord, the Lag of the Arrivals does hold sway here. My parents taught me well. If you truly seek balance, as I do, you will leave Amalus issues to the Amalus. It's for the good of the futhark."

Thadmeir straightened, looking down his nose. "Very well. But know this will weigh upon your judgement back in Danihem." Vahldan inclined his head. Thadmeir strode toward the shield circle. "Come, Urias." The circle parted to allow them passage. Thadmeir led the way without looking back. Urias gave him a look that urged him to caution. Vahldan tipped his head to reassure the Wulthus Captain.

Desdrusan looked like the cat that fell into the kennel. His words were more breath than voice. "I've had enough. You're an affront to the gods. You'll all regret this."

Vahldan shrugged. "I doubt it." Thunar's Blessing continued to tingle in his limbs. It felt intoxicating, but his head remained clear. "I see you came unarmed. I would offer to lend the futhark sword a final time, but clearly it's ill-suited to your style. Does anyone have a lighter blade our cousin can use?"

"Here, take mine." Arnegern threw his sword hilt first. Desdrusan backed away and it landed with a thud at his feet.

"I will *never* take part in such a mockery of justice," Desdrusan spat. "Jhannas!" The false lord pointed to have his guardian lead him from the circle back to the camp.

The moment had come. Vahldan watched as the big guardian methodically slung his shield to his arm, hand still on hilt, and headed for the circle's edge. Desdrusan crept behind and the men before him braced themselves. Jhannas arrived at the circle where Teavar and Herodes stood. Jhannas nodded gravely at his former fellow guardsman. Teavar glanced at Herodes, then both looked to Vahldan. Vahldan gave a slight nod, and they reluctantly stepped aside.

Vahldan sighed. They'd called his bluff. He couldn't be responsible for Amalus bloodshed outside of Desdrusan's or his own.

But rather than passing through, Jhannas pivoted, shield up, elbow to elbow with his fellows, blocking Desdrusan's passage. Jhannas's voice thrummed with threat. "You'd best take up that sword, if you expect to survive long. Difficult as it is for you, this time you'll have to bend over for something yourself."

Vahldan had never discounted Keffric's words. *'There are those not so loyal as they seem—even those very close to the fat man.'* He'd guessed correctly. The usurper was faced away, but Vahldan wished he could witness his expression.

Once he could see Desdrusan, the man's terror morphed into seething resentment, directed at Jhannas. "Have you forgotten what I've done for you, for your family? Do you know what you owe me?"

"I do." Jhannas hacked phlegm from his throat and spat in the usurper's face. "There's a partial payment, for my qeins. I'll let the son of Angavar deliver the rest of what you've got coming."

Vahldan stepped to Arnegern's blade on the ground. "Well, I suppose we'd best get on with this. And although I am willing to forgo shields, I really do recommend you take this." With the tip of Bairtah-Urrin, he flicked Arnegern's sword into flight, striking Desdrusan cross-wise on the chest. His girth delayed it from dropping. He raised his arms and cradled it at his elbows.

Desdrusan finally took the hilt in hand, but he let the blade hang at his side. Tears ran down his pink cheeks. "How can you all turn against me, after all I've done for this clan?" A grumbling murmur rolled through the onlookers.

Anger blew like a bellows on Thunar's Blessing. Vahldan stepped toward him, the forge flaring. The urge to chop this man down pulsed through him. "After all you've done to keep these men under the boot of the guild? After all you've done to fill your purse while those you supposedly led were reduced to groveling?" Eyes wide, Desdrusan raised the blade partway. Vahldan swung and soundly struck the blade, nearly knocking it from his chubby grip. On the backswing, he swished close to the bulbous belly, slicing the cloth of his silken tunic and drawing blood. The sight of it lured him on—urging him to finish this pathetic excuse for a man. He shook his head, pushing it down. He needed to do this right, to avoid losing himself.

Desdrusan backed away. "What do you want from me?"

"You ask that now? After allowing our once proud clan to be reduced to beggars; after all but ruining the futhark? Well, I suppose renouncing your status would be a start. Or, since it's clear that you sent savages to kill my father, perhaps you could set the record straight. You might start by admitting that you filled Aomeir's ears with lies about how Angavar stole my mother's virginity; how you then filled the Young Wolf with wine and rage, and put him on the Ananth-Jahn tarp, and then sent my father out there unknowing." The fat man was running out of room. Vahldan swung and knocked his blade aside again. "How the enraged drunk then came after my father, just as you planned; how you then threw this very sword to Angavar, forcing him to defend himself from an ambush, resulting in the accident that killed the Wulthus heir."

Desdrusan hit the shieldwall. The two shield-bearers pushed, thrusting him back toward Vahldan. He clanged Desdrusan's haphazard blade aside again, and brought the tip up to swipe at his opponents ear, drawing blood again. "Are you listening, coward?"

Desdrusan's bottom lip and chins trembled. "Go on, kill me. It's what you do. It's who you are—a killer."

Vahldan knew he was right, and the heat of temptation rose relentlessly. But... "In due course. Not before you admit it." He recklessly swung the blade, its tip swishing a finger's width from the usurper's nose.

"You want the truth? Fine. I admit it. I set the scene. But it was Angavar's rage that plunged a blade into Aomeir's chest. Now *you* admit it: the same sickness runs through your veins. It's clear that you feel it now. You can't control it, either. Go on, show them. Show what it looks like when a killer loses himself to savagery."

The clarity of Thunar's Blessing began to fray. His head began to fill with wool, the edges of his vision blurring.

He laughed, but Desdrusan saw he'd struck a nerve, and raised his voice. "Is this what you all want? After all of our years of peace and prosperity? Do you really want another deranged killer as your chieftain? Haven't you all heard tell of his grandfather? Of all the drunken rages? Of Beremund's sick debasing of your mothers and aunts when they were little more than girls? How he was blinded by the lecher's disease before drowning himself in drink?"

Vahldan forced a wry smile. "Beremund was your uncle, too, Desdrusan."

"Ah, but what I speak of is a taint, passed father to son, for generations. How many of you truly recall his father? How many recall Angavar as he really was before my supposed ruining of him, before he unleashed his murderous rage on his royal counterpart? He too was debauched. And while Angavar diddled himself over another man's woman, the wolves had their way in the longhouse, making their land alliances and strengthening the guild. They laughed at us for years! And I am to blame for begging of them? This boy's murderous forbearers had already brought the Amalus to the brink of ruin. I not only staved off the collapse Angavar wrought, I reversed our fortunes. It will all happen again if you let this... this scion of rage to return. This time it'll be worse! You all heard Freya's priestess foretell his doom. It won't be just his doom, it will be ours. Not just the doom of the Amalus, but of the Gottari people!"

Vahldan strained to maintain clarity as the inner fires raged. "They can hear past your lies. They hear your admission. You set up my father to usurp the dais chair, but it wasn't enough. You allied yourself with savages. You stooped to treason to accomplish the murder you don't have the stones to commit yourself. Murder of the rival you'd already cheated. I think these men can well decide which of us is best suited to restoring our clan's honor."

"Can you really hear me, brothers?" Desdrusan called, his top lip curling again. "Do you really think him capable of honor? He's already defiled the Mithusstandan by buggering his man-girl guardian."

The white noise was taking him; the periphery of his vision blurred; the hilt thrummed in his grip. It seemed the sword itself longed to slice this despicable creature's neck. Instead, he hit Desdrusan's blade again, harder, knocking it from his grasp—same as Auchote had. Vahldan charged forward, sword held high. The usurper backed until he tripped and sprawled, helpless. Vahldan put a boot on his chest, pinning him, sword poised to strike. The lions cheered.

Gods, he was so close. It would be so easy. *'Seize your destiny.'*

His arms tensed and he drew and held a breath. Desdrusan squeezed his eyes shut; the sword in Vahldan's hands called to him to be put to use—to swing, to chop. To kill!

Somewhere, through the white noise and the cheering, another voice came through: *'The honor isn't in the killing. It's in the justice.'*

Elan! It was always Elan. A killer's blood ran in his veins. But she kept him from losing himself. *'Sometimes death is the cost of it. The wisdom comes in knowing when it's truly necessary. And in preventing it when it's not.'* Yes, he could discern justice. He could find honor.

This was so much bigger than the pathetic worm recoiling helplessly beneath him. Killing Desdrusan would make him what the guildsmen hoped he'd be. *'I won't let them win!'*

Vahldan lowered the futhark blade, setting the tip right on one of his chins. Desdrusan's lips quivered and tears ran from his eyes when he opened them. Vahldan drew a breath, and his head began to clear. The Amalus around him roared for blood. Desdrusan croaked, "Go on, killer. Show them who you are. They'll love you all the more for it."

The forge cooled, and Vahldan saw clearly again. The tension left his arms, his chest. Beyond vengeance, this kill would fix nothing. Indeed, it would likely reinforce the status quo.

He recognized the broader outlook. He'd gone to the brink and found he could pull himself back. He withdrew the tip from Desdrusan's neck and stepped back, releasing a surge of gratification. It felt akin to the clear-headed power and control he found in Thunar's Blessing.

He smiled. "Sorry to disappoint. But you deserve to live with this disgrace."

"Shall we chain him?" Arnegern stepped in to pick up his sword.

Vahldan sheathed the futhark sword. "No need. He'll find no comfort here. And it's a long way back to Dania if he flees. Perhaps you could take up with your Paralatoe friends, Cousin. Oh wait—I take it Auchote would as soon kill you as smell you."

Desdrusan rolled and struggled to his knees, then his feet. "You'll all regret this," he huffed, wiping his face on his sleeve and yanking his twisted cloak straight. The fallen lord ran to the circle only to be shoved back. He began to bounce from one shield to another to another, trying to leave. The laughter and jeering of the Rekkrs grew raucous.

"Let him go!" Vahldan called. "He'll get his due soon enough."

The shield circle opened and the fallen lord almost fell through. Herodes kicked his butt as he scurried away, and the lions cheered. Badagis appeared at Vahldan's side. His father's first captain wrapped an arm around Vahldan. "Angavar's heir is an outcast no more! May he lead well and continue to ascend. All hail the rightful Lion Lord!"

Fists and blades were raised along with a throaty refrain. Arnegern began the chant, "Vahl-dan, Vahl-dan..." It grew to a cadenced thunder, echoing in the night.

It was overwhelming. Faces contorted with joy surrounded him. Vahldan continued to stare after Desdrusan, shaking off the last of the rapid pulse of his imbuement. The usurper was heading straight for the Wulthus side of the camp—sure to run straight to the guildsmen who'd originally installed him, and who'd protected him for years.

Vahldan's head swam. Could he lead well and continue to ascend? Could he pull himself from the brink like that again? It had been Elan's influence that had saved him. What would happen if they took her from him? Or was it *once* they took her? How would he navigate this treacherous new terrain without her?

Badagis filled his field of vision, arm around his shoulders. "He'd be proud of you."

"Would he?" *'Your father held such lofty aspirations.'*

"Of course!" Badagis grinned.

Vahldan wasn't so sure. What had he really done to earn this? Auchote still lived, and his Spali giant would've killed Vahldan if it hadn't been for Keffric and Elan. *'Your father was a gifted warrior, perhaps the finest in the realm.'*

Badagis released him with a fond pat to the side of his head. It made him feel like a child. "Trust me, son, you're going to make a fine chieftain. Just as your father knew you would."

'Gods, what will come of us if this falls to you?'

The big man's words sounded ludicrous. Badagis's assumption that he would become chieftain felt far from final. Vahldan would still have to convince the wolves, outmaneuver the guild, navigate the politics of the longhouse—all just to sit upon a lesser dais chair. He looked out over his celebrant followers, the steam of their breath hovering over them like a cloud.

Badagis chuckled. "Course, it still doesn't solve our problems with the guild. But you've put us in better shape to fight for what's ours." Was he that easily read?

Regardless, Vahldan realized his father's friend was right. The son of Angavar, rightful chieftain of the Amalus, had at least toppled the clan's usurper. Yet it wasn't done.

He might have taken the just course tonight, and avoided falling to the taint of his blood. But he hadn't taken back his clan's glory— not in a way that would lift him above the powerful forces he would still face. Not in a way that would win the hearts of the common herdsman.

His supporters began to drift away in small groups, likely to toast their victory. Gods, why did he still feel trapped, with an unsated longing still lingering within.

Vahldan suddenly knew what he had to do. He raised his hands. "Lions of the Amalus!" Everyone turned, their fervor fading. "It's true that we have won yet another battle. What came of tonight's trial is just. But, alas, my heart tells me it is not enough."

Men who'd been leaving drifted back. His close followers' grins fell away as they gathered near once more. "My brothers, I fear I know what comes next. They will tell you that this war is won, that the surrender of a gaggle of old priests makes it so. The wolves will want you to go back—back to your homesteads, to see to your flocks, to make ready for spring shearing and planting. They will ask you to resubmit to the yoke and whip of their markets, to serve their greed once more. But we warriors know it cannot be so. Not yet!"

Many were already nodding, and murmuring their recognition of the truth. He had them. Indeed, they were his to command. "The wolves don't want to face what we know. That this war was foisted by demons—demons that yet live. Those who dwell in Danihem cannot know as we do. Death's Grin and his ilk—the murderers who started this war, who killed and raped and burned through yours and your neighbors homes in eastern marches—yet live. This, we cannot allow, my brothers."

Now the lions voiced their concurrence. He went on. "We cannot let it happen again, and we know that as long as Auchote and his demon host draw breath, we will be waiting to face them yet again. For they shall return. If we let them go, they will easily regroup and regain their strength before they come. We lions are the true warriors of the Gottari. We lions are the front line—the true guardians of Dania. And, one way or another, we shall be the ones who face these demons again. Well, I say rather than waiting, we do so now, while we've got them where we want them. On our terms rather than theirs! I say, rather than waiting or hoping, we lions see this war done!" The warriors of his clan cheered and whooped and pumped their fists.

"Who will follow me? Who will hunt down the Paralatoe, and make each and every one of those demons pay? Who will help me to put an end to this war, once and for all?"

The cheering drowned out the last of his words, and they took up the chant again. "Vahl-dan! Vahl-dan! Vahl-dan!..."

Vahldan smiled and nodded. Now his course was set. He would keep the war alive. He was a killer, and he would take them back to glory. He could do so while aspiring to honor. He spotted Badagis among the jubilant Amalus. His father's right hand—the loyal captain who'd followed Angavar into a self-serving and ultimately futile war—was not smiling.

No, Badagis looked gravely concerned. It made Vahldan wonder what he knew.

CHAPTER 33—
STUMBLING INTO THE
MYSTIC

"I have had the honor of Urias's confidence. As Wulthus Captain of the longhouse, Urias long held a lofty perch from which to observe the workings of Dania's governance. And though some considered his influence too great, I, perhaps as well as any, was privy to his frustrations and deep concerns. I know how he once thought himself kept at the fringe of the Wulthus pack, suspected to conspire and meddle by both guildsmen and lions alike.

But I also know how deeply he cared for his people. I know how he always felt himself bound to something larger, tethered to a mystic power that was beyond ruling clans or the lords of men."—Brin Bright Eyes, Saga of Dania

URIAS DIDN'T MIND WAITING. The day had been exhausting, and he considered it a respite. He didn't even mind when the snow began to fall again. The snow was a nuisance, but his cloak was well-oiled. The suspicious glare of his escorts was disconcerting, but understandable. He'd only gotten into the Skolani camp because one of the sentries recognized him as the Wolf Lord's first captain. Still, he wished he hadn't been sent here.

Such an odd night. First he and the Wolf Lord had been repulsed from an Amalus tribunal. Now he felt unwelcome in another segment of the Danian army's camp. Unlike the lions, at least the Skolani offered him a seat by a roaring fire.

Finally the queen appeared. She came not from inside her pavilion, but strolling down the aisle between the lines of Skolani tents. She was flanked by two women he presumed to be servants or aids. Keisella's bare shoulders rose above her wrap. She was wearing sandals rather than boots, and her skin was pink, freshly scrubbed. Urias was most surprised by her unbraided hair, cascading wet upon her shoulders. He'd never seen a Skolani without her braids.

The queen smiled, clearly amused by his astonishment. He rushed to bow.

"Rise, Captain. I'm told your tidings are urgent."

"Lord Thadmeir deems them so."

"And you do not?" She raised a brow.

"It's not mine to judge, Queen Keisella."

"Come inside, then." She turned to her pavilion.

"My queen." It was the elder of her companions. "He is a male."

Keisella smirked. "That hadn't escaped me, Gahtala. But thank you for reminding me. Now go and fetch Sael. I'm sure she'd enjoy meeting with the captain, as well."

"Yes, my queen." The woman pressed her lips tight and left.

Keisella led him in. The first thing that came to him was scent, earthy and spicy. Then color. The temporary dwelling was more lavish than most homes, hung with tapestries and strewn with rugs and cushions. Hot coals glowed in a low brazier at the center.

"Forgive me, Captain, but it's late. You'll have to convey your tidings as I have my hair rebraided. Please, sit." She indicated the cushions surrounding the brazier. He tiptoed across a thickly woven Illyrican rug, hoping not to track mud across it. When he sat, the cushions nearly swallowed him, forcing him to recline awkwardly.

Keisella smiled. "Cozy?" She was amused again. "Pour our guest some wine, Annakha." He would've declined, but once it was in his hands he was grateful for its warmth.

"Annakha, my robe." The woman held up a robe, and Keisella dropped her wrap to her feet. The Skolani queen was completely nude, her milky skin taunt on her muscled form. Unabashed, she put her hands behind her for her aid to pull the robe onto her shoulders. He looked away and felt himself flushing. When he glanced, she wore both the robe and a satisfied grin. She was enjoying his torment. He supposed he deserved it. Actually, his brother did.

Keisella sat on a stool facing him. Annakha put a cup in her hands and began plaiting her hair. "So, Captain. The Great Wolf's tidings?"

"Of course. At this morning's parley, Lord Thadmeir negotiated on your behalf, as you bid. The Spali elders offer as a gift, in the hopes of partial reparation of the harm done, three-hundred head of their prized goats and a hundred of their finest ponies."

Keisella's eyes were closed. He wondered if she'd fallen asleep. He went on. "The livestock are, of course, yours as the leader of this campaign, to disburse as you see fit. And of course we could demand more. But my lord kept an eye toward their need in retreat."

"That's it then?" She kept her eyes closed.

"Well, they also offered chattel in the form of slaves. I hope you aren't displeased to hear that my lord turned this offer aside, with a mind toward a firm end to resentment." She still didn't open her eyes or speak. "But I'm sure we could still—"

"The Skolani hold no slaves," she interjected. "But that isn't what I asked."

"Forgive me?"

Keisella's blue eyes opened and narrowed on him. "Surely you aren't here merely to pass along a list of livestock. I'm asking for your real reason for coming, Captain."

Urias looked down. "My lord hopes you might ease a concern of his, Queen Keisella."

"Considering the uproar that echoes through the camp tonight, I'm guessing he seeks to lure me into Gottari politics. But certainly he understands doing so would test the limits of the Mithusstandan, does he not, Captain?"

"He does. But he hopes what he seeks will actually alleviate the sort of entanglement the Mithusstandan forbids."

A smile tugged at the corners of her mouth. "Let me also guess that this has to do with the ascent of the Young Lion."

Urias nodded once. He couldn't be surprised that she'd heard. "Now that Vahldan has secured a following among the Amalus Rekkrs, rumor speaks of his leading them in pursuit of the fleeing Paralatoe. My brother fears this will cause more harm than good."

Keisella clucked a laugh. "Harm? From the Spali? Even they now resent the Paralatoe."

"Not harm from without. May I be candid, Queen Keisella?"

"I've been wishing you would."

"Actually, Lord Thadmeir fears Vahldan intends to sunder our people—a divide along the very lines of our futhark."

Her smile faded. "He fears for the futhark? Or for the loss of the Wulthus advantage?"

Ouch. The woman was blunt. And incisive. "My lord desires the chance to seek balance with the man who's naming himself the new Lion Lord. Though Lord Thadmeir cannot speak of it openly, he believes that together he and Vahldan might restore something that has been lost. But he fears their chance will vanish if the Amalus don't return with us to Dania."

Keisella's stare hardened. "What would he have of me?"

"Only your assurance that the Skolani will abide by the terms of the foe's surrender, including our withdrawal to Dania. He plans to encamp above the ford at the confluence through the worst of the winter, to ensure the foe's concurrent departure. Lord Thadmeir hopes that before spring's thaw he can return to Danihem. My brother's first child is due in the spring."

"Fine," she snapped. "That too is as I intended—intentions

Thadmeir no doubt suspected. So I ask for the final time, Captain, for the real reason you're here. Come now, out with it. Our other guest will soon arrive."

Urias stared down into his cup. "My lord was hoping you could assure him that none of your warriors would accompany Vahldan, should he ignore Lord Thadmeir's demand to withdrawal to Dania... Not a single one, in fact."

"Ah—at last. You speak of Elan."

Blunt and incisive. It didn't seem right to meddle, but Urias couldn't dispute his brother's argument that this, more than anything, might sway Vahldan's decision. He nodded.

Keisella turned aside, lips pursed. She looked back at him. "You may assure your lord that no Skolani Blade-Wielder will accompany the Young Lion should he ride in pursuit of the Paralatoe. Not a one. He has my word."

The flap opened before he could thank her. A cold gust of wind chilled the warm space as Gahtala led in a hunched crone with stark white braids. The old woman kept her face to the floor as she shuffled to slump down on the cushions. She took her feet in her hands, curling one then the other to sit cross-legged.

"Thank you for coming, Wise One," Keisella said loudly.

The woman waved a dismissive hand. "Still not deaf, my queen." She turned toward Urias for the first time, revealing pale gray eyes, rheumy and teary, with wide, black irises. Eyes that were strikingly similar to Amaseila's.

"Nearly blind, yes. But not deaf." The old woman cackled at her joke. "I sense I already know your guest, but before you introduce us, I would have the Fierce One present, as well."

"Oh yes, I'd nearly forgotten," Keisella said. "Gahtala, go and fetch Icannes. Have her come quickly. None of her dallying." The woman bowed and left again.

The crone tilted her head back and let out a whoop. "Ah, such a merry meeting. At last. Have I not said? The Fierce One is as great a strand to this weaving as is this fine young wolf."

"Yes, yes—so you've said." Keisella sounded both indulging and put out at once.

The old woman cackled again and rocked her body. Urias's realized he was staring, something he knew the Skolani considered terribly rude. But her delight was so infectious. He felt as if he'd fallen under her spell. Perhaps he had.

"So?" Elan sat up from under the sleeping furs as Icannes entered.

Gods, Elan was as excited by Icannes's return as a tethered filly. "So what?"

"Don't be that way," Elan pouted. Icannes found herself wishing it really was her return that excited Elan. Ridding her of this curse was going to be tougher than she'd thought.

"Can't I at least take off my wet things and get into bed first? It's cold out there."

"Yes, but be quick," Elan said grinning. "Come—I've warmed it for you."

"How about a cup of the mead I brought?"

"Later." Elan patted the bed. "Tell me everything."

Icannes tossed the skin of mead on the bed anyway. "Everything? If you insist. No, I haven't heard from Mother regarding your hearing. I came straight here from the Gottari camp."

"Why? Why do you enjoy tormenting me?"

"Because it's so damn easy. You only prove your accusers right when you act like this. You're still fretting over him like a first-time mother who surrendered a son. It's unbecoming." Icannes draped the wet cloak over a stool by the brazier and sat at the foot of the sleeping pallet to unlace her boots.

"He was my duty. How am I supposed to stop caring what happens to him?"

"If only you'd felt so strongly about Sochana."

Icannes tugged off the first boot and turned to face the glaring silence. Elan's cheeks glowed. Damn, she'd gone too far. Gods of vengeance, she hated when those lovely eyes were sad or hurt. Especially when she knew she was responsible. "I'm sorry. That was harsh."

"How can you keep throwing it in my face? I know I've made mistakes, all right? The gods know I'll wear the scar of Sochana for the rest of my days. You said you understood, that you'd help make sure I didn't lose my blade."

"I do. I will. We can only hope the queen will understand, too." Icannes had her growing doubts. She knew it wasn't beyond Keisella to use Elan and then punish her for it, as well.

Elan's eyes shone. "You know my heart. Don't you?" She drew her knees to her chest and hugged them.

Icannes wanted to make Elan feel like she was home again, not make her back into a weepy girl. Icannes flung the second boot from her foot and crawled to prop herself on the pillows beside her. She gathered Elan in her arms and pulled her head to her chest. Elan snuggled against her, pleasingly warm and yet shivering.

She wanted things back the way they were. Sometimes she wished she was patient. "I do. And your heart is lovely. And stout. I know it's not fair, what they laid on you." She held her tight, like the battered girl she'd once brought in and sheltered. Elan sighed and relaxed into her.

"We'll get past it," she hummed in her chest. Icannes knew what she'd learned at the Gottari camp would incite Elan again. Now was probably as good a time as any to get it over with. "You can rest assured it's over now. Vahldan has regained his father's status. The lions have ousted the fat man, and named Vahldan their lord."

Elan sat up, her face alight. "That's wonderful."

Icannes nodded. "It's difficult to image anyone could undo what happened, even once they all get back to Danihem." A cloud passed over Elan's face.

Elan dropped her head back to Icannes's chest. "I suppose that's it then," she murmured. "It's really over."

"As I've been trying to tell you. It's been all but over for some time."

"Shhh. Can we just not talk?"

"Of course."

Acceptance was the first step. Icannes longed to be her champion again—the leader in her dream. But even that no longer seemed important. They were on their way back, whether Elan lost her blade or not.

The press of Elan's taut but yielding form against her hip and thigh, her breast squished against Icannes's ribcage, stirred another lost yearning. Not that sex was the answer. But it might play a part in restoring their bond. It might even help Elan to get over him.

Icannes slid a hand down to Elan's hip and said, "Just know, I will always be here for you. No matter what comes of this, I'll always take care of you." Elan stiffened in her arms.

"My princess?" Gahtala called from outside.

"What?" Icannes didn't try to disguise her annoyance.

"Your mother wants you."

"Now?"

"Her exact words were: 'Tell her none of her dallying.'" Gahtala's tone was smug. Her footsteps receded in slushy snow.

Elan turned from her. "Better hurry. That sounds serious." She huddled in their sleeping furs, making a cocoon that faced the other way.

Icannes sat at Elan's feet and pulled her wet boots back onto her still cold feet. "I'll be right back. Don't go to sleep on me." Elan released a breathy murmur that felt like a refusal. That confirmed it. She'd somehow misinterpreted Icannes's words. But rushing to try to correct it might make things worse. She'd have to leave it at that. For now.

∾

ICANNES ARRIVED at her mother's pavilion and Kukida opened the flap without announcing her. Meaning she would be considered late. She entered and was startled by the presence of a male visitor.

Urias looked fittingly out of place, as if he were trying to appear formal while reclining with a cup. And yet the smile that lit him was genuine. Her mother was dressed in a robe, her hair freshly braided. Beside Urias sat a grinning Sael—a strange scene indeed.

"My queen." Icannes bowed to her mother.

Keisella gestured for her to join them. "So good of you to find the time."

Icannes ignored the jab and bowed to Sael. "Wise One."

"Greetings, Fierce Daughter." The old woman's tone was full of mirth.

Icannes suspected the seeress was behind this strange gathering. "I'm honored. Perhaps we'll share a dream tonight." But her suspicion of Sael did not displace her suspicion of her mother's motives. Keisella always had an angle.

"May it be so, my dear," Sael replied.

Keisella said, "Now that things are as you insisted, Grandmother, may I finally introduce our guest?"

"Never mind formalities. I've waited too long for this. Come to me, lad." Sael beckoned Urias with both hands.

Urias glanced at Icannes, unsure. She nodded for him to do as he'd been told. He set his cup aside and went to kneel before Sael. Without warning, she grabbed his head, her mitt-like hands working their way from his hair onto his face, her rheumy eyes a hand's-width away. Sael's examination reminded Icannes of Urias's handsomeness. He was not striking like Vahldan. He was softer, his features less angular, his jawline less pronounced. But kindness shone from him.

Sael titled her head back. "Ah, there is power, lying deep, hidden. The blood of Usshvar is enduring, but the storm of your father's blood is soothed by your mother's calm reserve. Ironic, is it not? For a wolf to be the storm and a Skolani his tamer? Oh but the strength of such a comingling. Gods willing, so shall it come again in the line of the Bringer."

Urias smiled. "My mother was Skolani? That I have never been told. I knew my father's name, although I have no memory of him."

Sael sighed, her hands dropping to his shoulders. "Your father was as brash as a wolf can be. But he served Theudaric well. Which is why the Great Wolf honored Usshvar, bringing his son into the long-house even before his passing to the Banquet. It was rightful."

"And my mother," Urias ventured. "You knew her?"

"Knew her? I more than knew her." A rumbling laugh stirred like liquid in the seer's lungs. "Fierce Daughter, please confirm what I plainly see." Sael was changing the subject. "You've always found comfort in this fine young wolf. But even now, I sense you find his appeal grows within you, like warm tea heating your core on a cold morning. Appraise him well, then admit it! Before the gods, and to yourself."

Urias turned to her, confused and curious. Icannes had rarely felt so girlish. Indeed, there was a warmth growing within. She allowed her gaze to fall into the depths of his eyes. A fuller realization blossomed. The warmth became a molten heat, flowing from her stomach to her chest and up the back of her neck, prickling over her scalp. It felt reminiscent of Thunar's Blessing.

It suddenly seemed she should've always known. How could she not? And yet, in the span of but a few heartbeats she was sure. This man she'd known since childhood played a vital role in her destiny. She found her voice, "Yes, Wise One, I admit it. He is... quite appealing. More than I'd ever realized." She offered him a lopsided grin.

Sael laughed. "Of course you do. And you, son of the wolf? You have always been fond of our fierce princess. But something new emerges, does it not? A warm allure that now pulses with growing heat."

His gaze locked on Icannes, his smile fading. "It does," he finally said. "Since I first saw her as a boy, I've been fascinated by her. And

somehow only moreso tonight. I can't quite describe it. Like something that was always there but that I only now recognize."

Sael nodded. "Ah, that is well. Perfectly as it should be."

"Why, Grandmother?" Icannes asked.

"Why? May as well ask why the rains give way to the sun."

"But why now?"

"Ha! Because you've both hidden from it—for so long it now feels
strange. I had but to open your hearts to the blooming of a seed
planted long ago. Here we have the Guardian—protective and
nurturing; attentive, wise, and cautious; a force for temperance and
reflection; a source of teaching and healing. And the Fierce Warrior—
wreaker of upheaval; bold and curious; blessed with power and
swiftness; a bolt of righteous wrath; conqueror of all she deems
rightfully hers. One spirit of earth and one of fire! Drawn together,
seemingly against all odds. But not without the gods' own purpose.
For he whom the Bringer bestows shall need not just a Guardian, but
one with the potent blood of such a melding as this. The two of you
shall provide, and the resultant progeny shall see to Urrinan's
ongoing ride. As it shall be."

Urias stared at Sael. Was he awestruck? Outraged? He turned to
Icannes, and the girlish feeling returned—her cheeks hot. She
shrugged and looked away. How had this happened? She was never
the one who looked away.

Urias's bewilderment became apparent. "Forgive me, if you
please. But how do you...?"

The old woman placed a hand on his cheek. "How could I not
know all about you, Urias, son of Usshvar? Long have I seen you in
my Dreams—more often of late. It is well to have you here before me,
to touch you."

"You dream of Urias, Wise One?" Icannes prodded.

"Of course. All of his life. Is it so unusual, for a woman to dream
of her own grandson?" She heard him draw the same surprised
breath. Sael laughed again. "Your mother, who was my beautiful
daughter Ellasan, would have been proud to know you, Young Wolf.

She felt a strong bond with your father—one that nearly undid her. But the strength of their bond brought Usshvar back to Ellasan after you were born, and granted her a second child—a daughter, to stay at Ellasan's side. The daughter, too, is a Guardian—and a right fierce one, if I do say. It seems there are times when Freya's dreaded pull can be a blessing after all."

Elan! Elan and Urias were full-blooded siblings. It all made perfect sense. Their eyes! They both so easily drew Icannes into the depths of that same beguiling gaze. Both of them were so oddly comforting to the storms of her soul.

Urias stammered, "I... have a sister, among the Skolani?"

Sael's grin crinkled her nose. "Ah yes. And if all goes as is fitting to fate—if all of you heed destiny's call—both my grandson *and* my granddaughter shall play a vital role."

"A role in what, Wise One?" Urias asked.

"Have you not been listening? In the turnings of the Urrinan, of course. In this, my progeny shall bring me great honor. Just as the gods have foretold in my Dreams."

Icannes bit her cheek. Surely Elan's role in this was over. The Bringer had ascended. It was the role they'd all been prodding Vahldan toward all his life. He no longer needed his guardian. By rights Elan was hers again. And Icannes would never again take her for granted.

The queen stood. Icannes sensed amusement in her mother's hooded eyes. Keisella had known what was coming and relished witnessing its unfolding. Keisella said, "Now that we're all better acquainted, we should share a drink. We can toast what tomorrow must surely bring. Let us drink to surrendering to the gods' destiny. All that has come to pass, and all as it shall be."

Of course! What tomorrow must bring. They'd achieved their goal with Vahldan. The time had come to begin prodding the other players—herself and Urias included, apparently.

As if she'd been awaiting her cue, Annakha, who was Ursellya's and Sochana's mother, brought forth cups and a flagon. The woman had just lost her eldest daughter. Was that the gods' destiny? Icannes held the offered cup so that Annakha could pour. Their eyes met as she finished. "As it shall be," Annakha murmured.

"As it shall be," Icannes replied in refrain, and bowed her head to the mournful woman.

CHAPTER 34—
REGARDING DUTY AND
DESTINY

"Long have the seers foretold of the Urrinan—the prophesized coming forth of the Tutona onto the world stage. In their telling, the Tutona peoples would overturn mighty empires. Gottari and Skolani descendants would then rise to rule as the kings and queens of a hundred kingdoms.

In the seasons of the lives of those Urrinan touched, it would strike as a spiteful storm, riding on autumn winds. Its grip would then linger as a jealous winter.

Still, the Gottari and Skolani alike had long considered it a good and hopeful augur—spring's blessing upon their progeny. But few heeded the prophesy entire. Few foresaw the fallout for those doomed to the turmoil of bringing the Urrinan forth. Nor did they imagine the scale of the upheaval and tragedy that would come of its seasons' turnings. Only those who endure such a fate can conceive its full cost."—Brin Bright Eyes, Saga of Dania

ELAN WAS STILL awake when twilight tinged the sky through the smoke hole. Her arm wound itched. It was as if she could feel her flesh struggling to mend itself. Icannes's arm weighed heavily on her side, her breath hot on the back of Elan's neck. She carefully lifted the arm and rolled clear. She managed to dress herself without waking her sleeping mate.

She looked back at her fierce princess's face, so serene. Elan had to admit, it was wonderful being in Icannes's arms again. She could never feel this close to Vahldan.

Could she?

Sure, Vahldan thought he needed her now. But that was already changing. Yes, they had shared something special. But Icannes wanted her, knew her—like no one else ever could. Yes, she could perfectly picture sharing her life with Icannes. Elan was Skolani. She belonged among her people. In time perhaps her dreams would return, finally willing to offer her new direction.

But she knew she couldn't face moving on without seeing him one more time.

In the depths of night Elan had determined she must disobey, and go to him before facing the queen's judgement—this very morn. She had to let him know, to make him see. They'd been mere players in the workings of mortals and gods. But the parts they'd played were over. He would thrive in his new role. Without her. He would learn to trust himself, keep himself from getting lost.

And maybe if she convinced him, she could convince herself.

Either way, she had to go to him. She had to try.

It had to be done before the breaking of the camps began. Vahldan would not leave without seeking her out. She would not have him refused, told of their fate by a sentry and turned away. He would never accept it. He'd make a scene. Besides, she knew she couldn't face him if it happened after she lost her blade. He'd blame himself. Elan had to face him, now.

She stuck her head though the flap. Not a sentry in sight. She slipped out and drew a deep breath of frigid air. She realized she'd been all but holding her breath, like a kept secret.

Elan checked the aisles between the silent pavilions, thankful to find them empty. A low fog hung over the slushy, ankle-deep snow. Getting to him would take stealth and luck. Even her tracks in the snow were an issue. Elan first made for the healers' pavilion. It was the closest point to the Gottari camp. If she was caught, she was simply fetching herbs for Icannes's tea.

She came across a trail in the snow to the Gottari camp, with no one in sight. She cleared the last set of pavilions and sped her step across the clearing, walking in the existing tracks. She was going to make it.

"Halt. Stay where you are." The hulking silhouette emerged from the fog to block the way. "Well, well. Look who it is. I've been waiting for you, Elan." Her tone was pleasant. But the pleasure for this huntress was in having bagged her prey.

"For me?" Elan hated how meek her voice sounded. "Why would you wait here?"

"Don't be absurd. We both know why." The blood-bitch loomed over her. "I'm only surprised that it took so long. I suppose being a princess's pet makes running away difficult."

"It's you that needs a leash, Anallya. I'm only walking, not running." Elan fought the impulse to run now.

"Aw, pretty puppy." Anallya cocked her head. "Of course you're running. You were forbidden to leave the camp, and yet here you are. It's just that you got caught."

"I'm delivering a message. For Princess Icannes."

"As soon as I return you to your master, I will deliver her message. Come." Anallya snatched her right wrist and twisted. The burst of pain seemed like it should've been audible. The only way to avoid a sprain or broken bone was to turn until Anallya was behind her.

Anallya pushed, steering her back the way she'd come. Any drastic move risked her sword arm. "Icannes will be furious about this."

"Not true. In fact, I'm sure she'll be pleased. After all, it was she that had me watching for you. She bid me to bring you right back should you get loose." Icannes hadn't trusted her. Elan hadn't deserved her trust, but it still stung. "Things change, don't they, Elan?"

"You certainly haven't. Still a blood-bitch, same as ever." Rather than retorting, Anallya gave her arm a painful twist.

Elan spiraled toward panic. Facing Icannes would be humbling enough. But being brought to her by her blood-bitch made it beyond humiliating. As they came to the main aisle she heard a horse snort. Then hoof beats. Two horses, walking.

The riders' shapes emerged from the fog. Anallya pulled Elan aside to allow for their passage, but the riders drew to a halt. Anallya turned Elan so that she couldn't see.

"Release her." Keisella sounded as moody as the fog.

"My queen, it's Elan. Once again she has willfully disobeyed. Princess Icannes bid—"

"I said release her." Her tone brooked no debate. Anallya let Elan go. "Come, Blade-Wielder." Elan didn't know which of them Keisella wanted, but Anallya stepped to her stirrup with a bowed head. "On your knees." Anallya fell to her knees in the slush. "Hands and knees."

Once the blood-bitch was posed dog-like below her, the queen dropped her boot onto the small of her back. Anallya grunted. Keisella swung her other leg over and lingered a moment on her human mounting stool before stepping down. "Take my friend back to the corral, Blade-Wielder. Remove her tack and wipe her down. Perhaps a new set of shoes, as well."

"Yes, my queen." Anallya hung her head.

Keisella pulled her companion's horse toward Elan. "Come, Elan."

Elan swiftly realized the blanket-wrapped rider was her grandmother. Elan glanced to find Anallya glowering at her. It wasn't Elan's fault, but the blood-bitch would seek to make her pay somehow. She hurried alongside the horse and reached up. Sael clutched her hand in a soft leather mitten.

They arrived at Icannes's pavilion. The queen nodded at the banked fire. "Stir that up and feed it, Elan." Keisella opened her arms to Sael, easing her to the ground like a child.

The flames came to life. Elan dallied, digging for the driest logs. She wasn't sure if she was ready for this. She finally faced them, and bowed. "My queen, wise Grandmother, I fear our princess has yet to rise."

"We came to see you, Elan," Keisella said. This was it. Her judgement was at hand. She hoped her grandmother's presence boded well. The queen removed a woolen shawl from her shoulders, then helped Sael to sit on half of it before seating herself on the other half. Sael took off her mitts and held her hands to the fire, her nearly blind eyes staring into the flames.

"May I make you tea?"

"No thank you. This shouldn't take long." The queen gestured. "Sit, please."

Elan cleared the snow from the log across from them, pulled her cloak under her, and sat. "Am I to face your judgement, my queen?"

The queen, too, stared into the dancing flames. "Judgement? I suppose so. Certainly it's past time you faced a reckoning."

"May I first say that what happened was during the heat of—"

Keisella held up a halting hand. "I don't care to discuss the accusations against you. None of that matters."

"My queen?"

"What we wish to speak of is your duty, Elan."

"My duty?" Keisella nodded. "What of it?"

Sael's first words were morning-hoarse. "We wish for *you* to tell *us* of your duty, Granddaughter."

"Do you mean the Fulhsna-Utanni? I'm not sure if it's still mine. No one ever revoked it, you know."

Keisella scowled. "Who said anyone ever will? The terms of your duty were well-laid when you were assigned. Wouldn't the successful undertaking of any assignment include an understanding of its completion? Look not to others. Your duties are your own, Elan."

"What else, dear?" Sael prodded. "Besides the Fulhsna-Utanni, tell us of the other duties you shoulder?"

Both women scrutinized her. Elan sat up straighter. An image of Sochana flashed in her mind. "Well, there is my duty to the Skolani, to my sisters—particularly to my near-sister." They continued to stare. "And then there's my oath as a Blade-Wielder, to obey my queen and the elders, to maintain the sanctity of Dania's borders, to defend the helpless of my homeland, and to abide by the Mithus-standan."

"You seem to have left off part of that oath," Keisella chided.

Elan sighed. "Yes. I also vowed to renounce entanglement with the masculine."

"You understand that the blade is presented *after* this vow for a reason, do you not?"

"I do, my queen." Movement caught Elan's eye, at the pavilion behind the pair. Icannes's face peered through a crack in the flap. Her worry was apparent. "Forgive me, my queen, but is this about my blade?"

"Your blade was a gift from your mother, was it not?"

"It was."

"Cherish it, then. Never let it stray far from your hand, and it will ever bless you. As Ellasan would have it."

"Thank you, my queen."

Keisella raised her chin. "Now, as to your status as a Blade-Wielder." Elan feared her shiver was visible to them. "You know that we all make mistakes, that we all have lapses regarding our oaths?" Elan nodded, wringing her hands. "It's understood that a Blade-Wielder is human. Know that a Blade-Wielder can no more lose her status over a mistake than could a queen. Now, you must also recognize that making a mistake is quite different than having a change of heart. Do you recognize the difference?"

Elan swallowed and wiped her wet hands on her leggings. "I do." She wasn't sure how she'd answer the question sure to come next.

But the queen simply nodded. "Good."

Sael's voice was soothing. "Daughter of my heart. You speak of duty to your subject, to your queen, to the elders, to your sisters, and to your oath. But I ask you of a deeper duty. For the gods demand you heed a duty owed only to yourself."

"To myself?"

Sael nodded once. "Seek not to measure yourself with another's gauge. Appraise yourself not in another's light. Measure your duty in terms of your own—terms found not just in solemn thought, but also in the deepest exploration of your heart."

"I have. Or I thought I had. But it led nowhere."

"You speak of your dream, Granddaughter?" Elan nodded. "Oh, child. Why do you say your dream has led nowhere?"

Elan shook her head. Her eyes started to sting. "I thought I was to serve at the right hand of a leader, to complete a destiny. I thought I knew whose. Not once but twice."

Sael tilted her head back, her eyes skyward. "Ah, but you speak of seeking a destiny found in another."

"But that's what the dream seemed to tell me."

Sael hooded her rheumy eyes. "It's true—you may find your truest self while in service to another. But you mustn't confuse your destiny for theirs. Never will you find reward solely in spending yourself in service of another's whim. The completion you seek can be found only in the conviction of one soul." Sael pointed a thick finger at Elan. "Yours."

Elan felt exasperated. "So you're telling me I should've ignored the dream?"

"Of course not! Such dreams are a gift. One that can only be judged by the recipient."

"Then I can still find my destiny as a warrior, at the side of a leader?"

Her grandmother laughed, deep and throaty. "Ah, child. I will tell you all that I know of dreams. I know that they are gods-given. I know that some dreams are meant to guide us. But, oh, how fickle the gods can be. I know how difficult it is, sorting those intended to guide us from those that merely confound us. You cannot solely trust your heart, for the heart is easily lured with desire. And you likewise cannot trust your head, for the head is easily daunted by fear. Neither head nor heart can be trusted alone. Only when the two are united do we stand a chance of choosing our truest path. And the truest path is rarely one down which desire alone leads. Rarer still is it the one that seems safest. Seeking such a path—that is one's true duty. And only in doing one's true duty can destiny be found."

Keisella crossed her arms and gazed into the fire. "You say you are a warrior at this leader's side. But what if it's not meant to be? Some who serve at a leader's side are healers, or advisors. As Annakha is both for me. Without her, I would be lost."

"Forgive me, my queen, but no. My dream was very clear. I was a warrior, a guardian, riding beside this leader—spurring them to glory. Together we bring hope to our people."

The two exchanged a look. "So it could well be," Sael said. "And fitting, perhaps."

Keisella would not look at Elan. "As the Wise One said, you must follow both head and heart. Come what may."

Elan suddenly saw where it all led, saw the choice they were laying before her. "And so, as to my fate. Forgive my lacking, my queen. I know you said it was mine to know. But if you might reward me with your view on the state of my duty to the Fulhsna-Utanni?"

Keisella frowned. "If you truly need me to say it, I shall. I hereby declare the guardianship of Vahldan, son of Angavar, revoked. The assignation was given to a Blade-Wielder. The subject of it has risen to gain his own aegis. Hence, the Blade-Wielder's duty is complete. She needn't have any further concern for him, nor keep any further connection with him. There. Feel better?"

Elan found herself dearly wishing that she did. She drew a breath and released it, and ventured, "So I take it that to feel differently, and to act upon those feelings, would be to surrender my status as a Blade-Wielder?"

"Remember, a Blade-Wielder cannot lose her status over mistakes. Only over a change of heart. The action you speak of would require such a change."

"And the thing you're not saying—you both speak as if you believe my heart wishes to go with Vahldan. But are you warning me not to?" Neither woman stirred.

After what seemed the longest while, Keisella said, "Your heart is yours. We know we cannot change it. Nor can we dispute your dreams or alter your destiny. But we can appeal to your head. Remember Elan, the blood of a healer flows in your veins. We both believe your destiny could well be found in service to your near-sister. For Icannes, too, is destined to greatness. I might also remind you that with Vahldan's prophesied ascent rides his doom."

Elan looked to Sael, who rocked herself slightly. "You too, Grand-mother? You see my destiny at Icannes's side?"

Sael stopped rocking and pursed her lips. "I believe that destiny lies in the choosing. Ask not the blind to see for you, child. Only you can choose your path."

Again, Elan's eye was drawn to movement at the pavilion flap. Icannes's face was pleading and hopeful. Elan longed to go to her, to have done with it all, to accept her place among her people, at her near-sister's side. She'd already decided this. She hated the thought of riding with a Gottari host again—to be held in arm's-length awe and yet covertly ogled; for her viewpoints to be tolerated rather than discussed; to keep herself utterly apart from her companions, for every changed tunic, every washing, and every gods bedamned piss.

But she wanted it all in the open. She had to know. She faced Keisella. "And if I went with him, but then returned, would I face banishment?"

Keisella's gaze hardened. "If you go, you'd best not return. For you would be banished already."

"And should I have a daughter?"

Sael gasped, then composed herself and resumed rocking, softly humming in prayer.

Keisella shook her head. "At my mother's knee I learned the old ways of the Skolani. Under those ancient auspices, those banished are but ghosts, henceforth non-existent to our people. Their possessions are burned or buried. The telling of their tales is forbidden. No Skolani will ever utter a ghost's name again. In time, even their memory is banished, by Horsella's own hand. The banished perish from the existence of all who knew or loved them, forever. And so, by the old ways, a ghost's progeny never actually exists."

Cutting herself from contact with her people, from the only life she'd ever known, was horrible enough to contemplate. But the thought of having a daughter who would never know the world of her grandmother, her ancestral bonds utterly severed—it was unbearable.

Elan looked to the flap of the pavilion, but it hung closed. She was alone in her choice.

CHAPTER 35—OF
WOLVES AND LIONS

"The ascent of the Wulthus clan is an oddity worthy of consideration. Since history indisputably tells of the Gottari being ruled by Amalus kings at the time of the Arrivals, no few have speculated that the wolves must have been dissenters, rebels to an established system of rule. And since the Wulthus have ever been devoted to husbandry, rather than excellence in arms, one would surmise these early rebels to have been champions of the common man. Which would make the wolves eventual wealth—reaped from the levy of those who toil—and the power derived from it, an irony."—Brin Bright Eyes, Saga of Dania

VAHLDAN WOKE SENSING a presence outside of the pavilion. He checked the smoke-hole. It wasn't quite dawn. Heart hammering, he rose and hastily dressed, hardly daring to hope. As he laced his boots he heard voices. He dashed through the flap to find Belgar had been his sentinel. His cousin had stopped a visitor. Not the one he'd hoped for. But then, he knew he shouldn't have hoped. He scanned the pavilion circle anyway. She wasn't anywhere in sight.

He'd find her, though. It was his top priority.

Although Urias was unhoped for, his predawn arrival was unsurprising. Vahldan knew that rumor traveled fast in a military camp. Clearly Thadmeir had heard the Amalus news. Several Rekkrs of his host were already busy packing their gear. Several of the pavilions had already come down. Urias stepped to Vahldan's side. "So, you're really going?"

"We really are," he answered honestly. There was no reason to dissemble.

"You've come far, Vahldan. And quickly. Faster than I'd have dreamed possible."

"Aye, same here."

Urias crossed his arms, watching the bustle of the Amalus decamping. "It'll mean mouths to feed and quarrels to oversee and resolve."

"I suppose."

"Leading always seems so easy, to those of us who follow. We rant and complain over circumstance, with rarely a thought as to the difficult choices of those who create it."

"I suppose," he repeated.

Urias turned to him with a wry grin. "I suppose you'll soon find out."

Vahldan tilted his head. "I appreciate your concern, Captain. But I was born to this. My parents spoke of few things more often than of my eventual leadership."

"And I hear you're working on your patience." Urias winked.

"I am." Vahldan wished he could dislike him, but he found it increasingly difficult.

"Well, speaking of leaders, mine would like to speak to you before you leave."

"So I suspected. I doubted you came to see us off. I don't suppose he'd be pleased if I declined."

"I don't suppose. Perhaps as a favor to me you could accept?"

The gods knew Urias had done him a favor or two. Indeed, Urias may be one of those most responsible for making Vahldan's current status possible. "I suppose I can."

Urias turned and walked toward the Wulthus vanguard's pavilions. Vahldan fell in beside him, scanning the bustling Skolani camp as they walked. They too were pulling down pavilions, loading pack horses and wagons already lined up to leave. He didn't see any red braids. He'd have to keep this short and hurry straight over afterward.

They arrived at the Wolf Lord's pavilion and the Captain stopped at the flap. "Remember, he means well," Urias offered. "For our people, I mean."

"As do I."

Urias bowed and held the flap. Vahldan found himself alone with the Wolf Lord, for the first time. Four lamps blazed the space to virtual daylight. Thadmeir sat with his back spear-shaft straight in a chair, head bowed over folded hands, as if in prayer. "Lord Thadmeir." The Wolf Lord raised his gaze, appraised him, then beckoned him to an adjacent chair. He sat.

Their silence hung in the heavy tapestries surrounding them. They were stitched with scenes of the Danian countryside; of herdsmen and farmers, barns and livestock, families gathering their harvest. So different from his father's family's tapestries, which featured scenes of war, of glorious victory. Vahldan caught the Wolf Lord glancing at the hilt of Bairtah-Urrin. He looked like he'd swallowed a bug.

Vahldan didn't have time for this. "You asked to see me?" he prompted.

"Isn't it enough?"

"Isn't what enough, my lord?"

"You have the sword. Desdrusan is humiliated. Must you twist the blade in the wound?"

"My intent is not to wound. My intent has always been to right a wrong. And now I intend to finish this war, and bring the last of my father's murderers to justice."

"But you *have* inflicted a wound. And now you seek to keep it from healing. If you truly think Bairtah-Urrin is rightfully yours to bear, do you really believe it a wise start to separate the blades and to rend the futhark?"

"My intent is not to separate the blades, Lord Thadmeir. I would have you reconsider, and ride with us."

"But you know that won't happen. And you have no conscience about making a mockery of everything our forefathers built together. In fact, you think it's clever, riding off to glory. You seek to portray yourself as the hero and us as craven skulkers."

He tried not to smile. "I seek only our complete victory and the safety for our people."

"Nonsense! Let's not play at games. We both know what you seek. But I tell you, Vahldan, it isn't necessary. Nor is it wise. Now is the time to honorably finish what you started. Let us have gone with Desdrusan, but in a just way. If you gain the proper votes in the longhouse, which I believe you would, you can reenter the fold of lawfulness. Take what is yours in a fashion worthy of the tradition set by our two clans. Remember, ours are the clans that provided our people with generations of unity and security. Even in disagreement we've maintained the futhark. In the end, even your father knew it was so, and surrendered the blade. He submitted to balance. He left as he was bidden, rather than seeking to tear us apart."

Vahldan tensed, and the ugliness lurched. "You would use my father's honor against me? Angavar did what he thought he had to, for my family, for me."

"I understand you think your father was lured to his crime. I freely admit to holding no doubt that he was. But he'd already started down a dark path. He made powerful enemies by speaking dangerous words. Please, Vahldan. Think it over. Do not follow his example. Take the rightful path. The path to balance."

Vahldan leaned forward, trying to suppress the rising heat of the forge. "You can speak of balance? You allowed that... *pathetic prop* to keep this sword all these years, which was a mockery in itself. And now you would ask me to submit to the same farce—to become the same prop for the same powerful men? These are men who treat their fellow Gottari like chattel in the name of profit. So much for your so-called balance."

Thadmeir's mouth twisted. Urias opened the flap. "Is all well, my lord?"

Vahldan forced himself to sit back in his seat, breathing deeply to quench the glowing coals of the ugliness. Thadmeir's grin was halfway to a sneer. "Yes, we're getting on just fine." The tent flap closed.

"I didn't ask you here to argue politics. Nor to rehash the past." Thadmeir also settled back. His tone became a plea. "But don't you see, Vahldan? Our customs offer you a course forward. We are a people of laws, with a rightful homeland, and we're all the more secure and prosperous for it. Our system still embraces the ideal of consensus. It's far from perfect, and the gods know there have been liberties taken by the landholders and the guild. I'm offering you a chance to work from within, to change it for the better."

"From within a longhouse filled with men who protect their profits by keeping the voice of the common herdsmen from being heard?"

"Well, you could become their voice," Thadmeir said.

"You mean, I could play the role of their tireless yet compromising advocate, to make them feel heard in order to keep them in line?"

"And you honestly believe you'll accomplish more by riding off to play the war hero?"

"I do," he said without hesitation. "I believe that doing this will give *them* a voice. One that can't be ignored."

Thadmeir's face grew ruddy. "Easy enough for you. Go ahead, encourage a defiant tantrum. You rile those you think to be corrupt, and you will still be welcome at the tables of your pillaging Rekkrs. But what of the real herdsmen? The common men who don't have the means to ride off and play at war? What happens to them when you embolden them to stamp and shout? What happens when they find the markets for their wool are closed to them, or that their flocks have lost access to grazing? How will they feed their children?"

The forge was getting dangerously hot. Vahldan had heard enough. He stood and cursorily bowed his head. "Thank you for confirming it. I've come to see my father was right. Some rule is so corrupt it's beyond repair. Some systems must be broken and made anew to be fixed. Call it dangerous talk if you will. But the only honorable way forward, for me, for my followers, is to come to the longhouse as men of free will, with honest access to the means to feed our families—beholden to no master."

"I will offer once more, and once more only. Listen well and weigh my words. For our stands are not so far apart as you seem intent upon making them. Come back to Dania with us, as a man of free will. Allow me to speak for you to the council. I will tell of your service to victory. I will call for a pardon of your family's banishment. We can put it all to a vote—gain true consensus for the legitimacy of your claim to that sword. Then you can fight for your beliefs within the framework of our laws."

Vahldan stood straight as a post, fighting the impulse to grasp the hilt. "Or?"

"Bah!" Thadmeir waved him off. "Or go, and face your father's fate. For yourself and for the Rekkrs who follow you."

Vahldan hid a smile, knowing he'd rattled him. "You speak now of pronouncing banishment upon free Gottari men? Men whose only crime is to pursue our foes, to eliminate a threat? My lord, I seriously doubt it's a stance that will win the herdsman's heart." He bowed again, this time at the waist. "I thank you for your generous offer to grovel to your powerful friends on my behalf. But I think my odds are better with the Paralatoe." He turned and headed for the exit.

"By going you openly declare your intention to sever the futhark. All will see it and know it to be true."

The flame flared, and Vahldan stopped and turned back, the hilt calling to his hand. "No. We both know the futhark has long been dead. It's been propped up and presented as alive, like a rendering of a false god. But at least we two can admit it's not so. You can choose to believe it happened when my father's blade sliced into your brother's flesh, but that too is a lie. For the futhark truly died the moment your father allowed Desdrusan's words to stand as fact, when he knew them to be false." He started toward the exit again.

Thadmeir called after him, "Go, then. Pursue your glory, but it won't change the wool markets. Paralatoe trophies won't buy access to grazing for those you seek to woo. And winning glory won't be so easy as it was, without your own personal Blade-Wielder to see to your safety, to make you seem so valiant." Vahldan stopped short of the flap, but wouldn't turn back. "Oh, I'd nearly forgotten. You are aware that the Skolani are returning to Dania with us, aren't you? It seems a shame that you'll be severing yourself from those so crucial to your reputation."

The ugliness fogged the edges of his thoughts, his vision. He fought to resist the hilt as he turned. Thadmeir's smirk grew. "Oh yes, Vahldan. I have the queen's word. *No* Skolani warrior shall continue the pursuit of the Paralatoe. Every last Blade-Wielder is to ride for Dania, this very morn. In fact, if I know Keisella, they'll leave before the rest of us are ready to march."

The ugliness was winning. Gods, he longed to lash out. He turned away as his hand grasped the hilt, hurrying for the exit. Pain shot up his neck and to his temple. His vision blurred. His arms seized, the coiled muscles longing to fight. He willed his feet to carry him out.

He threw the flap aside, sucking in cold air. He took two dizzy steps and stopped.

The sun was up, streaming through the leafless branches to reflect on the slushy snow. He shielded his eyes and drew in more cold air, quenching the fires, seeking control.

A hand touched his shoulder, and he spun, the blade half out when the voice and the face registered. "It's me. Just me." It was Urias. A wolf, but an honorable one. "Sorry to startle you."

He drew a deep breath and pushed the blade back into the sheath. "It's... fine." His breath came in a jet of steam and his voice quavered with the last of the ugliness leaving him.

"Is everything well, Vahldan?"

"It was. But... I'm not so sure anymore."

Urias's concern morphed into puzzlement. Thadmeir's voice called Urias's name from within. Urias said, "I better go. Can you carry on alone?"

"I suppose we'll soon see." Urias frowned. "Go ahead. I'll have to manage."

Still looking concerned, Urias nodded and left him, alone amidst the bustle of decamping.

ELAN WIPED the cold sweat from her hairline, and holstered her axe on Hrithvarra's saddle. The ache in her shoulders seemed fitting. It matched the one in her chest. She bent to finish loading the firewood into the side-baskets of the Spali pack pony. She had no idea whether she'd need the wood in the days ahead, but it seemed wise to take it while it was ample. Besides, the chore gave her a bit of time alone to come to terms with her decision.

Only in hearing the approaching hoofbeats did she admit to herself why she'd drifted to this particular spot, overlooking the roadway back to Dania.

Now that her chance had come, she hesitated. Would it be painful, being a ghost? How would it feel to have those you'd known all your life gaze right through you, to look away as if you didn't exist?

She was drawn like a drunkard to a last cup of wine, even if they might only be offered a whiff. Elan walked to the treeline on the rise beside the road. The scouts had surely seen her, but the only one she caught looking did indeed turn away. She presumed at least one hidden archer held her in their sights. It was why she'd left her weapons with Hrithvarra.

The royal guardians appeared, and Anallya rode foremost among them. The sight of the blood-bitch caused Elan another moment of doubt, but still she couldn't turn away.

Elan stepped from the shadows. Sure as a ghost ruffling a pavilion flap on a windless night, she drew their attention. But, as with any specter, she was quickly dismissed and diligently ignored. Even Anallya forced herself to look away, curling her lip over having to do so. Elan smiled. At least there was one advantage to being a ghost.

The Skolani vanguard appeared. Elan caught a glimpse of her fair braids, and her heart fluttered like a sparrow's wings. She wasn't sure if Icannes had been commanded to stay away while she packed, or if it had been Icannes's choice. Her near-sister's absence during Elan's departure had nearly broken her will.

With stinging eyes she studied the profile of her proud face. Now Elan would always be the Bringer's guardian, but who would be Elan's? Who would have her back now?

What she both longed for and dreaded finally happened: her staring drew Icannes's attention. The stern face turned to her. Elan prepared for the worst: a fleeting look of disapproval, or diligent disregard. But instead, Icannes's face lit. Elan saw her joy in the moment, swiftly followed by regret and... Oh, the heartbreaking sorrow she'd caused her beloved protector. And Elan's own heart broke all over again.

Icannes reined and kicked Starfire, riding up to her, and the column continued on. Icannes leapt from the saddle and enveloped her in an immediate and unspeaking embrace. The power of it squeezed a sob from Elan's lungs and released the flow of tears down her cheeks.

"You shouldn't be up here. I shouldn't have come. Your mother, the elders—they won't approve."

"I don't care." Icannes's breath in her ear set her to tingling. "I'm glad you came. No one can keep me from telling the only person I've ever loved how much I'll miss her."

Elan tightened her grip. "Oh gods—I don't know how to live without you."

Icannes drew back to appraise her. "Oh please, dear heart. Tell me why."

"He needs me," she said.

"I need you too."

Elan wiped her tears with the back of her hand. "No, you don't. You'll be fine without me. I would have dwelled in your shadow." Icannes opened her mouth to argue, but Elan quickly went on. "And gladly so, my love. But there's more for me. I feel it. I know it. I've just been denying it. My dream—it's him."

Icannes's sternness melted, and sorrow again filled her eyes. She nodded. "I can see it's true," she whispered, and pulled Elan back into embrace. "I don't care what they say about ghosts. I love you and I will never forget you. And I'll always be here for you. Do you understand me, Elan? Always." Icannes drew back again, holding her hands.

Elan nodded. "I understand. I will always love you. Always."

Now her fierce princess's eyes shone with unshed tears. Icannes nodded. "As it shall be." Her beloved leaned to kiss her softly, squeezed her hands, and turned to remount.

Elan waited until Icannes rejoined the column. Her near-sister waved one final time. Elan replied with a sweep of her arm. Then she was a ghost once again. She turned and walked away.

She mounted Hrithvarra—her last childhood friend—and stroked the mare's neck. "It's just us now." Hrithvarra bobbed her head in fitting response. She sighed and set out, riding back toward the remnants of the camp, away from her people, never to rejoin them.

Elan was no longer a near-sister; no longer a granddaughter; no longer a Blade-Wielder; no longer Skolani. No longer could she even name herself the daughter of Ellasan.

She didn't know quite what or who she was. But she'd made her choice. And she was determined to find out.

THE RETREATING ugliness left Vahldan's head throbbing to the beat of his hammering heart. He made his way across the emptying camp, speeding his step around a line of loaded wagons, hurrying to get to the Skolani side. He cleared the column to find the site empty. The Skolani had already packed up and left. Gone back to Dania. As would the wolves and the rest of the Gottari.

His vision blurred. He'd actually gone through with it—he'd severed his own people. There was no going back. But it felt meaningless. He'd lost the only thing that had given him hope—hope that he could overcome the ugliness, find honor, reaffirm his true self.

Vahldan blinked to clear his blurry eyes and scanned the rest of the emptying campsite. His gaze alighted on the fuzzy image of an approaching rider, emerging from the forest.

Her auburn braids shone like a halo in the rising sun.

He started toward her, trying not to run. Hrithvarra was loaded with gear, pulling a pack pony which was also loaded—ready for a journey, but in what direction? Elan reined to a halt, her solemn expression stopping him in his tracks.

She'd come to say goodbye.

She dismounted. Vahldan sought to calm his breath, his frenetic pulse. Elan stood beyond reach. She was dressed for scouting, in her doeskin tunic and leggings, her newly rebraided hair pulled taut from her face. Her eyes were puffy. Gods, she was beautiful, even in sadness.

She reached to pull the neck of her tunic. "There's something I forgot to tell you." She withdrew the carving he'd given her and held it dangling from the cord. "It's about the kestrel."

Vahldan could hardly breathe. "What is it?" he managed.

"They're extremely loyal. Once they pick a mate, it's for life. I thought I should tell you, before I agree to keep this. There's really no understanding them without knowing it. So, now that you do, I can return it if—"

In two swift steps he wrapped her in his arms and pulled her tight. "Thank the gods," he said into her braids. "I can't do this without you."

Elan huffed in laughter and hugged him back. "Didn't I tell you not to put your trust in the gods? They're fickle, can't be relied on." She drew back and laid her hands on the sides of his face. "See me?" He nodded. "Hear me?"

"I do." Indeed, she was so clear. It seemed she'd banished the last of the ugliness.

"Good. Then hear this. There is no more you, no more I. There is only us. Believe me?"

"I do," he repeated, his hope renewed. Maybe they could banish the ugliness forever.

"Good. Because *we* can do this." She'd echoed his thoughts— their connection was stronger than ever. "Now," she said softly, "let's go finish this war. Together."

CHAPTER 36—TRACKING CHANGE

"*Many have questioned the Spali chieftain Auchote's wisdom in fleeing the pursuit of Vahldan's Amalus host by riding south, suggesting that surely Auchote knew his outnumbered Paralatoe would eventually be trapped along the seacoast. But one must consider how little choice the rogue chieftain had. Auchote had been renounced by the Spali people, precluding their riding east toward their former homeland. And with the victorious Skolani and Gottari marching west, and a difficult mountain range to the north, riding south was all but forgone.*"—Brin Bright Eyes, *Saga of Dania*

GODS BE CURSED, Elan couldn't ignore it any longer. The issue had grown urgent. She wasn't even a week into it, and there were already so many things she disliked about her new life. But this one gripe summarized them all.

She scanned her surroundings again, searching for cover. There was none. Just empty grasslands and her fellow riders—all men. These days Elan didn't waste a moment worrying about their quarry. She knew catching the Paralatoe was but a matter of time. Their trail was beyond simple to follow, and an ambush was all but impossible. No, during these long days in the saddle Elan's frequent concern, although mundane, was all too often a pressing one: finding places to pee.

To think she'd sacrificed everything—turned her entire world upside-down—for this.

Elan had hoped to hold it until they halted for the night. The gods knew privacy was precious out on this forsaken rumple of endless plains. Especially when you were the only woman. Especially when your companions had all gone months without female companionship. Well, without a female who would abide their touch, or even their ogling.

On they rode, the saddle pommel pressing against her pelvis. She couldn't stand it.

"I'm going to drop back for a moment," she said, reining Hrithvarra.

Vahldan raised a fist. "Hold!"

"No need to stop," she said. "I'll catch up."

Vahldan's smile was annoyingly patient. "It's fine. We'll wait."

She cursed under her breath and rode back against the scores of grim Amalus Rekkrs. A few tipped their heads respectfully. Others looked irritated or amused. But the worst were the few who seemed aroused.

Elan shouldn't have to ask them to look away. She refused to let them believe she cared. But there wasn't hill or vale to hide behind, and the grass had been laid flat by the snow.

She dismounted and began her awkward dance—squatting behind Hrithvarra's legs, holding her cloak to hide herself while she yanked her leather leggings and woven underpants down far enough to keep them dry. She couldn't help but shudder and sigh as the stream flowed.

Elan cursed herself. Why hadn't she foreseen how bad this would be? Icannes had tried to warn her. What other annoyances and awkward predicaments lay ahead for her?

She knew why she'd been willfully blind to what her new life might be like. She blamed her bedamned heart. It had outmaneuvered her head. And still there had been no reoccurrence of her dream. On any given day she might feel one way or another about her supposed destiny. But she'd made her choice. She was stuck with her new lot.

The worse part was, the root cause of her stubbornness—the fog of her feelings for Vahldan—left her more conflicted than all the other unsettled aspects of her life put together.

She was his guardian, not his bedamned traveling concubine.

Elan pulled herself back together, cleaned her hands on a scoop of snow, and mustered her dignity to mount and ride back to the vanguard. She passed the waiting lions with her chin raised, and rode on by Vahldan, who called to resume the march behind her. He trotted Ardua to catch up and ride abreast of her.

"I wish you wouldn't do that," she said, unable to veil her irritation.

"Do what?"

"You know what." How could he possibly not? "I told you I hate having everyone wait."

"I told you that you're not just anyone."

"I should be, though. I'm a guardian. A member of your host. Treat me like one."

He raised a brow. "What about my safety? I remember a time when you wouldn't let me out of your sight."

Elan scanned the empty plains, shielding her eyes and craning to one side then the other with exaggerated flair. "I think we can risk it. At least for the few moments it takes to have a piss in private."

He harrumphed and glared ahead. Evidently they were both pissed now. She shielded her eyes again and leaned forward. "Oh. Actually, there is someone out there. Coming this way."

"You've made your point, Elan. No need to brand my mount with it."

Gods, she hated when he got like this. Hated that and the pissing thing. "As your guardian, may I report that your captain, Arnegern, approaches... *My lord.*"

~

Gods, Vahldan hated when she got like this. Elan was cross. Again. He wasn't sure why. Again. It couldn't really be that he'd stopped to wait, could it? He knew he should know the real reason, but he didn't. And asking was usually a bad idea.

He'd imagined this so differently. On the morning she'd told him she'd chosen to come along with him, he thought she was saying she would *be* with him.

Although he wasn't even sure what that meant. He often asked himself what they were to one another. And each time he thought he knew, Elan proved him wrong.

He should've known. She'd gotten cross like this prior to the war, on the journey from Danihem to the queen's mustering camp. But somehow things had felt different this time.

Vahldan knew Skolani couldn't bond, of course. He hadn't expected a betrothal. But he also hadn't expected her to become more distant. He hadn't expected her to eat by herself, and to ride protective perimeters through the evenings. And he certainly hadn't expected her to continue to return only after he'd gone to bed, and then to sleep outside his pavilion, same as she had when he was in Desdrusan's custody.

He supposed at the very least, he'd expected to gain a friend—an ally. Instead he got a sulking ex-Blade-Wielder who evidently considered her duty to him to be a burden.

Vahldan halted the column again as Arnegern met them and reined in. "My lord, the scouts have followed the Spali trail into a forest ahead, due south of here. As my scouts approached the tree-line, the foe took shots at us from the trees."

"No one was hurt?"

"We fled safely. The Spali shot too soon. I suspect it was meant as a warning—a delay tactic. They're buying time. Attasar says he suspects that the Berezan River runs through the forest ahead. If so, I'd guess they're in the process of crossing it."

"Can we get there in time to catch them?" Belgar asked.

"It's doubtful," Arnegern said. "Besides, even at a gallop, it'd be dark when we arrive."

"Still, we ought to try," Teavar said. "After all, catching them is why we came."

"It may not be wise to rush in," Herodes said. "This is the first chance they've had to set an ambush."

"So we just let them get across this river?" Teavar asked. "What if they slip away?"

"If there is a river, we should be able to pick up their trail on the far side," Herodes said.

Teavar shook his head. "Ha. Should."

"What are your orders, my lord?" Belgar asked.

They all turned to Vahldan, waiting. Such was the life of a leader. He alone would decide. Urias had been right when he said it wouldn't be an easy thing to get used to. In this case it could be a matter of success or failure. Even life or death.

As anxious as he was to catch the Paralatoe and be done with this chase, Vahldan felt reluctant. It wasn't just caution. He knew in time they would finish this. But what then? Would it be enough? Could he then go back to Dania and reap enough support to avoid becoming ensnared by the guild? Thadmeir's words rang in his memory: *'Paralatoe trophies won't buy access to grazing for those you seek to woo.'*

He hated that the stiff had a point. One that haunted his thoughts day and night.

"We're not even certain there's a river, let alone that they're trying to cross it. We'll ride until we're close enough to put us in striking distance at dawn, but far enough to keep ourselves safe from counterattack in the dark. If there's a river and they've already crossed it, so will we." Vahldan turned to Arnegern. "Can your scouts get close enough to see what they're up to?"

"We're already trying, my lord. I sent them in pairs to swing wide and move in from the east and west. I told them to stay safe above all else. If the Spali are crossing the river, they're sure to be on high alert. Getting close enough before sunset seems unlikely. And approaching a Spali camp by night has proven risky in the past."

"I'll do it." They all turned to the surprise speaker. "After nightfall. Alone. You'll have the facts you need before dawn."

Vahldan saw Elan was serious. He shook his head. "No. Too risky."

Her scowl deepened. Clearly, she hadn't stated it as a request. She was, perhaps, the one person among them who didn't consider herself beholden to him. He tried making light of it. "Besides, I thought you came along as my guardian, just another member of my host."

Elan's eyes narrowed. "What better way for a guardian to serve than to provide the means for her subject to best achieve his goals, *my lord?*" She kept using the honorific as a slap.

Everyone fell silent, all of them waiting again. Had it really come to this? Was she really going to force him to either relent or to impose his authority? He realized that establishing himself as a strong leader was important. He suspected it was why Badagis had opted against coming along. In regard to Elan, it was a conversation that was overdue. But did she have to press it now, in front of everyone?

The silence stretched. The deepest voice among them finally broke it. "I can think of no one more perfect than a Blade-Wielder to handle this situation. And the gods have seen fit to bestow us with one." Vahldan shot him a look. Teavar bowed his head. "As I see it, my lord."

Vahldan looked back to Elan. She smiled. For the first time in days, it seemed genuine. "How can I argue with logic like that?" He inclined his head to her. "Go with our thanks, my guardian. May the gods protect you."

Elan wagged a finger. "Ah-ah-ah. Remember? We agreed to leave the gods out of it."

ELAN WAITED in a cove a bowshot from the treeline until nightfall. She raised up, gave the horizon a final look, and then ran. She wore Biter on her back and carried an arrow-nocked bow across the open expanse. Her feet fell silently. Her breathing was rhythmic but shallow. She scanned the shadowy, leafless trees ahead for movement and for a landing point.

It had been a while since she'd done any scouting, but she welcomed the familiar exhilaration. She ran through sparse, gray trunks, spotted a cluster of cedars, and made for it. She stopped and listened. Silence—nothing but a gust of wind through the branches. It was too cold even for night birds, let alone crickets. She settled on her haunches to look for her next vantage point. The rising full moon shone through the leafless trees to the east. It would only get lighter. There was no time to waste.

Elan worked her way west until she found the Spali's muddy trail. She darted and danced from cedars to tree trunks alongside the trail, and was soon moving downhill. The soft lap and gurgle of the river came to her. She hid behind a bushy hemlock above the spot where her quarry had forded the river. They were gone. But she couldn't assume they hadn't left a rearguard.

The river angled to the southwest. She searched in a semi-circle around the area before moving into the open. The moon was higher now. No sign of a rearguard, even on the far shore.

Elan stowed her bow and arrow, crept out and bent to study the hoof-churned shore. She gazed at the far banks. She needed to see more. She set her bow on her shoulders, drew Biter, and waded in. Her boots quickly filled and her leggings soaked through. The cold took her breath, and the fast current numbed her legs, but the water got no deeper than her waist. She climbed the far bank. It too was hoof-churned, but it seemed suspiciously less so than the near side. She followed the trail into the trees, but it diminished swiftly. Within a few hundred paces those who'd come this way had separated and swung back to the water in small groups.

The Paralatoe had gone to no small effort to make it seem they were continuing on a more easterly course. It was a heading that made some sense—a course that avoided the mountains to the south and would eventually lead them back toward the steppe. She went back and gazed up and down waterway. She made a logical guess and started downstream, wading along the wooded bank. Again, she didn't have to go far. Just beyond an oxbow, their trail reappeared, heading south along the near bank. She followed it until the landscape became rockier, with mossy foothills rising to either side of the river, hemlock and birch sprouting from the crags. She came to a well-traveled roadway—likely leading to a pass through the Pontean Mountains, out to the seacoast beyond. Attasar would have a good guess.

She'd seen enough.

The foe's trail would be as easy to follow through a mountain pass as it had been out on the open plains, though the way might present a greater risk of ambush. No wonder Auchote had made the effort to divert the pursuit at the ford. Any lead the Spali could gain was critical to their chance of surviving a crossing of the mountains.

Elan sheathed her blade and headed back, her boots squishing audibly in the still forest. The numbness in her feet and legs gave way to clammy discomfort. She came to the oxbow, and a view of the river opened before her. She stopped on the rocky bank, gazing at the reflection of the moon, blurred by the current. A memory of swimming in the moonlight with Icannes sprang to mind. Elan had waited all one warm autumn day at a Danian ford for Icannes's return from a scouting mission. When Icannes had arrived, Elan led her into the shallows. She'd scrubbed the paint and road dirt from her skin, and massaged her weary muscles. Afterward they'd wrapped up in a blanket, hugging away their giddy shivering.

It wasn't so long ago, but it already seemed like another life. She supposed it was.

The rocky bank wasn't muddy. Elan knelt to scoop a drink, cold and fresh—the best water she'd tasted in weeks. She dumped and refilled her skin. Her reflection wiggled in the current, her face dark with paint. She set the water skin aside and dipped her arms deep, washing the paint from them, then splashing and washing her face until it shone. The winter breeze braced her skin. She squeezed the excess water from the dripping ends of her braids.

On the night of their swim, Icannes had untied Elan's braids and washed her hair. Twining her fingers in her clean, unbound locks, Icannes had mused that Elan's daughters were sure to have gorgeous red hair. They'd imagined how their daughters might be near-sisters.

Elan's chest felt hollow again. She looked up to the moon, blinking away tears. It was the night of the first Fagna-Allramani of the new year. It was said that this first fertility ceremony after the solstice produced more daughters than any other full moon of the year.

Elan would never attend another. She would never see Icannes again. These men still called her a Blade-Wielder—her former identity was the reason they conceded this mission to her. But she was no longer Skolani. Resentment surged. She gripped two braids, pulling till it hurt.

Elan looked down at the Blade-Wielder in the water's reflection. Her hand grasped a fistful of pebbles. She slung them into the water, obliterating the image. She drew her belt knife and sawed, right at the jawline, again and again, flinging the auburn snakes into the river, one by one, the current carrying them off to the vast sea. After the last braid was cut, she watched until they were gone.

She sat huffing. The surface of the water grew smooth. And the Blade-Wielder was gone, replaced by a sad young woman. Alone.

Elan suddenly knew what she had to do, and what she had to say, and to whom. She got up, sheathed the knife and started to run.

Once she cleared the treeline, Elan headed straight for the

nearest camp sentry, making sure the man first heard and then clearly saw her coming. She passed him at a trot, offering a cursory nod. The sentry bowed his head.

Once in camp, she went directly to his pavilion. She entered without warning. He sat wrapped in a blanket before the brazier, looking forlorn but oh-so-beautiful.

Vahldan's face snapped up. "You're safe," he said. His eyes widened. "Your hair!"

Elan twisted out of the straps, letting her gear drop in a tangled heap. "It's nothing."

"But it's so short."

"Easier to wash." She went to him and he stood, looking uncertain. "We need to get something settled between us."

"What's that?"

"First, kiss me," she commanded.

Vahldan drew a sharp breath. She leaned in. At once, their arms wrapped and pulled. The kiss was powerful, urgent, almost painful, but it brought happy tears to her eyes.

Once their lips finally parted, he drew back, smiled and brushed back the loose locks that now fell into her face. He kissed her again, gentle now. It was luxurious, as sweet as any kiss Icannes had ever given her. She shivered.

He glanced down. "Your leggings are soaked. You must be freezing. Here, sit." She sat on his sleeping pallet and he dropped down at her feet. He diligently unlaced her boots and the wet cording on her leggings. He pulled the first boot off and rubbed her foot, warming it in his hands and blowing hot breath on her toes. Then he did the other.

Still rubbing her feet, Vahldan sucked on one big toe then the other. It felt deliciously decadent. He pulled off her leggings, then leaned in, bracing her calves with his palms and kissing the tops of her thighs, sending her skin to gooseflesh. A sigh escaped her. Elan leaned back on her elbows and raised up so he could pull off her underpants. He gently pushed her back flat, his torso parting her knees. He pushed up her damp tunic to kiss her stomach. She yanked it over her head and tossed it aside. Vahldan appraised her nakedness, his hunger apparent.

"We're going to get this right this time," she said breathily. Elan laced her fingers into his hair and pulled him to her sex.

Vahldan didn't hesitate to kiss and probe, but his effort was far too gentle. She pressed herself against his chin. She remembered how she'd learned, and encouraged him, "Yes, like that." He wiggled his tongue and she squealed. "Ooo, yes, perfect."

In mere moments her breath was coming in huffs. Her body heaved, and she came. But she knew it was just the beginning. They would not be denied. This time she would possess him, have him become a part of her. She hooked him under the arms, pulling him up to face her.

Elan laid her hands on his cheeks. "See me?" He nodded. "Good," she said and kissed him. Holding the kiss, she guided him home. He slid in and immediately began crashing into her. They banged hips recklessly until she pulled him down onto her, holding him against her. She needed to feel his weight. She had to slow it down to keep it going.

"You're here," Vahldan said into her tangled hair, almost sounding disbelieving.

"I'm here," she said. "I'm not going anywhere."

"See? I told you. You belong to me."

"Ah, there it is."

Still inside her, he grew still, seemingly holding his breath. "There what is?"

"The thing we need to settle."

"Now?"

"Yes, now. It's true—I belong to you. But..."

"But?"

Wrapping her legs around him, and using her best wrestling technique, she lunged and twisted, throwing him to the bed and landing on top. He'd slipped out of her. She gripped his cock, poising herself over the tip. "But you belong to me, too. We're equal part-ners." She grinned down, waiting. His breathing restarted, fast and shallow. "Agreed?" she teased.

"Yes," he hissed. She lowered herself, sliding him back in, reigniting their furious pace. He clutched her waist, pulling her with each stroke. She arrived just as he released, and they slowed to a languid withdrawal before collapsing together.

Elan raised up, looking down on him. "Still hear me?" He nodded. "Good. Hear this: I am no longer a Blade-Wielder. But I am not Gottari, either. And, yes, I belong to you. Our destinies are entwined. But you have to help me find my way to this new person. I... I am at your mercy. I have given myself to this—to you. But you have to give back. Include me. You have to listen."

"Didn't I just let you—"

"You *let* me?" Elan wagged a finger. "Ah-ah-ah. You have to *want* to listen. Understand the difference?"

Vahldan sighed and nodded. "I'm starting to. I'll try harder."

"Good. Thank you." She smiled, "*My lord.*" She tucked her fore-head against his chest.

"You are a gift. One I will try never to take for granted." He raised her chin with gentle fingers. "I'm lost without you." He caressed her kestrel charm, hanging from her neck.

"Remember? There is no more you, no more I. There is only us. That means two of us."

"I remember," he said.

Elan rolled off of him and onto her back. Moonlit sky appeared through the smoke-hole. "At least, there are only two of us for now."

Vahldan narrowed his eyes. "What's that supposed to mean?"

She grinned. "Who knows? It's said this is a fortuitous night for making daughters."

He didn't return her smile. "I am to have a son." Her breath caught in her chest, like she'd swallowed too much bread with no water. She rolled, turning from him. "Forget I said that. I don't know what I'm talking about." His tone was pleading, contrite. He leaned over her, trying to get her to look at him.

But Elan couldn't forget it, couldn't look. She knew exactly what he was talking about. She remembered every word the spooky seeress had uttered. He was talking about the prophecy. The son he mentioned was to be the grandson of the seeress. "She's not divine, you know," Elan said. "Amaseila said herself she's merely human. She could be wrong." Even though the bedamned woman hadn't been wrong yet. All that had happened since that day aligned too damn well with her forecast to dismiss her. "Haven't I been telling you? The gods are fickle."

He sat up. "I'm sorry. I just need to believe—at least that it's possible."

"What? That you're doomed? Be careful what you wish for."

He was silent a long moment. "She also spoke of the glory I would bring."

Elan rolled to him. "*That's* what worries you?" She softened her tone. "You've already won. It's already glorious. You, my dear, are the Lion Lord. No one can take it from you."

"It's not enough. I need more."

"What else? To actually be the gods bedamned Bringer?"

Vahldan looked away with a hurt expression. She realized how sarcastic she'd sounded. "My father..." He pressed his lips tight and shook his head.

She rubbed his back. "Go on. I'm listening."

"My father was the Lion Lord, too. He was the finest warrior in the realm. And he failed. I can't fail. I have to prove that..." He slumped.

"Prove what?" He shrugged. "To whom?" she pressed.

"To all of them," he snapped. She tilted her head and raised a brow. "I have to find a way," he said softly. "A way to lift my clan, my people. I have to find my way to the sort of glory that begets songs. My father was right. It has to be big. Something that changes things."

"Changes what things?"

"Everything." His smile was wry. He was being evasive. Maybe even self-protective.

Elan forced herself to smile back. She'd surrendered to him. Whether she believed in the bedamned prophecy or not, she realized that she believed in him. He still blamed himself; still worried about his worthiness; still feared he'd lose himself. She wouldn't pick the wound.

He would be a great leader. He was doomed.

And she belonged to him. They had come far tonight. They would grow together, be there for one another. She'd chosen this. She was his kestrel. "You will," she said. "I know it."

"We will," he said and lay back, pulling her into his arms again. It felt right—as close to perfect as she could've dared to hope it could.

CHAPTER 37—VIEW TO A WIDER WORLD

"Upon the Amalus arrival there, Akasas was a city that had seen finer days. Like many of the old Hellainic cities on the Pontean seacoast, it had ancient stout walls and a serviceable, protected harbor that opened to the mouth of the Berezan River. It had begun as a fishing village, and was later known for the amber that had been all but mined out of the surrounding mountains. It had been decades since there had been an imperial garrison in Akasas. Unlike neighboring Thrakius, its access to markets and trade routes was limited. And hence the city's fortunes had dwindled.

They say it was by happenstance, born of ill weather, that a fleet of Thrakian merchant ships had sought shelter there, just prior to the Paralatoe's arrival. None could have dreamed the impact on the world that such happenstance would bring."—Brin Bright Eyes, Saga of Dania

THE GROUP DISMOUNTED, and Vahldan's scouts led him to the top of a wooded ridge. They reached the crest and Attasar pulled aside the pine boughs.

And there it was. The sea. "Gods be revealed," Vahldan murmured.

If there was a feeling that was the opposite of the ugliness, he had it in this moment. He never could've imagined it. The blue of it was unlike any he'd seen, creased by a thousand white waves. He'd thought he'd had an image of it, but he saw that conjuring such a marvel in one's mind was all but impossible. How could anything be so vast? It was, at once, astonishing and clarifying.

The world had never felt larger to him. Perhaps fittingly, and in spite of all he'd gone through and achieved, he had never felt smaller.

"Yes, I'm certain of it now," Attasar was saying. "This is Akasas."

"It's what?" Vahldan asked, still gawping at the wondrous horizon.

"This city. It's Akasas, just as I suspected. I recognize the smaller walls surrounding the harbor keep. Though I've only seen them from the inside."

"There's a city? I hadn't noticed."

Attasar laughed. "No one forgets the first time they see the Pontean. I first saw it from Thrakius, right before sailing to the academy. The sight made the thought of sailing across it all the more frightening." The scholar pointed down the mountainside. "Akasas is there, my lord."

Vahldan appraised the valley below. The river parsed a small plain, and swelled to form a harbor on the inner side of a rocky shoreline that constricted its mouth. There by the harbor was a stone city, surrounded by stone walls punctuated by square towers. The space inside the walls seemed utterly filled with red-clay roofs at various heights and pitches.

He turned to Elan. She gazed out through hooded eyes, looking like she'd just woken from a dream. Vahldan remembered her saying that a walled stone city by the sea had been a part of her recurring dream—the one that revealed her future.

"The bastards really are besieging the city," Teavar said. "I must admit, he's a bold son of a nag, that Auchote."

It was only then that Vahldan noticed the Spali arrayed outside the city's walls.

"He may be daring," Arnegern said, "but he's a fool. And we have Vahldan the Bold on our side." Vahldan cringed but said nothing. He truly believed that the gods favored the bold, but he wasn't sure he liked the moniker. Surely he would find a way to earn a better one.

"He's desperate," Attasar said. "Probably hoped to frighten these Hellains into letting him in before we arrived. It's his last throw. There's nowhere left to run."

Vahldan studied the thin lines of the Paralatoe, more heavily manned outside the two gates of the city. The sight of them lit the forge and began to heat his blood. They would finally catch their quarry. He had to keep a clear head. He studied the lay of the scene. "Look at the tops of the walls. There are at least as many men inside as there are Paralatoe. Why don't they just muster a force and run them off?"

"I doubt they have enough warriors willing to do it," Attasar said. "Cities like this rely on the empire for soldiers. But the imperials have called back most garrisons for use in the war."

"The imperials?" Vahldan asked. "You mean the Tibairya?"

"Yes, my lord." Attasar suppressed a smile. Vahldan supposed it was indeed a dumb question.

"Tell me about this war," he said. Once you've asked a dumb question, may as well get all of the others out of the way.

"They name it The War of Two Empires. The Tiberian Empire versus the Sassanada Empire—a great but aging collection of kingdoms of the east. It began when Tiberia seized the realm of Trazonia, at the southeastern edge of the Pontean. The Tiberians sought to gain a direct trade route with the Peshtari and other merchants of the east, for spices and rare goods. But the Tiberians underestimated Sassanada's resolve. Not to mention the size and range of their armies. The war has dragged on for long years now. Most vitally, it continues to cost the Tiberians dearly. Eastern trade has been reduced to a trickle, and the price of goods continues to rise. Meanwhile, fringe cities like these have been left vulnerable, even to minor nuisances like Auchote's siege."

"It looks as though the whole of the town could escape in those boats." Teavar pointed at the docks on the harbor adjacent to the walled city, surrounded by a smaller wall.

Attasar smiled. "Perhaps not quite all, but you make a good point. I see there are quite a few merchant vessels in port. And they are indeed large ones. The city has likely sent for aid, but it's unlikely those ships will flee."

"Why is that?" Vahldan asked.

"The risks are greater than simply staying and waiting out the siege. The cost of sailing might be higher even than paying a ransom to the Spali."

"What's the cost?"

"Look out there." Attasar pointed. "See how rough the seas look, even from here? Trust me, it's much worse once you're out there. To sail in that, captains risk the loss of cargo, or even their ships. This is known as the season of storms. The imperials call it *hiatus*, and have laws that severely restrict sailing during the winter months. So captains risk fines, as well. Besides weather and fines, currently the risks are greater still. Because of the war, the Tiberian navy stays near to their ports, in Trazonia and Nicomedya. Which means the only ships out there belong to smugglers and pirates. Law-abiding captains want nothing to do with either."

"Smugglers and pirates," Vahldan mused, staring at the ships in the harbor and then out over the empty expanse of the sea again. Absorbing the circumstance did indeed keep the forge from growing too hot too quickly.

Arnegern cleared his throat. "This is all interesting, but may I make a suggestion?" Vahldan nodded. "The scouts say there are only two roads besides the one we followed here which offer Auchote a possible escape route. Since it'll soon be getting dark, I'd suggest sending squads to cut off each route. We could establish contain-ment yet today."

"And alert them to our presence in the process," Elan said.

"Perhaps," Arnegern conceded. "But they know we're coming. We have them outnumbered, and we'd have them trapped. We could attack on our terms."

Vahldan looked up at the late afternoon sky. "Getting in place would take time."

Teavar grunted. "If we're going to try, we'd best get to it."

Vahldan shook his head. "I don't like it. Feels like too much could go wrong." He needed this last battle to be decisive—and glorious. He turned to Elan. "What does my guardian think?"

Elan tucked the stray strands of blowing hair behind an ear. "I'd say attack. Fast. We made good time getting here. Auchote may not expect us today. Tomorrow he'll be more wary." She looked at him. "Surprise is a weapon. Why surrender it?"

She was right. The time had come. "I agree. Let's have done with this. We can do our best to encircle them on the approach. We'll split into three divisions once we're out of the pass. Arnegern will lead a third to the left along the river, and Jhannas"—he turned to the silent giant— "you'll lead a third to the right, skirting that forest. Teavar and Elan will ride at the fore with me. We'll go right across the plain, leading every rider who has a lance. I'm betting our skull-faced friend is at that main gate. We throw our best punch right at him. Agreed?"

All but Elan murmured their assent. Elan said, "Wise choice."

Vahldan smiled. "I remembered where to put my trust. And it's not in the gods."

"You're learning," she said, and went to mount Hrithvarra.

Vahldan's mounted Amalus host filled the vale, just over the ridge, out of sight from the slope that ran down to the city. His captains had gathered their divisions into columns. Arnegern led his group to the fore, to Vahldan's left. His vanguard and Arnegern's column would ride out side-by-side. Jhannas had the smallest division gathered off to the right. They would ride out once the main force was through the gap and onto the slope.

To the man, the mood and countenance was grim. Resolved.

Appraising his host, he recognized how ready and able these loyal men were to finish this war. Vahldan felt the same as they looked. His blood was hot but his head was clear. He was poised at the edge of imbuement. Better still, he felt like he could lead them all to Thunar's Blessing—like the high priest of a killing cult. One that would spill the blood of those who'd inflicted malice and spread evil upon the realm. The gods would sanctify this bloodshed. What he and his men were about to do would be honorable.

Vahldan walked Ardua to the apex, and reined to face them. He sat his helm on the saddle pommel before him and gripped the futhark sword's hilt.

Elan and Mighty Teavar flanked him—fully armed. His guardians looked magnificent.

Vahldan had but to raise his chin, and a hush fell over them. "Today, my brothers, we finally ride to meet our quarry. That these murderers deserve the lethal justice we shall deliver is beyond doubt." This was met with low murmurs of agreement and solemn nods.

The host fell silent again. "A wise friend told me that honor is not found in killing, but in justice." He glanced at Elan and she nodded. "Today we ride for justice, yes. But we also ride to glory. Glory that is found in honor, in bravery, in sacrifice." Heads nodded. Vahldan's voice rose. "Glory is the way, my brave lions. The way back to who we once were. Glory will deliver us. Glory will break the bonds of subjection—for our clan, for our people." The approving murmurs rose, punctuated by shouts of exaltation.

The forge flared. In its heat, Vahldan knew who he was. He was the Lion Lord.

He put on his helm, slung his freshly painted shield from his back, then drew Bairtah-Urrin and lifted it high. "Amalus Rekkrs! Let us serve our people as no one else can or would. Let us be the host that ends this war, now and forever. We ride together and strike as one. We ride to glory!"

He kicked Ardua and led them through the gap and over the crest.

Arnegern had never felt so quickly and fully imbued by Thunar's Blessing. He felt the hands of the gods at work, as if their mission, their leader, was divinely guided. Vahldan led the entire host filing through the narrow pass at a canter and started down the road, riding four abreast till the canyon opened to the downslope of grassy tundra. The walled city came to view under a low, late-afternoon sun that lit the tile roofs like a basket of apples. The host split into two and sped up, the clip-clop of hooves becoming a rumble.

Arnegern reined left and beckoned his division to follow. Staying to the road, running along the raised rim over the river, gave Arnegern a spectacular view of the entire scene. Spali cries pierced the growing rumble of their advance. Then shrill Spali horns blew. The three divisions of the lions' host were distinct now, his own in a lengthy snake, and Jhannas's breaking away to head west to ride the edge of the increasingly dense pine forest. The main division spread out into a flying wedge, with Vahldan at the tip—Elan and Teavar at his either shoulder. Gottari horns resounded, low and sonorous. They made the squawks of the Spali horns' sound like children's toys.

The host spurred to a gallop, red banners flapped overhead, and the rumble of Gottari warhorse hooves became a thunder that drowned out all other sound.

The Spali rushed to mount and assemble, forming up in a crescent to face Vahldan's thrust. It looked as though Arnegern's role would be easy. The foe spared not a single warrior to face his division's advance from the river road. He spotted Auchote, sitting ahorse amid a cluster of Paralatoe. Death's Grin was hiding behind his elite warriors, staying as far from harm's way as possible. An unheard Spali command set a volley of poison arrows into flight. A few horses among Vahldan's lines stumbled and fell, but far too few to cause the line to falter. Indeed, they seemed to spur to greater speed and cohesion. Another command set the Spali in motion toward the oncoming wedge.

Arnegern came around, skirting the harbor, heading directly for the eastern flank of the Spali line. He wasn't going to arrive in time to aid Vahldan's division against the Spali thrust.

The two sides crashed together with resound. It seemed scores of Spali instantly fell. The Gottari rolled through them almost without pause, with Vahldan and Elan still leading. The foe's formation disintegrated, and lone Spali horsemen galloped in all directions, many in flight, including no few toward his advance. Arnegern ordered his men to fan out to contain them.

His men sang out, happy to oblige, ready to seek glory. Thunar's Blessing ran through Arnegern, burning away all traces of fear and dread. At last, this was what they'd come for.

The highlight rivalry of the battle was playing out before him. Vahldan, Elan, and Teavar were targeting Auchote, of course. Death's Grin sent what seemed a dozen—about half of those he'd kept close —to meet them. The amazing trio was finally slowed, their blades flashing as they dealt with the superior numbers of Auchote's elite warriors.

Arnegern's fear came crashing back, but it was for the Lion Lord and his guardians. He had to refocus. The Spali who'd fled east drew near, shrieking and howling. These Spali were desperate. He called to his men, raised his shield and blade, and reined to target the nearest foe.

Vahldan had never felt the pulse of Thunar's Blessing more powerfully. As it had in the battle on the Oium Plains, his head stayed clear as the power burned brightly. As he had in his trial, he saw the fight as if his opponents moved in slow motion.

He slashed and sent a third Spali tumbling from his horse in mere moments. He and Ardua had drifted to the west as they fought. He glanced to find that Teavar had drifted east. Elan was between them, nearer to him. She was standing on her saddle as Hrithvarra galloped after a fleeing Paralatoe warrior. As the roan gained on their quarry, Elan leapt, landing on the fleeing mount's hindquarters. She instantly sliced the Spali rider's neck and threw him off. Vahldan turned to block the passing chop of a Spali straggler who continued galloping on. When he looked back, Elan had whistled for Hrithvarra and leapt back. He felt a surge of joy and pride for her.

Vahldan called to her and reined to meet her, and together they scanned the field. Those who'd been sent to meet them were either unhorsed or had passed on into the melee behind their advance. And Auchote and his bodyguards had vanished.

"There!" Elan pointed with her sword. "The bastard's saving himself again!" She was right. The last of Auchote's Paralatoe elite were in full flight, riding beneath the walls of the city, heading for a forested hillside to the west. They were only a half-dozen, but they rode in a protective array around their murderous chieftain. The walls above the Spali's progress were lined with men. Men who did nothing but watch.

Vahldan reined Ardua and set out, with Elan galloping right behind. "No, damn you—you will not escape," he said aloud. "Not again." The fire flared, the molten rage flowing from the crucible of his outrage into his limbs. He'd come too far. After all that had happened, he simply would not go back without Auchote's scalp on his reins. He urged Ardua to even greater speed, and the amazing mare responded. Seemed Thunar was willing to bless the horse, as well.

Jhannas's division was too far away to intercept Auchote and his guards, but the big Rekkr and his men had noticed their flight. "Arrows!" Vahldan called. "Stop them!" It was a long shot, but several drew their bows and fired. Luckily, one of the Spali guards' horses was hit, sending it bucking toward the city walls, putting one of Auchote's men out of the race.

The quality of the Skolani mares began to show as he and Elan gained on the Spali ponies. At a bellowing call from Auchote, two of his men peeled off to circle back and counterattack. The pair almost instantly flung javelins. Vahldan reined Ardua, but one of the javelins caught the gray mare in the chest. Ardua screamed in rage and stutter-stepped, but she did not stumble, did not falter. Elan passed along Ardua's front side and yanked the offending weapon from the horse's flesh. Vahldan was able to rein Ardua back on course, and the magnificent horse galloped on. Vahldan dispatched the shocked man who'd hit her, and the second Spali turned to flee again.

Just as Auchote and his final two guards made the treeline, Elan leaned back and hurled the javelin she'd yanked from Ardua's chest. The amazing throw hit Auchote's pony's hindquarters, and the beast started to buck and spin, slamming sideways into an oak trunk to jar the chieftain from the saddle.

This was it! This was Vahldan's chance to avenge his father's death, to begin to make right all that his enemies had wrought. He reined and heeled Ardua, but her breath came in heaves. The wounded gray abruptly crashed to her knees at the treeline, unable to keep herself upright any longer. Vahldan kicked his feet from the stirrups and leapt clear as she rolled. His poor, brave girl's eyes rolled and her mouth foamed. Likely a dose of Spali poison from the javelin's tip had taken its toll.

"He's yours! I've got the others," Elan called as she galloped on into the forest after the remaining guards. His kestrel had his back. This time Auchote would have no savior, no means of escape.

Vahldan got his feet under him and turned just in time to shield-block Auchote's first blade-stroke. His countering swing was wild, but it forced Auchote to back up a step, giving him space to gain a proper stance.

Death's Grin mirrored him, settling into his stance, once again fighting with two blades—a curved sword in his right and a long dagger in his left. Auchote's sinuous muscles rippled his tattooed torso and he grinned his infamous grin. Vahldan spotted the scar he'd left on Auchote's hand. This time Vahldan sensed the fear behind the façade. The fierceness was a well-rehearsed show.

Without hesitation, Vahldan attacked. His first hard stroke put his opponent into retreat. The wily fighter feigned a swing that would've left him open, and Vahldan fell for the ploy. Auchote twisted from Vahldan's eager counter, throwing a kick to Vahldan's knee. Vahldan stagger-stepped to avoid a fall, and Auchote landed a slash on the back of his shoulder. Pain pierced Thunar's Blessing, but he instantly realized his hauberk had saved his life. Still, the blow propelled him to the turf.

He landed hard, the ground stealing his wind. He sensed Auchote over him and twisted to parry the stroke he knew was coming. The flame roared, but the rising fear within it pulled the ugliness to the fore. Vahldan's head reeled, rage befuddling his movement, his clarity. This couldn't be happening. Not again!

He managed to roll away, but into Ardua's head, startling the floundering mare. Ardua's big eye momentarily found his before Vahldan pushed himself up, trying to regain his footing. Before he rose from a knee he was forced to parry. Auchote's hard stroke pushed him onto his butt. This time Auchote's curved blade skipped down to slide off the hilt to bash Vahldan's wrist guard. His sword hand went numb. He was forced to parry again, and the blade dropped from his weakened grip. He lunged to retrieve the blade, but the move allowed Auchote to step on his shield, pinning him in place, his sword hilt just out of reach. He lay bare to his father's murderer.

Vahldan quailed and lunged, trying to yank the shield free. Auchote kicked him again, this time in the chest, knocking him to his back. He could hardly breathe, could hardly see. The ugliness kept him down even more firmly than his rival. He longed to kill but had lost the control to do it. His confidence leaked away. He'd been so sure. He'd been bold. Had the gods betrayed him? Could defeat and death really be all that was left to him, after all he'd been through?

Death's Grin's namesake expression was the genuine item. "Ah, rabbit," he said in accented Gottari. "Just as we both knew." Auchote straddled him, the knife hovering to keep him down. His wicked rival raised the curved sword to strike the death blow. "The son is no Angavar. He is just a rabbit."

As Auchote set the blade in motion, the mare jolted to life, kicking and neighing angrily. Her hoof cracked audibly into Auchote's knee, sending the chieftain toppling. The Spali's swing went wild. Vahldan lunged again, slipping from the shield straps. His hand found Bairtah-Urrin's hilt. He pushed off with all his remaining strength, swinging as he rolled. Auchote's fall sent him to meet the arc of the blade, gashing the side of the skull of Death's Grin.

Auchote shrieked and landed with a thud. The chieftain had lost his sword but clung to the knife, both arms up to shield his tattooed face, blood gushing over it. Vahldan was back on his feet and over him, their positions reversed.

Vahldan saw the opening and wasted no time, thrusting the tip into the sternum of the man's tattooed chest, piercing his heart just as Angavar's had been.

Auchote's eyes widened in surprise. Death's Grin futilely swung the knife and missed.

Still pushing on the blade, Vahldan stepped on his wrist, trapping the hand that held the knife. Vahldan leaned over his victim. "I am the Bringer!" he bellowed. Auchote gasped. "I am beyond my father's wildest dreams. I will see empires crumble and then build them anew. Do you understand me?" The life left the bugging eyes of his nemesis.

Vahldan yanked the blade out and howled to the sky. When he

ran out of breath, he bent to his victim. "Never underestimate me again," he growled, to Auchote's gods and to his own.

He turned and staggered to Ardua and dropped down beside her, catching his breath. Vahldan laid the bloody blade aside, and pulled the dying mare's head into his lap. He stoked Ardua, calming himself and soothing her. "You saved me, my beauty." He sighed and she imitated it. "Thank you." It came as a whisper. "The least I can do is give you a warrior's death." He lifted his hand from her coat to stand, but she snorted and bobbed her head, pressing her nose to his hand. She didn't want him to leave her.

"It's all right," he said softly. "I'm not going anywhere." He shushed her and stroked her, and she settled again.

He stayed there, holding her and petting her, whispering his praise. She sighed again.

She died then. So peacefully. He was relieved. And so sad. Ardua died a hero, regardless of whether or not the poison had taken her. She had never stopped fighting. She had stayed loyal to those she loved, had given her last effort for them, even though she knew she would not survive them. Indeed, she had given her all, her very last effort, to ensure he would survive her. Vahldan knew these were lessons he should never forget.

He vowed then that he would hold Ardua's lessons dear, right up to his own doom.

The sound of hoofbeats came from the forest. "Elan?" he called. He snatched up the blade and got to his knees, using the sword as a cane to keep his balance on wobbly legs.

"Coming!" Elan called.

Vahldan drew himself up, setting into a defensive stance, but she appeared alone. Elan appraised the scene, taking in Auchote's body, and then Ardua's.

"You got both?" he asked. She nodded. She gazed out over the greater battlefield and he followed suit. Jhannas's men were riding up. Beyond them, the men of his division were looting corpses, running down stragglers, and rounding up Spali ponies.

Elan gave a single nod. "It's done, then."

Vahldan was exhausted, relieved, and deeply grieved all at once. And still angry. No matter how decisive it was, this victory had a cost. The remnants of Thunar's Blessing still gripped him. He suddenly knew what to do about it.

He stuck his sword in the turf, pulled his dagger and stepped to Auchote's corpse. He knelt, pulled his rival's tufted hair taut, and started to cut the trophy that had cost so much to harvest.

Vahldan, Lion Lord of the Amalus, stood and shook the blood from the scalp of his father's murderer. He tucked the trophy into his belt. "Yes, it's done," he finally agreed, though he knew his new life had just begun.

He was a killer. But he could discern what was just. He could act with honor.

He had led his clan to glory. He'd taken it back. Glory would be his song, and his sword would deliver justice for those who sang it.

His people would know these things of him, and they would praise and thank him for it.

∾

Elan kept a watchful eye on him. Vahldan was shaking imbuement, but he'd gone deep.

"I need to go over there," Vahldan said, pointing to the meadow below the walls. It was where the bulk of the Amalus host was gathering. Many were making a pile of the bodies of the foe. Vahldan's voice was hoarse and his countenance was hard.

Elan reached to him and vacated a stirrup, pulling him up on Hrithvarra just as she'd done the day they first met. This time he hugged her from behind. Tight. She had her own trophy to harvest, but it could wait. She looked over her shoulder. "See me?" He nodded. "Hear me?"

"I do."

"Good. Know this: I'm here." She tilted her head toward his host.

"As are they. The hunt is done. They need a leader now. We're with you. For whatever comes next. Are you ready?"

Vahldan's eyes seemed to clear as he and Elan regained their connection. "I am," he said. Indeed, Elan saw in his ardent gaze the young man she'd first met. This was the man who'd won over the giant they'd pitted against him. The man who'd volunteered to ensure the success of this war's initial attack. The man who'd led the Penance Line to redemption in battle.

The man who'd carved her kestrel.

Elan urged Hrithvarra to walk. Along the way, the men lining the top of the wall caught her eye. They stood silent, gaping. "They look frightened," she said, nodding up at them.

"The Spali were their besiegers. But our victory doesn't seem to have impressed them."

She laughed. "Oh, they may be impressed. Impressed with terror. We should try talking to them. Maybe seek some sort of barter. It's a long way home, and our supplies dwindle."

"We'll go and see what they're about. But I need to know some things first."

Elan couldn't quite guess what he meant, but he was clear of imbuement. And resolved.

Rekkrs bowed their heads, and a few raised bloody swords or spears in salute as he and Elan rode through the growing press, but no one was celebrating. Elan understood. Victory felt inevitable, but it had been long and painful in coming. Now that it was done, uncertainty crept in.

Vahldan pointed. "Up there, on that rise." She reined Hrithvarra, but let her friend walk slowly. Her dear one had done enough this day. "Here," he said. Vahldan gave her a final squeeze and slipped off. "Attasar," he called.

Arnegern and Teavar came to him alongside the scholar. Jhannas and Herodes came, as well. Elan dismounted and stood beside Vahldan as he gazed out over the scene, then over the heads of his host. He lifted his gaze to the city and then beyond it, to the harbor and to the sea. The rest of his host gathered near as he appraised the aftermath of victory.

Attasar kept his head bowed. "My lord?" the scholar finally prompted.

"Tell me more about those boats," Vahldan said. He'd become very calm.

"As I said, they're merchant ships, built to carry cargo."

"What are they worth?"

"It depends, of course," Attasar said. "The way they sit low in the water, I'd guess they remain loaded. It's likely this is just a stopover port. If any of them have already been to the eastern ports, they are likely loaded with exotic goods like spices and silk cloth. If that's the case, even the cargo of one of them could potentially be worth quite a lot."

"How much? Just a guess."

Attasar raised his brows. "A full load of eastern spices? One such cargo would likely be worth the whole of a season of the Gottari wool trade."

Vahldan looked as if he'd already guessed it, a slight smile tugging at the corners of his mouth. "And you said only smugglers and pirates would be at sea this time of year?"

"I did. Although this could be the home port of some or all of these ships. They could be loaded in preparation for the coming spring."

Vahldan shook his head. "Something about the look of the ships and the feel of this city tells me that's not so. Come." The Lion Lord strode down off of the rise, parting his followers, with his scholar and his captains at his heels.

Elan hurried to stay beside him. "What's on your mind?" she asked, though she suspected she knew.

"Remember when I said that glory was the way, but that it had to be big? Big enough to change things?" Vahldan stopped and turned to Elan. His smile was that of the boy she first met—full of wonder, with a world of burden newly landed upon his shoulders. But this time his eyes were clear, his demeanor assured. "I think I might have found something big. Maybe big enough to change things."

Gods' grace, this was no boy. This was the man she loved. Yes— she knew it in that instant. She loved him. Elan had chosen him, and she loved him. In the joy of realization, Elan flung her arms around Vahldan's neck and kissed him. "I always knew that you would," she said.

The setting sun dropped below a cloud and lit his angular face. Their gazes lingered, their connection more alive and vibrant than ever. Elan saw their future bright before them and knew that he saw it, too. "That *we* would," Vahldan said. "Remember, there is no you, no I, only us."

A raptor cried overhead. It was a hawk—a male—soaring on the wind, facing the city and sea. "I told you I'd get here," Vahldan called up to him. The bird flapped and swooped, streaking out ahead, over the city walls, heading for the seacoast and the vast expanse beyond. "I'll be right behind," he said with a satisfied smile.

He turned to her. "What do you think? Should we?" He held out his hand to her.

Elan took his hand. "I think we should." Vahldan started off toward the city's main gate, leading her into an unknown wider world.

EPILOGUE—AS IT SHALL BE...

"*I am not alone in having speculated about my parents' relationship, of what might have been different. What if my mother had avoided banishment? What if my father had found his way to destiny by another course? What if they had simply returned to dwell in Dania? Could suffering have been averted? Would the glory that was wrought still have come to be? These things are not mine to know.*

I am, however, certain that I am the product of one of the world's great loves; an epic and abiding love, as deep and potent and pure as can be shared by two beings in this life. I am reminded of it each time I hold my mother's gift—a kestrel charm, carved for her by my father. Just as it did for her, the kestrel provides me with a sustaining assurance and an enduring comfort."—Brin Bright Eyes, Saga of Dania

THE GATEHOUSE BELLS WELCOMED THEM. The remnants of crusty snowdrifts still lined the base of Danihem's walls, melting even in the shadows as the Wulthus host rode home. Thadmeir had received word of the birth of his daughter along the way. The wagons had been mired in mud. He hadn't made it in time.

It was disappointing, but Thadmeir was more distressed by the nebulousness of the tidings. It seemed both mother and babe were bedridden, and nothing the Gottari crones or the Elli-Frode prescribed seemed to bring them relief. Relief from what, it wasn't clear.

When the tidings arrived, Thadmeir had left the ponderous progress of the army behind, and had ridden in all haste with a small host of Wulthus Rekkrs. A crowd gathered on the commons as the Wolf Lord and his retinue entered the gates. Thadmeir feared the worst in appraising the villagers' solemnity. Had one of them—spouse or daughter—passed on since the message was sent?

Thadmeir leapt from the saddle, flinging the reins to a stable boy and rushing through the parting throng to the longhouse. At least two dozen Gottari matrons and crones lingered in the council chamber, hovering outside the residence drapes. The Elli-Frodei Gizar stepped before him at the entrance.

"How is she? Are they alive?"

Gizar's eyes widened. "Yes, yes. Both Priestess Amaseila and your daughter are alive, my lord. Both were weakened by the trauma of birth, but they seem to be recovering now."

"Thank the gods." Thadmeir moved to go past, but Gizar held up his hands.

"My lord, before you go in, I feel it's best you know."

"Know what, man?"

"The babe," Gizar said. "She's...odd."

"Odd how?"

"Well, her eyes, to start. Like your wife's, they seem imparted by Freya's communion."

Thadmeir waved the old man off. "She's young. All newborn's eyes are strange. In time many even change color."

"It's more than her eyes, my lord. She's so... aware. And, well, she never cries. Except when someone other than your qeins touches her. Then she screams like a demon from the underworld. Every time, no matter who else lays a hand on her."

"Bah. It's probably nothing. Just a sense of security found in her mother."

"Priestess Amaseila says the babe is blessed with *the Touch*; that she perceives the fate of others—of whomever she touches. She knows their dark secrets, feels their pains. Even foresees their deaths." The Elli-Frodei lowered his gaze. "My lord, I have come to believe. It is not without cause that she has named the babe Amaga."

Foreboding filled him. In the old tongue, an Amaga was not just an augur, but a harbinger of ill-tidings. "How could she name our child...?" He pushed past the man and went to his wife.

Amaseila was so pale, lying abed, smiling up at him. "Look, Amaga. Your father is come. As we foresaw."

The child was but a ruffle of orange hair at her breast. As if she'd understood perfectly, the babe disengaged from the nipple and turned her pale little face to his. He clearly recalled how startled he'd been by his first glimpse into his wife's eyes. In spite of Gizar's warning, he relived the moment. Wide, pale gray pupils with beady black irises appraised him knowingly. The look was with the regard of an adult, and decidedly unnerving.

Amaseila held the swaddled babe up to him. "Here, my darling. Hold your daughter."

"Should I? They say—"

"Never mind what they say. She'll know you. She recognizes her protector. Amaga is the progeny of the wolf. She and her father are to be as one."

The babe's swaddling hit his hands, soft. Amaga fell into his grasp, light as a puff of dried wool. Thadmeir brought his daughter to his chest, and she nestled against him. Her sigh was clearly one of comfort, of recognition.

He sighed, too. Thadmeir sat on the edge of her sleeping pallet, holding his babe to his chest. He reached for his beloved's hand. Upon their touch, Amaseila gasped. "Tell me," she said.

"I imagined you'd already know. We were victorious. The Spali have withdrawn."

"And the Bringer? You sought to convince him to return."
Amaseila was near breathless.

"I did."

"But he went on. Out into the wider world."

"Yes, Vahldan chose to ride on in pursuit of the Paralatoe. He's
reclaimed the futhark blade. He refuses to stand in judgement of the
longhouse. He took over four score of our finest young Amalus
warriors with him. If it hadn't been already, the futhark is truly
broken now."

The babe tensed in his hands, and her mewl sounded of displea-
sure. Thadmeir studied her scrunched up little face. Something had
clearly upset her.

"When mighty lion is cast aside, the Severing Son restores his
pride."

Thadmeir felt his face go slack. He turned to Amaseila, who
seemed to be in a trance. "Did you just call Vahldan the Severing
Son? Where, in Freya's name, did you hear that?" The image, clear as
yesterday, ran through his mind: of the young man, also seemingly in
a trance, bellowing at the Spali, proclaiming himself the Severing
Son.

"'Tis a prophecy, older even than our people's time in Dania."
Amaseila's head tilted back on the pillows, and her eyes rolled up as
she closed them. Her voice rang with the resound of the goddess:

"When mighty lion is cast aside
The Severing Son restores his pride
Tho' Lion's Son reclaims the blade
So too is spurned the futhark's glade
O'er rock and sea his fame is sought
Kingdoms quail as empire's wrought
Half a ring his will to carry
Wolf's half-ring withheld in tarry."

Thadmeir's hand drifted to the Nahtsrein's hilt at his hip,
fingering the half-ring writ with his clan's oath to the futhark.

Amaseila's eyes sprang wide, raptor-like, and locked on his.

"Thunder wakes when blades collide
The steed on which Urrinan rides."

The babe started to cry. Thadmeir hurriedly laid his tiny daughter upon her mother's breast. Almost instantly, Amaga fell quiet and her mother gasped and settled, cuddling her.

"Amaseila?" His qeins nodded, clearly herself again. "What does it mean?"

She smiled up at him. "It means all is as it shall be, my darling. As it shall be."

The End

The Severing Son is part one of The Sundered Nation trilogy. Part two is titled Bold Ascension.

GRATITUDE

I want to take this opportunity to thank you for spending some of your valuable time reading The Severing Son. I fully appreciate that, when it comes to entertainment, we live in an era of unprecedented diversity of choice. I continue to feel strongly that novels provide a unique type of immersion, and an incomparable means of exploring character. I'm guessing you share the sentiment, or it's unlikely we'd be meeting like this, here at the end of a rather lengthy novel.

I have never invested more of my own time, energy, and passion in any endeavor than I have in seeking to adequately convey the world of Dania and the lives of Vahldan, Elan, and those of their children. It's my fondest wish to be worthy of the telling of their tale. I can't wait to share the rest of The Sundered Nation Trilogy with you. I hope I've done well enough to have earned your interest in continuing to follow Vahldan and Elan into the wider world of Pontea in book two, Bold Ascension.

Speaking of gratitude, if you have enjoyed the tale thus far, and are so inclined, there are a couple of ways you can provide a real boost, to ensure that the saga of Dania carries on. The first—and easiest—is to tell someone else about it. Word of mouth is, by far, the most important way to bolster the success of any book. Beyond that, it's difficult to overemphasis the importance of reviews—particularly to a debut author such as myself. Nothing elaborate is necessary. I would be grateful for even a few simple sentences conveying what you liked best about the story.

In any case, I'm honored to have earned your time and humbled by your support.

As it shall be...
    Vaughn

ACKNOWLEDGMENTS

For almost as long as I've been writing I have imaged writing the acknowledgements for the debut you hold in your hands. Now that it's come to it, I find it an overwhelming undertaking. So many have contributed to my writing journey, in so many ways, I'm discovering how impossible it is to acknowledge everyone deserving of my gratitude. The list long precedes the start of my actual writing in the world of Dania. I have to go back to my sixth grade teacher, Mr. Raymond, who first put a copy of The Hobbit in my hands and encouraged me to lose myself in Middle Earth.

Looking back certainly brings to mind my parents, who both encouraged me in so many ways, but perhaps most importantly in that they never set any barrier or restriction on books or reading. Even in a household with a tight budget, I don't recall any request for more books or time to read ever being denied. Indeed, a blind eye was often turned to my reading well past my bedtime. My sister Colleen continues to be a source of support. But it was my oldest sister Marsha—a voracious reader herself—who became the first person to slog her way through the earliest manuscript set in Dania. Marsh made me feel not only that I could actually be a storyteller, but that I could excel at it. Although my parents and Marsha have passed on, I know my gratitude to them and their pride in me is something that echoes on. They are still with me.

Since I publicly proclaimed myself a writer (over a decade ago, but several years into my writing journey), many others have encouraged, inspired, and supported me. Those who read early drafts of stories set in Dania were immensely important to my growth and to the enhancement of this story and its world-building, including: Deb Wagner (my favorite fan!), Dan Brake, Cynthia Deane (my eagle-eyed aunt!), Eileen Kochanny, Colleen Murray, Laura Kieda, and Keaghan Cronin (the super-mama endurance reader!). Fellow writers who've read and offered vital feedback and camaraderie include Nicole Bates, Kim Downes Bullock, Valerie Chandler, Brin Jackson, Bernadette Phipps Linke, Juliet Marillier, Thomas Henry Pope, and Heather Reid.

I have had tremendous mentorship throughout my journey. I need to thank Cathy Yardley, who made me feel like I could call myself a writer, and who somehow convinced me to create my first spreadsheet. I'm also enormously grateful to Donald Maass, who has read multiple manuscripts, some of them several times. Don has provided a plethora of actionable critique, as well as an arsenal of storytelling tools. But more vitally, I need to thank him for believing in me, which lifted me toward belief in myself.

I am hugely indebted to Beth Balmano, whose meticulous and thorough editing allows this story to shine. Beth patiently saves me from my inability to master capitalization and from my uncommon proclivity for hyphenation. She also has a knack for providing assurance and positivity precisely when it's needed.

Returning to the topic of mentors (some of whom are also editors), I'm not sure how I can find the words to properly thank Therese Walsh—the Storywhisperer. Therese not only found her way to the beating heart of my storytelling, she made a map to teach me the route to a creative homestead I hadn't realized was mostly built. She checked the foundation, fortified the structure, and then provided the most gracious guidance possible to most every aspect of my effort to make Dania a special place. Thanks a million, T (for a start).

I owe a debt of gratitude to the entire Writer Unboxed community. I often say I don't know where I'd be without WU, but I'm certain that it wouldn't be here, writing the acknowledgements for my debut. I send my gratitude to everyone at WU who has inspired and aided my journey for more than a decade. Although I fear I can never provide a complete list, I have to single out Tom Bentley, Keith Cronin, Kat Magendie, Liz Michalski, Barbara O'Neil, Heather Webb, and Grace Wynter—all fine WU contributors who've gone above-and-beyond in their support and encouragement of me.

Lastly, but by far most importantly, I have to acknowledge my biggest supporter and inspiration, who is also my dearest friend— the brightest star in my life. I once wrote that without my wife Maureen, there would be no Skolani Blade-Wielders. But the senti-ment should be so much larger than that. Without her, there would be no Dania, no books, no writing journey. Indeed, without her love and guidance, there would be no me—not as I now exist. I simply can never thank you enough, but I'm all-in for a lifetime of trying. *Forever to lead, together to stand, unto death's door, and beyond.* I love you always, my Anam Cara.

About the Author

Vaughn Roycroft has aspired to write epic fantasy since his sixth grade teacher gave him a boxed set of The Lord of the Rings. He has spent many years seeking to be worthy of telling this tale. He lives with his soul mate in a cottage they designed and built themselves, near their favorite Great Lakes beach. When he's not writing, he's often walking the woods and beaches, trying to keep up with his energetic black lab.

CPSIA information can be obtained
at www.ICGtesting.com
Printed in the USA
JSHW050025141022
31624JS00003B/10